FROM THE DARKNESS

Susan Abel

Susan Abel

This novel is a work of fiction. Names, characters, places and incidents are either the product of the author's imagination, or, if real, used fictitiously.

Cover image – Fotolia Stock Image
Cover design by Cal Sharp, Caligraphics
Author photo by Katie Darby

ISBN: 9798708165428

DEDICATION

To my loving husband, Robb,
and daughters, Tara and Leah…
Without your encouragement and support,
my stories would never have become books.

To my inspirational parents who raised me
with the perseverance to overcome the many challenges
in my life, and who lead by example that through hard work and
dedication your dreams can come true.

And, to the many horses that have graced my life
with their trust, willingness to please, patience and forgiveness, while
reminding me of the importance of living in the present.

Love you all…

ACKNOWLEDGEMENTS

Many thanks to my husband, Robb,
and to my beta reader Pam Ullrich,
for their many hours of reading and feedback,
and to my editor, Natalie Bycraft,
for applying her knowledge of the written word to my work.

Collectively, your guidance and support
are helping me improve my writing and meet my goals.

You have to look deeper,

way below the anger, the hurt, the hate,

the jealousy, the self-pity,

way down deeper where the dreams lie…

Find your dream.

It's the pursuit of the dream that heals you.

~ Billy Mills (Makata Taka Hela)

PART ONE

BEFORE

1 – Betsy

Elk Head, Montana

July, 1999

Betsy White Cloud opened her eyes, her afternoon nap once again cut short by her discomfort. It seemed she couldn't rest much longer than an hour at a time anymore, day or night. Her aching bones felt a draft and she reached for her throw. But it had ended up on the cold floor of the century-old log and stone lodge she called home for most of her eighty-five years.

Hired as a housekeeper in her youth, there was never a day she felt less than a member of the O'Reilly, and now, Walker, family. It was a comfort to Betsy knowing she would never leave the estate she loved. Two Ponies.

Through blurred vision, she found her wire-rimmed glasses on the nightstand, slipped them on and struggled to swing her legs over the side of the bed to sit up. She immediately sought out the sepia-toned photograph hanging on the knotty pine wall across from her bed. In the image, the Blackfeet woman sat bareback astride her old mare, Flower. She had dreamt of galloping the Paint across the open range of Montana as a young woman, so fast their sheer speed had brought tears to her eyes. It had seemed so real – the distinct scent of horse, the thunder of hooves beneath her, her fingers laced tightly through mane, taut muscles stretching and retracting beneath her… bringing to life the sure joy and exhilaration of such a ride - one last time.

Grabbing her cane, she struggled to her feet and slipped on her house slippers, all the while shaking her head out of frustration, no longer able to bend over to put on her moccasins. They sat idle collecting dust on the floor of her wardrobe closet alongside her old riding boots. Betsy groaned her first few steps, stiff and ravaged by arthritis. Her knees had deteriorated beyond repair and were barely able to support her frail frame any longer. She had dismissed the urging by family and friends to have knee replacement surgery. Never would she trust a white doctor again after being unknowingly sterilized during a routine appendectomy as a teenager; the joy of motherhood torn from her as a means to curb the American Indian population. What would they take next, her life? She had already been denied the sacred privilege of entering the spirit world whole, but she sure as hell planned to leave Grandmother Earth on her own terms.

When she reached the kitchen, the lingering scent of sausage and biscuits greeted her. Betsy glanced at the stove where she once took pride in preparing meals for her loved ones and guests, but she had hung up her spatula a couple of years earlier, unable to stand long enough to complete a meal. With her guidance, Katherine Walker, the woman of the house, had become a good cook over the years, even compared to Betsy's high standards. This thought brought a smile to her weathered face.

While Katherine was out of town, the wives of Betsy's much younger twin brothers, Kimi and Nuna, took over the cooking for her husband, Steven Walker, bringing him meals or cooking at Two Ponies together with their families every Sunday. Her smile faded. The fact she could no longer take care of Katherine, the niece of her life partner, Joseph O'Reilly, as she had promised on his deathbed, left her feeling empty and without purpose. Now Katherine had to take care of her.

It seemed like only yesterday they were sitting together on the end of the dock on Pine Island Lake and riding the trails of Two Ponies as she passed down the lessons of her people, and of their brothers and sisters of the forest, to the little girl who was so eager to learn all she had to share. Where had all the years gone? But they had been grand years. Betsy felt honored to have lived such a full life at Two Ponies, a beautiful two-thousand-acre estate nestled in the Rocky Mountains, with the opportunity to care for her adopted family, sharing in their joys and comforting them through their sorrows. Most of all, she thanked the Creator for the good fortune to have been loved by a good man, their earthly time together cut short, but soon she would be reunited with her Joseph in the spirit world for eternity.

Betsy hobbled past the split-log staircase leading to the guestrooms upstairs, into the great room overlooking Pine Island Lake and the Continental Divide beyond. With both hands, she clasped the carved horse-head cane handle, her arms shaking to support herself as she gazed up at Joseph's portrait sitting center of the half-log mantle spanning the huge stone fireplace. A tear pooled and slowly ran down her bronze cheek as she studied the black and white photograph taken over sixty-five years ago.

She closed her eyes and recalled the sunny afternoon she had snapped the shutter, only moments after they had made love for the first time. The memory of them lying together in the tall grass under the swaying branches of the loan cottonwood in the back field, brought a smile back to her tired face as she turned and limped toward the massive front door of the lodge.

Katherine jogged up the side stairs and slipped off her boots before entering the side door of the lodge. Betsy had trained her well. Her half-wolf hybrid companion, Laddy, followed her through the door. She threw her fan mail on the table, all but one. That one went directly into the trash along with the others she had received from the anonymous heckler over the past few months, all postmarked from Ocala, Florida, with the same typed format and signed "Give it up!" She shook her head, dismissing it as she had the others, thinking some people just have nothing better to do.

"Betz?" she called out, slipping out of her vest and hanging it by the door. The old woman had become hard of hearing, so she began searching for her. Betsy should have been up from her nap hours ago.

She started by checking the library where her dear friend had made a habit of sitting and reading Joseph's historical novels, documenting the Western expansion, each afternoon. She must have known them word for word, having read them so many times over the years, yet she sat captivated as she turned each page. Finding the room empty, Katherine walked to the opposite end of the lodge again with Laddy on her heels to check the old woman's bedroom behind the kitchen. Perhaps she had taken a late nap that day or was back to leafing through her photo albums, a project she had begun a week or so earlier. The photo albums sat in a pile on her desk in an empty room.

"Where's Betz?" she asked Laddy, sitting with his head cocked in response to her question.

Next, she returned to the great room and glanced upstairs, but shook her head knowing Betsy hadn't attempted that dangerous climb with her knees for years. Pondering where to look next, she noticed Laddy focusing on the front door. Ajar a crack, he began pawing at the opening until he could push it open with his nose. Katherine followed, feeling certain Betsy must be taking in the sun on the front porch overlooking the lake, but she found her usual spot on the corner glider vacant. Suddenly, panic swelled in her chest as she turned toward Laddy making a strange whining sound out in the yard.

Katherine ran down the stairs toward the small family cemetery at the edge of the woods. The bench they had added for Betsy to sit and visit Joseph, just outside the fenced-in plot, stood agonizingly bare. When she reached Laddy pawing at the wrought-iron gate, Katherine came to an abrupt halt. Her heart sank to the lowest depths of her soul as she flung open the gate and dropped to her knees beside Betsy stretched out over Joseph's grave.

"No, please, no!" she shrieked, attempting to wake her, but in her heart, she knew she was already gone. Tears streaming down her face, she leaned over and buried her face in the old women's long silver hair and wept like a child. Katherine's worst fear had been realized.

"Oh Betz, I'm so sorry I wasn't here with you," she whimpered through her sobs. She had always envisioned being there to hold her hand as she passed from one world to the next. Yet this seemed more Betsy's way, always fearless and ready for the next adventure.

When she could cry no more, she sat up, brushed the hair from her dear friend's face and kissed her on the cheek. Katherine sat with her a while longer, uncertain her trembling limbs would support her.

How would she go on without her life-long friend? She had been her rock, always there to hold her up when her world crumbled beneath her. Betsy had become the closest to a caring mother she would ever know. She had never felt loved by her birth mother; her pregnancy with Katherine nothing more than a ticket to a comfortable life with her father, the son of a wealthy shoe factory owner in Boston. Betsy and her Uncle Joe had become her surrogate parents while visiting summers at Two Ponies from the age of ten, teaching her the important lessons in life, including the most important one - that she deserved to be loved. Following the death of her uncle and her inheritance of his mountain estate, she had moved West at the age of twenty to take ownership of Two Ponies, putting on hold her dream of riding in the Olympics to pursue her ambition of opening a girl's summer equestrian camp. Betsy had seen her through love, disaster, guilt, anger, joy, tragedy, births and deaths – the worst and best of times for nearly fifty years.

Now Katherine must carry on without her guidance and support. If it wasn't for Betsy, she may have given up on her dream of qualifying for the US Equestrian Team forever. Especially following the serious leg injuries she had sustained and the heartbreak of losing their dear friend, Billy Black, nearly five years ago. Lying beside Betsy's remains brought back the memory of holding Billy as he took his last breath in her arms. He had once been her lover, became a life-long friend of the family and was helping her train her horse, Major Command, when their disastrous past caught up with them. Billy sacrificed his life to save her and her family from a vengeful neighbor out to settle a score. Betsy had helped her move past the pain and guilt to continue with Major's training.

Katherine had just returned from a conditioning ride on her big bay gelding, covering most of their sprawling estate. In two weeks, the team would leave for the 1999 Pan American Games in Winnipeg, Manitoba, Canada, where they hoped to qualify for the 2000 Olympics. She had envisioned Betsy getting to watch her obtain her dream of competing next summer in Sydney, but now, her mentor would not see the day.

Betsy was so proud of her and her off-the-track Thoroughbred's progress over the past seven years. Determined to do all she could to make Katherine's dream come true, Betsy had been the driving force behind them earning the notoriety and sponsors needed to make the trip overseas by sharing their unbelievable story with the media. Katherine had returned to the world stage in eventing in her fifties, following a nearly thirty-year break, and would be turning sixty during the Games. Not to mention the nine-month interruption in their training as she recovered from two breaks in her leg, injuries she sustained during the near-death attack on her family, which in itself, was an extraordinary story. If that wasn't enough, she would be riding a fifteen-year-old retired racehorse that played a major role in her surviving the ordeal. Once the word got out, thanks to Betsy, equine and sports magazines and journalists couldn't get enough of her and her horse's incredible story. Now for Betsy, she needed to get to Australia.

Katherine stood up, wiped her face and met Laddy at the gate. Her faithful companion was getting up in years, too. Having rescued him from a bear trap in the mountains five years earlier, they could only guess his age at around five. Laddy whined, glancing between her and Betsy's still remains.

"She's gone, boy. There's nothing we can do."

Laddy's head and tail hung as he followed her back into the lodge where she would make the calls she had dreaded to her husband and their girls, Betsy's family and all their friends. Neither she nor her spouse of nearly thirty years, Steven, had any siblings or surviving family, but they had a huge extended family of friends and students that loved Betsy dearly. She had taken so much pride in cooking and caring for the thousands of girls that had passed through Two Ponies Summer Equestrian Camp over the past forty years.

Katherine collapsed into the desk chair in the library and dialed the office. It was nearly closing time at Steven's veterinary clinic, and he answered the phone himself.

"Honey," she said, her voice quivering. "… it's… Betsy." She didn't need to say more; Steven must have heard the pain in her voice.

"Oh no, Kat, I'm so sorry."

"I found her with Joseph." She took a deep breath, trying to hold back the sobs building in her chest again as she pictured Betsy's lifeless body lying over her uncle's grave. "I can't believe she's gone."

"I'll be right there."

Katherine gently placed the receiver down and stared at the phone. She couldn't make the other calls now. She would wait and notify their girls and others with Steven's support. She got up and took a throw off one of the chairs and returned to the gravesite to cover Betsy. Once a robust woman, her remains now resembled a frail child. She stopped short of covering her face, which looked as if she was napping, so peaceful with just a hint of her perpetual smile creasing the corners of her mouth. Katherine sat down on the bench to wait for Steven.

A cool freeze blew off the lake, snapping the red, white and blue flag like a wet towel at the top of the pole in the front yard. Katherine walked to the pole and lowered the flag half-mast, then returned to the bench where Laddy placed his head in her lap. She drew a deep breath. The scent of pine and the lake filled her senses as she looked out over the water, shimmering like jewels in the late afternoon sun. Katherine closed her eyes and imagined sitting at the end of the dock with Betsy on a summer day much like today during her first visit to Two Ponies as a child. There had been many lessons that summer, but one stood out now as the reality of death once again touched her life; first Joseph, then her father, two still-born sons, the loss of Billy Black and now Betsy. On the last day of that joyful visit, they sat swishing their feet through the cold mountain water as Betsy shared the Blackfeet legend of the creation of life.

That summer she had been reborn. She had found hope, the hope that she would someday escape her unhappy childhood and homelife, and find love, the love she had been denied by her mother. And, that summer she had fallen under the spell of what would become her life-long passion — horses. Her Uncle Joe and Betsy had opened the door to her heart and soul, letting the sun in so she could grow into the woman she had become. She cringed to think what might have become of her without them. The rejection of her mother and her father's neglect would have surely turned from hurt to anger as a teenager and who knows where she might have ended up. Between the love and guidance she received from Betsy and her Uncle Joe and the hours of sweat she had poured into her horses and riding, she had managed to stay out of trouble.

Katherine entered the cemetery, squatted beside the grave and rested one hand on Betsy's shoulder and the other on Joseph's headstone. "Thank you."

As the sun set on the saddest day of Katherine's life, she sat quietly in Betsy's favorite corner glider on the front porch. It had been an unusually hot summer for the mountain region of Montana that year, but a chill ran through her head to toe. The front door was open enough so she could vaguely hear Steven on the phone. He sat in the library making the arrangements for the excavation where Betsy would be laid to rest beside her beloved Joseph on Sunday. She tried to block out the image of the funeral parlor staff taking Betsy away earlier and leaned over and wrapped her arms around Laddy, burying her nose in his thick coat. His warmth and lingering puppy smell calmed her trembling frame as she stroked a velvet-soft ear.

When Steven's gentle hand rested on her shoulder, Katherine scooted over to make room for him. He clasped her hand. "They'll be here Saturday morning and promised to be done by noon, well before the girls arrive."

Katherine just nodded as she blew her nose and wiped her tear-streaked face with a tissue she extracted from the box she now carried with her. Contacting their two daughters had brought on another wave of sobs. They had texted their adopted, deaf daughter, Lisa Tyler, on their new cell phone. Luckily, it was a clear day and they didn't have to drive into town to get a signal. What a wonderful technological advancement, these new phones. It sure made it easier to communicate with Lisa and her deaf husband.

And they were amazed they were able to reach their only biological child, Josephine Walker, known to the world as the famous actress "Josie" Walker, on the first try. The girls were equally devastated. As Betsy had been like a mother to Katherine, she had become a grandmother to her daughters. Both girls would arrive the next day. Lisa booked flights immediately for herself, her husband, Daniel Tyler, and their little girl, Elizabeth, while Josephine would fly by private jet out of LAX with her director, Roy Higgins.

Roy, once a popular Western leading man and now an accomplished film director, and his family, had become close friends of the Walkers following his involvement in their rescue five years earlier. He had volunteered to help search the rugged Montana mountains with his chopper when she, Billy, Josephine and Billy's son, TJ, were missing and feared being held captive. While Josephine studied theatre and film at UCLA, Roy had helped her get a few bit parts and became so impressed with her acting, he cast her in a major role in one of his films. Who knew her daughter would become an overnight sensation as a result?

"I'm glad Lisa got to see Betsy again," said Steven, bringing her back from her thoughts.

Katherine turned to him. "Yes, it was nice they got to visit recently for little Lizzy's birthday."

Steven met her gaze. "Too bad Jo didn't make it… again."

"I know. I'm worried about her, Steven. She hardly said a word over the phone. I feel so out of touch with her."

Steven shook his head. "How long has it been now since her last visit?"

"Since she started her current film, nearly two years ago," she said, reflecting on her daughter's career. This was her first leading role, following the overnight success of her supporting role in Roy's western drama, *Across the Valley*, which earned her a nomination by the Academy. She didn't win an Oscar for her portrayal of the rancher's daughter, where she had the opportunity to show off her riding skills as well as her acting, but it had thrust her into the spotlight. Immediately, she had her choice of roles, but chose to work with Roy again on his next film, a romantic murder mystery set in Washington state.

"Betsy was so proud of Josephine's success," she said. "Never complained about her absence, but I know she missed her dearly."

Steven nodded. "As we all have. It's so strange having our little girl living so far away and having to go through a secretary half the time to talk to her."

"She hasn't been our little girl for a long time now."

"She'll always be our little girl," said Steven, with a weak smile as he wrapped his strong arm around her and gave her a squeeze.

"Sure, she will." Katherine returned his radiant smile. "I can't wait to see her." It had been nearly a year since their last trip to California to visit her and Roy and his family, while they filmed a portion of the film at a studio.

Steven sat erect, his mouth suddenly forming a line. "Is she bringing… what's his name?"

"Brad. She didn't say." They had both been disappointed they didn't get to meet her boyfriend last fall.

"Well, I'd like to meet this Brad guy." Steven shifted his weight and raised his right boot to rest on his left knee, tensely wagging it. "They've been living together for how many years now?"

"Only eighteen months," she said. "From what Jo says, he sounds nice and she seems happy."

"Have we seen him in a film?"

"I don't think so. No major roles, this will be his first."

"Thanks to Jo, no doubt," said Steven, his words edged with sarcasm.

"Stop, Steven. Let's wait to meet him before we draw any conclusions. I'm just glad both of our girls will be here Saturday. Saturday! Oh my God. Sports Illustrated! I forgot about the interview."

"Would you like me to reschedule it for you?" Steven turned to study her reaction.

"No, I can't after how hard Betsy worked to arrange it."

"What time are they arriving?"

"Around noon."

"Want me to pick them up at the airport before I pick up the kids? What's one more trip that day."

"No need, they'll be arriving in their own jet and are renting a van."

Steven smiled, nodding. "Of course, they are. Soon, you'll be as famous as our daughter."

"Highly unlikely."

"Well, it'll be a busy day. And maybe that will be a good thing; take your mind off things."

"No, I think it'll be a time of reflection. They're going to want to hear my story, and Betsy's a big part of it. If it hadn't been for her, I never would have started riding."

"You've got a point. It'll be a tribute, then."

"Yes, I like that. Speaking of which, I'm so pleased with the turnout planned for Sunday." When notifying everyone of Betsy's passing, she had invited over a hundred friends and students to attend a celebration of her life to be held following her funeral at Two Ponies Sunday. "But we'll keep the burial to just immediate family and close friends."

"Sounds good," said Steven. "Did you invite Sarah and TJ?"

"Yes." Billy's widow, Sarah Black Feather, their son TJ and Sarah's parents, lived down the creek a few miles east of Two Ponies.

Katherine couldn't recall the last time she saw TJ. She missed him. He had had a life-long crush on Josephine, and they had been so happy together as a couple, but ever since Josephine broke up with him, he had become scarce. He had even stopped assisting Steven on routine and emergency calls he so enjoyed. She imagined he felt rejected and embarrassed around her and Steven. Occasionally, they crossed paths in town when he was home summers from vet school, earning a nod or brief wave, but he avoided any conversation.

It had come as a shock to learn of the split, but it shouldn't have been with TJ attending school in Fort Collins and Josephine living on the West Coast. But she knew it had been more than just the challenge of a long-distance relationship, they had grown apart in other ways. As she and Steven had feared, the strain of being an interracial couple took its toll. Having an American Indian boyfriend must have been difficult for Josephine living amongst her rich white friends in California and they had heard from their daughter that TJ's

Blackfeet friends didn't approve of him dating a rich white girl. The bias went both ways.

The Walkers remained friends with Sarah, inviting her to family functions which she attended faithfully without TJ. She seemed happy, caring for her parents and taking up painting horses and wildlife which she sold at markets on the Blackfeet Indian Reservation in Browning. As they promised Sarah following Billy's death, they had continued to pay any balance on TJ's tuition. TJ excelled at school, earning nearly half his tuition in scholarships. The fact the Walkers were paying for his education had remained a secret. Even Josephine didn't know about it. Katherine and Steven feared if TJ found out, his pride would not allow him to accept their help. It was the least they could do for the son of the man that saved their lives. That same pride would most likely keep him home Sunday.

"Did Sarah say if TJ would be attending?" asked Steven, reading her thoughts as he so often did.

"Sarah didn't say for sure. It would be a difficult situation for him. I'm sure Sarah has mentioned Brad."

"Probably. But I hope he decides to come to at least the burial," said Steven. "Say, we need to pick out a photo or two for Sunday, right?"

"Yes. I already know one we'll display. The one of her and Flower hanging in her bedroom that Joseph took."

"Of course, perfect."

"But we'll need to find one of her and Joseph and a few recent pictures of her with her family and ours."

Steven stood up. "I'm going to fix a sandwich. Can I make you one? You haven't eaten all afternoon."

"I'm not hungry."

"You need to eat something. How about some chicken soup?"

Katherine nodded with a faint smile. "Sure." It was fitting, that had always been Betsy's fix all.

A few minutes later, Steven returned with her soup and set it on the table beside her along with a white envelope. "Look what I found in the trash. You must have thrown it out by accident - one of your fan letters." He sat next to her and took a bite of his ham and cheese.

Katherine cringed, recognizing it right away as the letter she had intentionally tossed earlier.

"You want me to read it to you?" he mumbled, still chewing.

"No, thanks," she said, sliding it beside her out of sight. "I'll read it with the others later." There was no reason to concern Steven with the ranting of some idiot. It would only upset him. As she stared at her soup, her thoughts returned to their loss. She realized, every meal she ate from now on would remind her of Betsy. "I knew this day was coming, but it didn't make it any easier."

"Eat, Betsy would want you to eat."

Katherine chuckled. "Yes, you're right, she would."

When they finished their meal, Steven draped his arm around her, his warmth and familiar scent enveloping her. Now she just needed her girls home.

2 – The Kids

New York City, New York
Saturday

A swath of early morning sunlight crept up the bedroom wall as Lisa rushed to pack for their return to Two Ponies. She smiled at her daughter, Elizabeth, darting past the door. Taking full advantage of her preoccupation, the four-year-old raced through the house galloping astride her play horse. They had just returned from Montana a month prior, having celebrated her daughter's birthday at Two Ponies, and ever since, all Elizabeth wanted to do was charge about the house on the stick horse her grandmother had given her.

"Slow down, Lizzy!" she hollered as the girl made another pass outside her room.

A few minutes later the little cowgirl, wearing her pink Western boots and matching cowboy hat, more gifts from Nana Walker, came to a halt beside her mother, out of breath.

Elizabeth pulled on Lisa's pantleg to make sure her mother could read her lips. "Can I ride Snickers again?" she questioned, still straddling the brown and black stick horse resembling Katherine's retired bay school pony she rode their last visit. To make sure her mother understood, she signed "ride" and "horse."

"Sure, sweetie. But please stop running. How about we put a movie in until Daddy gets home?"

Elizabeth ran and pointed to her favorite video, *My Little Pony.*

"Okay." Lisa slipped the video into the cassette player. Hopefully, she could return to her packing without any more distractions. They needed to be ready to leave for the airport as soon as her husband returned from the office where he had a couple of urgent matters to attend to before they left.

After getting Elizabeth settled on the couch with a snack, Lisa returned to packing in her quiet world. Sometimes it made her sad that she would never hear her daughter's laughter, but Lisa liked to imagine what her little angel might sound like. Having gone gradually deaf as a child, Lisa spoke quite clearly and could read lips effectively. But Daniel, who she met at a deaf college in New York, was born deaf. The couple shared a concern about their daughter's speech development growing up with two deaf parents, but she had adapted amazingly well. From an early age, Elizabeth was taught to sign, and just this year, they hired a tutor for children of deaf parents to make sure her speech advanced normally.

Her mind wondered back to the purpose of their trip as she pulled a couple outfits from her closet. The news of Betsy's death had not come as a shock. It wasn't so much her age as her noticeable lack of vigor and purpose during their recent visit. Picturing Betsy lying over Joseph's grave as her mother had described, she recalled how often Betsy had spoken of her life partner, nearly non-stop during their last stay. Perhaps she knew she would be seeing him soon. There had always been something special about Betsy, the way she seemed to sense things before they happened and knew what you were about to say before you said it. She often pondered if being Blackfeet had anything to do with how acutely intuitive and wise the old woman was.

And Betsy always knew the right thing to say or story to tell to get her message across to her as a child. Lisa wholeheartedly believed her wonderful stories that had been passed down from one Blackfeet generation to the next. Tales about the Creator and the spirits living amongst them, came to mind. And perhaps she still believed, wanting to imagine Betsy amongst the Sky People and her ancestors beyond the clouds. She liked the idea Betsy could still guide and protect her and her family as she always had, only now in spirit.

As she went through the motions of packing, her mind continued to travel back in time. She recalled a story Betsy had shared about

Katoyis, a mythical Blackfeet hero who had many adventures slaying monsters and wicked people. And another about the Little People, child-sized, benevolent, and shy nature spirits who were said to have a variety of magical powers, like the ability to become invisible or shapeshift into animals. When Lisa first lived with the Walkers at Two Ponies, Betsy had the room beside hers upstairs and when she had a bad dream, she would knock on Betsy's door. Then she would tuck her back into bed and tell her a story. Betsy would tell her that she had magical powers too, and that she was smart and strong like Katoyis. Or that she could turn into a bear or mountain lion like the Little People, and there was nothing to fear. And there had been a lot to fear in her life prior to the Walkers.

Lisa was the daughter of the Werdens, the family that once owned the adjoining property west of Two Ponies which encompassed the other half of Pine Island Lake. For centuries, the Werden clan had fancied purchasing Two Ponies and opening a hunting and fishing resort. In an attempt to force Katherine out of business and into selling the estate, her father and brother had schemed to burn down Katherine's barn full of horses. They had no use for the large barn and livestock, it was the eight-bedroom lodge they were after.

Her father, Jack Werden had enrolled Lisa at Katherine's camp that summer, unknowingly to Lisa, to obtain information and access to the school so they could plan their attack. She had become especially fond of her assigned mount that summer, an Appaloosa named Wompa, and when she learned of their plan, she hiked hours in the dark through the cold and rain to save the horses. The thought of any harm coming to her sweet boy, Wompa, or the other horses kept her pressing on. By the time she arrived, the barn was already burning, and in her haste to release all the horses from their stalls, Lisa became trapped at the back of the structure. Betsy had heard her screams, doused a horse blanket in the water tank and entered the inferno, guiding her to safety. Lisa would have perished that night, had it not been for Betsy.

Entering her daughter's room to pick an outfit for the day, her old *Black Beauty* book caught her eye lying beside the girl's bed. It had been Lisa's salvation as a child, all she had kept from her past life. She received few toys and no books growing up in the Werden household. So, when she checked *Black Beauty* out from her school library and fell in love with the story, she neglected to return it. She read it whenever her parents fought, which was often.

She had lived in constant fear; in fear of beatings by her father, in fear of her mother being pummeled, in fear of her much older brother and friends touching her in places she knew was wrong. There was no love to be found in the Werden home, not even from her mother who abandoned her following her husband's and son's imprisonment. To this day, she didn't know where her birth mother went or what happened to her and didn't care if she ever knew. She cringed to imagine what might have happened to her as a frail ten-year-old deaf child and ward of the state if the Walkers hadn't adopted her. It took years for the night terrors to end. Sometimes, Katherine would stay up and read Black Beauty with her until she fell asleep. Now Katherine would need comforting. Betsy meant the world to her mother and had remained the one constant in her life, raising and loving her like her own, just as Katherine had done so with her.

Lisa peeked in on Elizabeth before gathering a few more small toys to stuff in her backpack. It was always a challenge keeping the toddler occupied during flights. Her little fair-haired cherub sat grinning like the Cheshire Cat with her legs folded under her, munching on Goldfish crackers. She grinned at her beautiful miracle baby. Her pregnancy had come as a surprise, having given up after trying to conceive for over three years. Mother and daughter exchanged a smile and Elizabeth signed "love" before her attention was drawn back to the film.

She glanced at the Man-in-the-Moon clock hanging over Elizabeth's bed. Daniel would be home soon. They had an hour drive and nearly a five-hour flight followed by a two-hour drive before arriving at Two Ponies late that afternoon. She had a hard time imaging Betsy would not be there to greet them at the door with her beautiful smile.

Next, she entered the kitchen to pack a few snacks and drinks to add to her backpack and hesitated at the refrigerator door. Elizabeth's drawing from yesterday hung on the door with magnets. When Lisa learned of Betsy's passing, she wasn't sure how to explain her absence when they arrived at Two Ponies, so she shared the stories of the Sky and Little People. She explained Betsy had Blackfeet magic too, and she had turned herself into a bird and flew away to a beautiful place beyond the clouds to join the Sky People. A short time later, her daughter handed her a drawing of a red bird, cardinals were her favorite, and said it was Betsy flying into the clouds. It warmed Lisa's heart, imagining Betsy's perpetual smile knowing her people's legends lived on. Numerous times over the years, Lisa had suggested to Betsy she write them all down. But Betsy didn't write English as well as she spoke and read it and she would always say Joseph was the writer, not her.

While Lisa returned to her room to finish packing for herself, she wished she'd gotten the opportunity to meet Joseph O'Reilly. He had died long before she was born, but she had read all his books and felt a connection with him through his writing and from Betsy's and others' recollections. Everyone always said Josephine reminded them of her namesake, high-spirited and stubborn. But her sister did not share the importance of family Joseph wrote about in his books, at least not recently. She paused as she folded a blouse, recalling it had been nearly three years since she had seen Josephine. Lisa had hoped her sister would take an active role as Elizabeth's Auntie Jo, but despite all of her invitations to visit them in New York, she still hadn't taken the initiative, nor had she and her family been invited to California. Betsy had not been her first heartbreak. She had been mourning the loss of her sister for some time.

Perhaps it wouldn't hurt so much if they hadn't been so close growing up. After Katherine and Steven adopted her, her life became a real-life fairytale, a dream come true. She too, like Black Beauty, had found her happy ending – loving parents, Betsy as a grandmother, her own horse, and a little sister that adored her. She felt a warm tug at her heart recalling their fun times growing up together at Two Ponies. Little Bit, a nickname Lisa had given Josephine, became her shadow. Eleven years younger, she followed her everywhere, wanting to do everything her big sister did. Later they rode the trails and swam in the lake together, nearly inseparable. And, when Lisa moved to New York, they had kept in close contact, writing weekly. But following Josephine's move to California, living at opposite ends of the continent, they had grown apart more than just geographically. Telephone calls were useless for a deaf person and her family heard one excuse after another why she couldn't make it home over the past three years. The Walkers, and O'Reillys before them, had always celebrated Thanksgiving, Christmas and their mother's birthday together with their friends and neighbors at Two Ponies.

She considered the possibility Josephine's absence had something to do with her breakup with TJ, afraid of the possibility of confronting him in person. Lisa was so surprised when she learned Josephine had broken it off, and by letter no less, after all they had been through together. He deserved better. They seemed so happy. Lisa feared the death of TJ's father might have contributed to their split, considering he died protecting their family. Jo had to feel some measure of guilt and who would blame TJ for resenting the Walkers for his loss. Guilt hung over Lisa as well, knowing it was her older brother, Ricky Werden, her own blood, that had shot and killed Mr. Black Feather. She couldn't help thinking if it hadn't been for Ricky, not only would TJ's father be alive, perhaps TJ and Jo would still be together. Her mind understood she had no control over those events or their outcome, but her heart felt otherwise.

Lisa zipped up her suitcase. What a shame it would take such a somber event to finally bring her sister home. She looked forward to seeing her, yet a part of her feared the reunion. How much had Josephine changed?

Malibu, California

Josephine Walker sat on her bed, propped up against a pile of pillows, reading the script from her current film, *Secrets.* It's the story of a famous ballerina who loses her ability to dance following a car accident and can no longer handle the pitiful stares and comments of family and friends in New York City. She escapes West to work at a large dude ranch in Washington state where she leads a quiet, secret life, concealing her identity. There she meets a man doing the same, but for different reasons. While working at the ranch, she returns to her first love of horses, which she chose to abandon to pursue her dancing career. This hits home for Josephine having given up her prior life; her family, best friend and first love as well as leaving behind her heart horse, Bonanza, to become an actress. Her character finds love, but also finds herself in a tangled web of lies, deception and murder. Josephine could relate to her character's pain and planned to draw from her own traumatic past as she performed, just as her director, Roy, had taught her.

Growing up dreaming of becoming an actress, Josephine never imagined during her second year in UCLA's Theatre, Film and Television program, she would get the opportunity to accept a major role in a film. She had done a few commercials and bit parts, thanks to connections she made through Roy. Impressed by her work, he offered her a supporting role as the rancher's daughter in Across the Valley. She poured herself into her work and pushed everything and everyone aside that might come between her and the success she hungered for, including TJ.

When her dreams materialized, she was a bit shell-shocked by the immediate impact stardom made on her life, but she quickly adopted and relished the attention of being in the spotlight. Overnight, she had transformed from the naïve horse-riding mountain girl from Montana, her classmates had dubbed "Annie Oakley," to the envy of her peers. Suddenly, her face was everywhere from billboards to television commercials on an international scale. She wondered what her old classmates from high school thought of her silly pipe dream now.

But sometimes, Josephine missed the simplicity of being just a random young woman without the fear of paparazzi showing up to ruin a meal or a relaxing jog on the beach. The vastness of the ocean had become her mountains, the place she could still find some peace… find herself again, but soon her jogging routine was discovered and spoiled too. That was the only part she didn't like. The rest of it, the lovely glass house on the ocean, the beautiful clothes and glamorous parties, were a dream come true for the twenty-three-year-old.

When on location in Washington away from the city, she could once again find some quiet and alone time, going for a run or ride. When she did, she found her mind drifting back to the same memories playing over and over in her mind like an old movie she knew by heart. Being with TJ. Like her character, had her career been worth the sacrifice?

The print had become a blur and the script fell from her hands. It was a good script and a great part for her, sure to continue her sky-rocketing career, but she just couldn't get into it that morning. After hearing the news about Betsy's death, she had been pulled back to her roots.

Roy had flown her and Brad home the night before in his new Cessna to pack for their flight to Montana that afternoon. She had trouble sleeping and had packed earlier that morning while her boyfriend, Brad Donahue, slept in. He entered the bedroom without a word, his hair wet from a shower. She studied Brad as he paced between the closet and his suitcase lying open on his side of their bed. No relation to Troy Donahue, one of her mother's teen idols along with Alan Ladd and Tab Hunter, he could pass as Troy's grandson though, with his pretty face, gold locks, ocean blue eyes and slender yet masculine build. She guessed that might have been what attracted her mother to her father, another handsome sandy blond. But then, her mother had also been attracted to and had fallen in love with TJ's Blackfeet father. The parallels were intriguing between her and her mother. She found TJ with his black hair, chestnut skin, dark brown eyes and athletic build equally attractive as Brad who vaguely resembled her father. She often wondered if that's what might have drawn her to Brad. But he wasn't rugged like her dad, raised the spoiled, only son of an old money Tinseltown family of politicians and businessmen. She still wasn't sure what his father did, besides play golf and travel.

Josephine set the wad of sheets down. "I can't concentrate," she said. "I just can't believe she's gone," she pondered out loud. The news about Betsy had come as a shock and the guilt that soon followed hadn't helped, having not returned home to see her for years.

This was not Josephine's first experience with the loss of a loved one. She had lost her Grandpa Walker as a junior in high school. The thought of her grandfather always brought a smile to her face. He had a way of making everyone laugh with his funny one-liners and practical jokes. He had moved in with her family at Two Ponies following the death of her Grandma Walker, shortly after she was born. She looked fondly upon the years she shared the upstairs with Lisa, Betsy and Grandpa. She had always been grateful he passed in his sleep and that Betsy had found him. But she hadn't been so fortunate when TJ's dad, Mr. Black Feather, was shot. The image of him lying on his back in a pool of blood still gave her nightmares. At least TJ had been spared from carrying that memory throughout his life. Now Betsy was gone, who for all intents and purposes was her grandmother.

"What's the big deal?" said Brad, fragmenting her thoughts as he meticulously folded a pair of slacks. "All this travel and halting production on the film. Wasn't she just a cook and housekeeper?"

Josephine glared at him. "No!" Brad could be so… cold, insensitive sometimes. She recalled how sweet he used to be when they first started dating. Now, she oftentimes got the impression he only cared about his work. Slacks? What was he thinking? "You won't need to pack slacks, just a couple pairs of jeans and a few casual shirts."

Brad ignored her and pulled two dress shirts from the closet. "My mother had help too, Mexicans," he said. "She had so many functions to attend and I rarely saw my dad that I was nearly raised by these women, but I don't even know where they are now."

"Betsy was different. I've told you how she was a part of the family," she said, making sure her agitation was evident.

"I'm sorry. I didn't mean to upset you, sweetie." Brad sat on the corner of the bed. "How about I call in some lunch? Your favorite, Thai Taste?"

"I'm not hungry."

"Some shrimp coconut soup?"

"Okay," she agreed to quiet him.

"That's my Josie girl."

After Brad called in their order, he returned to the bed beside her. Brushing the hair from her face, he ran the back of his hand along her cheek to the nape of her neck where he planted a kiss. His hand moved to her breast. "We have time to kill before the food arrives."

"I'm not in the mood," she said, scooting away from him.

Brad sat up with a jerk. "Well, I can't wait to get this trip over with and get things back to normal, all this moping around is depressing. We have a huge production week next week – the murder scene and my best lines."

While Brad continued ranting on about how well he'll perform, Josephine pushed his voice out of her mind until he sounded miles away and curled into a ball on the bed. She had cried yesterday after her mother's call and felt tears welling again as memories of Betsy played like a silent film in her head. She remembered the evening Betsy had comforted her in front of the fire in the great room when her mother and Mr. Black Feather had disappeared and were considered in grave danger. Betsy wiped away her tears and told her stories about her mother as a girl and young woman.

"Don't worry, your mother will be fine," Betsy had said. "You remind me of her, and not just in the face, you're both strong women."

That was the day before their parents' vehicles had turned up at the Black Feathers' place. Three days later, they would learn just how strong they both were. She and TJ had recklessly ridden off ill-prepared into the mountains to find their parents. They hit rain followed by snow and nearly froze to death. And they may very well have done just that if it hadn't been for TJ constructing a makeshift tent and suggesting they combine their sleeping bags to share body heat. Up to that point, they had been just friends, in her mind anyway. But TJ hadn't hidden the fact he adored her since they were toddlers. She had fought any attraction to the tall, dark and handsome Blackfeet to appease her parents and avoid ridicule from her white friends at school. But that night she opened her soul to her best friend.

She had not only given him her virginity; she gave TJ her heart. Now an empty void took the place of the love and joy they once shared. Her heart ached whenever she dared to recapture their moments together. Would the scar ever heal? Could she ever give her heart fully to another? The worst part was knowing it was a self-inflected wound. She had been the one to break the promise they'd made to one another at the cabin their last Thanksgiving together. No matter the distance, time away, their difference in race, their parents or friends, they vowed to never allow anyone or anything to come between them. Sometimes the pain rivaled the agony she had felt when she feared she had lost TJ forever; shot in the back lying lifeless and face down in the river. When she was taken hostage, certain of her own imminent death, she felt no fear, certain there was nothing left to live for without TJ.

Miraculously, her father found TJ and between his care and Roy flying him to the hospital, TJ survived. She felt alive again. Tragically, it was Mr. Black Feather that didn't survive, taking a bullet meant for her father to save them all. It all still seemed like a dream, including her mother chasing Ricky Werden down and stabbing him to death with Billy's knife. She still woke up with visions of TJ lying in the river, his blood trickling downstream, of them hauling her mother away to be raped and killed and of Mr. Black Feather's body. She had no trouble producing tears for the camera reliving these events, especially imagining she would never see TJ again.

And now here she was, having not seen him for three years. Would she get the opportunity to see him again? Her hands shook at the thought of it, as much from anticipation as from fear. What would he think of her now? She glanced into the dresser mirror across the room; her hair colored redder than its natural auburn color, wearing as much makeup as a mannequin and having lost enough weight for her role that her face looked gaunt. She barely recognized herself.

Would TJ be at the funeral? Would he even talk to her and give her the opportunity to explain why she broke it off? Although, she wasn't sure she totally understood the "why" herself. But she felt she had to try. She hoped she could at least salvage their friendship… or maybe more.

Browning, Montana

Theodore James Black Feather whittled on a piece of dried pine on the back porch of an old stone building his three friends shared on the Reservation. He had helped them put on a new roof and replace the windows and doors of the once abandoned structure during his summers home from school. Each year he seemed to spend more time with them on the Res and less time at home with his mother and grandparents. TJ studied the object as it began to take shape in his hands.

"Another horse?" asked Talon, entering the doorway behind him. His old friend had adapted the nickname years ago, short for his surname of Eagle Foot, rather than going by his English name of Thomas. "What are you going to do with all those things?"

TJ glanced at the pile of carved animals growing in the corner of the porch. "I don't know, helps me think."

"Well, you sure have been doing a lot of thinking." Talon hesitated as if considering whether to ask him a question. TJ had a good idea what that question might be. "You're not considering going tomorrow, are you?"

Sure enough, he guessed right. Talon and the rest of his friends never approved of his relationship with Josephine to begin with. "I don't know. My mom wants me to go. Betsy was a close friend of our family."

"I think it'll be a mistake. Seeing her is just going to mess you up again, man."

"Maybe, I need to see her to… to move on."

"Is her boyfriend coming with her?"

"Shit," mumbled TJ, throwing the wooden horse as far as he could chuck it, having just sliced off its ears. He looked over to his friend. "Probably. Maybe seeing them together would help… you know, help me to put her behind me."

"Yeah right, look at you just thinking about the possibility. You nearly took your finger off. She's been nothing but trouble. We told you from the start she'd end up dumping you. You need to get laid and forget about that redhead."

The sound of gravel flying drew their attention to the truck and trailer pulling in the drive. TJ was glad for the interruption. The Standing Bear brothers, Noot and Matt had arrived with the horses after pulling them off a pasture nearby. Noot, short for Nootau which means "Fire" in Algonquian, was named appropriately, having a short fuse and explosive temper. Matt, short for Matuannaagd which means "He who fights," was born premature and fighting for his life and now feels he must live up to his name. Between the two of them, they were certain to find trouble nearly every weekend, the last no exception with TJ and Talon bailing them out of jail Friday night following a bar brawl. TJ had hoped forming a relay team would have channeled their friend's energy to competing on the track.

They formed their four-man Horse Nations Indian Relay Team two years ago, competing regionally against riders and teams from seven different Nations covering Idaho, Montana, North Dakota, South Dakota, Washington, Wyoming and Canada. Each team has three horses which are raced around a track by one rider. TJ earned the "rider" position by putting in the fastest times. The others help in the exchange. TJ races the first horse around the track, dismounts and mounts the next horse on the fly bareback. Talon, the "mugger," holds the next horse while Noot, the "holder," holds the third horse in waiting. Matt, the "catcher," handles the horse coming in.

Competing against five to eight other teams, the races run all summer and the champions of each meet compete in the Championship of Champions Race every fall. Their team, "Piegan Pride" hoped to win the North American Indian Days race held in Browning the following weekend to qualify for the championship in Washington State that September. If they didn't win that race, they would have the opportunity to qualify at two more races held in Montana in August. Last year, they qualified in Browning but placed out of the winnings at the Championship. After adding a faster horse, a gray part Thoroughbred gelding named Moon Cloud, for the final lap of the relay, the team hoped to take home the first-place prize that year.

"You ready to ride?" called Noot, hanging out of the passenger window. The three horses rattled around in the stock trailer anxious to unload and go to work.

"Sure," said TJ. "Let me get my bag." TJ jogged down the stairs to retrieve his backpack from his truck. Tossing his bag in the back of Matt's truck, he and Talon squeezed into the small pull-down backseats of the club cab.

"We going to practice again tomorrow?" questioned Matt, glancing back to TJ as he turned the rig around. He waited for a response before pulling out onto the road. "We could use another couple runs before the race next weekend. We all have to work this week."

"He's undecided about the funeral," said Talon, earning a nasty look from TJ.

"Sure," said TJ. "But can we make it in the afternoon?"

Noot snorted. "He's going!"

"I haven't decided yet."

Each of his friends snickered and shook their heads as Matt pulled out of their drive and headed toward the practice track which was nothing more than a graded area with stakes measuring the approximate distance of a track, but it sufficed.

When TJ returned home that evening following practice, he found his mother folding laundry in the living room. His grandparents worked on a puzzle in the corner of the room. Now in their eighties, TJ's grandfather was confined to a wheelchair, but his grandmother could still get around with a cane. They had moved off the Reservation and in with them a few years ago when grandfather could no longer drive. His grandmother never had learned to drive.

Sarah turned to him with a smile. "I knew you'd go."

"I didn't say I was."

"Oh, I thought since you came home…"

TJ rushed up the stairs, two at a time, threw his bag on the floor and plopped down on his bed. Why was his mother so hell-bent on him attending Betsy's funeral anyway? This needed to be his decision. He didn't need her nagging him about it. No sooner than he stretched out and closed his eyes for a nap before dinner, his mother entered the doorway.

"Don't you want to give respect? You loved Betsy."

TJ sat up. "You know why I don't want to go."

"Jo," she said, flatly.

"Is he going to be there?"

His mother clearly understood who he was referring to. "Yes, her boyfriend is coming. They're arriving this evening. Roy is flying them in. Wouldn't you like to see Roy? He did save your life after all." His mother's voice clearly conveyed her frustration.

He didn't mean to upset her. He just didn't want to see Jo, especially on the arm of some pretty, rich, white boy. Talon was right. He didn't need to reopen the wound she'd cut into his heart. The pain of her rejection and broken promises lay just beneath the surface, like an unhealed scab which could easily be torn wide open again to fester.

"I'm not going," he decided, springing up off the bed and throwing open his closet door. He wasn't even sure what he was searching for.

"You owe it to the Walkers if nothing else."

TJ turned to her. "What do I owe them? If it wasn't for them, Dad would still be alive!"

"No, your father made the choice to confront Ricky. He knew the danger. And he chose to save Dr. Walker's life. You can't blame them. And you would be dead if it wasn't for Dr. Walker. What's wrong with you? It's those boys… no respect."

"Not for whites. They can't be trusted."

"That's those boys talking. If it wasn't for the Walkers… you…"

"What?"

"I promised not to tell, but maybe you need to hear it." His mother took a deep breath. "The Walkers have been paying for your education."

"What, why?" TJ threw up his arms. "Oh, let me guess, they felt they owed us because of Dad? Perfect! You've been lying to me all these years about the life insurance and savings? Treating me like a child. What else haven't you been telling me? Where's your respect for me?"

"They were afraid you wouldn't accept their help if you knew."

"Damn straight I wouldn't have." TJ stuffed a few changes of clothes in a duffle bag.

"And they would keep paying, but I decided they've done enough. I'm selling the ranch."

TJ turned on his heels. "No, you can't sell it!" He couldn't imagine not having the ranch, it was all they had left of his father.

"Why not? What do you care? You're rarely home anymore. Always with those boys on the Res. Do you know how hard your father worked to keep us off the Reservation? See, no respect!"

"I know how much he poured into this place. I helped him do it. Don't sell the ranch. I'll take some time off from school, get a full-time job. If we win the Championship this fall plus what I'm saving from work, I'll be able to pay my own way. I'll return to my classes in January."

His mother opened her mouth to speak.

"I'm not going. I can't. Give my condolences."

TJ zipped up his bag, stepped past his mother in the doorway and left for the Reservation. Now more than ever, they needed to win the Championship in September.

3 – Interview

Elkhead, Montana

Katherine waited anxiously at the picnic table on the side porch, expecting the Sports Illustrated team to arrive any minute. It had become a bittersweet moment with Betsy gone. She had worked so hard and was so proud of herself for arranging the interview. They had been looking forward to the press team's arrival for weeks.

When the van pulled in, Katherine met them at the stairs.

"Katherine Walker?" asked a middle-aged man wearing a genuine smile with his arm outreached. This must be George; the man Betsy spoke with and who called her from the airport. She liked him already. The rest of the crew exited the van and lined up behind him.

She shook his hand with a nod. "Yes, you can call me Kat. I hope you found us without any trouble."

"The camp brochure with the map and directions was perfect. I'm George Freeman. I'll be conducting the interview, and this is my team," he said, pointing to each. "Sam James, director, Laura Mason, stills, Peter Bell, sound, and Freddie Grayson, video."

"So nice to meet you all. Welcome to Two Ponies."

"This place is huge. Is this your home?" questioned Laura, surveying the lodge from beneath her Yankees baseball cap as she stepped beside George on the stairs.

"Yes, I've been fortunate enough to call Two Ponies home for forty years." Katherine motioned toward her hat. "You and my husband would get along famously."

"A Yankee fan in Montana, cool. Will we get to meet him?"

"Sorry, he's picking our daughter up at the airport."

"Well, this place is gorgeous. Great backdrop," she said, looking in awe as she admired the lake view and peeked in the lodge windows as she explored the porch.

Sam, a tall and thin young man, greeted her next. "Hi, Kat. How about we set up on the front porch?" Before she could respond, he anxiously strode up the stairs two at a time and nearly jogged to catch up with Laura.

The sound guy, Peter, had a gray ponytail protruding from the back of his Aussie safari hat. He appeared all business, shaking her hand as he surveyed the lodge. "Any outlets on the porch?"

"Yes, there's one here," she pointed, moving a planter of begonias aside. "And one out front behind the table."

"Perfect," said Peter, tipping his hat before joining the others.

Freddie, a robust man, stayed back, reaching around George to shake her hand. "Nice to meet you, Ma'am. Beautiful property," he said in a Southern twang.

"Thank you, but why are you filming the interview?"

Freddie just smiled and pointed to George as he passed her on the stairs. Katherine turned to George for an explanation.

"We can always frame-grab stills from the footage if needed," said George, then whispered, "And, I have a friend at NBC that would love to see some footage of you and the location. They are interested in sending a team out after you qualify."

"If we qualify," corrected Katherine.

"Oh yes, the athlete curse if you count your chickens before they hatch."

"I suppose that's it," said Katherine with a chuckle. "Two Ponies is even lovelier that time of year."

"It's not bad now." George followed Katherine to where the team had congregated on the front porch.

"The porch won't do," said Sam. "I want the lake in the background."

"We could swing the chairs around," suggested Katherine.

"Wrong light, ambient light will only put you in the shadows," said Peter.

"How about we move these two chairs and table out onto the lawn, there in the shade of those trees," suggested Laura.

George studied the yard. "Yes, then we can get some shots from the lake with the cabin in the background and some with the lake and mountains behind you."

"Perfect!" said Laura and Freddie in unison.

"The lawn it is, then," said George, as each of the men carried a piece of the wicker furniture down the stairs. They set up the chairs with the small table in the center, turned slightly toward the cabin. "We'll want shots at the barn with the horse of course."

"Will you want me to ride him?"

"You bet!" said George, "You don't mind, do you?"

"I planned on it. My assistant trainer has Major groomed and ready to tack up whenever we're ready."

"Wonderful, we'll do the interview here first, then move to the barn. The interview will be Q&A style. I'll work from the recording to write the article. We'll run as many photos as space allows; normally three to six for a feature. Remember, the video is just extra. And I want you to know in all my years with the magazine, this is my first equestrian sport interview. So, have patience with me. In fact, there's only been a handful of features run outside of Thoroughbred racing. Your unique story and Betsy's persistence made it happen."

Katherine just nodded, glancing toward the open plot beside Joseph's grave at the edge of the yard. She closed her eyes. Just hold it together, she told herself.

Once Katherine and George were seated, power cords run and the lighting and mics set up, they did a few tests and were ready to go. Katherine felt anxious, even more than before, learning she would be filmed as well as recorded. She had never done anything like this before. Nervously, she curled her hair around her finger, an old habit from when she was a girl. Once she realized, she took a firm grip of the chair arm instead.

Laura, who doubled as makeup artist, put a few more pats of power on her perspiring face. "Relax, just pretend the cameras aren't there."

"Easy for you to say, you're on the other end," said Katherine.

"You've got this," said Laura.

"You ready?" asked George.

Katherine nodded, focusing on George as the video rolled and Laura snapped photos. George introduced himself, described their location, then introduced her and her goal. She took a deep breath and as soon as he began asking questions, just like starting a jump course or dressage test, she focused on the task at hand and relaxed.

"How long have you been riding?"

Katherine smiled. "It all started right here. I began visiting my Uncle and Betsy summers at the age of ten. They had two pleasure horses, a stubborn bald-faced gelding named 'Baldy,' which my uncle drove under harness, and a sweet Paint mare named 'Flower,' that was Betsy's horse and the first horse I ever rode. There was no big barn or riding arena then, just the old stable. I learned the basics of horsemanship right here on the trails at Two Ponies. Betsy not only taught me how to ride, but she also shared the magical connection and bond that can be nurtured between man and horse based on mutual trust that has carried me to where I am today."

Suddenly, the image of Betsy and Flower consumed her thoughts. Katherine folded her arms to keep them from shaking, and once again her eyes drifted toward the excavation hidden in the shadows at the edge of the woods.

George motioned with his hand across his neck, signaling Freddie and Peter to stop recording. "Are you okay? What's wrong?"

Katherine drew in a deep breath and gently wiped her eyes, not to mess up her mascara. She nodded in the direction of the gravesite. "Tomorrow Betsy will be laid to rest here at Two Ponies," she said on the verge of tears.

Laura gasped and covered her mouth in disbelief.

"I'm so sorry," said George. "I was so looking forward to meeting her."

The rest of the team followed with their condolences.

"We lost her just yesterday. She was eighty-five," said Katherine, her voice still faltering.

"You should have let us know, we would have rescheduled," said George.

Katherine shook her head and managed a smile. "How could I after how hard she worked to set it up."

"I'm sorry we didn't get to meet her," said Laura.

"Me too." Katherine took a deep breath, trying to calm her emotions.

"How about we give you a few minutes before we continue," said George.

"I'm good. Just a drink of water, please."

Laura handed her one of the water bottles they had set out. Katherine took a few sips, set the bottle down and nodded.

George proceeded with the interview with a thumbs up to Freddie and Peter. "When did your dream of qualifying for the US Equestrian Team become a goal?"

"Following my second summer at Two Ponies, I began riding lessons back home in Boston. That was the year of the 1952 Summer Olympics in Helsinki, Finland. I had never heard of the country, let alone the city. I watched as much of the Games as possible on our new black and white television, hoping to catch the show jumping. They didn't show much coverage of the equestrian events then, just some of the highlights, but enough to inspire me. After that, I set my goal to someday ride in the Olympics and win a gold medal. I was only twelve.

"I worked hard at my riding and my trainer began to see my potential. She started putting me on her best mounts and before long, she convinced my parents to purchase my own horse. It didn't take long for me to advance as far as I could on him, and for my sixteenth birthday, my parents bought me a beautiful Thoroughbred mare, Lady Jane of Rosehaven. This time, I had to catch up with her.

Lady was already competing successfully up and down the East Coast a couple divisions ahead of me. That's when my childhood dream took flight. Lady and I quickly advanced as a team and we might have qualified for the 1964 Games in Tokyo..." Remembering how close she had come then, made her pause.

"What happened?"

"I hadn't returned to Two Ponies in four years. My trainer had convinced me I needed to compete each summer if I was serious about making the team. Then my Uncle Joe died, and I returned for his funeral. That was when I learned he had bequeathed the estate to me. I decided to leave one dream behind to obtain another. I moved West with Lady to take ownership of Two Ponies and open a riding school, a girls summer equestrian camp."

"How old were you?"

"Twenty."

"Wow, big decision for a young woman to make. How did your parents and trainer feel about it?"

"My trainer was extremely disappointed to say the least. My father supported the move, but my mother… well, she disowned me… we never spoke again. My mother and I were never close." Katherine hesitated. "I didn't have a happy childhood. I suppose that played in my decision. I had always been happiest here."

"Any regrets?"

"No, not at all. I missed Two Ponies, Betsy and… well then there was Steven."

"Your husband?"

Katherine blushed. "We were best friends as kids and then teen sweethearts."

"He's a large animal vet, I understand. That must come in handy."

"Yes, it's nice to have him involved in Major's conditioning and overall health."

"So, what stands between you and qualifying for Sydney?"

"Since we didn't qualify at the World Equestrian Games, Major and I must medal at the Pan American Games the end of this month in Winnipeg. If we don't, we could still qualify in team or individual jumping at the FEI Show Jumping World Cup in Las Vegas this spring."

"How will you train and keep your horse in condition through the winter with the cold and snow?"

"We will spend September, October and the beginning of November at a facility in northern California, conditioning and schooling cross-country and show jumping. Then we'll return home for the holidays and school mostly dressage in our new covered arena through the winter, giving Major's legs a break from jumping. If there's one thing I don't need to worry about, it's his jumping."

"Tell us about your horse, Major Command."

"Well, he's not a youngster anymore. We're both getting up in years for competing at this level. A friend of mine found him while working at a Thoroughbred farm in California. They had just retired him from racing, and he was about to go to auction."

"Could he have ended up at a slaughterhouse?"

"Unfortunately, yes. Many retired racehorses that have givèn their all making money for their owners and trainers, are discarded when they can no longer produce. It's incredibly sad." Katherine shook her head. "Thank goodness, Billy saw his potential and picked him up for me to try as an upper-level school horse. It didn't take long to realize how special he was, and I started training him for myself. It was a long shot, and it's taken seven years of hard work, but he's now thriving on the eventing circuit."

"Billy, would that be the Blackfeet assistant trainer you tragically lost a few years ago?"

Katherine's smile faded. "Yes, Billy Black Feather." Katherine once again found a lock of hair to coil around her finger. "He was much more than an assistant trainer… he was a dear family friend."

"I'm so sorry for your loss. Do you feel comfortable telling us about your abduction?"

Katherine reflected for a moment. She had expected questions about their ordeal, but she realized there was no way to prepare her emotions for recalling that fateful day. "It'll be five years this fall. Major and I had a chance of qualifying for the 1996 Olympics in Atlanta." Katherine wrung her hands. "It's a long story…"

"Take your time."

She breathed in softly like smelling a rose and exhaled slowly as if to flicker a flame, just as Betsy had taught her to calm herself. "Our neighbors had desperately wanted to purchase Two Ponies to combine with their adjoining property to open a hunting and fishing resort. When my Uncle died, and I inherited the estate, they tried to pressure me into accepting an offer. I refused. This was nearly forty years ago. I went on to open my riding school which required a large set-up loan with escalating balloon payments. They, my neighbors, discovered I was having trouble making the final payment and on the verge of losing Two Ponies and felt certain they would finally get the opportunity to acquire the property. But when I qualified for a loan extension, they became desperate and set fire to my barn full of horses, knowing that loss would force me out of business and I would need to sell the property or lose it to the bank."

"How awful. Did you lose any of the horses?"

"No, thankfully we didn't. The father and son left evidence behind which led to an arson conviction and were sentenced to fifteen years in prison. The father died a few years into his term and when the son got out, he was out for revenge. He blamed me for his father's death and the loss of his family's estate. He had it in for Billy, too, who had taken the life of his older brother in self-defense many years earlier. He left us a letter and map instructing us to ride into the mountains to a location on Eagle Crest River. He threatened to harm our families if we went to the police or didn't follow his instructions. We suspected he didn't intend on us returning home."

"What a frightening situation."

"Billy had a strategy to end it once and for all." Katherine paused to take another drink. "But things didn't go according to plan… and Billy and I ended up being held captive in a mountain cabin just south of the Canadian border by the son and his gang."

"How terrifying."

Katherine could feel the fear take hold as she revisited the anguish and anger she felt that day. It must have been evident in her eyes.

"Can you go on?"

Taking another deep breath, Katherine nodded. Her defenses kicked in as she began recalling the events as if they happened to someone else, almost an out-of-body experience. "Our kids… my daughter, and Billy's son, discovered our tracks and followed us. The very situation we were trying to prevent, putting our family at risk, the kids rode right into. Billy's son was shot, and our daughter was also taken hostage."

"Did the boy survive?"

"Yes, thanks to Steven. He followed the kids' tracks and found him shot in the back and left for dead on the bank of the river. A perfect stranger who volunteered in the search, airlifted him to the nearest hospital. After the helicopter left, Steven followed ours and our abductors' tracks to the cabin. There was a confrontation… and Billy took a bullet to save Steven."

"I'm so sorry."

Katherine remained silent attempting to maintain her composure. With moist eyes and a strained voice, she continued. "He died saving me and my family. All the abductors were dead but one, Billy's murderer, the neighbor's son." Katherine shook her head. "I was so angry… when he attempted to escape on horseback across the border… I chased him down."

"On Major, into a forest fire with only a knife, I understand?"

She nodded her head, taking another gulp of air, feeling like she was drowning. "Billy had taught me how to use a knife. Looking back, it was pretty insane. But I had to try to stop him."

"Did you know he was armed?"

"No, I didn't. All I knew was Billy wasn't going to die in vain. And what kind of future would we have fearing for our children's safety the rest of our lives? I couldn't let him get away. And, if I'd been riding any other horse, I probably never would have caught up with him." Katherine stared out over the lake; images she'd prefer to forget began playing in her head.

"What happened when you caught up with him?" George asked, bringing her back in focus.

"I think the only reason he didn't shoot me as soon as I caught up with him was because he knew he was low on ammunition and the law was still after him. He charged us by surprise from out of the woods, ramming his horse into Major so hard both horses fell… legs intertwined…" Katherine's voice trailed off, as she relived the terror. "I was knocked unconscious and came to the sound of a single gunshot. Immediately, I feared he had shot Major, but his horse had broken its leg and he had put him out of his misery. He said I was next." Katherine took another sip of water. "As he moved supplies from the dead horse to Major, I tried to move, but I couldn't. I had broken my leg in several places. I was lying there helplessly awaiting my imminent death when my dog, Laddy, attacked him, giving me a fighting chance. Laddy took his last bullet and we struggled over the knife… Billy's knife. Seriously wounded, Laddy somehow attacked him again and I won the battle."

"I understand the dog survived."

"Yes, Laddy recovered just fine."

There was a moment of silent refection between them before he asked, "Have you recovered?"

"I don't think you ever fully recover, mentally that is, from such an experience… never. It changes you. I think I became stronger in some ways… yet tainted by the knowledge these things don't just happen in the movies or to other people… they can happen to you.

You no longer take tomorrow or your safety for granted."

George shook his head in disbelief. "You're an amazing woman. A real fighter. And here you are, five years later, still pursuing your dream after surviving such an ordeal. A true testament to overcoming adversity. What an amazing story of courage, strength, perseverance and dedication – the essence of an Olympic athlete. Thank you for sharing your amazing story. We wish you the best of luck in obtaining your dream of qualifying for the US Equestrian Team." He leaned across the table and shook her hand.

"Thank you, I hope I get the opportunity to represent my country in Sydney in 2000."

Katherine hadn't noticed she was trembling until they shook hands. Recalling her ordeal had left her drained and unsteady. It had been a miracle she and her family survived, and she still had a difficult time coming to grips with the fact that she had killed a man and that Billy was gone.

With the interview over, the men began tearing down their makeshift set. As the women walked past the great room window, Laura caught sight of Laddy inside.

"Is that Laddy? I'd love to get some shots of you with your dog and horse," she said.

"Sure, let me get him."

Laura gasped as Katherine led her hero from the lodge. "That's no dog!" she said in disbelief. "He's huge."

"He's a wolf hybrid."

"He's beautiful! Can I pet him?"

"Laddy will have to answer that question. Reach out your hand and stay quiet." The cautious canine sniffed her hand and circled her smelling her legs, then sat beside Katherine. She nodded to Laura.

Laura stroked Laddy's head as he leaned into her leg, enjoying the attention.

"He likes you. He doesn't like everyone."

Laura snickered, "I'm glad."

"I have to be especially careful with strange men."

"I'll tell the fellas to keep their distance."

"Thanks!"

When they all reached the barn, Major was led out into the sunlight by her assistant trainer, Jessie Collins, his well-groomed blood-bay coat glistening like a polished apple in the afternoon sun. Katherine introduced the crew to her long-time friend and after a series of poses, Jessie ran Laddy back to the lodge while she tacked Major.

The crew shot stills and video footage of her jumping and performing a few dressage movements in the arena. After a tack change, they followed her out to the back field where they captured the pair galloping and jumping some cross-country obstacles.

As the team began packing up, George joined Katherine and Jessie back in the barn while they tended to Major.

"This will run in this week's edition," said George, as Katherine rubbed Major down in the crossties. Resting his hand on her shoulder, he added, "Thanks again for sharing your story. In all my years as a feature writer, this is by far the most incredible story I've ever heard. It could make the cover."

"Really, the cover!" said Katherine.

"Wow!" Jessie's head shot up from taking Major's splint boots off. "How cool – now I know two celebrities!"

Katherine shot Jessie a warning glare. Betsy had taken special care not to reveal that the famous actress Josie Walker was her daughter. The last thing she wanted was for George to go in an entirely different direction with the story or get the word out to his friend at NBC who her daughter was. Josephine insisted they keep Two Ponies under wraps so she'd always have one safe place she could go to get away from the press.

Jessie quickly added, "My best friend and favorite horse!" She gave Major a pat. The big gelding tossed his head as if in agreement.

After they shared a laugh, Katherine walked George out to their van, now packed and ready to leave. Each of the crew members shook Katherine's hand, wishing her the best of luck, and once again giving their condolences.

Laura gave her a hug goodbye. "Good luck," she said, then handed Katherine her card. "I'd like to stay in touch."

"I'd like that too," said Katherine, slipping the card into her pocket.

George honked and Laura waved out the passenger window as they pulled out the drive.

"That went well, don't you think?" said Jessie, having just finished rinsing Major off. "Sorry about the celebrity comment."

"Quick thinking, though. Thanks."

"Well, you and Major will be famous when that article comes out, especially if you make the cover."

Katherine smiled, taking notice of her friend's youthful expression, dimples punctuating her freckled face and looking much younger than her forty-two years. Jessie hadn't changed much from the kid that first attended Two Ponies Equestrian Camp as a beginner student nearly thirty years ago.

"Betsy would have been pleased. Hope her magic will work and the story will attract another sponsor or two."

Jessie's smile faded. She lurched toward Katherine, embracing her. "Oh, Kat, how can Betsy be gone?" Jessie patted her back. "How are you doing? It must have been tough today without her."

Katherine just realized with everything going on, the two women hadn't had an opportunity to talk in private since Betsy's passing. Nodding, Katherine replied, "I'm okay." Then stepping back at arm's length, she looked into her friend's orange-flecked eyes. "At first, I was devastated, but I think she was ready. She read all Joseph's books again, looked through all her photo albums and was so pleased with herself having arranged this interview for me."

Taking a wet towel, Katherine rubbed away the sweaty marks left by the bridle as Jessie scraped the excess water from Major's coat with a squeegee.

Jessie looked over the tall gelding's back. "You think she willed herself to die?"

"No, I think she knew her time was near. She always spoke about death in a peaceful way, the natural course of things… with no fear. She's with her Creator now, reunited with Joseph and Flower. I'm finding peace in that. I'll miss her terribly, but she'll always be with me… here." Katherine placed her hand over her heart.

Jessie became choked up again and walked around Major to give her another hug. "Oh, Kat. Me too."

"Don't cry, Jess, Betsy wouldn't approve. Let's smile like she always did and enjoy this beautiful day."

Jessie released her hold, dramatically wiped her face on her sleeve and raised her chin. "Okay, then… let's eat lunch, I'm starved!"

Katherine chuckled, nodding. "Betsy would love that. She would have fed the world if she could. There's some leftover chicken, we can make sandwiches."

"Sounds good. Then I need to head home. It's Mom and Dad's sixtieth anniversary," called Jessie from the tack room as she returned Major's saddle and bridle. "Dane and I are taking them out to dinner. Mike gave Dane the day off so he could babysit Cole. Mom drove to Great Falls to pick out a new dress for the occasion, and to buy Dad a new hunting jacket."

It came in handy since Cole came along, that Jessie's husband, Dane Collins, a sheriff with the Elkhead police department, worked for his father, Mike Collins, the chief of police.

"Wow, sixty years. How are your folks doing? I haven't seen them since spring."

Jessie reappeared. "Dad's knee is acting up and Mom is managing her diabetes, but they're good. They still have their small herd of Angus with our help, and little Cole is the joy of their lives."

"That's wonderful. It's hard to imagine the little ones are four, but what a fun age. We sure are enjoying little Lizzy. Can't wait to see her and the girls this evening." Katherine checked her watch. "Steven's probably left for the airport from the office by now."

"We made sure he had a light schedule today," said Jessie, who worked as one of Steven's vet techs at the clinic. "Dr. Hanley offered to switch Saturdays, but Steven insisted on working this morning. As least Dr. Hanley will be on call tonight and tomorrow. It sure has been nice having another vet on staff the past few years."

"No kidding! I love having Steven visit while I'm on the road. And when I'm home, we get to spend more time together too. It's like we're kids again, going on dates… riding and fishing together."

"You two are so cute."

"Cute?"

"Yeah. You know; always holding hands, ogling each other..."

"It's Steven, he's the hopeless romantic."

"It's sweet. Dane never shows affection in public," said Jessie, sweeping up the crosstie area. "But, back to tomorrow. I'm really looking forward to seeing Lisa and Jo, especially Jo. It's been so long."

"Us too." Katherine felt Major's chest. Still hot. "Say, you go ahead. I know you're hungry. I'll tend to Major and be right up."

"I'll have yours ready. Mayo?"

"Butter, salt and pepper, please."

As Katherine began walking Major to cool him out, she watched Jessie stride up the drive toward the lodge, her carrot-red ponytail swinging with every step. She was so happy for her friend, happily married and finally blessed with a beautiful son after having tried for years to conceive. But she would miss Jessie's companionship and expert assistance with Major again this fall in California. Since Jessie's son Cole was born, another of Katherine's local students had replaced her, yet Jessie continued to do some instructing over the summer and on weekends. The camp had been shut down four years earlier. Between her traveling, Betsy's decline and Jessie becoming a parent, there was no other option. It had been a difficult decision.

Her school horses were like her children, but she found good homes for them, many going to past students and a few gifted to students on the Reservation. And it was helpful that most remained under Steven's care so she could keep tabs on them.

Jessie's replacement, Sadie Two Crows, had also advanced through the ranks of student to camp leader to assistant trainer. The Blackfeet young woman had been one of the many girls from the Reservation to attend Two Ponies Equestrian Program over the years on scholarship, including her older sister, Sally Two Crows. A single twenty-three-year-old with no commitments, Sadie became the perfect candidate to replace Jessie on the road. She was great with Major, too, but Katherine missed Jessie's humor and wit. After spending more time with Sadie, she discovered the two women couldn't be more opposite. Sadie barely spoke, ate like a bird and focused on advancing her riding skills with aspirations of showing nationally herself someday. Jessie never shut up, ate like a horse, and was content competing locally with her home-raised and trained Paint mare, Crystal, in Versatility Ranch Horse classes. For Sadie, growing up on the Reservation and having never left Browning or Flathead County, accompanying Katherine to shows across the nation had to be a dream come true for the young woman.

Once Major was cooled out and dry, Katherine returned him to the crossties for a good brushing. The big Thoroughbred attentively followed her every move, anticipating his post-ride treat.

"Okay, I won't make you wait any longer." Katherine set down her brush, and offered him a reward from her pocket, a grain and molasses cookie. Major snatched it from her outstretched palm. As the gelding chewed, he eyed her other pocket.

"Oh, you're such a smart boy, aren't you?" Katherine patted his neck and retrieved another treat from her reserve stash.

As he chewed, Katherine wrapped her arms around the bay's silky neck, needing a little equine therapy. Drawing on Major's warmth, calm and strength, she felt herself relax. It had been a stressful forty-eight hours. Her boy nudged her, seeming to feel her sorrow. Horses were like that, so simple yet so complex.

"Betsy's gone, but we'll be okay," she told Major and herself. "She knew we would be okay."

Katherine reflected on how much she would miss her biggest cheerleader. Every accomplishment from here on out would be bittersweet without Betsy to celebrate with.

Slipping a light sheet over Major, she quickly fastened the straps and hooks, and led him out to the front pasture.

"Take care of yourself. We have a big event coming up." Katherine slipped off his halter and watched him trot out to where Bonanza and Dandy were grazing. After giving each of them a nip on the rump, he stretched down to feast on the ample mid-summer grass beside them, his tail swishing in sequence with the others like a choreographed dance.

Katherine had moved Major from the old stable to the main barn after they closed the summer camp. Since the big Thoroughbred ruled the herd, she didn't worry too much about him getting injured. And it helped to have him out and moving about all day at his age, instead of standing in a stall or smaller paddock. When she returned to the barn, she glanced down the aisle of the large structure that once housed a full string of school horses. Now, it only held their three personal mounts. Two retired school masters, Blackjack, who was born at Two Ponies and now used as a guest mount, and the kid's little bay pony, Snickers, now shared the old stable run-in and paddock. This helped with barn duties, especially when she was out of town, with two less stalls to clean. As she hung Major's halter and lead rope back on the front of his stall, she glanced at the brass name plate on the stall door which still read Lady. After all these years, she hadn't been able to bring herself to replace it.

Feeling spent, Katherine planned to take a little nap after Jessie left to feel refreshed for the girls' arrivals. Finally, Josephine was coming home.

4 – Homecoming

Josephine silently sat in the back of Roy's Cessna while Roy and Brad conversed up front; Roy piloting and Brad sitting shotgun. Their words didn't reach her above the rumble of the aircraft as she stared out the window overlooking the green tapestry lining the floor of the valley below. Long late-afternoon shadows of the Continental Divide muted half the basin in contrast to the brilliant sunlit range opposite it. For a moment she imagined TJ and herself on horseback navigating a ridge below.

Memories of their first summer home together following their freshman year at college, flooded her mind, turning the scenery below to a blur. She smiled recalling how every other weekend, TJ would take off from his summer job and they would escape to the mountains on horseback, fishing all day, sitting around the campfire at night, laughing and sharing stories from school. Eventually, one of them couldn't stand it any longer and pulled the other into their small tent or onto a blanket under the stars. She focused in on a distant, still snow-capped range to the north; could that be the mountain where they first made love? Closing her eyes, she imagined the heat and electric sensation of his bronze skin against hers, of his tongue exploring her from head to toe.

Suddenly, a tap on her shoulder startled her eyes open. She turned to find Brad looking at her inquisitively. Was she blushing?

"What were you dreaming about? Hope it was me."

"I wasn't asleep, just resting."

"You should take a nap. You look tired."

"I can't sleep when we're in the air. I'll sleep well tonight. I always do at Two Ponies."

Brad moved to the seat beside her. "Will we be able to share a room, you know, unmarried?"

Josephine took a deep breath. Did he think about anything else? "I can't speak for my parents, but I'd prefer we didn't." She turned away, returning her focus out the window. "I'll have my old room and you can take your pick of the remaining guest rooms."

"How many other people are staying over?"

"I believe it'll be just Roy, my sister Lisa and her family."

He gently stroked her head, regaining her attention. "I'm looking forward to meeting your family."

"Really?"

"Sure. I know how important they are to you. And, what's important to you is important to me."

There he goes again. He had a way of being a royal jerk one moment and a sweetheart the next. "Thanks, they're all looking forward to meeting you too."

Following a shared smile and a kiss on her cheek, Brad returned to the front seat. Josephine resumed her study of the rugged landscape below, now able to push thoughts of TJ aside, for the moment anyway. They would be landing soon at Great Falls International Airport where they would pick up a rental and drive to Two Ponies.

Josephine felt excited one moment, apprehensive the next. She looked forward to seeing everyone but felt guilty at the same time. How had she stayed away so long? She glanced at Brad. Question answered. Every time she had brought up a visit to Two Ponies, he had come up with some excuse not to go. It was always work or more convenient to visit his folks instead. He managed to avoid meeting her parents when they visited California with one excuse or another. More of his jerk moments, but as a grown woman she should have stood her ground and insisted they make the trip home. Why had she caved in so easily? Deep down she knew the answer. TJ.

Katherine awoke to warm panting breaths in her face. Laddy stood over her, tail wagging.

"Okay, I'm awake," she said, giving him a pat on the head.

She had dozed off on the great room sofa while leafing through family photos looking for pictures of Betsy with Joseph, with their family and of Betsy with her brothers and their families. She soon realized Betsy spent more time behind the camera than she did in front of it. It felt strange waking up to such a quiet house, but it wouldn't be for long with the kids and Roy arriving soon. Katherine glanced at the grandfather clock across the room reading nearly five o'clock.

As soon as she sat up, Laddy's focus turned down the hall leading to the side door, then back to her. A low whine escaped as his intense gaze summoned her. "You're close, boy. It's almost feed time."

The accuracy of animals' body clocks never failed to amaze Katherine. She knew in addition to Laddy, her horses would be patiently grazing, waiting for her and Laddy to appear. But if they dared to be late, she could count on finding the herd congregating by the gate in order of dominance. Laddy led the way to the coat rack by the door, tail wagging vigorously. There were few mornings or evenings at this elevation that didn't require a jacket, even mid-summer. Katherine slipped into a light windbreaker and her boots, nearly tripping over the excited canine as she exited the door.

While Laddy's feet moved in the direction of the barn, his head and gaze turned to her every few strides, making sure she was following. His big tongue hung lopsided out the side of his mouth while he appeared to be smiling. He loved bringing in the horses. The rush of the herd galloping to the gate, no doubt set off the half-wolf's instinctual reaction to the running of animals as if on the hunt. Off he ran toward the small herd at the back of the field. After quickly disbursing their grain, she opened the gate. The horses filed into their stalls on cue, Major leading the way with Laddy bringing up the rear. Katherine tossed a couple sections of alfalfa hay to each horse while checking their water. She was grateful to find Jessie had filled their buckets earlier. She needed to get back to the lodge to prep for dinner.

Thankfully, she had plenty of food in the freezer to feed eight for supper that evening and for breakfast in the morning, having had no time to shop the past two days. But she was not prepared for the nearly one hundred guests they expected the following day for the celebration of Betsy's life. Kimi and Nuna offered to cook for Sunday, but Katherine didn't want to bother the women who were also mourning along with their families. Instead, a compromise was met. She ordered several cold cut and cheese platters, dozens of rolls and a large veggie tray that the brothers offered to pick up on the way home from their meat processing plant today to bring with them tomorrow.

Betsy's twin half-brothers, Mukki and Tahki, were much younger than Betsy and lived most of their lives on the Reservation. Betsy had been separated from her brothers for years after their mother disowned her for moving in with a red-headed and bearded white man she swore was a demon spirit. But they reconnected at their mother's funeral and remained close ever since. When the Walkers purchased the old Werden property for back taxes, the brothers and their families moved in as their neighbors. Betsy had often expressed her gratitude, knowing her family would be looked after by her and Steven after she was gone.

Betsy gone… it still didn't seem real. But at least some good would come from it — Josephine's return. A faint smile formed on her lips, wondering if Betsy might have planned it that way. Katherine shook her head. That would be ridiculous, but then again, she wouldn't put it past the perpetual schemer always wanting the best for her and her family. Betsy may not have been related by birth or marriage, but she was just as much a member and the glue that had held her family together.

Her dear friend was selfless, considering everyone's interests and well-being above her own. Betsy knew they missed Josephine terribly, and she hadn't hidden the fact she agonized over having become more of a burden in recent years. No matter how many times Katherine told her it was their turn to repay all the years of care and devotion she had bestowed upon her and her family, Betsy would say, "no need, it was my honor… my chosen path."

"Well, Betz, if it was your plan, it worked. Our girl is coming home."

As Katherine began shredding the thawed pre-cooked pork for barbecue sandwiches, she still felt divided about Josephine's homecoming, thrilled yet a bit anxious. She hoped Steven wouldn't say something to Brad or about him to Josephine that would taint their stay and lessen the chances of future visits. Then there was TJ. Even though they would love to have him attend tomorrow, Katherine feared what might transpire between him and Josephine, not to mention him and Brad. But in the end, her excitement won out.

Once she browned the meat in barbecue sauce, she moved it to two slow cookers to keep warm. The rest would have to wait until later. Laddy followed her to the great room where she waited to see who arrived first, Steven with Lisa and her family, or Roy with Jo and Brad.

"Who's it going to be, Laddy?"

A few minutes later, the wolfdog jumped to his feet, ears pricked forward, and trotted to the side door. Katherine peeked out the large great room window. It was Steven. She scurried to the door and led her unhappy companion into her bedroom and closed the door. Laddy howled out of frustration, but it was for the best. The big canine stood level to Elizabeth's face and Katherine couldn't trust him not to try to play with the little human in all the excitement and knock her over in the process.

While Katherine gave Lisa, Daniel and Elizabeth a hug on the porch, Steven insisted on retrieving their luggage without Daniel's help. Katherine escorted her guests into the great room to show them Betsy's photos. Little Elizabeth begged to see the horses, and for a moment Katherine pictured herself the evening of her first visit to Two Ponies, anxious to see the horses. She gave the same answer to Lizzy as Betsy and her uncle had given her — after dinner.

Any trepidation Josephine felt disappeared the moment they pulled into Two Ponies and she saw her dad removing two suitcases from the back of his truck. She rushed to give him a hug and felt her eyes well up. "I'm back!"

Her father set the bags down abruptly on the drive to embrace her. "Welcome home, Jo. I've missed you… we've all missed you."

When she stepped away and her father got a good look at her, his expression turned from joyful to a look of surprise and perhaps a little concern.

"I lost a little weight for my role, Dad. Don't worry, I'll gain it back."

She followed his gaze eventually resting on her new carrot top, a much brighter red than her natural auburn. "Your hair… Oh, don't tell me, your role?"

"No, actually that was my idea."

"Now you really take after your Great Uncle Joe."

"Funny, I hadn't thought of that." Following a shared chuckle, the purpose of her visit resurfaced. "Where's Mom? Is she doing okay?"

"She's inside, I just pulled in with Lisa and her crew. She's managing. It's been tough. Are you okay?"

"Yeah. Not sure it's really sunk in yet."

Roy stepped up and shook her father's hand. "So good to see you, Steve. Sorry it had to be for such a solemn occasion." Roy rested his other hand on Steven's shoulder. "I'm so sorry about Betsy."

"Thanks, it's been hard, especially for Kat."

"I can imagine."

"Thank you for making the trip."

"Sandy and the girls send their love and condolences. Sandy wished she could have joined us, but April is traveling this weekend and she's with the grandkids."

"How are the twins?"

"Great, growing like weeds."

Josephine noticed Brad hanging back and took him by the arm. "Dad, this is Brad."

Brad stepped up flashing his "I'll win you over with my handsome good looks" smile, as he shook her dad's hand a little too enthusiastically.

"Good to finally meet you," said her father, with skeptical undertones as he studied her boyfriend through narrow slits. Josephine took a deep breath and prayed Brad wouldn't have a jerk moment and say something inappropriate.

"Great to meet you, sir."

Relieved, Josephine slipped her hand into his with a quick squeeze of approval, not going unnoticed by her father.

"I'll get our bags." Brad returned to the rental for their suitcases joined by Roy. Josephine sighed in relief, so far so good, just thirty-six more hours to go.

Steven picked up the luggage he had set down.

"Let me help, I can take something," she said, finding Lisa's backpack.

As they climbed the side stairs, her father leaned in and whispered, "When things quiet down later, let's get caught up… just the two of us, okay?"

"I'd like that." Josephine smiled to herself. Guessing she knew where this was going, recalling his interrogations when she brought boys home from high school. It was sweet, her father still feeling the need to protect her, even though she was a grown woman now.

Once introductions were done, including Laddy, who quickly settled down once he got a good sniff of all their guests, Katherine left everyone in the great room to finish preparing their meal. She pulled what she needed from the fridge to make a salad and piled it on the counter. Next, she opened two large cans of pork and beans and poured them in a saucepan to warm. Katherine was pleased when Josephine joined her in the kitchen.

"Can I help?"

"Sure. Just need to make a salad. You can cut up that cucumber." She noticed her daughter smiling as she easily located the best knife for the job still located in the same drawer beside the sink. Katherine smiled back, recognizing the familiarity of the moment having prepared so many meals together before she left for California. "Do you cook much now?"

Josephine laughed. "No. Not that I don't remember how. You and Betsy taught me well. When we're on location, food is brought in and when we're home, Brad prefers to eat out or order in. He likes sushi and Thai mostly."

Katherine cringed, glancing at the barbecue. "Oh."

"Don't worry, Mom. He'll enjoy whatever you serve."

"I hope so. I can finish the salad. Can you stir the beans?"

"Sure."

For several minutes, they stood at the counter within a couple feet of each other in silence. A million questions raced through Katherine's mind, but she didn't want to drill her daughter right away, so she kept it light and conversational.

"How was your flight?"

"Good. Glad Roy could bring us. I prefer his private jet to a charter jet."

For an instant she had forgotten her daughter was now a celebrity and didn't fly commercially anymore. "Yep, good old Roy. Glad Brad could join you. We've been dying to meet him."

"I'll bet, especially Dad."

Again, mother and daughter shared a lively smile. "How are they getting along?" asked Katherine.

"Okay, I think," said Josephine, stirring the beans more intensely. "They're different."

"Yes, they are."

"So, what do you think?"

"He's certainly handsome and seems like a nice young man. I wish you could stay longer. I would love more time to get to know him better. Any chance of extending your visit?"

"I'm afraid not. We need to leave first thing Monday morning. Everything is on hold until we return. Most of the actors went home for the weekend but we have local extras, livestock and their handlers, and stunt doubles still on the clock."

Katherine gently took a hold of her daughter's hand, forcing her to stop stirring and make eye contact. "You keep that up and we'll have bean soup. Is everything okay?"

"Sure," she answered too quickly. Confirming her suspicion Josephine's answer might not be entirely true, her daughter bit her bottom lip — her "tell" when nervous about something or hiding something. Katherine gave her that mother knows better look and Josephine confessed, "Well, sort of."

Katherine leaned in. "Come out to the barn with me later to turn the horses out for the night. We can talk then."

Josephine nodded with a tentative smile. Katherine imagined the worst as any mother would with her youngest child living so far away with a man they didn't know. She couldn't wait to find out what the "sort of" was about.

Following dinner, Lisa and Daniel took Elizabeth down to the barns to see Snickers and the other horses as promised. Katherine and Josephine cleared the dining room table as Steven started a fire in the great room. Brad awkwardly followed Steven.

Josephine became noticeably uncomfortable about leaving the two men alone, with frequent glances in the direction of the great room every trip to the dining room. She would stop mid-task and lean an ear in their direction to listen for any conversation between them. Katherine had to chuckle to herself, finding herself doing the same. It sounded like normal chatter between strangers, discussing the weather and the details of their home. The massive lodge always made an easy topic.

Once Lisa put Elizabeth to bed, Katherine gathered everyone in the great room to share stories while leafing through Betsy's old photo albums. A poignant mood soon filled the room as laughter mixed with tears. Katherine sat on the sofa between Steven and Josephine with Lisa and Daniel sitting opposite them in two chairs across the coffee table. Brad sat in the corner, lost in the dancing flames in the fireplace as he tapped the arm of his chair, appearing to count the seconds until they headed upstairs. Katherine paid special attention to Josephine observing the same.

"Come on over, there's room here on the couch," Josephine said to Brad, scooting in closer to Katherine and patting the seat of the sofa beside her. Brad squirmed in his seat, then hesitantly joined her.

"Oh, this is one of my favorites… my thirteenth birthday when Betsy gave me my first Western saddle," said Josephine, pulling him closer, no doubt hoping to see some interest. "She was so pleased to see how much I loved it."

For a moment Katherine became lost in her own recollection, the day she found her first saddle in the old stable tack room with a big blue bow attached to the horn for her own thirteenth birthday. She had to hold back the surge of emotions running straight to her heart.

Josephine waved Lisa over to take a peek at the photo.

"She gave me my first Western saddle, too, remember?" said Lisa.

Josephine glanced up so her sister could read her lips. "Sure, that was your first year with us, when Mom and Dad gave you Wompa. Here, I saw some pictures from that year," said Josephine, thumbing through another album. Lisa leaned over to see.

"Here," said Brad, getting up from the couch and motioning with his arm. "You… can… have… my… seat," he said loudly, going out of his way to make eye contact with Lisa. Katherine imagined Josephine must have coached him on making sure Lisa could read his lips.

Lisa glanced at Josephine and grinned. "Thank you," she said to Brad, scooting in next to her sister. Katherine guessed Lisa knew he meant well and obviously had no experience communicating with the deaf. How would he know it was easier for Lisa to read lips at a normal cadence? But Katherine couldn't explain the speaking louder part, although it seemed to be a common reaction for many people as if they were trying to communicate with a hearing-impaired person rather than a deaf person.

Josephine didn't hide her disappointment when Brad returned to his seat in the corner. Her daughter's "sort of" reply played over in Katherine's mind. Since they arrived, the couple seemed very much in love one moment, holding hands and smiling at one another, then she felt a disconnect the next, like now. Could she be looking too hard to find something? Brad was difficult to read, his actions fluctuating like the wind between what seemed sincere to appearing fake or rehearsed. How good of an actor was he? She knew he grew up rich, like herself, surely getting every little thing he desired. But she wondered if there were other parallels too; like growing up alone and feeling unloved. Is this how she would have turned out, had it not been for Betsy and Uncle Joe? Her heart went out to him, and even more so to Josephine trying so hard to involve him and make him feel a part of the family, as Betsy had done with her. But was it too late for Brad? She feared perhaps so. Believing there is no better judge of character than an animal or child; both Laddy and little Elizabeth had steered clear of him all evening.

When the flames turned to ambers, Lisa and Daniel signed goodnight and lumbered up the stairs to their room, looking exhausted after their long day of travel.

Katherine stood up. "I need to turn out the horses."

"I'll join you," said Josephine. "I've been looking forward to seeing Bonanza. We won't be long," she said to Brad, who didn't look pleased about being left alone with Steven again.

As soon as they exited the side door, Josephine turned to her. "I hope they'll be okay in there alone together."

"They'll be just fine. Don't worry, I warned Dad to go easy on him."

A nearly full moon hung low in a clear cobalt-blue sky as they strode down the drive toward the barns. "We should have grabbed a jacket," said Katherine. "I should have known better."

"Ha, me too. Montana nights. Soon as the sun goes down, the cold comes out."

The mother and daughter shared a brief chuckle as they walked side by side. Blackjack and Snickers greeted them with a soft nicker as they approached the old stable. Josephine rushed to the split rail fence to stroke their faces. "Jack looks great. How old is he now?"

"Twenty-nine. Hard to imagine he'll be thirty this January and that he's never left the property."

"And this little guy?" she asked, patting the pony's soft nose.

"Not sure, probably in his late twenties too."

"What a cutie. Remember Dusty?"

"Sure, and Snickers is just as great with the kids."

"Yeah, Lizzy couldn't wait to see him. I'll help Lisa tack him up to give Lizzy a ride after everyone leaves tomorrow."

"Lisa would like that. She's missed you too."

Again, they fell silent. Katherine could read the guilt on her daughter's face even in the shadows. She knew Josephine hadn't made an effort to visit Lisa and her family either.

The moment they slid open the main barn's heavy doors, Josephine rushed to Bonanza's stall, slid in and wrapped her arms around her boy's generous neck. "Hi, Bo Bo, I sure have missed you… you big lug."

Stepping into the tack room, Katherine grabbed a few carrots from the refrigerator. She handed one to her daughter.

"Thanks." Josephine broke the carrot in half and offered it to Bonanza who eagerly accepted the treat.

Katherine watched her stroke Bonanza's honey colored neck. They had managed to keep the big Buckskin in good condition in Josephine's absence, using him for a couple lessons each week. After Josephine fed her boy the other half, she gave him a lingering hug and Bonanza reciprocated by resting his big head on her shoulder. Katherine could swear she saw her daughter's eyes glistening in the faint light.

"We're both glad you're home," said Katherine, handing Josephine the other carrots as she exited his stall and moved onto Dandy. "Are you happy, Jo?"

Josephine hesitated with her response as she fed her father's handsome gray a treat. "Yes, mostly."

Katherine raised her brows. "Mostly?"

"I love my work. Roy is great. The script is great. The house is great. The parties are great, but…" Josephine ran her fingers through Dandy's silver mane as if searching for her next words.

"But, what?"

"But I miss you, Dad, Bo… Two Ponies."

That sounded a bit canned and too easy, thought Katherine. There had to be more to her "sort of" response earlier and her "mostly" answer just now. Before she could think better of it, the real questions that had been nagging her all day just popped out.

"Is it serious with Brad? Do you love him?"

Josephine's jaw dropped, turning her attention from Dandy to her. "Why would I be living with him if it wasn't?" she said, defensively.

"Oh, sweetie, I'm sorry. It's just been so crazy; hardly seeing you, then the fame, and you living so far away with a man we've never met. I'm just sensing something isn't quite right. I know you're not a child, but you're still my little girl. What kind of parent would I be if I wasn't concerned?"

"It's been a big change for me, too."

"Of course, it has." But Katherine couldn't let go of the sense something wasn't right between the couple. Sure, she hadn't been around her daughter for a while, but this was still her little Jo. She knew her daughter better than anyone and something was bothering her. Josephine could have just answered "yes" to both questions, but she hadn't, avoiding the "do you love him" question altogether. Katherine had a feeling Josephine wanted to talk to her about something but just didn't know how to go about doing so.

"Is he good to you?" she probed further.

Josephine took her time closing Dandy's stall door before answering. "Sure," she said, barely above a whisper.

Another evasive answer, but before she had the opportunity to dig deeper, Josephine unexpectedly let go, as she began pacing around her in a circle. "We get along fine most of the time, but sometimes he's a bit selfish and immature. He likes to have things his way. And he's moody." She became more animated as she spoke. "One moment he's pouting, not wanting to make the trip, the next he's telling me how much he's looking forward to meeting my family. He can be so sweet, then be such a jerk." Josephine's marching came to a halt. "Are all men like that?"

Katherine set her hand on her daughter's shoulder. "I think you already know the answer to that question." All Josephine had to do was look to any other man from her life, her grandfather, her father, Roy, and TJ, for the answer.

"Okay. You're right, he's a spoiled brat." Josephine drifted toward Major.

"I'm sorry Jo, but no relationship is perfect or easy. They all take work, but the good times need to outweigh the bad."

Josephine stood in front of the Thoroughbred's stall, hands in her jean pockets and studying the rafters, oblivious to Major's antics. Impatiently, the big bay tossed his head up and down, anticipating his treat.

Abruptly, she turned toward Katherine, shaking her head. "I just don't know how I feel about him half the time. It's like he's two different people."

This comment didn't come as a surprise after what Katherine had observed of the young man so far. She felt bad for Josephine, yet it touched her knowing her daughter still felt comfortable sharing her concerns with her. Sure, they had kept abreast of each other's lives, discussing Josephine's work and her progress with Major over the phone and during their few trips to the Coast, but nothing personal or meaningful, until now. Suddenly the gap between them closed.

While Katherine worked through a thoughtful response, Josephine finally fed Major his treat and blurted out. "I've thought about breaking it off."

"Does he know you're not happy?"

"I don't know. If I did say something, he'd just ask why. How do you tell a grown man he needs to grow up?"

"Perhaps you need to take a break… see if you're happier with or without him."

Josephine started pacing the aisle again. "How can I while we're filming together? And then there's the press, and they don't miss a thing. We're Hollywood's hottest couple, you know?" she said with a bite of sarcasm. Then she took a deep breath, her tone leveling out as she added, "A breakup now would hurt the promotion of the film. I can't do that to Roy… I owe him that much."

"You owe it to yourself to be true to your heart first. Roy will understand."

"There's more to it than that. We'd still have to work together. There's love scenes, Mom!"

"I see what you mean." Katherine hadn't thought about all of the ramifications. She motioned with her hand. "Can you get the gate?"

Josephine opened the entrance to the front pasture and extended her arms, forming a barrier. Katherine opened the horses' stall doors and the three geldings trotted in single file out the barn door and through the pasture gate. Katherine slid the barn doors shut behind them.

"Maybe I'm just being too hard on him, expecting too much," said Josephine, closing the gate. "He's had such a sheltered and privileged life. Quite the opposite of…" Josephine gazed out into the dark of the night, appearing miles away lost in her thoughts, or perhaps years away.

Did she dare say it? "The opposite of TJ?"

The mention of his name brought Josephine back with a jerk, but she only drew a deep breath. Her daughter studied the driveway as she shuffled her boots through the gravel. Katherine knew she had hit a nerve, perhaps the real underlying issue with Brad wasn't entirely Brad.

"You haven't asked about TJ once since you broke up. Sometimes a person can say a lot by not saying anything at all."

Josephine smiled affectionately. "That sounds like something Betsy would say."

"She did, to me many years ago when I wouldn't mention your father when we were estranged. He was on my mind more than I cared to admit to her, or to myself."

"Okay, maybe I do miss him." Josephine seemed content to end the conversation there and began to lead the way back to the lodge. "We should get back."

"Aren't you the least bit curious if TJ is coming tomorrow?"

Josephine stopped in her tracks and spun around, a look of fear in her eyes. "Is he?"

"I don't know. He's invited."

"When did you see him last?"

"TJ hasn't returned to Two Ponies since the breakup. I've only run into him in town a time or two, but he only nods. He's still attending CSU, but no longer assists your father. Sarah has mentioned he spends a few nights at the ranch with her and her parents when he's home from school, but spends most of his time hanging out with his old high school friends on the Reservation."

Josephine shook her head. "Don't tell me, Talon, Matt and Noot."

"She didn't mention any names specifically, but Sarah's not too happy about it. She said TJ's changed."

"That's sad." Josephine kicked a pinecone from the drive. "I hope it's not because of me."

"You can't take the blame, TJ's a grown man making his own choices."

"True. All but one. I made that choice for both of us."

Katherine gasped, recalling Billy making that exact point the night before he died. Her mind drifted back, picturing them sitting by the campfire together when he told her he still loved her. She had dismissed his comment, saying things ended up the way they were meant to be, her with Steven and him with Sarah. Then he reminded her she had made that choice for both of them.

"How has he changed?" questioned Josephine, bringing her back to the present.

It took Katherine a moment to respond, her thoughts still circling in her mind. "Sarah says he's been disrespectful to her… and her white friends. She blames it on those boys."

"They never did like me, that's for sure. Didn't approve of us as a couple." Josephine seemed to reflect for a moment before adding, "They said I would dump him eventually… and they were right."

Again, Katherine recalled her choice so many years ago. "You just followed your heart."

"Did I?"

As the women approached the lodge, Katherine gently took Josephine by the arm. "Only you know the answer to that question."

Steven stood waiting outside the side door to catch his daughter on her way in from the barn. "C'mon, let's sit a bit." With his arm around her shoulders, he escorted her out onto the front porch, leaving his wife with a knowing grin.

Josephine smiled and took a seat across from him at the wicker breakfast table, running her fingertips over the woven arm of the chair.

Surprising Steven, she spoke first. "I know, Daddy. I've been a terrible daughter, gone so long. I'm sorry. I'll do better from now on, I promise."

Maybe she didn't. "I'm glad to hear that, your mother and I sure missed having you home, but…" Steven glanced through the window beside them into the great room where Brad still sat in the corner, lost in the fire. When he returned his focus to Josephine, her expression revealed she knew. "Are you happy?" he continued. "Do you love him?"

Josephine's mouth formed a lopsided smirk, her focus dropping to her lap. "Mom and I just had this discussion. I'm fine." She hesitated, shifting her focus to meet his eyes. "Brad is good to me."

Steven found it curious that Josephine dodged both of his questions. "I'm glad, but know if you ever need to talk, I'm here for you, we both are."

"I know, Dad." Her expression turned inquisitive. "You don't like him, do you?"

"He's just not what I expected is all. And it didn't help hiding him from us for three years."

"It hasn't been that long." Josephine took a deep breath. "I just wanted to… you know, be sure."

"Are you?"

Josephine squeaked, "Sure," then added more faintly as she went, "Maybe… not really… not yet…" Following a hesitation, she added, "Okay, no, I'm not sure and if it hadn't been for Betsy, I…"

He could tell she had admitted more than she had meant to. "You'd still be hiding him from us?" he filled in, half-jokingly.

"Probably," she admitted, light heartedly.

"I'm glad you're taking your time. And whether you want to hear it or not, I'm going to say what's on my mind." Steven tilted his head and grimaced. "I just don't see the connection between you two, the way you look at each other and interact with each other. When I was his age, I adored your mother and I didn't hide it, like…"

"Like TJ?" she blurted out.

Steven raised an eyebrow. Ha, he had hit on something! "Yeah, like TJ."

"Not all guys are hopeless romantics you know."

"I just want the best for you."

"I know."

Now that she brought up TJ, Steven decided to push the topic a bit further. "Haven't seen much of TJ the past few years. We miss him."

"Yeah, that's what Mom said. Do you think he'll come tomorrow?"

"Talking from experience, if he's still hurting, probably not."

"The last thing I wanted to do was hurt TJ. But it just couldn't have worked, him here, me there, living two different lives. I broke it off before it got any more difficult."

"For him, or for you?"

Josephine looked surprised. "Well, for both of us."

"Are you sure?" he said, patting her on the shoulder as he stood up. "I better go see if your mother needs any help."

His daughter looked shocked that he left her on that note, but he wanted to give her something to think about. Or perhaps he was being selfish, wanting Jo to break it off with Brad for his own reasons. The guy just seemed so fake. Steven didn't trust him. Lurking in the corner of his mind, he would love to see Jo get back together with TJ and maybe… just maybe she'd return home and give up her fancy beach house, the parties and celebrity lifestyle that frightened him to death. He had read so many sad stories about Hollywood stars struggling with drug or alcohol addiction, involved in sexual exploits… Steven shook his head at the thought of his baby girl no doubt being subjected to all that and more. This Brad was a total unknown. How many woman or men had he been with? Was he just using his daughter? He figured Jo would just go off to college for a few years and return to start up a local players group or write a screenplay or something… here at Two Ponies, or at least in Montana! Never in his wildest dreams did he imagine the level of success and stardom she achieved so quickly. He would keep a close eye on this Brad guy and pray TJ showed up the next day. Funny how things can change. Not long ago, he hadn't approved of TJ. Now, he prayed they'd get back together.

Josephine sat in the dark on the porch, her arms crossed to the cold breeze blowing off the water. She stared out across the lake without focus. Her father's question had rattled her. Had she been fooling herself all along, thinking she had broken up with TJ to spare him from any more pain, when she might have been acting selfishly? Could it have worked? Had she given it a fair chance? The pressure from friends and the media had won out. How would she have explained a poor American Indian boyfriend in Montana to all her rich and famous friends? Pure and simple, she had become a Hollywood elitist! Maybe she did belong with Brad. Mr. Brat and Ms. Snob!

Eventually, Brad came looking for her. "Here you are." He sat beside her, sliding his arm around her. "You're freezing."

Dismissing his comment, her thoughts elsewhere, she said. "I love it out here. I can't believe I stayed away so long."

"You've been busy becoming one of the world's most desired actors. I'm going to head upstairs. You coming?"

"No, I want to sit out here for a bit longer. You go ahead. I'll see you in the morning."

Brad flashed her a smirk, registering somewhere between disappointed and pissed. "Okay then, good night." He gave her a little peck on the mouth.

"Good night."

Josephine sat long enough for Brad to make it upstairs before searching out her parents. Their bedroom was dark, but she could see a light still on in the kitchen. She found them standing side-by-side washing and drying the last of the dishes, gazing into each other's smiling eyes. That's what she wanted someday, right there, to have a relationship like her parents. Their love for each other was obvious to anyone who took the time to notice; how they tenderly spoke to one another with respect and genuine affection, sometimes seeming to communicate without saying a word.

When her father turned to put away some glasses in the cabinet, he noticed her standing just outside the kitchen. "Jo, we thought you had gone to bed."

"Not without saying goodnight. I always did when I was home, remember?"

"Sure do," said her father.

Josephine gave her dad a hug as they exchanged a kiss on the cheek.

"Where's mine?" teased her mother.

Josephine hurried to give her a hug and kiss, too. When they broke off their embrace, Josephine noticed how tired she looked. "You okay, Mom?"

"Yeah, it's just been an emotional rollercoaster kind of day."

"It sure has been. Good night, Mom and Dad," said Josephine. "See you in the morning."

"Good night, sweetie," her parents said in unison as she turned for the stairs.

Josephine thought she heard them say "jinx" as she left the kitchen. Sometimes her parents seemed like two halves of the same person, more so as the years went by. She wondered if it was possible for her and Brad to grow together over time.

The upstairs was quiet and dark except for a sliver of light emanating from beneath the door to her room. Had she forgotten to turn a light off earlier? Opening the door, Josephine was shocked to find Brad laying shirtless on her bed with the nightstand light on, reading a People Magazine he'd brought with him.

"Look, this is a great picture of us," he said, pointing. Her illusion of them becoming like her parents shattered.

"Shhh," said Josephine, rushing to close the door behind her. "What are you doing in here?"

"I thought we'd have a little fun. I think these walls are pretty soundproof. I can wake up in the other room for appearances if you want."

"Please leave," she said, disgusted as she handed him his shirt.

Brad sat up and raised his hands in compliance. "Okay, no need to get pissy. Good night, Jo."

"Good night!"

No sooner than she had slipped into her nightshirt and into bed, she heard light tapping on her door. "Now what," she hissed, figuring it must be Brad making another attempt.

But when she jerked the door open, she found Lisa.

"Can I come in for a few minutes?"

Relieved, Josephine waved her sister in with a smile and put Brad and her frustration out of her mind. Suddenly, it felt like the old days when they were kids, but it used to be her sneaking into Lisa's room after bedtime. Following a lingering hug, Josephine turned the overhead light on so Lisa could read her lips. They sat on the bed facing each other.

"I didn't know when we'd get another chance to be alone," said Lisa, still speaking with the same slight speech impediment, void of any "t," "d" or "r" sounds in her child-like little voice.

"I know, it'll be hectic tomorrow with all the guests."

Lisa reached for her hand, gently squeezing it. "I missed you, Little Bit."

Josephine laughed louder than she meant to, covering her mouth. "You haven't called me that in forever." The old nickname brought back treasured memories of following her big sister everywhere. "I've missed you too. I'm sorry…"

"Don't," Lisa interrupted. "You're here now and that's all that matters… just don't stay away so long again, okay?"

"Okay, I promise."

While the sisters got caught up, they giggled like a couple of teenagers at a sleepover. Lisa told funny stories about the challenges of childrearing and married life and Josephine shared astonishing tales from Hollywood parties she'd attended and awkward situations filming. Eventually, they got serious.

"Are you happy, Jo?" asked Lisa.

"Why does everyone keep asking me that? Do I look unhappy?"

"I can't tell, you are a great actress you know."

Josephine laughed, "I love my work, I love my home. Can you believe it, I have my own house?"

"Yes, I've seen the pictures."

"I'm sorry, Lisa, I should have invited you all out. I've just been so busy." Lisa gave her a feeble smile, deservingly so following such a lame excuse. "And thank you for all the invites. I would love to visit you and see New York, really. As soon as we wrap up this film this summer, I'll make the trip East. I promise. It would be fun to see some plays on Broadway together."

"Sounds great." Lisa furrowed her brow. "But you didn't mention Brad."

"I can't say if he'd be able to make the trip."

"No, I meant when you listed what made you happy. You mentioned everything but your relationship. He's very good looking, I can see the attraction… but are you in love with him?"

Was that all there was to Brad, his good looks? "I don't know," she admitted. "It all happened so fast and then we were working together. It got complicated."

"I can imagine. Is he good to you?"

Here we go again. "Yes, we get along just fine, well, most of the time."

Lisa nodded. "We can all say that."

"Really? Daniel is so sweet. I can't imagine you two having a fight. Anyone can see how much he loves you and Lizzy."

"We have our moments, like all couples do."

Josephine had to think about that a moment. Even she and TJ had the occasional fight and disagreement, although they had been rare.

"Do you ever think about TJ?" whispered Lisa, reading her mind.

Josephine squirmed a moment. Did she dare admit her recent thoughts about him? But, who better to keep a secret than Lisa? "Just between you and me, all the time. And, more so lately."

"Do you still love him?"

"I don't know. I haven't seen him for three years. But, when I play our times together over in my head, it seems like just yesterday… the details are so clear." Josephine brushed her fingers across her lips. "Maybe I'm just in love with the memory of us. It's been different with Brad." Then she added as more of a question than a statement, "Maybe I'm just older now, not a hopeless romantic kid anymore."

"What's wrong with being a hopeless romantic?" Lisa smiled. "I still feel the same way when I'm with Daniel after ten years… same as when we first started dating."

"You two have something special, like Mom and Dad. I'm so happy for you."

"You had something special, too."

The smile left Josephine's face. She stood up and glanced out the window overlooking the lake, the moonlight reflecting off the still water like a mirror. Wincing, she knew Lisa was right. She and TJ did have something special and she had tossed it aside, convincing herself it could never work.

Josephine turned her focus to Lisa. "Perhaps," she said, before once again studying the glistening surface of Pine Island Lake. In a daze, the images of her and TJ skinny dipping and laughing as they ran naked to the cabin to make love played in her mind.

"Jo, are you okay?"

Josephine turned from the window again so Lisa could read her lips. "Maybe I did blow it, you know, with TJ. It was terrible for me to just drop him like that, in a letter no less. I just felt so pressured by my new friends. Maybe we could have made it work? It seemed like the right thing to do at the time, but now I think it was just the easiest thing to do."

The sisters once again sat on the bed across from each other.

"You need to talk to him," whispered Lisa.

Josephine shook her head. "And say what? That I'm thinking about us while I'm living with another man?"

"Say you're sorry. Tell him what you just told me. That you felt pressured to break it off. That you should have given yourselves more time to work it out. Let him know you're having doubts about Brad. Just tell him the truth."

"I'm afraid."

"It's TJ, you'll be fine."

"What if he hates me now? Dad said if he's still hurting, he won't even come tomorrow."

"I hope he does. Sounds like you need some closure one way or the other."

Josephine gave her sister a hug. "You're so smart, thanks."

"We better get to bed, long day tomorrow… sad day. It's hard being home without Betsy."

"I know. A part of Two Ponies is gone, and it'll never be the same again."

The two women hugged again. "Good night, Jo."

"Good night. I'll think on what you said."

"I'm glad. Love you!"

"Love you, too."

Quietly closing the door, Josephine set her purse on the bed beside her. She opened a zipped pocket full of notes and business cards and searched until she found the bent and worn photo of TJ she still carried. He stood shirtless with shoulder-length hair, smiling his gorgeous smile; coal black tresses resting on broad shoulders. As she studied the image, she could feel the love and affection in his deep mahogany eyes. God, he was beautiful, inside and out. She should have been proud to call him her boyfriend, yet when any of her college friends in LA asked if she had a steady guy, she had denied it. Why had she felt ashamed? She shook her head in frustration. She hated herself for feeling embarrassed because of the color of TJ's skin. It was like high school all over again. She thought moving to California, she wouldn't have to pick between her friends and TJ any longer. She was wrong… things hadn't changed… she hadn't changed!

Josephine hid the photo once again, turned the nightstand light off and threw herself onto her bed. Eventually, she slid between the cool sheets and studied her room, the moonlight softly illuminating every detail. It hadn't changed either. She closed her eyes and willed herself to fall asleep, putting her conflicting fears and anticipation to rest for the night as well.

5 – Hide-and-Seek

Sunday Morning

Josephine awoke to the feeling of warmth on her face. A blinding sliver of sunlight, peeking above the jagged skyline, cut through a gap in the curtains. She squinted to read the alarm clock on her nightstand and jerked upright in bed, threw her legs over the side and rushed to her closet. She had overslept. When she opened the closet door, the faint scent of horse welcomed her. It came as no surprise finding her old Western boots and barn coat right where she'd left them.

Fully dressed, she quietly opened her bedroom door and peered down the hallway. All was quiet. Tip-toeing past Brad's room and down the stairs, she used the downstairs bathroom off the kitchen hoping to avoid waking anyone. Just as she exited the bathroom, she paused to glance in Betsy's room. Her wardrobe closet doors stood open, revealing nothing had been touched. She jumped as someone place their hand on her shoulder.

"Oh, hi, Mom." Josephine ran her thumb over the handle of Betsy's cane leaning against the wall just inside her room. "I should have been here for Lizzy's birthday last month."

"She'd be happy you're home now."

Josephine nodded, offering a pathetic guilt-ridden smile. "If you'd like some help with Betsy's things before I leave, just let me know."

Her mother looked drained and appeared to have aged ten years over night. She still wore her night gown, robe and slippers and had hastily pulled her gray-streaked auburn tresses into a messy bun.

"I'll see. I don't know if I'm ready just yet," she said, avoiding eye contact, but it wasn't hard to miss her red and swollen eyes. "It was difficult enough sorting through her things to find something to dress her in. I chose the old Blackfeet outfit she wore on the cover of Uncle Joe's book." Both women glanced at the photo of a youthful and slim Betsy sitting bareback on her sweet mare, Flower, while posing for Joseph. "She had lost so much weight, it fit her perfectly."

Once again, guilt ravaged her heart for having been gone so long. Josephine sighed trying to imagine Betsy, a robust woman most of her life, having lost that much weight.

Her mother shuffled into the kitchen to brew some coffee. As the coffee percolated, she removed two pounds of bacon, two dozen eggs and the milk from the refrigerator, setting them on the counter. "I see you're going for a ride," she said, pulling a mixing bowl from the cabinet.

Josephine was surprised her mother had even noticed her clothes in her condition. "Yeah, I could use some quiet time, unless you need help."

"No, go. There's not much to do." Her mother stood at the counter beating the egg and milk mixture with a blank expression, her thoughts obviously elsewhere. She seemed to be doing so well yesterday, but the reality of saying her last farewell to Betsy today must have hit home this morning.

"Want to join me? I can help you when we get back."

Her mother turned to her with a fragile smile. "Go enjoy your ride, but Bo hasn't had his breakfast yet."

"I'll feed."

"Great, thanks Jo," she said, setting the bowl in the fridge. "Take Laddy." The canine immediately appeared in the kitchen, having heard his name.

"Sure, if he'll follow me."

"Once he knows you're bringing the horses in, he will. Not sure if he'll follow on the trails, though, but he could use the exercise." Without another word, Katherine turned and went back to prepping for breakfast.

Josephine could tell her mother needed some alone time too and gave her a gentle hug from behind on her way out.

"I'll save you a plate," she called after her.

Mother was right. Laddy not only followed, but gleefully led the way to the barn. After being unprepared last night, Josephine was glad she thought to slip on a coat that morning. Even though a chill still ran through her body as she strode down the drive, she didn't mind. She welcomed the familiarity of the cool Montana mornings and evenings. They were nonexistent in Los Angeles or where they were filming in central Washington, bordering the high desert where it is much milder and drier. She also missed the scent of the lodge pole pine and blue spruce, intensified by the morning dew. As she neared the barn, the perfect blend of evergreen and horse greeted her.

Laddy went about his business of bringing in the horses while Josephine smiled at the familiarity of it all. It was like she had never left, everything still in its place in the barn; the same old dented coffee can in the grain bin, same antique, black-handled scissors hanging on a nail in the same spot. She quickly rationed out the grain per the instructions on the front of each stall before she brought the horses in. While they ate, she filled the front pasture water tank.

Suddenly, Josephine felt she was being watched. She immediately turned toward the lodge, half expecting her mother to join her after all, but no one was there. Then she noticed Laddy standing at attention, focused down the fence line. Shielding her eyes from the early morning rays cutting through the treetops, Josephine searched the pasture. She thought she saw something move at the far end of the field. Laddy must have seen it too, and took a few quick steps in that direction, then froze again.

"Laddy, come!" she called. Josephine feared it might be something he'd tangle with and get injured. Feeling relieved when he immediately came to her side, she patted him on the head. "Good boy, Laddy." While the tank filled, she continued to study the fence line, but saw no more movement. She figured they had caught a glimpse of a mule deer.

Josephine turned the hydrant off and when she stepped back into the barn, six eyes and ears were fixed on her. After cutting open a bale of hay, she tossed her big Buckskin gelding a section, then opened Dandy's and Major's stall doors. She had to hurry to man her post with her arms extended to make sure the horses didn't try running up the drive instead of through the front pasture gate. Major nipped at the old gray's rump and the two geldings frolicked as they trotted to their favorite grazing spot. Laddy chased after them but quickly lost interest the moment the horses stopped playing.

As she allowed Bonanza to finish most of his hay, she followed Laddy through the tack room into the office, where he laid down on the cool tile floor, panting. Josephine strolled around the room studying the pictures on the walls. Her eyes were immediately drawn to the large framed portrait of her mother, around her age, jumping her old Thoroughbred event horse, Lady. The pair sailed over a huge oxer. She recalled how excited she was to ride the tall red mare a few times as a toddler. Flanked on either side of the portrait, hung group shots of students before Two Ponies Equestrian Camp closed and photos of many of her mother's favorite school horses spanning nearly forty years. She recognized Texas, Stormy and little Dusty among them and a picture of herself jumping Blackjack when she still rode English.

Josephine had grown up schooling dressage and jumping alongside her mother's students and helping prepare new lesson horses for their beginner riders. But, when she started high school she switched to Western, competing with her school's interscholastic equestrian team in speed and action classes and competing in barrel racing at local rodeos. Her mother had balked at the idea in the beginning, but it didn't take long before she became the best show-mom around. Bonanza was fast and agile for his size, earning her several prizes and buckles. Since she left home, she often reflected on how disappointing it must have been for her mother who planned to purchase a talented eventing mount for her daughter to compete regionally, and ultimately, nationally as she had. Josephine couldn't help noticing there were no photos of her cowboy hat and buckle days displayed.

But in the far corner of the room, covered in dust and cobwebs, hung a photo of her and TJ riding double bareback on Cisco alongside Mr. Black Feather. Josephine took the picture from the wall and carefully dusted it off as if she were wiping the cobwebs from her mind, bringing the memory back to life. It was the day TJ received the Medicine Hat Paint as a twelfth birthday present from his father. A plethora of emotions bombarded her. First the joy of recalling the fond memory, followed by a wave of sadness as the loss of their lifelong friendship and the death Mr. Black Feather swept through her. She wiped her burning eyes as she touched the image of TJ's smiling face. They were just kids, but TJ had already sworn his devotion to her years earlier. She replaced the picture and shook her head. What was she doing? If she didn't get moving, she'd run out of time for a ride.

"C'mon, boy," she said to Laddy, who sprung to his feet.

Quickly, she pulled Bonanza from his stall, slipped his bridle on, and climbed the fence to mount him bareback. The moment she laid across his back, before she had a chance to swing her right leg over, he started off at a trot, forcing her to complete the maneuver on the move. Good thing she shortened her reins and grabbed mane as she mounted. Bonanza pranced up the drive toward the trailhead with his head held high, ears forward and tail swishing, reminding her of their barrel racing days.

"Well, we'll see how long that lasts." She knew he mostly sat around getting fat while she was gone."

As they trotted up the drive, Laddy split off toward the lodge and jogged up the stairs to rest at the side door, no doubt looking for Mom. He sure was loyal to her. Guess he won't be getting any more exercise this morning.

When she reached the trail, she cued the Buckskin to pick up a canter and her worries swiftly lifted as the pair quickly covered ground. Sunbeams flashed between the aspen in strobe light fashion as Bonanza'a body heat began to radiate into her legs and seat. Now she truly felt at home as the pair moved as one.

Nearly to the creek, Josephine pulled Bonanza up to a walk. "Guess I'm out of shape too," she said, feeling a bit sore already.

Josephine had been doing some riding on the set, but nothing too strenuous, just enough to complete a scene or take a relaxing walk into the hills seeking some quiet time away from Brad and the crew. She knew Bonanza had been getting some work, ridden occasionally by a few of Jessie's students, so she considered them both in about the same condition. She found herself longing for the summers she rode with TJ every day, including long rides into the mountains for days during their last summer together. Looking back, that had to be the best summer of her life — the summer of 1995.

When she reached the stream, Josephine allowed the gelding to stretch down for a drink. She thought out loud as Bonanza siphoned the clear mountain water from between his lips.

"I need to thank mother for keeping you," she said, giving him a pat on the shoulder. "She probably hoped you would lure me home more often. That strategy didn't work too well, did it?"

Bonanza began pawing the water and Josephine quickly pulled his head up fearing he might roll as he had a habit of doing in the past. She shivered at the thought of a surprise cold bath if Bonanza plunged her into the freezing water. Just before she cued him to cross the creek, she imagined listening for TJ and Cisco downstream, ready to play their game of tag. Then much to her surprise, she swore she heard plopping sounds in the distance. It couldn't be, but Josephine gathered her reins and picked up a trot following the current of the tributary in the direction of the sounds. Heavy foliage along the winding creek banks blocked her view, not seeing any more than fifty feet ahead. Periodically, she stopped to listen, but only the gurling sound of water running over the rocky riverbed broke the silence of the forest. When she gave up and turned back, a heavy branch snapped in the woods. For an instant, she believed she saw something rush between the trees. She took a deep breath out of frustration. What was it with her this morning? Chasing ghosts, that's what, haunted by the memories of her past life. When she returned to the trail, she shot up the bank and galloped the straight trail through the open field, pretending TJ was chasing her.

"I won!" she said to Bonanza, bringing him down to a trot at the woods. Abruptly, she pulled Bonanza up to a sliding halt. No! She had lost… lost her best friend…lost her first love and perhaps the love of her life. Sure, she had won fame and fortune, but was she truly happy? She didn't seem to have the answer when her mother, father and Lisa all asked. Why couldn't she have just said yes? Josephine looked down the trail leading to the cabin on the lake and spun Bonanza around one hundred and eighty degrees and picked up an easy jog trot toward home. Too many memories lived at the cabin. No more chasing ghosts!

She needed to put TJ behind her and move on with her life, once and for all. Then she could focus on her relationship with Brad and things would be better between them again. She was living her dream after all. If TJ showed up today, she would express her regret in having not broken up with him in person and take whatever she had coming. She deserved it. And if TJ didn't come, it didn't matter, she told herself. She had made her choice and there was no turning back now. Josephine glanced at her watch and cued Bonanza into a smooth lope. Brad would be waiting.

Only the Walkers and White Clouds gathered for Betsy's burial at the edge of the front yard. As the two families held hands, her mother read the same American Indian version of a poem attributed to Mary Frye, that had been read at Joseph's funeral.

I give you this one thought to keep,
I am with you still – I do not sleep.

I am a thousand winds that blow,
I am the diamond glints on snow,

I am the sunlight on ripened grain,
I am the gentle autumn rain.

When you awaken in the morning's hush,
I am the sweet uplifting rush,

of quiet birds in circled flight.
I am the soft stars that shine at night.

Do not think of me as gone,
I am with you still in each new dawn.

The poem brought tears to Josephine's eyes with its lovely message. It seemed like something Betsy would say and believe. She wished TJ was present to hear it. Damn, why did TJ keep creeping into her head?

While she glanced over at Brad standing just outside the cemetery, his hands clasped in front of him, Josephine swore she saw someone duck behind a tree deep in the woods behind him. No, not someone, TJ. Great, not only could she not keep him out of her thoughts, but she kept imagining seeing him everywhere; in the pasture, at the creek and now in the woods.

As the casket was lowered and the attendees all held hands, her mother clasped her hand so tight Josephine was afraid to let go for fear she might topple over out of grief. She had never seen her mother so distraught and felt relieved when her father put his arm around her shoulders, steadying her as they each tossed a daisy, Betsy's favorite flower, onto the coffin. Her father then directed her mother back to the lodge and the others followed.

Josephine stood frozen in place, staring into the hole as the funeral crew began filling it in. Morbid thoughts accompanied by feelings of sorrow and guilt consumed her.

"I'm so sorry… Betz… I should have…" was all she could manage. She wasn't aware of the tears streaming down her face until Brad rushed to her side and pulled her into his arms.

"Are you okay?" he whispered in her ear, wiping a streak of tears from her cheek.

"I will be. It's just so hard."

Brad gave her a gentle squeeze. "I'm sorry, I now see how much she meant to you and your family."

Josephine nodded, drying her face the best she could with her hands. When she looked up into Brad's eyes, she felt a connection like she hadn't felt in a long while. He did care and she felt reassured that if she really needed him, he would be there for her. As Josephine leaned her weary head on his shoulder, Brad gave her a gentle kiss on the top of her head then guided her across the yard and up the front stairs.

TJ took a deep breath, fearing Josephine had seen him that time. What was he doing, following her around all day? Why hadn't he just attended the celebration with his mother and confronted her? When he showed up at home early that morning, his mother had happily greeted him at his truck, assuming he had changed his mind about accompanying her to honor Betsy. He had walked right past her to the barn to bridle Cisco, leaving her upset and disappointed with him yet again.

When he dared to carefully glance from behind the large tree trunk once again, Josephine was bent over in anguish. He wanted to rush to her, to hold and comfort her. Instead, he watched in revulsion as Brad embraced her. He had to turn away; his eyes shut in agony. That should be him! Not that pretty, rich boy who was probably just using Josephine to advance his career. As Josephine looked up at the leech, TJ had a clear view of her eyes and there was no mistaking the affection she felt for him – the same expression once reserved for only him. TJ felt gutted. His torment turned to rage as Brad leaned over and affectionately kissed her on top of her head. He had to turn away, wanting desperately to punch something. He couldn't find his breath, crushed by the weight of everything he'd lost, what she had taken from him… taken from them both.

His blood boiling with jealously, he anxiously waited for the couple to join the others in the lodge before making a mad dash through the underbrush back to Cisco. He didn't feel the branches dragging and snapping against his skin as he ran. He just needed to get away – away from the image of his Jo in the arms of another. The guys were right. He should have stayed away.

Josephine waited anxiously, hoping TJ would accompany his mother to the celebration, but Sarah arrived alone. However, that didn't stop her from continuing to look over every time her parents opened the door to greet new guests. Who was she kidding? She cared if he showed up, no, she needed him to walk through that door. Lisa had made a valid point. The only way she could finally move on with her life was to face TJ in person. Even after the last guest departed, she held some hope he might still show up, but he never did.

Sadie glanced at her watch again. TJ said he would come by an hour ago. She shook her head in frustration and checked her hair in the mirror for the umpteenth time. She had even left Betsy's memorial early to get home in plenty of time to prepare for his arrival. She wanted everything to be perfect. She had slipped into a revealing top and tight jeans, fixed her hair and cooked one of his favorite meals, pork chops with scalloped potatoes and green beans.

TJ had stopped by the night before, after their practice, and Sadie had asked him if he wanted to ride along with her today since he had a falling out with his mother. But he had declined, saying he wasn't planning to attend. She knew why. He still wasn't over her. Too proud to confront Little Miss Perfect after she dumped his ass. Josephine… with the perfect parents, perfect home, perfect skin, perfect body, perfect hair! Sadie scoffed at her reflection in the wall mirror. Why couldn't she get her hair to be full and wavy like hers? She'd tried everything, body building shampoos, conditioners and every kind of curlers.

Sadie had grown up in Josephine Walker's shadow, wishing she could take her place. She'd had a crush on TJ as long as she could remember and could never understand his infatuation with this rich, white bitch, especially when she treated him so poorly at school; avoiding him in the halls and siding with her white friends against him. Sadie first attended Two Ponies Equestrian Camp only as an excuse to be close to TJ. He was always hanging around Josephine at the riding school. But she soon came to admire Katherine and fell in love with her horses. Sadie had grown up the daughter of an alcoholic mother and an absent father. Her much older sister, Sally, who had attended the riding school years earlier had pretty much raised her. Not only did Josephine have TJ wrapped around her finger, she had the mother of her dreams. And how could she not envy Josephine as a successful movie star. But, to her surprise, that development had proved to work in her favor, opening the door for her to have both TJ and Katherine to herself. Someday, Josephine would be jealous of her!

She hadn't mentioned she was seeing TJ to Katherine, and she liked it that way for now. When TJ finally wakes up and realizes Josephine is never coming back, she'll be there to pick up the pieces. Sadie could picture them now, married and with a family living off the Reservation on his beautiful ranch just down the river from Two Ponies and Katherine. It would be perfect! But TJ was not there yet.

Sadie laughed to herself. Like some perfect rich and famous white girl is going to marry a Blackfeet! TJ was delusional. She wished he had been there today to see her perfect blond boyfriend. Sadie knew from the start it would be just a matter of time before she broke it off with TJ. The only reason they ended up together to begin with was because of the frightening experience they shared, almost dying and all.

Sadie stepped outside the small slat board cabin onto the front porch. She sat deep into the ragged and sagging couch they had moved outside when they replaced it with a nicer one from Goodwill. She searched the road which stretched for miles across the open range, spotted with lights from cabins and mobile homes, running between the Reservation in Browning and the mountains. Another brilliant Montana summer sunset cast an orange sheen over the barren land, turning the dust to gold.

As the sun disappeared behind the Continental Divide in the distance, the air turned cold. Sadie grabbed a few pieces of wood that TJ had cut and stacked under the porch and returned indoors to start a fire in the potbelly stove. After washing her hands and checking the mirror one more time, she curled up by the fire and waited. Where could he be? Sadie suddenly sat erect, her mind reeling. Had he gone to Two Ponies after all? Had TJ and Jo arranged to meet secretly afterward? She jumped from her seat, slipped on a jacket, and returned to the porch. She strained to identify a vehicle approaching from the west, leaving a trail of dust in its wake. Its headlights cut through the now dark prairie, rising and falling with each small swell of the nearly flat road. She prayed it was TJ.

Her heart skipped a beat as his truck pulled in her drive. They met in the front yard.

"I was worried. You okay?"

"Practice ran late," was all he said, putting his hands in his pockets, focusing on his boots.

The moment they entered the cabin, Sadie noticed several

scratches on his face. "What happened?" she questioned, touching the deepest cut across his cheek.

"Moon Cloud spooked and ran me through some brush." TJ pulled away and sat on the couch.

Okay, highly unlikely, but she wasn't going to push it. "I cooked dinner, your favorite, pork chops. You hungry?"

"Sure."

TJ was acting strange; distant, distracted. Something had happened besides a shying horse. She put a plate together and stuck it in the microwave. "So, aren't you going to ask me about today?"

TJ scowled. "Were there many people?"

"Yes, a lot of old students and families came. I overheard Kat ask your mom about you."

"What did she want to know?"

"Oh, just how you were doing – that they missed you." Sadie thought for sure he would inquire about Jo. When he didn't, she volunteered. "And Jo and her boyfriend were there."

"Yeah, my mom said they would be."

"Is that why you didn't go?" Silence.

She handed him his plate and sat beside him. "It's okay if you still miss her. I understand."

He turned to her, managing a meager smile. "You do? That's so sweet. It's hard to just turn off your feelings after caring about someone for so long." TJ stretched over and gently kissed her on the cheek.

What was that? She wasn't his sister! They had been seeing each other intimately for nearly two years. When she turned to kiss him on the mouth, he turned away and took another bite of his meal. For a moment, her face felt hot with anger, but she had to remember time was on her side. Jo would be leaving again, and she wasn't going anywhere.

"This is great, thanks," he said. "I haven't eaten all day."

"You should take better care of yourself." Sadie ran her fingers through his shoulder length hair. She was glad to see he was growing it long again. "Since you're taking this semester off from school, you could move in with me. I forgot to tell you. Sally is planning to move in with her new boyfriend. She's practically living there now. I was going to look for a roommate, but I'd rather you moved in. Between the two of us we could handle the rent, utilities and groceries. Then I could take care of you."

TJ turned toward her. "I'll think about it. Maybe if we win next weekend."

That was a start. She'd certainly be cheering the team on at the races that Saturday. Sadie smiled and gave her man a hug. Well, he might not be totally her man yet, but he would be in the end, one way or another.

At daybreak Monday morning, Josephine woke from a disturbing night's sleep. Several times through the course of the night, she had sprung up in bed from a frightening recurring dream. Each instance she found herself riding Bonanza through a dark forest during a severe storm with lightning strikes and trees falling all around her. The fear and anxiety lingered, and Josephine wondered what it meant. She doubted dreams could warn you of any specific danger, but she had learned in her psychology class that dreams could tell us something about ourselves. What was she running from? What was she afraid of? Josephine made herself shake off such thoughts and start her day. They were just dreams, after all.

She didn't have time for another ride before they left for the airport, but she felt drawn to the woods beyond the cemetery. Although she had been distraught and her vision blurred following Betsy's burial, she could swear she saw TJ peek from behind a tree trunk. Her mind would not rest until she did all she could to eliminate the possibility.

Josephine dressed and quietly exited the lodge from the side entrance, the farthest door from her parent's room, and walked around the lodge to the front yard and cemetery. It was so strange seeing the new headstone beside Joseph's. Again, her heart ached knowing Betsy was gone forever as she passed the wrought iron enclosure.

The woods were dense, but she pressed on, carefully maneuvering her way through and around the underbrush. She meticulously studied the ground for any sign of passage as TJ had taught her: overturned mossy rocks, broken twigs, or perhaps a footprint. When she reached a thick stand of saplings, she looked up to determine her best route around it. That's when she saw them — a couple of branches, snapped and left dangling just as they used to mark their trail for each other. Had TJ been there and left these branches as some sort of message to her, or had it just been a coincidence?

There was only one way of knowing. She would call him as soon as she had a private moment after they returned to Washington. Besides, she still needed to apologize, and she knew she would find no peace until she did. She should have told him in person, or at least over the phone, when she broke it off. How cliché and cruel to have written him a "Dear John" letter after all they had been through together. TJ deserved better. She had been weak and regretted it ever since. Like Lisa said, she needed a proper closure to their past. She would find the strength and courage to right her wrong, and perhaps he might forgive her so they could at least be friends again.

Josephine returned to her room to pack. She had the whole flight to think about what she would say.

The soonest opportunity to call TJ came the day after Josephine returned to filming on location in Washington. The site, comprised of a leased fifty-room lodge, a huge old barn, several corrals and outbuildings, was set on a couple hundred acres perfectly placed with a majestic mountain range as a backdrop. Roy and Brad were shooting the murder scene in the barn, leaving her alone at the lodge.

The large ranch acted as part of the set and served as living accommodations for the cast and crew. Just like rehearsing her lines for a film, she had rehearsed what she would say to TJ countless times over the past twenty-four hours, but she still had butterflies when it came time to make the call. She sat on her bed, legs crossed, her heart beating faster with each unanswered ring.

Sarah answered on the fourth ring. "Oh, hi, Mrs. Black Feather, it's Jo," she said, in shock. Josephine hadn't thought to prepare herself for Mrs. Black Feather to answer.

"What a surprise," she said. "It was so good to see you Sunday. But, please call me Sarah, we're all adults now."

"Sure. Old habits die hard. I… I was hoping to talk to TJ."

More awkward silence. Apparently, Sarah was at a loss for words as well. Finally, she spoke. "I'm sorry, Jo, he's not here… he isn't living here any longer. I'm not sure where he is at the moment."

Josephine stood and began pacing the room. "Oh."

"He's living on the Res with Talon, Matt and Noot."

"So, the old gang is back together." She pulled the curtains open enough to search the set down by the barn for Brad and Roy. Only a few extras and staff were milling around outside the barn. They had to be filming indoors.

"Yes, and I'm not happy about it. TJ has changed. He kept spending more and more time there and finally moved out on Saturday."

She recalled her mother mentioning Sarah's concerns. Josephine was tempted to ask exactly how he had changed. But how could she when she hadn't been in touch with either of them for so long. "Do they have a phone?"

"Afraid not. I imagine he'll be returning home for more of his things."

"When you see him, please let him know I called." Josephine left her cell phone number. "He can reach me at that number anytime."

"Can I tell him what this is about? You know he'll ask."

"I just wanted to explain..." Explain what, why she broke her son's heart? "I was hoping to see him at the funeral."

"He should have been there. You see, that's what I mean. He's changed." Sarah sounded on the verge of tears. "But I know where he'll be this weekend. They've been competing all summer at the Indian Relay Races. They're racing Saturday at the North American Indian Days at All Chief Park in Browning."

"Thanks, but I already left and I can't get away again so soon. Please take care and I'll try to make it back for the holidays."

After they said their goodbyes, Josephine plopped down on her bed. She stared at her phone in a daze. It was all disturbing news – TJ changing, not living at home, and now she may never know if it was him in the woods. She really did need to get a grip! Why had she even called to begin with? Silliness, all silliness. She shook her head, slipped her phone in her pocket and stomped out of the lodge. Perhaps she could still catch the end of the murder scene. Brad wanted her to be there, but she had given the excuse she had a headache earlier. Now she really did have one.

All week, Josephine kept telling herself she didn't care if TJ returned her call or not, yet she made certain she carried her phone on her or had it lying nearby every moment. By Friday morning, she couldn't stand it any longer. She couldn't get TJ off her mind no matter how hard she tried. She must see him! She ambushed Roy between takes while Brad was busy chatting with a couple cast members.

"We're back on schedule, right?" she asked her director, nonchalantly.

"Yes, thank goodness the weather has held." Roy turned to her suspiciously. "What's up, Jo?"

As much time as they'd spent working together over the past three years, he'd come to know her well, too well sometimes. "It's my mom's birthday Sunday and then she'll be leaving Monday for the Pan American Games in Winnipeg. I'd like to be there to celebrate and see her off."

Roy surveyed her from above his glasses. "You haven't been home in years and now you need to visit twice in a week? What's this really about?" Before she could answer, he must have read her scrambled expression. "TJ." And it wasn't even a question.

"I thought he'd be there. That I'd get to finally explain things in person, like I should have done in the first place. Then I swear I saw him watching the burial from the woods."

"Watching you, you mean."

"I suppose. I never meant to hurt him, you know that, right? It just couldn't have worked out."

"You trying to convince me or yourself?" Roy guided her behind a trailer away from Brad and the others. Several seconds passed as his face contorted, apparently trying to find the right words. Josephine leaned in, encouraging him to speak. He opened his mouth, but shook that thought off, and after another awkward silence, finally spoke. "I see you with Brad. It's not the same, is it?"

"As with TJ?"

"Yeah."

"No, but we were just kids with silly teen crushes and unrealistic dreams."

"Then why do you need to see him?"

Josephine took a deep breath. Roy always had a way of cutting through the crap. In a moment of weakness, she blurted out the truth rather than any of the excuses she had been feeding herself all week. "I've been thinking about him a lot lately. I can't get him out of my head."

Eyebrows raised in surprise; Roy rubbed his chin between his fingers. "Having some regrets?"

"I don't know. Doubts, maybe."

"Have you mentioned this to Brad?"

"How can I?"

"Hmm…" Roy scratched his scalp. "This could turn ugly."

"I just need to see TJ and sort things out first."

"I've noticed you haven't been as focused lately. I wondered what was going on."

"Will you?" she begged.

"What? Fly you back?"

She nodded. "I need to know if he still cares… if it's really over. Then I'll be able to focus on my work again. On Brad again."

"Okay, get packed. I'll take you right after we cut for the day. We'll return Sunday afternoon."

"Perfect!" Josephine gave him a hug. "Thanks, Roy."

"Well, can't have our star all distracted, now can we?"

Josephine smiled and rushed back to her room to throw a few things in an overnight bag. She had a feeling Roy wouldn't turn her down. He had become like a grandfather to her, watching over her and looking out for her best interests since she left home.

Roy had known her and TJ as a couple and he really liked TJ. He had never pressed her for an explanation following their breakup and he didn't hide the fact he felt a little leery of Brad's intentions in the beginning. But when Brad became a part of the cast, he hadn't brought it up again. The dynamics had changed. No longer was Brad just her boyfriend, he had become an important part of his project. And the press coverage of them as a couple had helped promote the film. She knew this put Roy in a tough spot, making him even more endearing to her, agreeing to fly her home to see TJ.

When she called home and spoke to her father, her return trip turned into a surprise visit for her mother. He didn't ask any questions, glad to have her home again so soon and for the opportunity to spend the day on the lake fishing with Roy.

While Brad sat finishing his lunch, Josephine studied the young man she had chosen to share her life with for the past two years. Did she love him? When he noticed her looking his way, he gave her one of his winning smiles. She smiled back, but something was missing. Where was the overwhelming desire to be close to him like she had always felt with TJ? Or was she looking for something that just didn't exist in an adult relationship? Was she just holding on to the memory of a childhood fantasy? She needed answers and hopefully this trip would provide them.

When Josephine returned to the set, she picked up her script and reviewed her lines one more time. With new-found enthusiasm, she delivered a stellar performance in a sensitive scene. The tears came easily, considering the emotional state she was in. Why had it taken her so long to realize what she needed to do? Thanks to Lisa, she had finally woken up. After they completed shooting for the day, Josephine told Brad about her return visit, explaining the importance of seeing her mother again, which wasn't entirely fabricated. She hadn't gotten to spend much one-on-one time with her last weekend. Brad didn't say much, only wishing her a smooth ride before joining the cast for dinner. That seemed a bit too easy, she thought. Maybe he was having doubts too. No need worrying about that now. She had to confront TJ first.

Josephine arrived at the fairgrounds in Browning late. Her father received an emergency call right before she planned to leave and her mother already had her truck hooked up to the trailer, packed and ready to depart for Winnipeg. The cheers from the crowd let her know a race was in progress. She worked her way through the throng of spectators and up the bleacher stairs to get a view of the track from the elevated railing. The competing teams were about to make an exchange of horses in front of the grandstand, the next leg of horses in waiting. The riders raced their mounts around the track jockeying for position before the switch. A young woman stood beside her with some sort of program in her hand.

"What race is this? Who's racing?"

The woman nearly threw the sheet at her, not taking her eyes off the track while screaming for her favorite team. Josephine quickly glanced at her watch then to the schedule, her finger running down the list of heats and team members, finally resting on the current race and the name, TJ Black Feather, rider for team Piegan Pride. This was their race!

Josephine studied the teams on the track. Immediately, she recognized Talon holding a flea-bitten gray in line with the other horses and handlers preparing for the exchange. Matt stood beside Talon, most likely ready to catch the horse TJ was riding in on. Four of the horses, out of a field of six, came out of the far turn in a tight group, racing down the homestretch. They were so tight; she couldn't identify TJ right away, but just before the pack approached the switch area, she recognized him riding a chestnut. In one fluid motion, TJ slipped from the bare back of the chestnut, ran a few strides and hopped onto the bare back of the gray effortlessly, and charged for the rail. Other transfers didn't go as smoothly; one horse rearing in anticipation of the exchange, spooking another. The spectators, mostly of American Indian decent, erupted as all the teams eventually made a clean exchange of horses. The six-horse field spread out around the first turn but three of the horse-and-rider teams began to pull away from the others down the backstretch. No horses were in waiting, this was the final lap!

Leaning over the rail, she strained to follow TJ as the three raced in a tight pack going into the far turn. With another light-colored horse in the group, she had to look for the Piegan Pride team colors of red and black to identify TJ. He was positioned just to the outside of the lead horse, a black running on the rail. A bay ran just behind him and to the outside. As they came out of the far turn, he gave his horse his head, pushing for what was left of the big gray. Then the bay made a move on the outside, pressing TJ and his horse tight between it and the black horse. The three horses ran neck and neck toward the finish!

Caught up in the excitement, Josephine screamed, "Go TJ!"

She froze as TJ glanced toward the grandstand, his eyes locking with hers. The rest seemed to play out in slow motion. As TJ turned to focus on her, his mount swung to the outside as well, running into the bay. For a moment, she feared the gray's and the bay's legs might tangle and a horse and rider would go down, if not both of them. The crowd drew a unified breath. Thankfully, there was not a spill, but TJ's gray had faltered when he broke stride. The bay overtook TJ and the black to cross the finish line first.

Josephine gasped! What had she done? Standing frozen in shock for a moment, she watched in horror as TJ turned his mount on his haunches and galloped back toward her. She panicked and ran from the bleachers, pushing her way through the mass of spectators back to her father's truck. How could she face him now after causing him to lose the race? If he were angry with her before, he'd be furious now.

TJ frantically searched the crowd. He felt certain he'd heard and seen Josephine cheering him on. After pacing his horse several times back and forth in front of the grandstand, he ran out of the track and into the parking lot, racing up and down the aisles between vehicles trying to locate her. For an instant, he thought he recognized Dr. Walker's truck as it disappeared into a cloud of dust leaving the fairgrounds. Moon Cloud was breathing heavily and dripping in sweat beneath him. He would not risk the horse's health on the slight chance they could catch Josephine before she hit the highway, if it was even her. TJ turned back toward the track and their trailer.

By the time he reached their rig, his team had rinsed off and cooled out the other two horses, which stood quietly tied to the trailer. The guys did not look happy. Talon stayed back but Noot and Matt came at him at a furious pace.

"What the hell!" screamed Matt, tossing a cigarette to the ground and smashing it with the heal of his boot.

Noot took a hold of Moon Cloud's bridle. "What happened out there? Where did you go?"

TJ dismounted. There was no sugar coating it. "I thought I saw

Jo in the stands. I got distracted." He stared at the ground. "I'm sorry."

"You're sorry?" Matt stood with his arms rigid at his sides. "Are you crazy? You had that race won. Now we have to come up with the money for another entry!" Matt paced back and forth within inches of him. TJ half expected him to reach out and grab him, shake him up or worse. He deserved it.

Noot released Moon Cloud, threw up his arms and turned to walk back to the truck. "You're losing it, bro," he called back to TJ.

Talon leaned silently against the truck, shaking his head.

TJ led Moon Cloud to the trailer and slipped off his bridle, replacing it with his halter. Avoiding eye contact with any of his team, he led the gelding to a nearby hose to rinse off the sweat. As he scraped the excess water off the gray, he knew what his friends were thinking. To qualify for the Championship of Champions Race, they needed to win at least one race of the remaining tour stops, two of which were a longer drive in Montana and the rest out of state, all requiring overnight expenses. Hopefully, they would qualify at the next meet in Montana at the Phillips County Fair in Dodson held the first week of August.

When he returned, the other horses were loaded, and his teammates were waiting for him outside the truck since the vehicle had no air conditioning. It had to be over eighty degrees. He quickly loaded Moon Cloud, secured the back gate of the trailer and approached his friends.

"I'll cover the entries. We can camp. I have everything we'll need; tents, sleeping bags… I'll even supply the food."

Matt and Noot turned and climbed in the truck without a word, slamming the old Dodge pickup doors so hard they rattled in exclamation. TJ slipped in the back seat opposite Talon, who wore a lopsided smirk.

"Sadie came by right after the race looking for you. She looked pissed. She wants to see you before she leaves for the big show in

Canada Monday," whispered Talon. "Forget about the redhead, you belong with Sadie. In case you haven't noticed, Sadie is one fine babe. And the chick is crazy about you!"

TJ just nodded. On the drive home, TJ stared aimlessly out the window, trying to recapture the image of Josephine cheering him on in the stands. He closed his eyes and the vision of her ponytail swinging in rhythm to her waving arm, came to life — all five seconds of it. TJ smiled to himself. Seeing her there meant more than any race or winnings ever could. There was no other explanation. She had come to see him ride.

6 – Promises

While preparing dinner, Katherine heard a vehicle pull in the gravel drive. She glanced out the kitchen window and was surprised to see Josephine home already from visiting some old school friends. Katherine checked her watch and exited the lodge to meet her on the side porch.

"Hi, Jo, back so soon?" she called to her daughter as she exited Steven's truck. The moment Josephine lifted her focus at the top of the stairs, it became clear she was upset. "What happened?"

Josephine offered a half-hearted smile. "Nothing really. I missed someone I was really hoping to see."

"I'm sorry, sweetie. But I'll take any additional time we can spend together."

This brought a genuine smile to her daughter's face. "Where's the guys?"

"Where do you think?" Katherine led the way toward the front porch.

"Still fishing?"

"Yep. They must be biting." Katherine shaded her eyes, searching the large portion of the lake visible from their vantage point. "But they'll be getting hungry soon."

"There they are," pointed Josephine.

Katherine followed her daughter's finger in the direction of Pine Island.

"That's always been Daddy's favorite spot," said Josephine, turning to her. "When are the guests arriving?"

"Oh, I meant to tell you, no guests this year. We got to see everyone last weekend, and I really wanted to spend as much time as possible together, just the four of us. Kimi was so kind to drop off some cupcakes earlier."

"I should have baked you a cake."

"The cupcakes will be fine." Katherine entered the lodge, holding the door for Josephine. "How about a ride together in the morning? I'm sure Roy will want to get out on the lake with Dad one more time before you leave."

"Sounds wonderful," said Josephine. "I was disappointed we didn't get the chance to go out together last weekend. Who will you ride?"

"I'll take Major out. It'll be good to put some miles on him before the long trailer ride."

"This is so exciting, Mom. Wish I could join you in Winnipeg, but no way can I get away again so soon. Keep us posted on your progress, okay?"

"I sure will."

"You still leaving Monday?"

"Yes, first thing that morning as soon as Sally drops Sadie off."

"I wish I could stay another day to see you off and see Sally… and Sadie. I didn't get to spend much time with either of the sisters last weekend. But I was surprised to learn Sally broke it off with Sam and is seeing someone else so soon. They'd been together forever. Is Sadie dating anyone?"

"I don't know. Sadie isn't much of a talker."

"She is a quiet one. I don't recall her ever seriously dating anyone, do you?"

"No, now that you mentioned it. But it makes her more available to travel."

"I'm glad she's working out for you."

"Yeah, Sadie is great with Major, but I sure miss traveling with Jessie. Sadie is, well… Sadie."

"I never really hit it off with her either. She can be so moody and serious about everything."

"Yeah, not too many laughs. But I'm lucky to have her."

Josephine turned to Katherine; her expression suddenly glum.

"I'm sorry it's not me. I think you always hoped, I'd… you know, follow in your footsteps."

"You doing what makes you happy, makes me happy." Katherine had long gotten over the disappointment of her daughter's lack of interest in competing in eventing. "And, by doing what you love most, you've became one of the best at your craft. I couldn't be prouder."

"Thanks, Mom."

"But I would love the opportunity to tell you in person more often. I know you're busy but know that pop-up visits like this one are welcome anytime."

Josephine smiled and gave her a hug. "I will visit more often, I promise."

After team Piegan Pride dropped their horses off at the pasture, an uncomfortable and silent ride home continued. TJ couldn't blame the fellas for being disappointed and angry with him. He deserved it.

When they pulled in the stone house drive, he wasn't surprised to see Sadie's blue Ford Escort parked out front. Matt and Noot snickered between them, breaking the silence.

"Hope she didn't see the redhead," said Matt. "What are you going to tell her?"

TJ had the door open before the truck came to a complete halt. "Nothing, I'm not even sure what I saw."

As he ducked out of the pickup, he heard Noot say something that sounded like, "He better have seen something… blowing the race like that."

Sadie exited her vehicle and leaned against the driver door; arms crossed.

TJ tried to assess her expression as he approached. "Hey."

"What happened, TJ?" she said, sounding more sympathetic than pissed off, which came as a relief. "It looked like you were in perfect position to pull away and win the race. Moon Cloud looked strong."

"Yeah, well, I got distracted."

"No kidding."

TJ was hoping she'd say more to give him a better indication of what she did see. He stalled, focusing on his feet with his hands in his pockets. After shuffling a few stones around with his boot, he looked up and said, "I thought I saw an old friend I haven't seen for years," which wasn't entirely untrue.

"Who? Couldn't it have waited?"

"It was stupid, I know. I'll make it up to everyone."

Sadie slid her arms through the gaps between his arms and torso and gave him a hug. "I was hoping you'd win, so you could move in with me." Judging by her next comment, he must have looked pathetic. "It's okay, you'll win the next race for sure." She gave him a squeeze and a kiss. "Can you come over tonight?"

"I'm pretty tired."

"Just for a little while? I'll fix you some dinner."

"You don't always have to feed me, you know?"

"I enjoy cooking for you."

"How about we just go pick up some pizzas, I owe the guys."

"Oh, okay," she pouted. "Tomorrow then? I was hoping for a little alone time before I leave Monday morning. I'm going to be gone over a week you know," she whispered in his ear.

TJ just nodded.

"You promise?"

Another nod. "Let me take a quick shower," he said, already moving in the direction of the back door. "I'll be right out."

"Okay."

Seeming herself, he must have lucked out and she hadn't seen Josephine. He would come up with some excuse not to visit Sadie tomorrow as well. He didn't say he would. All he could think about was Josephine. He had to see her somehow… and soon!

That evening, Katherine sat at the head of the table staring at a cupcake covered in candles resembling an upset porcupine. Thankfully, Josephine hadn't tried to fit all fifty-nine on the small cake. While her daughter searched for some matches, Steven disappeared out the side door. She guessed he had snuck out to retrieve her gift from his truck. Roy sat at the table with a silly grin across his face. Steven must have shared what he got her, and Roy apparently approved. This raised her curiosity even more. He always managed to come up with something special. She was surprised and disappointed when Steven returned to the dining room with his arms full of envelopes instead. He must have picked up the mail from the post office following his emergency call earlier.

Josephine approached the table. "I found them," she said, opening the box of matches.

"Would you look at this?" said Steven. "Ever since the Sports Illustrated article ran. Letters from all over the country."

Josephine's jaw dropped. "You're getting more fan mail than I do! Do you read them all?"

"Sure, it's fun," said Katherine. Well, most of the time, she thought to herself. All but the ones from Florida. "Do you read all of yours?"

"Most of the time," said Josephine, before noticing her director's skeptical expression. "When I have time," she added.

"Ha," said Roy. "We have someone that handles most of it."

"It's still hard to grasp my little girl is a movie star," said Steven, shaking his head. "And now my wife is a celebrity." He set the pile of mail down on the far end of the table.

Steven took a seat beside her as Josephine lit the candles. As they sang to her, a montage of images from birthdays past sped through her mind; her first wonderful birthday at Two Ponies with Betsy and Uncle Joe, the summer of her sixteenth birthday when Steven gave her her lucky gold stirrup earrings, her twenty-first birthday that she'd rather forget when Steven found her and Billy together, many birthdays with just Betsy after a long day working the camp, then many more with Steven as her husband and the girls at different ages. Several of those years, Betsy invited over twenty friends and family members, her birthday becoming the social event of the summer. Today it was just the four of them. Katherine wished Lisa could be there, but she worked weekends and couldn't get away again so soon. But more than Lisa, she missed Betsy. Katherine sighed and blew out her candles. She made the wish that Josephine would never miss another one of her birthdays. She knew it was most likely a wasted wish, but that's what filled her heart as she shared a warm smile with her daughter.

After they finished their cupcakes and milk, Katherine opened her gifts. Roy pulled an envelope from the seat of the empty chair beside him and handed it to her. Inside, she found a sweet birthday card signed by Roy and Sandy containing a few photos of their grandkids and a Visa gift card.

"Oh, thank you, what a lovely card. The pictures are great. I can't believe how big they are already. And you really didn't need to include a gift. Bringing Jo two weekends in a row was plenty."

"I figured you could use the card for gas this week," said Roy.

"I will, tell Sandy thanks too."

Next, Josephine slipped her what appeared to be a handmade card. "Sorry. I didn't have a chance to shop for a card or gift."

"You just being here is gift enough."

Katherine studied the drawings and hand-written birthday wish and could feel her eyes well. "You used to always make my cards. I still have them all. Thank you, Jo."

Josephine leaned over and gave her a hug. "Love you, Mom. Happy birthday!"

Instead of offering her a gift, Steven stood up and collected the pile of envelopes in his arms. "Where do you want me to put these?"

"Just set them down on the kitchen table," said Katherine. "I'll read them later."

As Steven left for the kitchen, she played along as she began collecting their plates, becoming more curious about his gift by the minute.

"Hey, I've got an idea. Let's read them together," said Josephine, springing up to stop her father.

"No, I was hoping we'd all watch a movie, something light and fun before it gets too late," she said, fearing there might be another letter from her heckler in Ocala. "Jo, pick one out for us."

"Sure." On her way to the movie cabinet in the great room, Josephine reached down and picked something up from the floor. "Can I read just this one?"

Katherine panicked, setting the stack of dessert plates down on the table in a clatter. She rushed from the table to take the envelope from her daughter. Josephine laughed, holding the letter behind her, turning to evade her mother's grasp. "Oh c'mon, Mom."

By this time, Steven had returned from the kitchen. "I must have dropped one." Seeing the game Josephine was playing, he joined in and snatched the letter from Josephine just as Katherine was about to grasp it from her daughter's hand. Katherine reached to take it from him, but he held it too high.

"What?" he asked. "Why can't we read it? You afraid it'll be embarrassing?"

Meanwhile, Roy sat chuckling at the scene playing out before him. "Now I want to see it too," he said.

Katherine couldn't breathe. "No!" she yelled, as Steven opened the envelope, still holding it beyond her reach.

"Oh, it's sweet, Kat," said Steven, reading the note over his head.

She released a held breath in a whoosh, relieved it was a real fan letter. Steven read the short note written in script within a lovely card with a picture of a jumper on the front.

Dear Ms. Walker,
You are an inspiration to all of us senior riders. I belong to an aging horsewomen's eventing group in Georgia and you're our hero. We wish

you the best of luck in Winnipeg and hopefully in Sydney next year.
We'll all be cheering for you!
Pam Summers
p.s. That's me and my Wellesley, center.

"And look, she enclosed a picture." Steven handed Katherine a photo of seven elderly women on horseback in dressage attire, the woman in the middle holding up a sign that read "Go Katherine and Major!"

Katherine smiled, passing the card and photo on to Josephine and Roy. Then the message dawned on her. "Senior?" she snipped. "Aging Horsewomen!"

"Big six-o next year, sweetie," Steven teased. "Happens to the best of us, got to accept it."

"Ha! Look who's talking, Mr. I won't take a senior discount," said Katherine. Steven had turned sixty earlier that year and insisted on not revealing his age in public. "Talk about denial!"

They all broke into a fit of laughter, Roy's robust cackle overpowering everyone else's. Once the teasing and laughter subsided, Josephine left to pick out a movie.

Steven patted her on the back. "You're my hero, too, honey."

Still, he hadn't given her a present and her expression must have been telling. Steven smiled broadly and reached out his hand. Suddenly, she recalled her sixteenth birthday when she had opened all her gifts, all but one from Steven.

"Tell Jo we'll be a little bit," he said to Roy.

Katherine stood and clasped his hand. Steven led her out the door and down the stairs. She knew where they were heading. The moon was full now and lit their way as they walked hand in hand through the aspen grove to the top of the hill overlooking the lake. For an instant, she recalled the night so many years ago, a night much like this one, that she watched Billy walk into the lake from that very spot, presumed drowned. Steven squeezed her hand, bringing her back to the present. He led her a little further down the path to the old bare log, now completely covered with graffiti. The log had become a landmark where the girls etched their names and dates into the old tree trunk. Katherine sat down on the log and traced the carving of their names framed within a heart. Steven had revealed his work to her the night of her sixteenth birthday when he gave her the earrings she still wore every time she competed. Steven sat beside her and reached into his back, jean pocket and extended another small blue velvet box to her. What could it be this time?

When she opened it, the moonlight reflected off a horse-head-shaped gold locket. She opened it and gasped. Inside was a picture of Lady on one side and Major on the other, her two heart horses.

"It's perfect! I love it!" Katherine handed it to him and turned. "Can you see to latch it?"

"I'll try." It took a few tries before it hung securely around her neck, appropriately resting over her heart.

Katherine turned back to face him. They embraced and passionately kissed like they were kids again.

"We better head back," said Steven. "They're waiting on us."

Holding hands, the happy couple walked back to the lodge. She wondered if Steven shared her thoughts, as their pace quickened along the way, anxious to finish the movie so they could celebrate her birthday as one.

Following the most romantic lovemaking they'd shared in a long while, Steven dozed off beside her. It had been a long day for him with the emergency call early that morning, fishing out in the fresh air all day, patiently watching The Black Stallion for the umpteenth time, not to mention their romp in the hay. She was tired too, but she couldn't rest until she returned to the kitchen. Quietly, she padded her way across the lodge, through the library, great room, dining room, and into the kitchen to look through the mail still in a pile on the counter. There it was! Another letter postmarked from Ocala, Florida. Thank goodness that letter had not slipped from

Steven's grasp earlier.

Tearing open the envelope, Katherine read the typed message:

Hello Katherine,

I hope you get this warning before you leave for Winnipeg. If you insist on showing up at your age with that used-up nag, I can promise you your trip will end in tragedy. It's people like you that give the sport of eventing a bad reputation, pushing horses and riders that have no business competing as this level to the point of disaster. Besides, you had your chance.

Give it up and stay home!

Katherine crumpled up the letter and tossed it and the envelope in the garbage, then stood there, transfixed on the trash can. Who is this person? Then she seized the wad, flattened it out on the counter and read the note again, reading the words "you had your chance" out loud. What could that mean? Suddenly, she knew the answer. She knows this person, or this person at least knew her back when she was competing with Lady four decades ago when she was a shoo-in for the 1964 Olympic team. This time, she returned the note to the envelope, folded it in half, and slid it into her housecoat pocket. Just in case something did happen, and she suspected foul play, she would have it for evidence. Only then did it occur to her, she should have kept the others too. Well, she has this one, but where can she hide it that no one would find it? She wrapped her robe snuggly around herself, tying it tight at the waist, then quietly exited the lodge into the frigid night air still in her slippers. Katherine walked out to her truck. Through the passenger door, she opened the glove box and slide the letter into her vehicle's manual, confident no one would find it there.

Unable to put the note out of her mind, Katherine ended up in the library with the desk lamp pointed away from their bedroom door. She began leafing through the folder of documents on her desk, ready to take on the trip. There, she found it, the list of entrants. Katherine pulled it out and ran her finger down the long list of names, trying to think back forty years to her competitors at the time. None of the names sounded familiar. She ran through the list a second time with the same result. She stuffed the stapled sheets back into the folder. This meant nothing. Women marry, like herself, and change their names. Or it might not even be a competitor or anyone dating back to her early show career. It could just be some nut case. She couldn't imagine what she might have done for someone to wish her and her horse harm.

Katherine slid back into bed and curled up beside her husband, his warmth and masculine scent calming her. She contemplated telling him about the threat letter, but she didn't want to worry him right before they left. Katherine dismissed the letters once again as just some bored person who had heard her story and had nothing better to do than harass her. She closed her eyes and thought about her ride with her daughter in the morning. With a smile on her face, she drifted off to a sound sleep.

Following a glorious ride with Josephine Sunday morning, Katherine. along with Steven, wished their daughter and Roy a safe flight back to Washington to resume production on their film. It was a short but sweet visit and Katherine had high hopes that more frequent visits from their daughter might become the norm. Soon after they pulled away, Steven left to check on a few of his patients at the animal hospital.

Katherine sat at the picnic table on the side porch waiting for Sadie to arrive to prepare for their departure in the morning. Laddy looked up at her with a questioning expression. He had become glued to her side ever since he saw her suitcase come out that morning, knowing this meant she'd be leaving again.

"Sorry, Laddy. But this trip won't be as long as the last one, I promise." Laddy laid his head firmly on her lap, which had become his MO when demanding her attention. Her and Steven referred to it as "chinning." She stroked the soft top on his head and ruffled his ears. "That's a pretty pathetic look you've got going there, boy."

Katherine worried about Laddy home alone with Betsy gone, but Steven agreed to take him to the office and along on calls when he could. And Jessie said she would spend time with him when she came to teach her lessons. The wolfdog would enjoy their company, but he would miss her terribly. She wished she could make him understand how much she would miss him too, and that she would take him along if she could.

She planned to leave before daybreak in the morning so they would arrive at the show grounds before dark. They would have three days for Major to recover from the trip and acclimate to his new surroundings before the competition began on Friday.

As she waited, her thoughts returned to who she might have crossed forty years ago. She knew she needed to push the whole notion of someone wanting to harm her and her horse from her head, but her mind kept going there. Major needed one hundred percent of her focus on him and competing at the Pan American Games. Not on some crazy lunatic. Katherine got to her feet and marched toward the barn, needing to do something besides fixating on the letter. Unfortunately, there would be plenty of idle time during the eleven-hour drive ahead of them. But for today, she would have plenty to do to distract her from such thoughts.

First on her list, they needed to clip Major's bridle path, face and fetlocks and give him a bath. Katherine pulled the clippers and extension cord from the cabinet in the tack room and set them down on the shelf in the wash rack. Next, she grabbed a five-gallon bucket from the feed room to flip upside down and use as a step stool to reach the head of her tall Thoroughbred. Major could be a bit of a jerk when getting clipped. He did his best when someone steadied his head and distracted him with some pats, so she would wait until Sadie arrived. After finishing with Major, they would run down their packing list one more time.

When she heard Sadie pull up beside her truck and trailer, Katherine strode out to the barn to greet her with Laddy leading the way.

"Hi, Sadie, I have everything ready to clip Major."

"Great," said Sadie, with less enthusiasm than the word deserved. She knelt down and gave Laddy a better welcome, stroking his coat repeatedly. "How you doing, big fella?"

Katherine led the way into the barn. "You okay? You look tired."

"I'm fine," she said, then added, barely audible, "Just a little disappointed."

This was highly unusual for Sadie to invite Katherine into a conversation about any aspect of her personal life. Katherine became very curious. "What happened?" she asked, pulling Major from his stall.

"I was hoping the Piegan Pride team would win yesterday at the races. You know, to represent our tribe at the Championship of Champions Race this fall."

"I'm sorry. That's TJ's team, right?" said Katherine, clipping one crosstie as Sadie secured the other. Already knowing the answer to her question from Sarah's updates on TJ, she added, "Will they get another chance?"

"Yes, there are several more races they can qualify at, but it would have been nice to do it here at home." Sadie reached down to plug the extension cord into the outlet.

"That is too bad. I'm feeling a little disappointed too," said Katherine. "Roy flew Jo home for a short surprise visit over the weekend for my birthday, but I wish she could have stayed to see us off tomorrow morning. She did wish us luck and got to visit a few old friends from school on Saturday."

Sadie sprang up, looking shocked by the announcement. "Right," she said, sharply. Katherine noticed a sudden change in her young apprentice's mood, her eyes narrowing as she straightened her back.

"When did she leave?"

"They just left a short time ago. It was great to see her again so soon. We went on a lovely trail ride together this morning. It had been years."

Sadie ran her hand over the saddle mark on Major's back. "I see you rode Major." Katherine could feel the tension exuding from the young woman. Major felt it too, flinching under her touch.

"Yeah, he did great."

"Surprising she'd come home again so soon after being gone so long." Where did that come from? Sadie's focus turned from Major to her. Her lips parted for a moment before pressing into a straight line. Katherine sensed she was about to say something, then thought better of it. Instead, she turned away and unwrapped the Oster clippers. "Ten or forty blade?" she asked.

"The ten. We'll work our way down from the bridle path. That worked well last time."

Without another word, Sadie attached the blade, setting aside the forty for his ears and muzzle. Okay, that was strange, but that was Sadie. Back to business. Katherine slid the bucket beside the right side of Major's front end and stepped onto it. In response, Major raised his head, his eyes suddenly rimmed with white. He knew what was coming and Katherine knew what to expect. She wished people were so easy to figure out.

Katherine stroked Major's neck. "Oh, c'mon, boy. We've only done this a million times."

She guessed he either had a bad experience getting clipped in his past life or just didn't like the noise or vibration of the clippers. But he was consistent, that was for sure. "Animals of habit," she thought out loud.

Sadie plugged in the clippers into the extension cord and sprayed the running blade with cooling lubricant before handing them to her. The extra cord allowed Katherine more flexibility moving around the big gelding. The last thing they needed was for Major to get tangled in the cord as he fidgeted in the crossties and fling the clippers from her hands onto the concrete floor.

When she finished with his face, Katherine glanced at his pasterns. "His legs look good. But let's pack the clippers in case we need to give him a touch-up later in the week."

Sadie just nodded and quietly wrapped the clippers back up in the towel. She remained silent unless spoken to for the remainder of the afternoon, bathing Major and packing last-minute items. Katherine couldn't help but wonder what had upset the girl.

As Sadie retrieved her jacket from the office, preparing to leave, she surprisingly cheered up. "I'll see you bright and early in the morning. Can't wait!" Yet her face didn't quite match the fervor in her voice.

"Great! See you then and don't forget your passport."

"Got it!" Sadie gave Laddy a pat and left for her vehicle.

Katherine watched her pull out. Josephine was right, Sadie sure could be moody. Not a real people person, that's for sure. Again, she missed having Jessie as a traveling companion. Yet she must be grateful to have Sadie, no matter how strange she could be. At least she was great with the animals.

She returned to Major's stall and threw his light sheet on for the night and gave him a couple horse cookies. He had been a good boy. Spa days were always a challenge for him, having to stand for such a long period of time. The hot-blooded Thoroughbred preferred schooling to grooming, anything that set him in motion.

But even more than training, Major loved to compete. It seemed he could tell the difference between schooling shows and the shows that counted, no doubt picking up on her vibe. She looked forward to their three days to settle in and school before dressage on Friday, then Steven would join them for cross country and show jumping over the weekend. Dressage never did capture his interest. Hopefully, he would get to see them qualify.

As she watched her beautiful boy chew, her mind drifted back to the letter. She had been so busy that afternoon, she had been able to put it out of her mind. Every time she recalled the comments about her and Major being a detriment to the sport of evening, it raised the hair on her arms like a dog's hackles. How dare someone imply she would endanger her horse… that they were not prepared! They had followed the book, moving up divisions gradually and successfully, earning the chance to qualify for the team like everyone else. Several senior riders and horses Major's age and beyond have competed at the highest levels successfully without incident. Yet, she could feel a seed of doubt had been planted.

"We're ready, right boy?"

Katherine closed Major's stall door and strutted to her truck. Laddy, who had been laying on the cool concrete floor of the wash rack, sprang to his feet and followed her. Leaning in the passenger door, she extracted the letter from the manual and read it again. Two statements stood out, "I can promise you it will end in tragedy" and "You had your chance." The other comments about them not being prepared seemed more like a cover for what was really on this person's mind. This person hated her and didn't feel she deserved a spot on the team and was trying to justify it somehow. It had to be a competitor and someone she knew when contending for the Olympics decades ago. She returned the letter to her glove box. The question was, how much did this person hate her and was it enough to make good on their threat?

As she lumbered toward the lodge, Laddy kept stride with his head strategically placed at hand level. He was always more demanding of her attention before trips. When she neglected his invitation, he nudged her fingers with his wet nose. Katherine stopped and knelt on one knee and gave her faithful companion a good rub. Running her fingers through his thick coat soothed and revived her. She sprang to her feet and threw a pinecone for Laddy to chase. In the five years she'd had him, he never chose to fetch one. He would chase it, bite it, then leave it, as if he was above such menial dog games with wild wolf blood flowing through his veins. Katherine chuckled. She would miss him too, but she could look forward to his jubilation upon her return. Hopefully, they would have plenty to celebrate!

7 – Getting Even

Ocala, Florida

The sun still lay hidden just below the flat Florida horizon as Karen Lutz zipped her suitcase closed on the edge of her bed. Lifting the large bag and rolling it to the front door of her mobile home was no trouble for the seventy-year-old. She had maintained her upper body strength from cleaning stalls and performing other tasks at the barn where she worked. She heard a vehicle and glanced out the window to see if her son, Stanley Lutz, had arrived. The flood light out front remained on, illuminating the gravel street of the trailer park, but it was just her neighbor leaving for work. Karen checked her watch and poured another cup of coffee. If there was one thing she could count on with Stanley, it was him running late. Knowing this, she had allowed some extra time to make sure they arrived at the Ocala International Airport in time for their flight to Winnipeg. She had saved every spare dime for the past year for this trip and she wasn't about to miss their plane.

Her granddaughter Kayla Lutz would be competing for one of the coveted US Equestrian Team spots at the Pan American Games. Kayla's mount, a ten-year-old Hanoverian mare, Joyous Occasion, owned by Erica Shields Eventing, was already en route along with three other horses via the farm's large diesel truck and slant-load four-horse trailer. The trailer housed a good-size dressing and tack room up front, complete with sleeping quarters which extended out over the fifth wheel. Kayla accompanied Erica and the horses on the long drive north and would sleep in the trailer the duration of the games while assisting with the other horses and riders. Karen and her granddaughter both worked at Erica's facility to pay for Kayla's lessons and show expenses. At twenty, Kayla would be the youngest on the US Equestrian team, if she qualified.

In addition to accomplishing so much so young, her granddaughter had overcome more than her fair share of adversity. Following the drug overdose of Karen's only daughter, Valerie Lutz, Kayla came to live with her at the age of four. Shortly after, Kayla was diagnosed with acute leukemia. It had been painful for Karen to see her only grandchild born into a drug addict's world without a father, then to grow up feeling different and singled out because of her affliction. But unlike Valerie, Kayla was born with horses in her blood. Kayla's riding became her only joy, giving the girl the strength and purpose she needed to continue the fight. Without horses, Karen felt certain Kayla would have given up and wouldn't be here today. It took a fighter to survive the years of treatment and therapy that followed. Kayla now lived a normal life thanks to early detection and years of treatment and therapy.

Once Kayla fully recovered, she advanced quickly, earning the opportunity to ride one of Erica's top prospects at the age of sixteen. When the pair began showing promise, Erica hired Kayla and started backing her, doing all she could to help her afford to show the mare. For four years, Kayla and Joy schooled and competed as a team, working their way up one division at a time. And now here she was, so close to qualifying. But there was a limit to Erica's generosity. If Kayla qualified, it was agreed it would be her responsibility to cover the cost of travel to Sydney for herself and the horse, including airfare, hotel and meals, which would come to tens of thousands of dollars.

They needed to secure as much backing as possible from the limited amount of equestrian companies offering sponsorships. Competitors fought for sponsors as hard as they fought to qualify. Kayla had a great story which had landed one endorsement, but they would need more. In Karen's mind, if anyone deserved to go, it was her granddaughter. And this would be their only chance. Erica would be putting Joy up for sale either following the Pan American Games or the Olympic Games depending on the outcome. The trainer was getting up in years and looking to cut back on her projects and overhead. Karen would be paying on Kayla's medical bills the remainder of her life. She would never be able to afford a quality prospect for her granddaughter, nor was it likely she would get the opportunity to ride a horse like Joy again.

Kayla was all Karen had left to live for. Having lost her daughter to drugs and her son and her son being a good-for-nothing alcoholic, this was her last chance to get it right as a parent. Her granddaughter had given her a second chance as a mother, and she would do whatever it took to make Kayla's dream come true. The dream of every young eventer – the opportunity to qualify for the Olympics.

Nearly forty years ago, Karen had a dream too — to have a student of hers qualify for the Olympics. Never having the opportunity to compete with a world-class horse of her own, she had been given the once-in-a-lifetime opportunity to train a super talented horse and rider. And, she had come so close. If only her student had gotten the opportunity to ride and medal at the 1964 Summer Olympic Games in Tokyo, she would have become one of the nation's top eventing trainers with a beautiful barn full of quality horses and riders to perpetuate her success, instead of cleaning stalls at someone else's barn. With a medal-winning student, Karen's reputation would have been bolstered, earning her the recognition from her peers and income she deserved after all the years of sweat she had poured into her riding and training career. She had taught this girl from the ground up for eight years, finding her the perfect horse to carry them to the top as a team. She even closed her riding school in Boston to take an instructing position at Centenary College in New Jersey, in order to follow her star student, who just so happened to be the daughter of one of Boston's most prominent families with pockets deep enough to make it all happen. They were at the top of their game, placing high at nearly every event and would have surely qualified for Tokyo — until the girl's betrayal. Her dream ripped from her grasp by a rich, stupid, spoiled brat. What hurt most, the girl had become like a daughter to her.

That girl was Katherine O'Reilly.

Nearly forty years ago, they had sat down at a restaurant for dinner with her parents to discuss that summer's show schedule, but they never got as far as ordering their meals. Without warning or any discussion with Karen, Katherine announced her move West to take ownership of an estate she had inherited, taking her horse, Lady Jane of Rosehaven, with her. Karen stormed out of the establishment following a few choice words expressing her disgust, earning the attention of every patron. How could Katherine have been so selfish and unappreciative after all she had done and sacrificed for her and her horse. They were so close to what she thought had been their shared dream, only to throw it all away.

She had lost the farm she leased, her star student, the best horse she'd ever have the opportunity to train, and her reputation in a matter of seconds. After that, she didn't get another chance. Clients that could afford a horse like Lady didn't come along every day, not to mention Katherine's natural talent. Just recalling that day, made her blood boil. Four decades of hatred swelled within her, yearning for retribution. The fact that her plan to get even might also benefit her granddaughter's chances of qualifying and earning more sponsors, made her revenge all the sweeter.

Karen and Stanley would arrive a day before Erica, Kayla and the horses, and the other riders and families flying in. She was banking on Katherine not arriving as early either, so she could get a lay of the land. She needed to find the perfect spot, or spots in case the first one failed, to take out Katherine and her so-called wonder horse. She had first heard about her old student and her ex-racehorse in a feature article in a sport horse magazine about four years ago when Katherine returned to competing on the national stage. This week, the Sports Illustrated story came out, no doubt capturing the attention of more sponsors. No way would she allow Katherine O'Reilly, well, Walker now, to qualify in Kayla's place. This overprivileged brat needed to learn how it felt to have her dreams crushed, and to be forgotten and dismissed by the eventing community overnight.

She had seen Katherine at the Rolex Three-Day Event in Lexington, Kentucky earlier that year and almost approached her. It would have felt good to tell her what she thought of her and her nag, but Karen was glad she had restrained herself. Because now, she needed to be stealthy, get in, do what needed to be done, and get out without being recognized.

A knock on her door brought Karen back from her scheming. She unlocked the deadbolt.

"Hi, Ma," said Stanley.

"Hi, Stan. You did good, only fifteen minutes late this time."

Stanley smirked. "This your only bag?"

"Yeah, to check anyway. I have a carry-on and my purse." Karen fetched her two bags off the couch while Stanley grabbed her suitcase.

As soon as they were on the road, Stanley started in. "Tell me again why you're spending all this money, not to mention the wages at the garage I'll be losing? They could replace me while we're gone, you know." Stanley worked as an auto mechanic at a locally owned garage in town. They had been threatening to replace him for years. He was often late to work too, if he showed up at all.

"Like I said, as soon as she's disqualified and Kayla qualifies, we'll return." Karen turned toward him from the passenger seat of his old truck, feeling the need to justify her actions to her son and herself one more time. "I told you why. She ruined my life, my only chance at the Olympics and now she could ruin Kayla's chances by earning every sponsor out there." Just the thought of Katherine coming out on top raised her blood pressure and her tone. She continued, becoming animated, hand gestures accentuating every point. "That rich bitch doesn't even need the money, owner of some huge estate with thousands of acres and her husband's a doctor, no less. It's time she feels some pain, that she's the loser, that something doesn't go her way. Now is my chance to finally win." Even though it would be vicariously through her granddaughter's achievements, she would come out on top.

"Win what?"

"Win over Katherine O'Reilly!" was her knee-jerk response before adding, "Not only are the sponsors at stake to fly Kayla and Joy to Sydney, there would be the endorsements following the games to those who medal. The money will roll in."

"What if she doesn't qualify or medal?"

"Of course she will."

"I think you want it so bad, you're delusional. This whole plan of yours is crazy stupid."

"You're one to talk, going to prison for assaulting a police officer!"

"And, I don't want to go back."

"Don't worry, we won't get caught."

"This is all about you getting even. You're just out for revenge. Kayla's just an excuse."

Karen wanted to slap him. How dare he accuse her of using her granddaughter. But she needed him for her plan to succeed so she restrained herself. Stanley had a mean streak almost as bad as his father's, and he could be unpredictable. If she pushed him the wrong way, he could turn the vehicle around right then and there.

"It's all about Kayla, first. The rest will be a bonus. Of all the other competitors, she's the one that poses the biggest threat to Kayla's chances. Besides, I gave her plenty of warnings. She'll just be getting what she deserves."

"I'm getting a bad feeling about this. We should just turn around and forget about it," he said, pulling his eyes from the road.

"Look where you're going!" she screamed, pointing to the oncoming traffic. "You said you'd do it!" she shrieked, then quickly softened her tone, almost begging. "You're not backing out on me now, are you, honey? You know how important this is to me. If you love me…"

"Okay, okay. I said I'd do it, didn't I? I just don't see why we can't wait to see if she qualifies first."

"Katherine or Kayla?"

"Both."

"Kayla will, but it's not enough. We need the sponsors, remember? If we don't take her out now, we won't get another chance. I'll make it up to you, I promise. When Kayla is a medal winner, she can open her own training facility and we can live there rent-free. It'll be perfect. Just remember, not a word about our plan to Kayla. She doesn't know anything about Katherine or what happened between us years ago."

"That should tell you something."

"What?" Karen wiggled in her seat. She knew what was coming.

"If you can't tell Kayla about it, it's not the right thing to do."

Karen laughed. "You're one to talk about right and wrong. Just keep your big mouth shut and everything will work out fine."

Stanley shook his head and Karen was relieved he dropped the subject and drove in silence the rest of the way.

They gained an hour flying from the Eastern to Central time zone, arriving in Winnipeg that afternoon. After picking up their compact rental car at the airport, Stanley drove while she read him the directions. Unfortunately, they ended up losing the hour they'd gained making a wrong turn. After arguing whose fault it was the rest of the drive, they pulled up to the show grounds office around four o'clock.

"Why didn't we check in at the hotel first?" Stanley slipped the vehicle into park. "I need to stretch. I feel like a sardine in this piece of shit car."

"I have no idea when Katherine is arriving, hopefully not until tomorrow or Wednesday. I need to start planning the attack tonight. You wait here while I get our passes."

Karen showed her driver's license to the show secretary behind the desk. The elderly woman glanced between Karen and her ID, furrowing her brow. Karen felt like she was back at the airport under the scrutiny of a customs officer. Did she look nervous? Karen took a calming breath. What was she nervous about anyway? They hadn't done anything yet.

"Are you a parent, trainer or both?" the woman asked, still studying her suspiciously.

"I'm Kayla Lutz's grandmother. She's competing this week."

Another woman peeked from around the corner of the adjoining room. "Need any help?"

"Got it, thanks!" she said, again turning her attention to Karen. "Normally family members don't arrive until the opening ceremony."

"My granddaughter and I work for her trainer, Erica Shields. They'll be arriving tomorrow. I'll be helping out." What does she think, I'm some terrorist or something? She knew security would be heightened following the 1996 bombing in Atlanta, but this was ridiculous.

"I see." The woman began sorting through a box of business envelopes which were in alphabetical order. She found the one she was looking for and peeked inside. "Okay. We have two general admission tickets and one parking pass for you," she said, handing her the envelope.

"I'd also like to pick up my granddaughter's show packet."

Another frown. "Just a minute."

The woman got up and left the office, disappearing down the hall into another room. Karen wrung her hands as her stomach churned. With Kayla's competitor pass, she would gain access to the cross-country course in advance and wouldn't be questioned when snooping around the dressage arena. Finally, the woman returned with a canvas competitor bag and a large envelope. Karen let out a sigh and quickly glanced through its contents. She found Kayla's dressage number, jumping penny, an event program, competitor schedule, advertising material including a number of small promotional gifts, and her competitor pass.

"Thank you. Where will Erica Shields Eventing be stabled? I'd like to call her to let her know and save her the trouble of stopping at the office when she rolls in with her big rig."

"She'll still need to check in as soon as she unloads."

"Of course."

The woman slid a large, laminated diagram across the counter between them and pointed. "Here she is. Barn F." Karen followed her finger. "Turn right at the dead end and it'll be the second from the last barn. Two bags of shavings are already in each stall."

"Great, thanks! How's the weather looking?" said Karen, gaining her confidence.

The woman seemed to relax as well and smiled. "So far it looks good for this week, but we could see some rain by the weekend."

"Thanks!"

When she returned to their car, Stanley looked anxious. "Did you get what you needed?"

"Sure did. Now we can go check into our room."

The closest and cheapest hotel she could find was about a twenty-minute drive from the show grounds.

"Is that it?" inquired Stanley, looking glum as they pulled in.

Karen nodded, grimacing. "The photo in their ad must be twenty years old." The sign reading "Paradise Inn" was half lit and the paint was peeling off the front of the two-story hotel, which looked more like an old motor lodge with its rooms opening directly to the outside. "You check us in, Stanley," she said. "And request a lower-level room at the back. Here's my driver's license."

Once they unloaded the car, they walked to the diner next door.

"After it turns dark, we'll check out the dressage ring first then the cross-country course."

Without taking his eyes off his meal, Stanley replied, "Good, we'll have time to stretch out and relax a bit. After that plane ride and drive, I feel all tied up." Stanley glanced out the window. "I'll run across the street to that gas station store and pick us up a few beers."

"No drinking until we get back to our room," she demanded. "I need you to be… you know, to remember everything."

Stanley glanced up. "Okay. Will it take long?"

"It'll take as long as it takes."

Just as dusk fell over Manitoba, Canada, Katherine and Sadie pulled into the 1999 Pan American Games show grounds. During the straight eleven-hour drive, there had been little idle conversation between the two women, only when necessary as they took turns driving, giving directions or discussing stops for gas and food. Katherine passed the time singing along to songs on oldies stations. It helped her keep her mind off the threat letter, but nothing could totally erase it or her concerns. Hopefully, now that they arrived at the Games, there would be little time for worrying.

Both women scanned the large facility laid out before them, decked out in advertising and signage everywhere. Katherine found the show office without any trouble.

"Please keep Major occupied while I check in," she said to Sadie. Major had taken the ride in stride, having become accustomed to long hauls following so many trips East over the past few years, but he had to be ready for this one to be over.

The cool Canadian air welcomed her the moment she stepped from the truck, even cooler than a summer evening at home. Major announced his arrival the moment Sadie opened his drop-down window. A distant whinny replied from one of the barns. Sadie talked to the big gelding as he stretched his head as far out the window as the trailer tie would allow. The girl spoke softly, and it occurred to Katherine she spoke far more to animals than she did to people.

Only one office light burned directing Katherine into a room with a row of desks dividing it in two, one side for competitors and the other for staff. But no staff were present. Since the door had been unlocked, Katherine called out, "Hello, checking in!"

A plump, elderly women with thick glasses appeared down the hall and entered the room. "You just caught me before I locked up for the night. We have someone out in the barns all night for stall check-ins, but I can get you everything you'll need now and save you a trip back in the morning to get your packet and bag." She glanced out the window at Sadie patting Major followed by a couple of impatient loud bangs. "If your horse can wait."

"Sure, we drove from Montana, a few more minutes won't kill him."

The woman smiled. "All I need is some identification." Katherine produced her driver's license. The woman glanced at it and handed it back to her, hurried out of the room and vanished down the hall again. A few moments later she returned with her competitor bag and packet.

"Here you go," she said, handing it to her. "Let's see what barn you're in." While the woman scrolled down a list, Katherine checked the contents of her packet. Pointing out her barn and stall on a diagram of the show grounds, she said, "You're in Barn F. Turn right at the dead end and it's the second from the last barn. Stall 21. Your shavings are in the stall."

"Thanks!"

The woman followed her to the door to lock up. "Good luck!"

"Thank you. You have a nice evening."

Karen led the way around the stadium where the main dressage ring was set up. "It'll depend on her ride time Friday, but here, take this," she whispered, handing him a small makeup mirror she extracted from her jacket pocket. "All you have to do is position yourself in the sun as close to the ring as possible and shine the mirror's reflection at her horse. Make it quick flashes like a strobe light.

Shouldn't take but two or three."

"Someone could see me," said Stanley, with skepticism and a bit too loudly.

"Keep your voice down," she hissed. "Not if you're careful. Watch your back and who's beside you and shine it from within your open jacket so no one can see what you're doing."

"What if the sun isn't out?" he whispered to her satisfaction.

"We'll worry about that if and when, okay?"

Stanley stared at her from beneath a furrowed brow.

"That's where plan B comes in," she said.

"Plan B?"

"Didn't you hear a word I said last week? Follow me." Karen pulled a mini flashlight from her pocket and started off toward the cross-country course. Once they walked beyond the reach of the closest floodlight, she turned on the flashlight and pulled out a map of the grounds, focusing on the cross-country course. "This way," she pointed.

Karen studied every cross-country jump, walking to the next hoping to find the perfect obstacle to pull off her plan. Her legs were getting tired and she could tell she was losing what little focus or interest Stanley had to begin with. About halfway through the course, following the second water obstacle, they walked uphill through a group of trees. At the base of the hill, she saw it! A huge cabin jump, nearly fully enclosed with small openings on each end, framed by shrubs.

"There!" she pointed, quickening her strides to the jump. "That's perfect!"

"For what?"

Stanley kept pace as they approached the over four-foot high, five-foot wide and fifteen-foot long rectangle log cabin with a wood-shingle roof. She couldn't have designed it better or placed it in a better location for her purpose. The course lane ran between two stands of trees a good distance from the taped-off spectator area.

Picturing the ambush in her mind, she described it to her accomplice.

"You'll climb inside. Stay out of view." She ducked into the box with her flashlight, waving for him to follow. "See, there's plenty of room."

Ducking down from his stocky six-foot stature, Stanley looked in. "Looks pretty cramped to me. How long will I have to stay in there?"

Karen turned toward her son, shining enough light his way to read the expression on his face. "Could be as long as ten hours." Stanley opened his mouth to no doubt object, but she continued before he had the opportunity to. "You can't be seen going in, so it has to be before daylight. And to be safe, you'll have to stay hidden until at least an hour after the last rider finishes the course."

Stanley winced. "If you weren't my mother, so help me!"

"Shhh… take a pillow or something to sit on and I'll pack you some sandwiches and drinks. Then I'll signal you."

"Oh, right, The new fancy portable phones. I wondered how they played into it."

"Cell phones. You'll need to turn off the ringer and put it on vibrate like I showed you. I'll be standing over there in the trees. I'll let you know when she's over the hill. You'll be able to hear the horse's hoofbeats as they approach. Just before he reaches the jump, you make a loud banging noise inside. I brought a hammer."

"The horse won't get hurt, will it?"

One thing she could credit her alcoholic son for was his love for animals. "If things go our way during dressage and Katherine's horse spooks and is penalized for a disobedience, this might not even be necessary."

"You didn't answer my question."

"No, he'll just stop or spin. The first refusal, run-out or circle is penalized twenty points, second, forty points, and the third, she'd be eliminated. If she or her horse falls, she's eliminated. Either way, she would either collect enough error points to put her out of contention or be eliminated."

"Well, I hope we knock her out in dressage."

"Me too."

"If not, what if someone hears the bang?"

"It'll happen so fast they'll think it's a hoof or clump of dirt hitting the jump."

"Okay. Can we get back to the hotel now?"

On their way back to their vehicle parked alongside Barn F, Karen noticed a woman hand-grazing a big bay gelding, with her back to them. She couldn't help but notice how beautiful the horse was, not paying much attention to the woman. As they approached the pair, the woman turned toward the barn aisle light. It was her! It was Katherine! Karen held her breath as she dropped her focus to her feet as they passed. Once they were out of earshot, Karen tugged on Stanley's shirt sleeve.

"That was her," she whispered. "No, don't look now."

Once they were safe within their car, Stanley turned toward her. "Do you think she recognized you?"

"No, it was too dark. Besides, she was looking into the barn." Then the worst of it just occurred to her. "Shit, she must be stabled in Barn F too, same as Erica's horses!"

"What rotten luck, out of all these barns. This is a sign, Ma. We should give it up and head home."

"Don't be silly. It'll be fine. I look a lot different than I did forty years ago." Karen flipped down the passenger side visor mirror and studied her wrinkled face and gray hair in the dim light. "I'll wear a hat and sunglasses as an extra precaution." She flipped the visor back up into place, her focus returning to Katherine and her horse. "I need you to follow her into the barn to see where her stall is in relation to Erica's, so I can avoid her as much as possible."

They watched her meander around in and out of the light emanating from the barn, until a young woman with a dark complexion and black hair came out and joined her. They spoke for a few minutes then led the horse into the barn together.

"Go now," she said. Stanley froze with his hand on the door latch. "You okay?"

He shrugged his shoulders. "Yeah, I guess. I'll just walk through like I'm looking for someone's stall."

"You are, silly." The mother and son co-conspirators shared a chuckle. "Go!"

She watched Stanley sashay toward the barn looking conspicuously casual. He glanced toward her a moment before disappearing down the aisle. Karen anxiously waited until he reappeared, looking more worried than when he entered, if that was possible. He slid into the car straight-faced.

"What?"

"Her stall is right across from the last of Erica's stalls."

"You've got to be kidding me!" Karen took a deep breath. "It's okay. I'll just have to be careful. Hopefully, Joy won't end up right across from her."

"With our luck, she will be."

"Stop it, Stan. Let's get some rest."

"Sounds good. I'm ready for a beer."

"Or two… or ten."

"Leave it be, Ma."

"You have a problem and the sooner you admit it, the sooner you can fix it."

"Fix what, that I drink a few beers?"

"A few too many."

"I'm a grown man, you just need to mind your own business."

"Just go easy this week, then you can do what you please."

They drove back to their room in silence. As soon as they parked, Stanley left for the store across the street. Then Karen noticed a pool hall next door and knew she wouldn't see him until morning.

Tuesday morning, Katherine woke at dawn feeling anxious. She needed to check on Major. Regardless of the long drive and not checking into the hotel until after midnight, she had woken up several times with the fear someone might harm her horse. She lightly shook Sadie's shoulder.

The girl answered without moving or opening her eyes. "Yeah?"

"I'm going to the barn. I'll feed and be back to join you for breakfast."

Sadie nodded and rolled away from her to face the wall. Katherine quietly exited the room.

When Katherine arrived at the showgrounds, she was surprised by how many more trailers had rolled in overnight. She noticed license plates from several different states and provinces, but a large truck and trailer with Florida plates caught her attention. She parked beside the rig, got out of her truck and began snooping around.

"Can I help you?" said a girl's voice, startling her. When she turned, a young woman about her height with dark brown hair, pulled up into a high ponytail, peered at her from under a USEF visor. "Oh, I thought I recognized this truck and trailer," was the best Katherine could come up with. "Where are you from?"

"We're from Ocala, Florida. Who are you looking for? I might know them."

"I can't remember their names, met them at Rolex this year."

"We were there, but without a name I'm afraid I can't be any help. Where are you from?"

Katherine hesitated, but this girl posed no threat. "Montana. I'm Katherine Walker, my friends call me Kat."

"Hi," she answered tentatively. "Am I considered a friend?"

"Sure, we are now."

"Well then, hi, Kat!" she said cheerfully. My name is Kayla Lutz. Are you here to compete for the games?"

"Yes."

"Me too."

Katherine couldn't help looking surprised. The girl looked younger than Josephine. As soon as she realized her mouth was gaping, she smiled. "Sorry, you just look so young."

"That's because I am. I'll be the youngest rider on the team if I qualify."

"Wow, congratulations on coming this far at your age. You must be a wonderful rider."

"It's all Joy, my horse… well, my trainer's horse, actually."

"She must be lovely. I'd love to see her. What barn are you in?" asked Katherine.

"Barn F."

"Me too! I'm heading there now."

"Me too! I just need to get some tack from the trailer. I'll look for you."

"Great!"

The girl disappeared into the trailer before Katherine could ask what stall she was in. Stopping at her trailer first, Katherine unlocked the tack compartment, opened the grain container and grabbed a premeasured bag of Major's feed. Sadie had already stacked two bales of hay in front of their stall. Major greeted her with a shrill whinny, ready for his breakfast since many of the horses were already eating. Katherine was happy to see some shavings on the gelding blanket, a sure sign he had rested well last night and felt comfortable and safe in his new surroundings. That's always a good start.

"Hi, handsome," she said, making him back up so she could enter his stall and empty the bag into his feed bucket. Katherine pulled off his sheet and wraps while he ate. She was pleased to see he had drunk a fair amount of water, another sign he wasn't stressed. She always feared the possibility of colic following a long haul. As she pulled the shavings from his long black tail, Kayla walked up to the stall.

"Hi again. Who is this?" she said smiling, her eyes gliding over Major head to hoof, approvingly. "He's gorgeous."

"Thanks! This is my boy, Major Command."

"I love blood bays. Joy is a chestnut."

Katherine stepped out and latched Major's stall door. "Which one is she?" said Katherine, glancing down the barn aisle.

"We're almost neighbors," said Kayla. The girl led her across the aisle and three stalls down. "This is Joyous Occasion."

"She's lovely. Her face reminds me of a chestnut mare I had years ago. She was a sweetheart."

"Joy is a typical redheaded mare. But, if she was easy to handle and ride, my trainer would have sold her years ago and I wouldn't be here today."

"Lucky you," joked Katherine.

Kayla laughed and Katherine joined in.

"Sounds like a party over here," said a woman about Katherine's age, quickly approaching them.

"This is one of our barn neighbors," said Kayla. "Katherine Walker from Montana."

"Nice to meet you," said Katherine.

"Erica Shields. Nice to meet you, too. I've heard about you and your horse. Saw the Sports Illustrated article. The retired racehorse, right?"

"That's us. And I watched you compete in the seventies on Alexander. You were a fantastic team." Katherine glanced at Joy. "And your mare is beautiful."

"Thanks," said Erica, turning to the girl as if Katherine was no longer standing there. "Where's Karen? She was supposed to meet us here an hour ago."

"I'm sure she'll be here soon."

"I hope so," said Erica, then the woman turned to her. "Good luck."

"Good luck to you and your team this week," said Katherine.

"Thanks!" Erica moved on to the next stall and began tacking a big black stallion.

"I better get moving," Kayla said to Katherine, "I need to finish stalls. My grandma and I help out. I'll introduce you to her later. And my uncle is here to watch me too."

"I'd love to meet them. See you around."

"See ya!"

Katherine felt for the girl, her and her grandmother working so she could ride and compete. She recalled how lucky she was at her age to own a wonderful horse like Lady and not have to worry about finances. What would this girl think if she knew she had it all years ago, about to qualify for the US Team, only to toss it all aside? For a moment, a pang of guilt mixed with a touch of regret needled her conscience. Perhaps she could help this girl in some way. Katherine looked forward to meeting her grandmother.

Running late, Karen hurried and parked. She entered the barn from the nearside, taking the risk of passing Katherine's stall. She knew Erica would be upset with her for oversleeping. She had a difficult time falling asleep, worrying about Stanley out all night. The last thing she needed was for him to get into one of his brawls and end up in jail in a foreign country. She left him sleeping off a hangover.

Karen hesitated a moment, glancing down the aisle. There were a few people milling around, but none of them were Katherine. Just as she was passing Katherine's stall, the stall door opened and out stepped her old student!

"Good morning!" said Katherine, cheerfully.

Karen forced a smile and pulled her cap down further. "Good morning," she said, not stopping.

Thankfully, Katherine quickly exited the barn. Neither Kayla nor Erica were around. She stuck her head into their barn's green with gold trim curtained tack stall, finding it empty. When she checked the stalls, she found the big black missing. Erica must be schooling him. Just as Karen exited the barn on the far side leading to the schooling rings, Kayla approached her with a wheelbarrow.

"Geez, Grandma, where have you been? I had to do all the stalls and organize the tack room myself this morning."

"I'm sorry, dear. I overslept." Karen turned to make sure Katherine hadn't returned and let out a pent-up breath.

Kayla gave her a hug. "I'm glad you made it okay. How was your flight?"

"Good. The hotel, not so good. But we'll make do."

"The aisle still needs to be swept. Can you do it while I lunge and hand graze Joy? She's been a little up."

"Sure. Is Erica pissed?"

"Uh, yeah. And I didn't know what to tell her. You could have called."

"I guess I should have, but I just woke up about thirty minutes ago." Knowing how inquisitive and friendly her granddaughter could be, Karen had to ask. "The barn looks like it's filling in. Meet anyone?"

"Sure. There are famous riders from all over the world. This is so exciting. Even if I don't qualify, it'll be the experience of a lifetime."

"Oh, don't be silly. Of course, you're going to qualify." Karen grabbed the broom from the tack stall as Kayla located the surcingle, lunge line and whip.

"I met a really nice lady I'd love for you to meet. She's gone now, that's her horse, the big bay."

Karen shuddered. "What's her name?"

"Katherine, but she said I could call her 'Kat.' We're going to school together later. That's why I want to work Joy a little bit first. I want her do well when we ride together."

The color must have drained from Karen's face, judging by Kayla's reaction.

"Are you okay, Grandma?"

"Actually, no. I'm not. That's why I'm late. I think I'm going to return to my room and lie down for a bit. I might have caught a bug on the flight. I'll send Stanley later to help out with the evening feeding and stall cleaning."

She couldn't tell if Kayla looked more disappointed or concerned, or perhaps a little of both.

"Okay. I hope you feel better."

"I probably shouldn't have even hugged you." Karen coughed. "I better go."

"Take care, Grandma."

Karen hurried off, stopping at the end of the barn to make sure Katherine wasn't nearby. Just as she approached her vehicle, a truck with Montana plates pulled away. What were the chances they'd end up in the same barn… then Kayla making friends with Katherine? What a mess!

Kayla set the lunging equipment down on one of the director chairs set up outside the tack stall and began sweeping the aisleway. Her grandmother was acting so strange, perhaps it was because she wasn't feeling well. But there was something else she just couldn't put her finger on. Kayla was surprised her grandmother could even afford to make the trip. Now, she might not be able to work off part of her expenses as planned. Hopefully, she'd feel better soon.

Once she finished in the barn, she groomed Joy in her stall and prepared her to be bitted and lunged. That always worked to take the edge off. Kayla couldn't explain why it became so important for her to impress this woman she only just met. But she really liked Katherine and hoped they both might qualify for the team so she could see more of her in Sydney. She seemed like a great lady and Kayla suddenly wanted to know more about her, her horse and Montana. She had always wanted to travel west to the Rocky Mountains, but she was fortunate to have had the opportunity to leave the state of Florida with Erica's help. Maybe someday.

Kayla led Joy to one of the round rings designed for lunging. Not all showgrounds had them, but it sure was nice when they did. Without any distractions from sharing a space with other horses, Joy worked well. So well, Kayla stopped after only fifteen minutes. She didn't want to tire her out. When she returned to the barn, she found Erica sponging off Joker, the black stallion.

"Did Karen ever show up?"

"Yes, but she left right away. She's not feeling well."

"I'm sorry to hear that. Don't be kissing her or anything, please! The last thing we need is to all come down with some crud this week."

"I'll be careful. Uncle Stan is going to come help later."

"Stan? I guess some help is better than none." Erica rested her hand on Kayla's shoulder. "Try not to overdo it, okay? I'll help out, too. We need you one hundred percent. How did Joy do?"

"Great, I'd like to school her after lunch if that's okay?"

"Sure. I still have Magic to ride this morning. Then I think I'll just lunge Jet this afternoon, following your lesson. Kerry, Mel and Joan arrive tonight."

"Oh, I thought I'd just take her through her paces on my own today… get her settled. I was going to ride with Kat this afternoon."

"Who?" asked Erica, collecting what she needed to tack up Magic.

"The woman from Montana. Remember? You said you knew who she was."

"Right, that's fine. A light workout today will be good. We'll do a lesson tomorrow morning, early, before the others."

"Great, thanks!"

Kayla took her time cooling, bathing and hand grazing Joy while Erica rode Magic so they could head out to lunch together. This would be her last chance to have Erica to herself. When the other women arrived, Erica would spend all her free time with the paying customers. Her trainer treated her differently when her other students were around.

When Kayla and Erica returned from lunch, she found Major's stall empty. Katherine must have headed out to school already. She quickly tacked her mare and searched the schooling area, locating the big bay in the farthest ring. Katherine and Major were walking on a long rein, quickly covering ground with the gelding's long strides. This was the first time she got a good look at him. He looked heavier boned than most Thoroughbreds she'd seen, resembling a warmblood more than a racehorse.

"Hi," she said, surprising Katherine from behind.

"Hi there. Just getting warmed up," said Katherine, as Kayla caught up with her and Major. "Joy is stunning, even prettier under saddle."

"Thank you. So is Major."

"You're very fortunate to be riding with Erica. She does a great job with her horses and riders."

"Oh, I know. And to be riding Joy is an honor."

Katherine gathered up her reins and proceeded into a lively trot. Kayla watched them glide along as she walked Joy a few more times around the ring. By the time she cued for a trot, Katherine was cantering – beautifully collected and uphill. She passed them on the diagonal, working a serpentine pattern, followed by a few figure eights. Joy felt wonderful, light in her hands and fully engaged. She caught Katherine glancing over, smiling approvingly. Kayla smiled back. This was fun! She rode with Erica's other riders often, but she always felt inferior not riding her own horse. And the competition between the women was fierce, sometimes sucking the pleasure out of her riding. But when she and Joy were competing in the ring or on course, just the two of them, she could block out everyone and everything. It was the only time she felt truly free, focusing only on Joy. Together, they were perfection!

Neither she nor Katherine asked for any lateral work or advanced movements from their mounts that day. She imagined it was a fun workout for the horses, too. Joy felt strong yet yielding, rare for her, especially the first day at a new venue. She considered her horse might be picking up on Katherine and Major's great vibe, as she had. While they cooled their horses out, they got to know each other better. They compared living in Montana to Florida and shared funny experiences with horses. When Katherine spoke of her daughters with so much pride and affection, Kayla couldn't help but feel jealous. How wonderful it would be to have such a loving and caring mother. Her grandmother did her best, and she loved her dearly, but she wasn't her mother – forced to raise her in her parents' absence. She tried not to think about having to return to Ocala. She would miss her new best friend.

8 – The Games

Friday

A cool breeze blew through the barn aisleway as Katherine sat in a comfy, canvas folding chair in front of Major's stall. She had the leg she injured five years ago propped up in the other chair in front of her. It had been feeling pretty good, but this morning during their inspection, which is designed to evaluate the horse's fitness to compete, her leg had begun to ache. As she trotted Major in hand in front of the veterinary delegate and the ground jury, a sharp pain radiated down her leg. Katherine had pushed through the discomfort in front of the panel, completing the inspection, and figured it was just her arthritis predicting the expected rain over the weekend.

She checked her watch. Soon, she would need to start getting ready for her dressage test. Anticipating their ride in about two hours, a spurt of adrenaline raced through her veins, overriding any pain. Closing her eyes, the familiar scent of horse and pine shavings along with the sound of Major chewing the few remaining pieces of hay, calmed her. She played every element of the test over in her mind, even though both horse and rider had them memorized. Dressage would be Major's biggest challenge. With this caliber of talent competing, they had to score near the top to stay in contention. She didn't worry as much about the cross-country or show jumping components with her strong and talented jumper. Katherine took a deep breath and smiled. They were as ready as they'd ever be. No sense in stressing about it. She needed to have fun. If she had fun, Major had fun, and that's when the magic happened.

It had been a fun week, spending time with Kayla and getting to know one another. They had forged a great friendship in only a few days. Funny, the oldest and youngest competing, yet they connected right away. She could sense Kayla had an old soul for her age and found the girl charming and a true inspiration after learning the physical obstacles the young woman had overcome to get there. And she was a joy to converse with, smart yet funny, a welcome change from Sadie.

She had met Kayla's uncle, Stanley, who seemed about as moody as Sadie. An opportunity to meet her grandmother hadn't arisen since the poor woman had taken ill upon her arrival. She even missed her granddaughter's dressage test earlier that day. The girl did well, earning a respectable score, but like Major, jumping was Joy's strong suit. Katherine had kept so busy and entertained, she hadn't thought much about the threat letter. But as the first leg of the competition neared, she began taking more notice of people and spending more time parked out front of Major's stall.

"Hey, time to get you two ready."

Katherine's eyes flew open and she jumped, startled by Sadie standing over her. "Right." Katherine sprang to her feet and started for the trailer.

Sadie kept pace. "The expo is huge. There's so much to see. You need to break away from the barn one day."

"Did you buy anything?"

"Not yet. Going to wait until the last day. That's when everything goes on sale."

"Smart thinking. I'll get changed while you groom Major. Take the saddle and I'll bring the bridle."

"Will do."

Katherine pulled her dressage clothes from the tack room closet Steven had built for her above the saddle racks. She dressed, then retrieved her cosmetic bag from the front seat of her truck before heading to the restroom. After emptying her bladder, she put her hair up, applied a modest amount of makeup and put on her lucky gold stirrup earrings. Katherine studied herself in the mirror and straightened her stock tie. She was ready!

When she dropped off her makeup bag at the trailer, Katherine grabbed Major's dressage bridle, which Sadie had cleaned, and headed for the barn. The big bay's head raised and turned toward her; ears pricked forward. He knew the routine by now… he knew it was show time. Sadie had his coat as slick as satin, his mane braided, and his long tail pulled at the top and cut blunt at the bottom just above the ground. He was one handsome boy. Katherine glanced at her watch. Time to warm up.

Just as she mounted, Kayla approached. "Good luck, Kat."

"Thanks, and congrats!" said Katherine. "You and Joy had a lovely ride."

"Thank you. You both look beautiful," said Kayla, stroking Major's neck. "I've got some work to do first, but I'll be watching. See you at the exit gate."

"Great!" said Katherine.

The girl gave her a thumbs up and rushed toward Erica's stalls.

Sadie silently wiped the dust from Katherine's boots and stuffed the end of a small towel in her back pocket to give her boots a once over before entering the ring. Sadie hadn't said much to or about Kayla all week and seemed a little put out by her hanging around all the time. It was difficult to imagine Sadie being jealous, but that's the impression Katherine was getting. She would try to spend more free time with her the remainder of the event.

Katherine studied the late morning sky. The clouds had cleared, and it was already inching toward eighty degrees. The stormfront expected to blow in overnight would bring cooler temperatures and rain. The cooler temperatures would be welcomed, but she prayed the cross-country course would hold up. A wet course meant poor footing and slower times. The first horses to ride would have the advantage before the course became torn-up and sloppy. They drew a midday ride time, but that was a worry for another day. First, they had to have a brilliant ride today. She left for the warm-up ring.

Kyle Schmitt easily found his seat in the large stadium. Katherine Walker and her horse, Major, would be performing soon. He hadn't watched much of the dressage so far, spending most of his time watching other sporting events and spending time at the expo, but he wasn't about to miss this team. He traveled all the way from Alberta to see them compete. Kyle had followed the pair's progress in sport horse magazines, and most recently in Sports Illustrated, in addition to following the USEF results for the past five years. A horse enthusiast for as long as he could remember, Kyle had to see the hometown pair perform, even though Elkhead, Montana, was no longer his home.

Ever since he escaped into Canada on horseback following the death of his older brother, Jake Schmitt, he lived on a small ranch just across the border. It was nice of Ricky Werden to leave all that money behind when he fled for the border after killing Billy, affording him the opportunity to purchase the property and live comfortably. Kyle later learned from his sister, Tammy Butler, that Katherine had chased Ricky down on Major and killed him. The fact she had rid the world of that useless sack of shit, made him like her and her horse all the more.

Perhaps his brother deserved to die, getting involved with the likes of Ricky again. He chose to be a part of Ricky's crazy scheme to take revenge on Katherine and Billy, for the money. Afraid to defy his brother and Ricky, Kyle had gone along with their plan until the opportunity to help Katherine, Billy and her daughter escape presented itself. Unfortunately, it didn't work out, but others came to the rescue. The day Jake died, he gained his freedom, but there hadn't been a day since he didn't regret standing up to him sooner. He could only look ahead now, living his own life on his terms.

His partner had stayed behind to take care of the animals on their small ranch; a dream come true for Kyle. Never allowed to have a single pet growing up at home or with Jake, he enjoyed sharing his life with as many animals as they could afford. He still had

Strawberry, the roan mare he had ridden across the border, along with a few good Quarter Horse mares he bred each year. He finally got his first dog, a Shepard mix named "Shep," and added a few head of cattle, some chickens, turkeys, pigs, a few cats and even a ball python named Henry to his menagerie. Besides only getting to see his sister in Montana once a year at the holidays, he was happy.

Kyle checked the program for Katherine's ride time again. She was scheduled to ride her test in about thirty minutes. He had a great seat in the second row, close to the center of the ring. The sun was beating down on the bleachers and he wished he had worn his straw cowboy hat instead of his felt one. He took it off for a moment, but the glare was too intense, so he slicked his hair back and returned the hat to his head.

The bleachers were full. He purposely chose the second seat from the end of a row, hoping no one would buy the single seat on the end to give him more space. He planned to move to the end seat if it remained empty. So far, his plan was working. Another US rider was performing, and his test looked flawless. Kyle revered the skill of the rider and training of the horse as they danced across the ring. He looked forward to watching Katherine and Major.

Kyle hadn't seen them since that tragic day five years ago. He had thought about walking through the barns to find them, but he felt unsure how Katherine would react if she noticed him. As far as he knew, he was still wanted as an accomplice to the abduction and murders in the states. But he sure was tempted to locate Major one evening after everyone left. Kyle had admired the big bay from the first time he'd laid eyes on him when he and Jake had taken Katherine and Billy hostage. He'd never seen a Thoroughbred racehorse in person before, only in pictures. Today, each horse looked prettier than the last. Kyle was in his glory, until some guy slipped into the seat beside him. Dang! He wondered if the man even owned the ticket, but he wasn't about to ask and cause a fuss. The guy was about his age, but he didn't look like he belonged; unshaven, wearing a flowery shirt, bulky windbreaker in this heat and a Florida Gators cap.

When Katherine entered the stadium and circled the dressage ring to warm up, Kyle scooted to the edge of his seat. They made a beautiful team, Major's brilliant blood bay coat glistening in the sunlight, Katherine sitting tall in the saddle as beautiful as ever. Much to his surprise, the fella next to him seemed just as interested in their performance. Kyle was about to start up a conversation with the guy, when the pair entered the ring and saluted, capturing his full attention. He watched Katherine and Major's every move with admiration and fondness. When Kyle glanced over, curious to see the stranger's reaction, the man abruptly got up and rushed down the stairs, disappearing out of sight. Kyle found his behavior odd and followed him. If anyone was familiar with anxious behavior, it was Kyle. This man had the same expression he imagined he wore when he was about to do something he didn't feel comfortable doing.

At the bottom of the stairs, Kyle searched the crowd and picked out the man's blue and orange cap right away. He stood at the rail beside some attractive young ladies. This guy must be some kind of pervert, was his first thought. Again, Kyle was familiar with men like Ricky and his brother, predators who preyed on women like pieces of meat to satisfy their hunger. Kyle moved closer as Katherine and Major cut across the ring at a canter coming straight toward them. Just before the pair reached the rail only yards away, the crowd gasped as Major suddenly reared, nearly coming down outside the perimeter of the ring. Kyle knew from watching years of Olympic dressage competition, that they would have been eliminated from the entire event if they had left the ring, even with just one hoof. When the man noticed Kyle watching him, he swiftly rushed through the crowd toward the exit. Kyle shook his head, glad he had scared him off. When he took the man's spot on the rail, something cracked beneath his boot. It appeared to be a now-broken makeup mirror.

He figured one of girls must have dropped it. Kyle watched the remainder of Katherine's ride from the rail, which was flawless. Ending with a lovely square halt at X, the crowd erupted in applause. Major's disobedience was unfortunate, and he hoped it wouldn't take them out of contention.

Katherine and Sadie shared an umbrella as they jogged from their hotel to her truck Saturday morning. Halfway to the show grounds, Katherine had to turn the windshield wipers on as the rain intensified from a sprinkle to a heavy shower. She cursed under her breath. It would have to rain cross-country day, but at least the news report they watched during their continental breakfast showed it letting up by noon.

"Hopefully, the weatherman was right, and you won't be riding in the rain," said Sadie, sipping on a cup of coffee.

"Yeah, but it'll be sloppy and slick."

"What's your ride time again?"

"Geez girl, we just went over the schedule last night. Two forty." Katherine glanced over at Sadie staring aimlessly out the window. She had been even quieter and more withdrawn than usual this trip, making Katherine wonder what had changed. "A penny for your thoughts? You look a hundred miles away."

"I think I'm a little homesick."

"Really?" Katherine thought out loud. She never figured Sadie as the homesick type. And homesick for who? "Her sister? Or just maybe…" Recalling her discussion with Josephine, she had to ask. "Is there a special boy you haven't told me about you might be missing?"

That snapped Sadie out of her trance. Interesting, thought Katherine. Maybe there was a secret someone in Sadie's life. "Not really," she said. "How's your leg?"

Well, that confirmed it! Her ambiguous answer and change of subjects could only mean there was a man in her life. But Katherine knew better than to dig any deeper. It would be to no avail with Sadie. "It's good. I brought some Advil to take before my ride."

"When are you expecting Dr. Walker?"

"In time to watch our course, if his flight is on time." Katherine glanced at the truck clock. "He should be mid-flight. Wish Josephine could have made it too, but they're shooting some time-sensitive scene this week."

"Is she planning any more visits home soon?"

"Not that I'm aware of."

And that was it. Sadie turned away to resume her blank stare out at the countryside. Katherine could swear if she asked her what they just passed by, she'd have no idea. "I'm going to walk the course again first thing."

"Good idea." Sadie nodded, pulling a slicker from the passenger door storage bin and setting it down on the console. "I'll have him fed and his stall cleaned by the time you get back. Are you planning to school him this morning?"

"No, just a couple warm-up jumps before we go on course. Yesterday's warmup and dressage test will be enough. He'll be fresh, but that will be good. This is a very taxing course and we'll have a difficult jumping course Sunday."

They rode the rest of their drive to the show grounds in silence. Unfortunately, the quiet time gave Katherine the opportunity to think about the threat letter. She didn't worry for herself, she felt it was Major who was more vulnerable. There had been the dressage incident, but she couldn't imagine how anyone might have purposely caused her horse to rear. She chalked that up to Major looking for a distraction from their dressage work, his least favorite discipline. Her horse knew the routine now after several years of attending events and begun anticipating the second day of jumping and galloping on the cross-country course, which he loved, distracting him from their flat work. And Katherine couldn't imagine how anyone could interfere with her and her horse on the cross-country course considering there are jump judges at every obstacle, not to mention thousands of spectators.

With that final thought, she tucked her fears away and looked forward to walking the course with Kayla when they arrived. The girl had tended to Erica's horses yesterday afternoon following dressage while her trainer walked the course with her three other students who all have ride times this morning. When Katherine offered to have Kayla accompany her, Erica gladly approved, saving her another walk through the course and allowing her to focus on her other students and their horses. It had become apparent to Katherine that Kayla didn't receive the same amount of attention from Erica as did her paying clients, but the girl never complained.

Kayla got up and cleaned stalls before daybreak, so she'd be ready when Katherine arrived. "Hi, Kat," she called to her. "I hope you don't mind I threw Major a little hay. I fed early and he was getting impatient."

"No problem, thanks!" Katherine hollered back as she fed Major his grain. "How's your grandmother doing? Better, I hope."

"Yes, she's planning to watch my cross-country ride later."

"That's great. I hope I get to meet her afterward."

"Me too!" she said. When Katherine stepped outside Major's stall, Kayla added, "We might be on the course at the same time, with only one rider between us."

"That's very possible," said Katherine, throwing her horse more hay. "We may not get a chance to watch each other."

Sadie soon appeared with Katherine's jumping saddle in one arm, a metal collapsible saddle rack in the other, and Major's bridle hanging from one shoulder. Kayla couldn't quite figure out Sadie; one moment she seemed so friendly and talkative, then aloof the next, not making eye contact or replying to a greeting. Kayla would love to be in Sadie's shoes, working for Katherine.

As Kayla hurried to dump the last wheelbarrow full of manure in the designated area, she reflected on how fast the week had flown by; keeping up with her job and preparing herself and Joy to compete. She was having a great time, especially her rides and chats with Katherine. They got along so well; it was easy to forget they were competing against each other for a spot on the team. A few US riders, including Erica's student, Betty Swanson on Magic, had outstanding dressage scores. Her and Katherine came up a little short, just outside placing in the top fifteen so far. Kayla had scored ahead of her friend, but if Major hadn't spooked, their placings would surely be reversed. But they each had strong jumpers, so Kayla felt confident they would move up following cross-country and show jumping. She'd be thrilled to qualify but would be equally thrilled to see Katherine qualify after reading her story in the copy of Sports Illustrated Erica had loaned her that week along with the bits and pieces Katherine had shared with her. What an amazing story. She was proud to be considered her friend.

Kayla just needed to give the aisle in front of their stalls a quick sweeping. Katherine grabbed their broom and helped her finish. They had only an hour before the course would be closed and the competition began. Once finished, the youngest and the oldest competitors strode off to walk the course together.

All through the nearly four-mile course, averaging four-foot plus high jumps, some spanning as much as eight feet and dropping up to six feet, Katherine shared tips and discussed how to approach each obstacle and the striding between combinations with her as if she were an equally seasoned competitor, asking for her opinion. It made Kayla feel special, something Erica never did.

"I think this is the best line between the two skinnies, don't you?" said Katherine, pointing out a route between the two narrow chevron jumps.

"Yes, I agree," she said. But looking ahead to the next question, she felt goosebumps raise on her arms. She stopped mid-stride and took a deep breath. "That's the jump I'm worried about."

Katherine looked up from pacing the strides between the combination. "The keyhole?"

"Yes, sometimes Joy refuses them."

The two women approached the brush jump, totally framed by a wreath of ivy. "Make sure you focus through the jump on to the next one ahead. Get your spot and go. It's amazing, but horses can actually tell by the position of your seat bones, or how you're balanced in the stirrups, where you're looking. If you dwell on the jump, so will Joy."

"Right," she said, nodding. Then Kayla turned to Katherine. "It's really nice of you to be giving me advice... with us competing against each other and all."

Katherine turned to her. "The horse and rider teams that perform the best collectively this week, and this week only, will qualify. But there will be many equally talented and perhaps even more deserving teams that won't. I've already reached my goal, to be competing at this level again on an incredible animal. All we can do is our best, right? And let the eventing Gods handle the rest."

"I wish my grandmother felt that way."

"I'm sure she does. And I'm sure she'll be proud of you no matter where you place."

Kayla just nodded. She felt pressured to produce results with all the years of work and money her grandmother had invested in her riding, not to mention for Erica who would price Joy accordingly.

"I'm not so sure," said Kayla. "She keeps saying I'm going to make the team and medal and how wonderful it'll be for my career as a trainer, as if it's already happened."

"I have a story to tell you," said Katherine as they walked side by side down a long stretch of lane they would soon be galloping along against the clock. Katherine told her about her days competing at her age and the pressure she felt from her parents and trainer. "It kind of ruined it for me. That had a lot to do with my decision to leave it all behind."

"You were so close."

"It wasn't my time. And maybe it won't be my time now either. I try to put the journey ahead of the destination. Don't get me wrong, I'd love to qualify, but I won't be crushed if I don't."

"That's a good way to look at it."

"And you're so young, Kayla. There will be many more Olympics in your future. You're a very talented rider and the way you connect with your mount is special. You have endless potential."

"Thank you, but I'm not so sure I'll have a future in eventing. Joy will be sold this year. I can't imagine getting the opportunity to ride another horse like her and we sure can't afford to purchase one… not ever."

"I'm sure Erica will give you another chance on another horse."

"She's cutting back and planning on retiring the next year or so."

"There are other trainers."

"Sure, all looking for clients with money. I told you the only reason I ended up riding Joy is because of how difficult she is. I'll never find someone willing to give me another chance with such a talented horse."

Katherine stopped and took her by the shoulders. "Never say never. You have your whole life ahead of you. Look at me, forty years later, and here I am!"

Kayla smiled. Katherine was such a positive person, even after all she'd been through in her life, and the girl felt certain her friend had barely scratched the surface with what she had shared of it. Sometimes when Katherine was in the middle of one of her stories, she would pause, and Kayla could see the pain in her eyes. Then she would switch topics, usually to one of her daughters or her grandchild and her face and eyes would light up with joy in place of the sadness. Katherine was a special lady.

When they completed the course, Katherine turned to her and gave her a hug. "Good luck, Kayla. Godspeed!"

"Good luck to you, too, Kat!"

The women parted, Kayla to meet up with her grandmother for lunch and Katherine to meet up with her husband.

Karen arrived at their designated meeting spot early, a picnic table in front of the barbecue vendor, to make sure they got a seat. The aroma of cooked pork filled the air. She immediately spotted her granddaughter from a distance, her tall, lean stature topped by her favorite Kentucky Horse Park cap with her long brunette ponytail swinging with every stride.

"Hi, Grandma! How are you feeling?" she asked, giving her a hug before taking a seat across from her.

"I'm feeling better. Thanks for meeting me here. I need to stay clear of the hay and dust for now. You hungry?" Karen opened the white paper bag and slid a sandwich and fries to her.

"A little. I can eat half now and the rest later. I don't want to eat too much before my ride."

"Right. How did your walk go?" Karen still couldn't believe it had to be Katherine of all people that Kayla had to befriend this week.

"Great. Kat is so helpful," she said, taking a small bite of her sandwich. "She's so sweet, taking the time to help a competitor."

"That's nice." All she had heard from her granddaughter all week had been Kat this and Kat that. When they had dinner a couple nights ago with Erica and her students, Katherine and her horse came up frequently in their conversation. They all had read about her abduction, her ride up the river into the fire and taking revenge on her captor for the death of her friend. The women joked about never wanting to cross a woman like Katherine, and here she was planning to do that very thing. It was difficult hearing how her granddaughter was so impressed by Katherine's courage and strength and couldn't imagine anyone wanting to hurt someone as nice as her new friend.

When orchestrating her plan, Karen had marginalized all

Katherine had been through to get there, focusing only on how she had done her wrong forty years ago and how she stood between Kayla and her dream. Her anger and jealously toward her old student, coupled with the love for her granddaughter, had blinded her… taken her to a dark place. Katherine had become an obstacle, no longer a living, breathing or feeling human being. Now her plan felt all wrong. With the veil of her hate lifted and the evilness of her plan exposed, she really did feel ill.

"Grandma? Are you okay?"

Karen searched her granddaughter's eyes, as if searching for forgiveness in her deep gray eyes. "Lunch isn't settling well. I think I'll go back to my room and lay down for a bit. I don't want to miss your ride later."

They wrapped up the remainder of their sandwiches and Kayla walked her to her vehicle. "Want a ride back to the barn?"

"No thanks, I'll walk," said Kayla. "I hope you feel better."

"I'm sure I will. I'll see you at the finish line. I wouldn't miss this for the world."

"Great, see you then!" Kayla smiled and waved as she left for the barn.

As soon as Kayla walked out of sight, Karen broke down in tears. How did she get here? How had she sunk to this level? To a place so low, her granddaughter would hate her if she learned the truth. She risked losing the only thing that mattered in her life, Kayla's love and respect. She had to end this now!

Karen quickly punched Stanley's number on her phone, but it only rang. Then she recalled they had set the phone on vibrate. If he wasn't holding or wearing it, he wouldn't know he was getting a call. And he wouldn't be expecting one until this afternoon. She locked her car and started for the cross-country course. Each time she dialed Stanley her hands shook more; to the point where she misdialed a few times. Karen imagined him sound asleep inside the cabin jump, sleeping off another hangover. He had been out late again and probably only got a couple hours sleep before she woke him before daylight. Karen had handed him a flexible cooler with a few sandwiches and a couple bottles of water along with the hammer and the phone on his way out the door.

Riders were on course and Karen had to stop twice at spectator crossings to wait for competitors to pass through the lane. Once she reached the cabin jump, she got as close as the taped-off area would allow. The shrubs did a good job of not only framing the obstacle but concealing the inside of the large cabin jump. That's why she had picked it, but now she had no chance of getting Stanley's attention. Karen stepped away from any other spectators and dialed Stanley again. No answer. She checked the time. Katherine would start her course in thirty minutes.

Just outside Barn F, Katherine slipped into her protective vest, secured it, and put her helmet on. She glanced toward the parking area one more time hoping to see Steven before mounting Major. Quietly, Sadie led them toward the warm-up area near the starting box as she tightened and secured her helmet strap. The announcer's voice rang out across the complex, keeping everyone abreast of each competitor's progress through the course. Just as she picked up the reins and Sadie set her free, she heard a rider was down at the number twelve jump and a loose horse was heading toward the barns. Suddenly, a gray rider-less horse galloped by, setting Major and other nearby horses into their instinctive flight response to possible danger. If one horse was running from something, perhaps they needed to also. Not having gathered her reins yet and riding only on the buckle, Major scooted from under her and spun in the direction of the free horse. Katherine nearly came unseated but managed to stay on by gripping with her legs until she gained control. Pain shot through her bad leg, almost bringing her to tears.

Sadie rushed to her. "Are you okay?"

"My leg," she said.

"You okay to ride?"

"I think so. I'll just walk a minute and see how it feels." On her second lap around the outskirts of the warm-up area, the pain subsided, but she feared if tested again, it might not hold up. She decided to carry a little insurance. Major had become so solid over fences she hadn't carried a crop in a while. Today she didn't need him to try to cut out. "Think I'll carry a crop today, just in case."

"Okay," said Sadie, already heading to the trailer to get it.

Still focusing on her leg, she turned in the direction of a familiar voice calling out to her. "Kat!"

Her handsome husband strode toward her. She waved. After nearly fifty years, he still took her breath away. She could still see the young towheaded boy admiring her through the deepest sky-blue eyes.

"I made it!" he said.

"Barely," she teased; her leg forgotten for the moment.

Steven gave Major a pat as he smiled up at her. Katherine leaned down so they could kiss. As they did, she whispered, "Thank you for coming. I sure missed you."

"Say that again."

"I missed you!"

"Music to this old cowboy's ears."

"What happened? Did your flight run late?"

"Yep. Then I had to wait for a rental. There's some huge event taking place around here."

"Ha, ha!"

"Hi, Dr. Walker," said Sadie, returning with the crop.

"Hi, Sadie," he said, then turned to Katherine. "Thought you weren't riding with a crop any longer."

"Just feeling it might be a good idea today." Without giving Steven the opportunity to question her decision, she slid the crop in her tall boot and added, "I've got to warm up then head straight to the starting box," and picked up a trot.

"We'll be right behind you," said Sadie. "You've still got about twenty minutes."

Following a warm-up canter and a few jumps, Katherine headed for the start of the course. When she glanced back, she was surprised to see Sadie and Steven appearing to have an engaging conversation as they followed. She hoped Sadie didn't mention her leg. It felt better and she didn't want to worry Steven. Major was calmer than usual which helped her calm down. Normally, it was the other way around. No sooner than she met with the cross-country steward, they were announced in the hole with two riders to go ahead of them. Steven and Sadie approached her.

"Major looks great," said Steven, keeping pace as she moved closer to the starting box. "How's the course?"

"It will be a good test of our training at speed and precision. But we're ready!"

Following an update on a few of the riders on course, the announcer called her to the on-deck position, next to go. She thought, how funny they always find an announcer from the UK with a wonderful British accent, giving the event a touch of class.

"Next up, we have Katherine Walker onboard her Thoroughbred gelding, Major Command, from Elkhead, Montana, number sixty-three," said the announcer, calling them into the starting box.

"Well, here we go."

"Good luck, Kat!" said Steven, with a wink.

Sadie gave Major a pat on the hind end. "Have a great ride. See you in eleven minutes."

Katherine waved back. As she circled in the box to face the starting line, the nerves hit her like they always do; until the second the buzzer goes off. Then it's all about Major and the next obstacle. She stroked her boy's neck. "Let's do this."

She shortened her reins as the crowd became a palpable hum, her senses as sharp as the tips of Major's ears, working back and forth between the anticipated course and her. Katherine could feel her big bay gather himself beneath her. They were ready. She glanced at her watch as the buzzer sounded. And they were off!

Stanley is startled awake by a knock along the top of the cabin jump followed by a splattering of dirt up against the backside of the jump. The riders are on course! How long? Had he slept through that Walker women's ride? He hadn't felt his phone vibrate from his mother's call. Stanley dug the phone out of his back pocket, but it wouldn't turn on! "Shit, I forgot to charge it last night!" He peeked out at the end of the jump between the shrubs trying to locate his mother, but with no luck. He heard another horse approaching. "Shit, shit, shit!" As more horses traveled the course, passing over him, all he could think was that might have been her and how pissed his mother will be if he messed up again.

Then he noticed the announcer commenting on how each rider navigated the rainbow trout water obstacle, which came two obstacles before his jump. He began timing how long it took from the time they passed through the water to the woodsman cabin jump and felt confident he could still pull off his mother's crazy scheme.

Kyle situated himself on a knoll where he could view several of the cross-country jumps from one vantage point. He could follow each competitor as they navigated a tricky combination of narrow jumps set on an angle, which he couldn't remember the name of, then on to the keyhole jump, most of the second water obstacle and then down the lane a bit to an uphill bank a distance away before disappearing into a stand of trees. There he would lose sight of them until the course turned back toward him and down a slight hill to a huge box resembling a log cabin.

He wouldn't budge until Katherine and Major were on course. Then once they disappeared into the woods, he should have enough time to hurry to the cabin jump where he could see a few more jumps down the hill. A rider on a gray horse approached the narrow jumps in front of him. Chevrons, he recalled. The horse and rider team had awkward striding between the jumps and nearly cut out of the second one but stayed within the flags. They took the keyhole with no trouble. Kyle raised his field glasses, strung around his neck, to watch the pair go through the water and trees and down to the cabin jump. Wow, how exciting! He couldn't wait to watch Katherine and Major navigate the course. Just then, the Elkhead team were announced on course.

Using his binoculars, he watched for the pair to appear over the hill. Several minutes later, Major galloped into view. Katherine rode him perfectly through the chevrons, taking each jump on an angle straight through the combination, saving strides and time. Kyle hooted and clapped along with the other spectators. The team galloped off at a nice steady pace toward the keyhole. He followed them down the bank and through the water obstacle and into the trees before he rushed to the cabin jump.

Stanley heard the Brit introduce Katherine and her horse as on course. He tensely waited for the next announcement on their progress.

"Katherine Walker and Major Command have made it through the rainbow trout water obstacle successfully. No faults, clean course so far."

Intently listening, he squatted and gripped the hammer, ready to strike. He could hear his heart pounding in his ears. Soon he heard hoofbeats becoming louder and louder as they approached until it sounded as if they were just out front. He hit the top of the jump, producing a loud bang. The sound echoed within the small space, sending him off balance and tipping him over onto his backside. Then another bang, not of his making, rang out! Stanley covered his ears and curled into a fetal position as the crowd reacted to some sort of mishap! Had he banged too late? What had he done?

Kyle smiled as Katherine and Major approached the log cabin jump. He was the closest spectator with a front row seat. They looked strong and had completed over half the course clean without any penalties. Just as Major gathered himself to take the cabin jump, he thought he heard a bang. The big bay gelding reared and pivoted to the left, so high he nearly fell over backward, sending Katherine flying into the stationary obstacle. Major finished his one-hundred-eighty-degree spin and trotted off, away from whatever spooked him. Without considering the consequences, Kyle jumped into action to reach Katherine first. She had slid to the ground in front of the jump, conscious but looking dazed as she reached for her arm in pain.

"Are you okay?" For an instant, they made eye contact, and a faint look of recognition flashed across her face.

"My… horse!" she choked out, "Is he… inured?" He guessed she must have had the wind knocked out of her.

Kyle glanced over to see Major walking toward them. "He looks fine."

The jump judge was now beside him, radioing the emergency crew. "Lay still, don't move. Help is on the way," the woman told Katherine.

Kyle sprung up as a crowd outside the lane buzzed with chatter. Major was avoiding a couple people attempting to catch him as he tried to return to Katherine. Boy, if he didn't look concerned about her. Kyle slowly approached the Thoroughbred, hand extended. Major smelled it and allowed him to gather his reins, then the big bay gave his arm a push. For a fleeting second, he thought Major remembered him. He had always heard horses have great memories. He saw no blood or injuries and Major walked squarely as he led him toward Katherine, but before he could reach her, an Indian girl ran up and took the horse from him, without so much as a thank you. Kyle slipped back amongst the spectators as an ambulance pulled up. He watched intently as the medics tended to Katherine. She didn't appear to be seriously injured, perhaps a broken arm, but they applied a neck brace and placed her on a board, he hoped just as a precaution.

Swiftly, a man brushed by him, pushing his way through the crowd. It was her husband, the blond doctor. It took Kyle a moment to remember his name. Steve, that was it, Steven Walker. Kyle put more distance between him and the doctor, walking up alongside the tree line to watch from a distance. What had he heard and where did it come from? Was he the only one that noticed the bang? Then something colorful caught his eye lying on the ground between the woods and the cabin jump. That something was a blue and orange Gators cap!

Waiting on deck to start her cross-country course, Kayla heard a rider was down and there would be a delay. She could see a crowd of people gathering in the distance around an EMT vehicle at the cabin jump. Kayla began trotting Joy toward the scene, fearing it might be Katherine who she knew was on course ahead of her. Then what she dreaded was announced.

"Katherine Walker has taken a fall at the woodsman cabin jump. It appears horse and rider are not seriously injured."

Within seconds, Kayla reached the ambulance. They had Katherine on a board, checking her vitals. Suddenly, her grandmother came into view, watching in horror. Kayla jumped off Joy and approached her. Her grandmother looking pale and shook-up for never having met Katherine. She feared it must be bad.

Before Kayla could get a word out, her grandmother exploded. "What are you doing? You're due to ride any minute!"

"They're delaying everything. That's my friend Kat I told you about. Is she okay? Do you know what happened?"

"She just took a tumble. She'll be fine. You need to get back to the start, now!"

Instead, Kayla handed Joy to her and entered the circle of people tending to the fallen rider. As they lifted Katherine to carry her to the ambulance, her friend saw her. Katherine motioned for the EMTs to stop.

"Kayla!" Katherine called out in a weak voice.

"We need to get you off the course, Ma'am," said one of the medics.

"Just one minute, please. Kayla!"

Kayla approached Katherine. "Are you okay?"

"I'll be fine."

"But you're eliminated!"

"Go. It's your time. Go make the team for both of us!"

Kayla nodded with a smile. She turned, wiped the tears welling in her eyes and searched out her horse with purpose.

"I'm ready," she said to her grandmother.

"You must hurry," said Karen, holding Joy as Kayla mounted. "Good luck!"

Kayla trotted toward the starting box just as she was called on deck. She would ride for her grandmother and trainer, but mostly for Katherine.

Katherine felt better seconds after whatever they injected her with for pain. When they placed her into the emergency vehicle, they confirmed her arm was broken. One of the two medics, a woman, stayed with her while the man slid into the driver's seat. Steven climbed in and took a seat beside her.

"I'm her husband. How is she?" Steven asked the woman.

"Just a broken arm so far, but she took a good knock to the head and may have a concussion. The helmet and vest helped, but she should have her neck and back x-rayed to be on the safe side."

Steven turned to her. "You going to be okay, sweetie, if I get my car? I can meet up with you at the hospital."

Katherine nodded.

Steven asked the medic for the address and if they could drop him off at his vehicle. "I'm in Row D, near the entrance, a black SUV."

The medic handed him a release to sign and another sheet with instructions and directions, then moved to the front of the vehicle. As they drove slowly over the course, each bump jostling her arm, reminded her of the break.

Steven gave her a gentle kiss and squeezed the hand of her good arm. "I'm so sorry, Kat."

She knew he was referring to the competition as much as her injury. "It's okay. It was a hell of a ride getting this far."

"What happened?"

"I'm not sure. There was a loud noise, Major spun around and I lost it. Hit the jump pretty hard."

"What kind of noise? From where?"

"I couldn't tell. The next thing I knew, I'm on the ground," she said, then motioned for him to come close and whispered, "But, the strangest thing… I swear I saw Kyle."

"Kyle Schmitt?"

"Yeah."

"When, before you fell?"

"No right afterward. He was the first person to get to me. His hair was shorter, and he had a beard, but I'm pretty sure it was him."

"You were pretty shaken up, honey."

"No, I'm sure now. We spoke to each other. I recognized his voice."

"Could he have something to do with this?"

"How, why? I don't think so. Kyle was very fond of Major and he tried to help us escape, remember? He has nothing to gain by harming me or my horse. And, he wouldn't have approached me if he had anything to do with it." Silently, Katherine considered the threats from Ocala. Perhaps it was time she told her husband about them. "But… I have been receiving some threat letters."

"What? Where are they?"

"I threw them all away, well, all but one. Just short notes really."

"What did they say? Why didn't you tell me? Where is it?"

"It's in my truck. I didn't want to worry you and I figured whoever it was, was just some nut that wouldn't actually act on their threat."

"The last note you got and didn't tell me about didn't end so well, remember?"

"I'm sorry. I should have told you." Katherine described the letters and told him where to find the one she saved. "Sadie has the truck keys. And please check in on Major for me."

"Will do."

The vehicle stopped and the door opened. "Is that it?" asked the driver, pointing to the rental car.

"Yes, thanks," he said to the medic, then turned to her. "I'll see you at the hospital. Love you."

Katherine offered a weak smile. With another squeeze of her hand, he exited out the back.

9 – Forgiveness

From a safe distance, Kyle hurried to follow the Indian girl leading Major. When she led the horse into Barn F, Kyle stopped just outside the entrance and glanced around the corner. The girl tied Major to the front of a stall about half-way down on the left and began removing his tack. He hoped Katherine's husband would come to check on the horse. He felt certain Katherine would insist, especially since he was a vet and all. This would be his opportunity to share what he saw with the Walkers.

He knew since Katherine was unable to finish the course, she would be eliminated and out of contention for the Eventing Team. But he had read in the Sports Illustrated article that if she didn't qualify here, she planned to compete for a place on the show jumping team or as an individual in jumping next spring. That would mean she and her horse might still be in danger. Kyle put two and two together and felt certain this guy with the gator hat, working independently or on someone's behalf, intentionally caused her mishap in the dressage ring yesterday and on the cross-country course today. Someone wanted her out of the competition. Hopefully, Katherine was not seriously injured, and they were lucky Major appeared to come away unscathed.

Kyle hid around the backside of the barn away from the parking area, glancing occasionally around the corner as he waited for Steven. Only minutes later, the doctor strode up and into Barn F. Kyle waited for him to exit.

After Steven brought Sadie up to speed on Katherine's condition, he gave Major a thorough exam. He checked each leg for any abrasions or heat and had Sadie walk and trot him up and down the aisle. Major appeared to be fine. He looked forward to giving his wife a clean report.

"You have him handled for this evening?" asked Steven.

"You bet, Dr. Walker."

"Great, thanks. Kat said you have the Ford keys. I need to get something from the truck. I'll need the room key too, to get her a change of clothes. Hopefully, she'll be coming home with me sometime today."

"They're in the trailer, hanging just inside the door on the right." Sadie reached into her jean pocket producing the trailer key, then explained where to find the trailer and truck.

"I'll return the truck and hotel keys to the trailer and hide the trailer key under the wheel well," said Steven. "Please keep an eye on Major. Call me if he starts to get sore or doesn't finish his feed?"

"Sure, I'll just get something to eat and watch the rest of the cross-country until feed time."

Steven pulled his bill clip from his back pocket and pulled out a twenty. "Here, dinner's on me. We'll meet up at the hotel later. I'll be checking into the adjoining room tonight, hopefully with Kat. We may need to fly her home on my flight tomorrow afternoon. Kimi or Nuna can pick her up at the airport. If that's the case, I'll drive back with you and Major."

"Sounds like a plan. Give Kat my best. See you later."

As Sadie walked Major out the back of the barn to rinse him off, Steven hurried out the front. The lot was full of every sized rig parked in rows, at least four-deep. Katherine's was in the second row, parked tightly between two large vans eclipsing their small two-horse trailer.

He found the truck and hotel keys right where Sadie said he would find them. As he locked the trailer on his way out, he heard gravel crackle as someone approached him from behind within the tight confines of the trailers. A perfect place for someone to ambush him! He wheeled around ready to defend himself.

"Kyle?" Steven was shocked. Katherine was right, but it was still a surprise to see him again. He slowly lowered his fist. "What are you doing here?"

"I need to tell you something. It's about Mrs. Walker's safety. It's a long story. Can we talk someplace?"

Steven considered what Katherine had said earlier and Kyle sounded sincere. "Sure." Steven unlocked the truck passenger door and told Kyle to have a seat, then walked around the front of the vehicle and slid into the driver's side. "Okay, let's hear it."

Kyle first asked about Katherine's and Major's condition, then went on to tell him about his escape five years ago, where he now lives and how he had followed Katherine and Major's progress over the years. Steven was glad he had survived the fire and made a fresh start for himself. It made sense that he would be interested in his wife and horse's career and that he didn't have anything to gain from Katherine's fall. Then Kyle described what he saw yesterday and today.

Steven clenched his jaw and reached across the cab to open the glove box. Kyle jerked away reaching for the door handle. "I swear, it's the truth. I didn't have anything to do with it!"

Steven raised his hand. "Calm down, Kyle. I'm just getting a letter."

Kyle relaxed back into his seat. "You had me worried there for a moment."

As Kyle must have suspected, Katherine's handgun rested in clear view within the open glovebox. Steven slid the truck's manual out from under the revolver, which fell open to the note. He removed it and returned the manual to the glovebox and closed it. Kyle curiously watched him as he read it to himself.

"I just learned today that my wife has received threatening letters," he told Kyle. "This is one of them. She hadn't thought much of them until today. I'm going to take the note and your description of the man to security. Perhaps they can locate this guy for questioning."

Kyle lowered his eyes to his lap and shook his head. "I was worried about your wife and her horse. I wish I could help more but I can't…"

"Get involved, I know," finished Steven. He knew Kyle had risked a lot by exposing himself to Katherine and himself as the only witness to a potential crime, considering he's still wanted in the States. "Don't worry, I won't mention you by name, only that some stranger told me what he saw. I'll just say I was in such a hurry to reach my wife that I didn't get a name."

"Thank you," said Kyle, opening the truck passenger door. "Please tell Mrs. Walker I'm sorry about her arm and about her being eliminated. I hope she qualifies in show jumping. Wish her good luck for me."

"I will. Thank you, Kyle. You gave a good description and maybe the jump judge saw something and heard the noise too. Hopefully, the authorities can get to the bottom of this."

"I hope so. Bye, Dr. Walker."

"Bye, Kyle. And good luck to you, too." Kyle exited the truck and disappeared into the maze of trailers and out of their lives once again.

Steven tucked the note in his pocket. He would visit the show security office in the morning with the letter and share Kyle's description of the man. He didn't want to take the time now. Who knew how involved it might get reporting such a thing? Steven wanted to return to Katherine as soon as possible, and he still needed to pick up a change of clothes and some toiletries from the hotel room in case she ended up spending the night.

All of this was very disturbing. The letter, the attacks on Katherine and Major. Why? Who was this guy!?

Karen's heart felt like it might beat clear through her chest it was pumping so hard. She was glad Katherine's horse appeared not to be injured, but seeing Katherine hauled away in an ambulance to the hospital totally freaked her out. She had tried to stop Stanley, but this attack was all by her design to begin with. If only she could take it all back. Kayla appeared more concerned about her new friend than she did her ride. But whatever Katherine said to her granddaughter, seemed to motivate her once again. Hopefully, she would do well enough to keep her in contention and all of this would not have been in vain.

With the course shut down after Katherine's fall, ride times were running about ten minutes behind. Karen stood at the finish line. She had watched her granddaughter take the first few jumps then disappear into the woods. The announcer gave periodic updates as she rode the course. Karen guessed Kayla should be nearing the half-way point and the keyhole jump about that time. If they had one refusal, they would be charged twenty penalties and forty for the second. On the third, they would be eliminated. She prayed Kayla would not have an issue with the keyhole jump this time.

"Kayla Lutz has cleared the second water obstacle, riding a clean round so far," came the latest update blaring from the speaker just above her head where she stood. She knew the rainbow trout water obstacle came after the keyhole, so they did not have a refusal. The next five minutes seemed an eternity waiting for Kayla to appear over the hill and down the final stretch. There, she spotted the green and gold colors of Erica's barn on a chestnut horse in the distance. That had to be Kayla and Joy. Three more jumps lie between her and the finish. For the moment, the terrible thing she had done to her old student was blocked out. This is what she had sacrificed so much for, for so many years. Her excitement built with every cleared obstacle.

"Go Kayla!" she cheered as Kayla and Joy raced past her toward the finish line.

Erica greeted Kayla at the finish just as Karen did.

"Great ride!" said Karen, giving her granddaughter a hug.

"Good job, Kayla," said Erica, holding Joy as Kayla dismounted.

"Joy didn't even look at the keyhole! What a tough course, but we cleared everything," said Kayla, glowing with pride. "How was my time?"

"You lost time taking that alternate route through the first water combination and I saw a few wide corners," said Erica, sounding disappointed.

"The course is pretty slick and torn up from the rain," said Kayla, trying to justify her caution.

As Erica began walking Joy toward the barn, with Karen and Kayla keeping pace, she added, "You'll have a time penalty for sure."

Kayla's beautiful smile full of joy and accomplishment only seconds ago, disappeared. Over the loudspeaker, it was confirmed that Kayla Lutz, onboard Joyous Occasion, rode a clear round but with time penalties.

Karen opened her mouth to speak, but Erica anticipated her question. "We won't know until the end of the day," said Erica, referring to whether or not Kayla would remain in contention. And even if she did, they still had show jumping tomorrow. Then she added, "There's always the chance she could make it as an alternate."

That didn't sound too promising. Karen put Joy's tack away while Kayla cooled and rinsed off her mount. Watching the girl go about her task like a wounded creature, broke Karen's heart. She knew what was on her granddaughter's mind. If she doesn't qualify, will Erica put Joy on the market immediately or give the pair the chance to qualify in jumping next spring? But with Erica cutting back, selling school horses and limiting her clients, the latter seemed unlikely. The only reason Erica had held on to Joy this long, was to see if the mare might settle down as she matured and see how far Kayla could take her to increase her value. The opinionated mare would be a difficult sale either way with her stubborn and moody disposition. Joy liked Kayla but never performed as well for other riders, including Erica. Perhaps Kayla would get a chance at the Olympics yet, but they would still need sponsors to get there.

That thought brought her back to Katherine. She will no doubt try to qualify in jumping next spring in Las Vegas. Katherine and Kayla could end up competing against each other again. No more nasty tactics. Luckily, they had not been caught… not yet anyway. Stanley still needed to exit the jump undetected. Karen tried calling him again. No response.

When the last horse sailed over the cabin jump, Stanley peered out the end of the obstacle. As the last of the spectators began hiking across the field toward the barns and parking, the jump judge removed her headset, gathered her paperwork and followed them. Apparently, no one heard the bang prior to Katherine's fall or suspected any foul play or they would have checked the jump by now. His mother's plan had worked perfectly. She would be pleased. He heard the medic tell Katherine she had broken her arm and he saw her horse being led away through an opening, apparently uninjured. Thank goodness. He had done good and was ready to celebrate. After spending the day cramped up in such a small space, he couldn't wait to get out and have a drink. But they had agreed he would wait at least an hour after the competition before exposing himself.

Stanley exited the confines of the jump, stretched, and surveyed the area. No one was around. When he reached for his cap in his back pocket, it wasn't there. "Dammit," he spat. After checking inside the confines of the jump, he figured it must have fallen out of his pocket on his way out that morning. Slowly he backtracked his steps searching for his hat. It wasn't hard to find. Thankfully, he had dropped it in the roped off section of the course where spectators were not allowed, or someone might have picked it up. He slipped it on and pulled the bill low over his face and headed straight for Barn F.

Karen checked her watch again. It had been over an hour since the last competitor left the course. He should be arriving soon. After the cross-country competition had completed, Erica invited everyone out for a dinner on her to celebrate their progress as a team. The course had turned out to be a challenge for many of the competitors between the poor footing and difficult course. Kayla and Joy remained in contention, along with Betty and Majic, going into show jumping the next day. Karen had offered to stay behind to feed and water all the horses so they could beat the dinner crowd. She needed to wait for Stanley, but also wanted to get back on Erica's good side after being absent most of the week. Karen guessed she wouldn't have to worry about seeing Katherine anytime soon. When she finished feeding and picking stalls, she sat impatiently waiting for Stanley in the tack stall. Karen checked the time. He should have been back by now. Just as Karen rose to her feet to go looking for him, Stanley pulled open the curtain.

"I did it!" he said, out of breath.

"Shhh," whispered Karen. "I tried to call you. Where's your phone?"

Stanley reached into his jacket pocket. "Right here. Dead as a doorknob. I forgot to charge it."

"Of course, you did." Why would she be surprised. "Did anyone see you or suspect anything?"

"No. I saw the horse is okay. She wasn't seriously injured, was she?"

"She'll be okay. A broken arm, I heard." Karen got up from her seat. No use in mentioning her change of heart to Stanley. The damage was done.

"Glad it's over. I heard Kayla did good. Let's get dinner. I'm starved," said Stanley, leading the way out of the barn. "We still leaving tomorrow?"

"Yes, right after Kayla jumps." Karen stepped up her pace to match her son's. "She rides at ten-thirty."

"How's it look? Will she qualify?"

"It'll be close."

"Good thing we did what we did then."

Karen took a tight grip on her son's arm, stopping him mid-stride. "Kayla must never know what we did. You understand?"

Stanley pulled his arm away. "Okay, I got it the first hundred times you told me."

Karen's guilt burned like a searing brand to her conscience. She would forever regret what she did to this woman. Having turned Katherine into something evil, a non-human obstacle to Kayla's success, she had allowed her hate to cloud her judgement. Katherine turned out to be a good person, willing to help a young woman reaching for the same dream. Karen's hands shook as she searched for her keys in her pocket to unlock the rental. She would have no reason to live if Kayla learned what she had done. Karen could barely breathe at the thought of her granddaughter hating her. That would mark her final failure.

Katherine returned to her room from x-ray just as Steven arrived. "Perfect timing," she said, "How is Major?"

"He's fine, not even a scratch." Steven hung a change of clothes in the small locker beside the restroom.

"Oh, I'm so relieved."

"Sadie is taking care of him. How are you?"

"Better now that you're here." He gave her a gentle hug and a peck on the cheek as she got situated in her bed.

The nurse that wheeled her from x-ray, still in the room, opened the drapes. "There, that's better," she said, allowing late afternoon rays into the sterile room.

"They took slides of my arm, shoulder, back and skull," said Katherine. She looked to the nurse. "Did I leave anything out?"

The nurse chuckled. "You covered it." She turned to Steven. "She suffered a mild concussion and a clean break to her fibula bone."

"Thankfully is my left arm," sighed Katherine, considering she's right-handed.

The nurse gave her a shot. "This should handle the pain, but just push the button if you need anything. The doctor will be in soon." On the way out the door, she added, "Try to get some rest."

Steven pulled a chair up beside her bed and took a seat. "Have you eaten?"

"Yes, while I was waiting to go to x-ray. It was actually pretty good."

Steven leaned toward her. "Can you tell me again what happened out there?"

"We were going just fine, making good time. Just as we reached the cabin jump, there was a loud bang, like I said. I just couldn't stay with him." Katherine figured she'd better come clean about her leg. "I probably could have stayed on, but Major spooked earlier when a loose horse raced by and my bum leg began aching. Think I aggravated it when he reared and spun, gripping to stay on."

Steven got up and closed the door to the private room and reclaimed his seat beside her with a suddenly serious expression. She knew that look and braced herself. "What?"

"I spoke to Kyle."

"You did? Where?"

"He approached me when I stopped at the trailer for the truck and hotel keys. He said he had something he needed to tell me about your safety."

"My safety? What did he say?"

"He witnessed a man he believes deliberately spooked Major during your dressage test."

"How?"

"He said the man sat in the aisle seat next to him then walked down to the base of the stairs on the rail when you began your test. Kyle said he was acting suspicious. At first, he thought he was going to harass a group of young women, so he followed the guy. The man reached the rail beside the girls just before you approached the barrier closest to the stands. A moment later, Major spooked."

"That doesn't mean much."

"There's more. The man noticed Kyle watching him and nearly ran from the stadium. Kyle found a makeup mirror lying on the ground right where he had been standing at the rail. The sun was opposite the stands. Kyle thinks he used the sun's reflection to spook Major."

"I could see where that might work, but I never saw anything."

"Where would you be focused at that moment, straight ahead or down the ring?"

"Ha, like I always told my students, focusing up and a few strides ahead through the corner."

"Exactly."

"What did he look like?" she asked, nervously curling a strand of hair around her finger.

"He said he was a big fella, about his age, fifty something. Kyle said he looked out of place with a bright colored jacket, tennis shoes and a sports cap."

"Well, that doesn't give us much, does it?"

"That's not all. Kyle believes the same man caused your cross-country fall."

"How?"

"Perhaps he shot something at the jump with a sling shot or used a BB gun from the woods."

"No, I meant how does Kyle know it was the same man?"

"Sorry, I left out the most important detail. The hat the man was wearing at the dressage ring was an orange and blue Florida Gators cap. He saw the same hat lying near the cabin jump. Not too many of those lying around in Winnipeg."

Katherine gasped. Kayla's uncle, Stanley, who the girl had introduced her to, wore such a hat. "That doesn't mean anything," she said in a huff, refusing to believe Kayla had anything to do with her mishaps.

"I plan to report it to security in the morning. Maybe, they can locate this guy."

"No!"

"No?"

"Don't report it. I have my reasons."

"Care to share them with me?"

"I think I know who it is, but it's complicated. Trust me. I need to handle this on my own."

Steven's eyes narrowed; his jaw clenched. "Kat? I don't like it. Not one bit. Why can't you tell me... after all we've been through?"

Katherine was already thinking ahead to tomorrow. "I have to get out of here tonight. I need to talk to someone first thing in the morning. It'll be my only chance."

Steven shook his head. "Damn, woman."

"I'm sorry, hon, I have to do this. Please."

"Okay, I'll give you until tomorrow morning, then we're going to the authorities. If we can prove foul play, you might get another chance to qualify."

"No, that's done. How do you think the other competitors would feel, a rider claiming someone caused their horse to refuse a jump? We had our chance. I'll go to Vegas in the spring."

"Let's get you taken care of. I'll find the doctor," said Steven, still sounding agitated with her as he stomped out of the room. And who could blame him. But she needed to confront Stanley alone.

Steven returned with the doctor and after setting her arm and applying a cast Katherine was discharged that evening with instructions to follow up with her doctor at home. Thankful she didn't have to stay overnight. Katherine looked forward to resting in peace with Steven in their hotel room that evening while she planned how to approach Stanley.

Sunday morning, Katherine woke up in a panic. What time was it? She quietly sat up enough to read the radio clock over Steven's shoulder. He lay asleep beside her. It read eight o'clock. Katherine relaxed some, having not overslept, but she didn't feel rested. The cast on her arm made it impossible to sleep on her side. Unaccustomed to sleeping on her back, she hadn't slept well. Thanks to the pain pills, she felt little to no discomfort as she swung her legs over the edge of the bed and sat up. She panicked when the room began to spin, until she recalled her concussion. She lowered her head for a moment, then slowly stood up, steadying herself against the wall with her good arm. Katherine headed straight for the window. When she drew the curtain, a light but steady rain ran down the window blurring her vision of the parking lot below. Her truck was gone. Sadie had already left to feed Major.

Last night, Sadie had brought her up to speed on the standings and she was pleased to learn Kayla still stood a chance of qualifying. She prayed the rain would let up in time for the girl's show jumping ride mid-morning. Katherine sat back down on the bed and rubbed her aching head. They said she might experience headaches and dizziness and to get plenty of rest. She considered laying back down for a bit, but she couldn't rest until she spoke to Stanley. Tenderly, she reached over and caressed her husband's arm.

"Sweetie, I need your help to get dressed."

Steven groggily sat up and read the time. "You need to head over this early?"

"Yes."

"How are you feeling? How's your head?"

Katherine opened her mouth to explain about her headache and dizziness but caught herself. "I'm fine," she said, instead. She would share how she was feeling later, she didn't want any resistance from her husband about going to the showgrounds this morning. This would be her only opportunity to confront Stanley.

"Okay then, let's get you dressed."

Steven carefully helped her pull on her jeans and slip into a button-down short-sleeved shirt.

"How about you run downstairs and pack a little breakfast to go for us while I finish getting ready. I'll take a bagel and cream cheese… and grab an apple for Major."

"Will do."

"Oh, and where are your binoculars? I'm going to need them."

Steven shook his head. "Of course, you will." His face showed his restraint. "They're in the back seat of the rental. I'll pull them out for you."

"Thanks, hon."

As Katherine brushed her hair and put on a little makeup, she glanced at her cast in the mirror. Did Stanley act alone on his niece's behalf? Or what about the grandmother who seemed to be avoiding her all week? She never did get to meet her. Well, she's going to meet her today if it's the last thing she does. Katherine felt certain both of them would be at the stadium that morning to watch Kayla jump. After all, one or both of them went through a lot of trouble to eliminate Kayla's competition. For Kayla's sake and the sake of their friendship, she needed to be certain if they were involved. Then she would decide if she would go to the authorities.

Katherine met up with Steven in the lobby. "Still need to do this alone?" he questioned again.

"Yes," she said firmly. Steven knew better than to question her further when using that tone. "I need you to get me as close to the stadium entrance as possible, then I'll meet you at the barn afterward and fill you in."

Steven gave her another curious look. Katherine knew he was dying to know what this was all about, but good old understanding Steven remained patient. God, she was the luckiest woman alive.

She surprised him with a tender kiss on the cheek. "Let's go!"

Katherine arrived at the stadium just as they announced the first rider had entered the ring. Thankfully, the rain stopped, and the sun was beginning to peek through a thin layer of clouds overhead. The course was beautiful, full of colorful and creative obstacles, and her heart ached because she wouldn't get the opportunity to ride it with Major that day. She didn't go to the barn first because she wanted to catch Stanley and the grandmother by surprise in the stands. Suddenly, she recalled her first conversation with Erica. She had said her grandmother's name, but she couldn't recall what it was. Whatever her name, she hadn't shown up that morning to work, or any other time Katherine was at the barn that week.

After showing her husband's ticket at the gate, she entered the first section closest to the entrance instead of taking his front row seat, center of the arena. Katherine climbed halfway up and found a single empty seat on the aisle. She awkwardly pulled the field glasses from her purse with one hand and began searching the stands which were already about half full while keeping an eye on newcomers. Row by row, she studied the crowd, looking for Stanley. The big man wouldn't be hard to miss, especially if he had retrieved his bright blue and orange hat!

It took about a half hour to search the stands. No sign of her uncle. She glanced up at the large clock above the jumbotron. It read ten o'clock. Kayla rode in thirty minutes. She had been so preoccupied; she hadn't been watching the riders or keeping track of their scores. Again, she scanned the entrance as more people filed in. And there it was! The Gators cap! An elderly woman walked beside Stanley as he carried some refreshments. Katherine couldn't get a good view of her face from above. She waited for the pair to pass her section, then rose from her seat and followed them from a distance until they took their seats. Thankfully, there were empty seats behind them. Katherine walked up the aisle quickly, her face turned in the opposite direction. She had to scoot in front of a group of women to reach the seats behind Stanley and presumably Kayla's grandmother

Katherine took a deep breath, leaned over and whispered between them, "I know it was you."

Stanley swung around so fast he spilled his drink on the old woman's arm.

The grandmother turned. "Katherine," she gasped, her eyes full of fear, yet with a look of recognition.

She knows me? It took a moment for Katherine to recognize her old trainer. The forty years had not been kind to her. "Karen? You're Kayla's grandmother?"

Eyes locked, all the pieces began to fall in place. The words "you had your chance" from the threat letter and the "why" was now clear. Karen not only wanted to eliminate the competition, she wanted revenge!

Stanley started to rise out of his seat, searching for the fastest escape route. Karen firmly gripped his thigh, pulling him back to his seat.

Karen turned away, staring aimlessly across the stadium. "Hello, Katherine," she said, shockingly calm.

Katherine's anger burned through her veins like a wildfire. How dare she threaten my safety and the safety of my horse! Katherine took a deep breath in an effort to contain her emotions for Kayla's sake. "We need to talk," she said. She didn't care about Stanley any longer. She knew Karen was behind the assaults. "But first, let's watch Kayla's ride. You went through a lot of trouble to give your granddaughter the best opportunity to qualify."

Silently, they watched the rider before Kayla complete the course. Only now did Katherine learn that only two riders had gone clean with no jumping faults or time penalties so far. The challenging course tested horse and rider with difficult combinations and tight corners.

"I tried to stop it.," said Karen, now focused on the rider in the ring. "But I couldn't reach Stanley in time. Kayla know nothing. "

Katherine wasn't sure how to process that piece of information. She had still planned it for months, flown here with the intention of eliminating her and her horse, not to mention putting them in danger.

When the rider finished his course and Kayla entered the arena, Katherine moved into an empty seat beside Karen. Again, they locked eyes. Katherine no longer saw fear in her old trainer's gaze, rather a combination of pride and sorrow. Not until that moment had Katherine thought much about what might have come of Karen after she stomped out of that restaurant in Boston so many years ago. What Kayla had shared of their family history now held new meaning; her grandmother having been a trainer years ago and being the inspiration behind her riding, the tragic and untimely death of her mother, her grandmother stepping up to raise her, and the stress and cost of Kayla's health issues resulting in the family now living in a trailer park.

Looking back, she had been a thoughtless, spoiled young woman thinking only of herself. Karen had sacrificed a lot for her, for the dream they once shared. The dream Katherine had tossed aside to pursue another. Her trainer had been her salvation during a difficult time in life while dealing with her dreadful mother and absent father. Karen invited her into her home, helped her with her homework and was always there when she needed her.

Under different circumstances, then and now, this reunion might have been a joyous one.

Side by side, they watched Kayla and Joy navigate the course, holding their breath in unison as she approached each obstacle. Following the last tricky combination, Joy came down on the wrong lead and tossed her head several times, breaking stride, causing the team to take the corner wide, losing valuable seconds. The chestnut mare continued to toss her head, straining against the martingale, as they approached the last obstacle of the course, a wide oxer. Both Karen and Katherine gasped as Joy chipped in too tight to the jump, not giving them enough room to clear the top rail. Down fell the pole, penalizing them with four faults in addition to a time penalty. Regardless, the two women stood and cheered as she crossed the finish.

Katherine turned to Karen. "She might still have a chance. There are several riders to go yet."

Karen looked at her cast. "I'm so sorry."

"I am too." Karen's confused expression prompted Katherine to continue. "You were good to me. It was wrong and selfish of me to walk out on you like I did."

Karen somehow looked satisfied. She gathered her things, allowing Stanley to leave. "It was all me. Please don't involve my son. He just did what I told him to do."

Katherine nodded.

"Are we going to the authorities now?"

"No."

"No?" Karen's defeated eyes welled up. "It was a terrible thing I did."

"Me too," said Katherine, resting a hand on her old mentor's shoulder, now slumped with age. "Go to Kayla. She needs you."

Katherine got up and walked away without looking back.

10 – Confrontation

Washington State
September

TJ retrieved the worn and tattered sheet of stationary from his jean pocket and unfolded it. It was so wrinkled he could hardly make out Roy's letter, having read and folded it again over a dozen times since he received it. He stared at the address Roy had given him, still surprised the world-famous actor and director remembered him at all, let alone replied to his letter. Luckily, Roy still lived at the same California address he had given him years ago and his wife had been so kind to forward his correspondence to their shooting location in Washington. It had been a short response but contained the best news possible.

Hi TJ,
So good to hear from you. I half expected to after Jo asked me to fly her to Montana to see you last month. Too bad it didn't work out. She still cares, I can tell you that much. You're welcome to stop by when you're in Walla Walla next week. Just show the security guard this note. I've told him to expect you. The address is Box 212, Route 9, Yakima, WA. Per your request, I haven't mentioned your visit to Jo. Good luck with your race and with Jo!
Roy

Thankfully, they qualified for the Championship of Champions Race at the Crow Fair at Crow Agency in Montana nearly a month ago. They had arrived at the Walla Walla Fair Grounds yesterday and would race soon. TJ felt certain having qualified for an event so close to Josephine was a sign he was meant to see her.

Folding the letter once again, he slid it back into his pocket and approached his team members. Talon set a smudge pot on the trailer fender and lit up the small bundle of sage. When it began to smoke,

TJ, followed by each team member, drew the smoke over their head with their hands. This would bring them good luck from the spirits. Matt extinguished the smoldering pile.

"Let's go win this thing," said TJ.

The guys hooted and chanted while they bridled the horses. As they led the horses onto the track in single file, the stands hummed like a disturbed beehive. Tribe members from the seven nations and states, along with hundreds of spectators from all over the country, filled the bleachers. The track was dry and fast. Some of the guys' families and girlfriends attended. TJ imagined having Josephine waiting for him at the finish next year.

TJ's racing heart, beat in time with the rhythmic thumping of a drum that filled the air as they approached the track. When it came time for the final heat, the Championship of Champions Race, the Piegan Pride team was introduced as they entered the track. After informing the crowd of where they were from and how they qualified, each team member's name and age, as well as the name and breed of each of the team's horses, were announced over the loudspeaker to the cheer of the crowd. The large field of winners from each competition would truly test each team's skill and speed.

In place of a starting gate, each "rider" led the first horse of the relay to a white chalk line in the dirt stretching across the width of the track. The other members led their team's horses to the outside rail, lined up in order of go. As soon as all the riders and their horses resembled any sort of line, a horn would sound, signaling the riders to mount bareback from the ground and immediately race off to jockey for position for the first lap of the three-horse relay.

TJ led Tomahawk, a quick Appaloosa and Thoroughbred cross, onto the track. His coloring, referred to as a Leopard Appy, sported black spots across a white coat from head to tail. The flashy gelding painted in traditional war markings drew cheers from the crowd as they lined up. TJ wore their team colors of red and black, which made for a striking addition to the pair's flair. Tomahawk liked to anticipate the start, so TJ had to hold him by the reins firmly while grasping mane to aid in his flying mount.

A few of the horses, strange to one another, fussed, shifting back and forth, one spinning in a circle disturbing the whole line. Finally, when the horses formed some resemblance of a line, the horn sounded. The horse to TJ's left reared nearly over backward as his rider attempted to mount, causing him to fall into TJ. TJ managed to stay on his feet, but Tomahawk lunged forward to join the rest of the horses racing away, nearly pulling the reins from his hands. Running to keep pace, in one vaulting effort, TJ leaped onto the back of the gelding and swung his leg over. Kicking and howling, he sent Tomahawk off in a dead run to chase down the rest of the field already rounding the first turn. The Appy had good speed, not as fast as Moon Cloud, who would run the last leg, but faster than Sky, the middle horse of the relay. He had to make up the lost ground before the first switch. On the backstretch, he remained about ten strides behind the pack. The horse that reared ran a good distance behind him. On the far turn, the horses began to spread out and TJ managed to pass two of them through a narrow opening on the rail. The crowd cheered in approval of the risky move. A clean and fast exchange would be crucial to catching the front runners.

Talon, the "mugger," stood holding Sky, a long-legged, chestnut Appendix Quarter Horse, which is half Thoroughbred. Built and bred to run fast, he just didn't have Tomahawk's or Moon Cloud's heart. Sky, also the most skittish of the bunch, had a tendency to shy away from him as he approached. Talon stood on the far side, out of his way, where he could help steady Sky as TJ ran toward them to mount. TJ flew off Tomahawk's back as Matt, the "catcher," grabbed his reins. He ran about six strides and leaped onto Sky's back, grabbing the reins from Talon to perform his best exchange of the summer with him, earning cheers from the crowd as he got to the rail ahead of one of the horses from the lead pack.

TJ quickly closed the gap between him and the others on the first turn, passing a couple on the backstretch, but the front two were still well ahead of him. Gaining some ground, he came down the homestretch just behind them. The second and last exchange had to go as smooth as the first if they were stood a chance at winning. Again, Matt stood waiting to catch Sky, as Noot, the "holder," held Moon Cloud for the final lap.

This exchange was a mess for all three lead teams, including Piegan Pride. TJ had a smooth mount, but the other two riders collided when they mounted in front of him, their horses spinning around and cutting him off. Once the two horses got straightened out, they made a mad dash for the rail just in front of TJ. Moon Cloud felt strong and TJ positioned himself just behind the two lead horses, letting them set the pace through the first turn. On the backstretch, TJ made his move on the outside, but so did the second-place horse, forcing him to go three-wide into the far turn. One horse fell back on the homestretch, leaving the win between TJ and the home team from Washington. The cheering was deafening as they raced neck and neck. TJ asked Moon Cloud for all he had left, and the strong Mustang and Thoroughbred cross delivered, crossing the finish line by a neck to win!

TJ trotted the gray around the track to cool him down as the announcer read off the team's information again. Talon, Matt and Noot ran up to him, patting his leg and Moon Cloud's neck. He could hear the hometown section from Browning cheering above the rest of the spectators. TJ was thrilled with the win, but all he could think about was seeing Josephine tomorrow and giving her the news. Now TJ had the money to continue his education for another year. If they could win again next year, he could finish his last year and earn his degree. Then he would be worthy of Josephine's hand in marriage. After what Roy said, he felt pretty confident she would accept and perhaps even return home to Montana after completing the film. He couldn't wait to see her tomorrow; to kiss and embrace her again.

Now he just had to break the news to the guys that they wouldn't be leaving in the morning. Having the win and purse money in their pockets would make it easier. He won the race, now he needed to win back the heart of the woman he's loved all his life.

The sound of a rooster crowing woke Josephine from the same reoccurring dream; riding Bonanza through a terrible storm, darting lightning strikes and falling trees. She sprang up to a sitting position, her forehead perspiring and hands clammy. Josephine wiped her brow and studied Brad fast asleep beside her, glad she hadn't woken him.

He had been especially clingy since her return from Montana last month. At first, she relished the attention, allowing her to keep thoughts of TJ at bay. But she missed her quiet time, with few opportunities to break away from the cast, crew and especially Brad. If they weren't filming together, Brad shadowed her every move. Since Roy had a meeting that day with some investors that flew in yesterday, they wouldn't start filming until noon. So, Josephine planned to take advantage of the break and go for a solo trail ride that morning.

Josephine peeked out between the blinds. Just as the weatherman had promised, there wasn't a cloud in sight. The sun, just breaking over the range to the east, painted the sky a rainbow of colors, from its flaming red center radiating out to vibrant orange, yellow and green against a dark blue canvas. She quietly changed into the clothes she left in the bathroom overnight and tip-toed out of the room.

She could smell fresh brewed coffee down the hall before reaching the commercial kitchen, which now acted as a commons area for all of the cast and crew. Josephine poured herself a cup and stepped out onto the patio to admire the sunrise before heading to the barn.

"Good morning!"

Startled, Josephine turned to find Roy sitting at a table against the wall behind her.

"Oh, Roy, hi. I didn't expect anyone to be up so early with the late start today. I can't remember the last time we didn't start at daybreak."

"So why aren't you sleeping in with the rest?"

"Going for a ride." Josephine glanced back at the prism of color now starting to fade into pastel shades. "Beautiful morning. I needed some quiet time."

"To think?"

"I suppose, or perhaps to not think."

"I know what you mean. Something about being on a horse slows things down."

"Exactly." Josephine set her mug down. "I better get moving."

"Where are you going to ride? You know, just in case."

"Ha, my parents always made me leave a note on the refrigerator. My mom said Betsy and her Uncle Joe used to make her do the same before she left for a ride. Think I'll head toward the lake. Maybe go for a swim."

"It'll be cold this early."

"I'm from Montana, remember?"

Roy smiled and nodded. "Right!"

Josephine turned and stepped closer to her director. "Don't tell Brad, okay?" she whispered.

"Sure, see you at noon."

"Thanks."

As Josephine started for the barn, she turned and waved. Roy waved back wearing the silliest grin. Josephine just shook her head and stepped up her pace.

Roy did have a meeting that day, but not until ten o'clock. He expected TJ soon and Josephine going for a ride would work out perfectly to give them some privacy. He planned on keeping Brad occupied with a special project all morning, helping re-write a scene.

He knew helping TJ might not be in his best interest or the film's, but as a hopeless romantic at heart, he would always put love above money. Besides, they had only another week or so of shooting and had completed all of the love scenes. If Josephine and Brad did break up, it most likely wouldn't affect production. Ever since the day he saved TJ's life and the poor boy lost his father, Roy felt he had a stake in his welfare. It felt good giving him and Jo one more shot. They were so much in love, the kind of love that comes along once in a lifetime, if you're lucky. So many of his Hollywood friends never found it, flittering from partner to partner or marriage to marriage. He had been blessed to find Sandy and he wanted the same happiness for Josephine and TJ.

Just as he finished his second cup of coffee, an old pickup pulled up. He barely recognized TJ with shoulder-length hair and his matured stature. He was no longer the boy he rescued five years earlier, but a man.

Roy jumped up to greet him. "Hi, TJ. Good to see you." The men shook hands.

"Hi, Roy. It's been a while."

"Sure has been, I barely recognized you."

"I haven't changed that much." He surveyed the ranch. "Wow, some place. It's huge."

"I can give you a tour later, but you need to depart on your mission now. Jo left about fifteen minutes ago for a ride. Follow me, we'll get you a horse." Without a comment, TJ followed him into the barn. "Here, this one should do," he said, stopping in front of the stall of a black gelding. Roy left TJ looking over his mount as he pulled a bridle and saddle from the tack room.

"I won't need the saddle," said TJ, already in the horse's stall, stroking his neck. He took the bridle from him and slipped it on over the black's ears. "He's a pretty one. Using him in the movie?"

"Yes. His name is King. We lease him and the others from a nearby ranch." TJ led the gelding from the barn and hopped on his bare back in one fluid motion. "Wow, I'm impressed. I haven't been able to do that for years. She headed for the lake, that way," pointed Roy. "Just over that butte."

"Thanks, Roy."

"Good luck!"

TJ loped King in the direction Roy had pointed. When he cleared the ridge, a large lake spread out below, bordered by willows and cottonwoods. He could make out the rear of a horse with its tail swishing between some trees. TJ trotted about halfway then dismounted and led King toward the chestnut horse grazing on some lush grass. He tied King to a tree and walked toward shore. Josephine lay on her shirt in a bed of grass with wet hair, wearing only a bra and underwear. Her jeans and boots lie in a heap beside her. God, she was beautiful; her new bright red hair fanned out behind her head, and she wore a size or two larger bra than he remembered. He hadn't been the only one to mature over the past three years. His gaze rested on her silk black panties then traveled down her long tan legs to bare feet with bright red nail polish. His heart skipped a beat as he suddenly became aroused. He nearly jumped back on King to ride off before she noticed him. Was this a mistake? But she had come to see him race, he had to remind himself. TJ stepped behind a willow, took a deep breath and cleared his throat loud enough for her to hear him. Through the branches he watched Josephine scurry to slip on her clothes as she looked every direction searching out the source of the noise.

"Hello? Someone there?"

TJ peeked from behind the tree, finding her nearly finished with buttoning up her blouse, and answered. "It's me Jo, TJ."

Josephine turned away in shock, fumbling to finish buttoning up her shirt. "TJ, what are you doing here?" He had to smile as she smoothed her blouse and ran her fingers through her wet hair before she turned around.

"I had a race not far from here yesterday. Thought I'd drive up for a visit. I hope you don't mind. Roy told me where to find you."

Josephine turned, her face radiating with a warm smile. TJ's heart melted.

"Hmm, that Roy," she said. "He neglected to mention anything about it."

"Well, here I am," he said, walking closer.

"How did you do in the race?"

"We won! Wish you could have been there."

She blushed as he drank her in from head to toe. "You look amazing… all but the hair."

Josephine snickered. "My dad doesn't like it either, but I like yours. I always liked it long." She glanced over at the horses. "I see he put you on King." As she walked past him toward the black, his senses filled of her sweet scent. Josephine stroked King's shoulder. "He's a good boy. I ride him sometimes."

TJ walked beside her. "It's good to see you… for longer than five seconds."

Josephine turned toward him with a confused expression.

"At the race in Browning."

Embarrassed, she turned her flushed face toward the lake. "Right, the race. I was home to visit Mom for her birthday and to send her off to Winnipeg. I…"

"You don't have to explain, Jo. Roy told me. That's why I'm here."

Josephine bit her lip and walked toward shore, gazing out across the lake. "I wanted to see you face to face, to explain… how sorry I am about how I…"

"That's the past," he interrupted. "Only today matters." He dared to step closer.

"It that a Blackfeet thing? Living in the here and now. You sound like Betsy."

"I'm so sorry about Betsy. I should have been there."

"I think you were."

Now it was TJ's turn to blush from embarrassment. "I should have been there with you."

When Josephine turned and found herself face to face with him, he heard her draw in a shallow breath and slowly exhale. TJ clenched his fists to resist reaching out and pulling her to him. Their eyes met and he swore he recognized that "look." Her "come take me" look. She stood trembling but did not step away. TJ slowly reached for her face, ready to retreat, but she held fast. He cradled her beautiful face in his hands. "Oh, Jo. I've missed you so much."

Josephine draped her arms over his shoulders. He pulled her face closer. As she leaned into him, she eliminated any doubt. She wanted him. Still framing her face with both hands, he gently kissed her on the lips. He could feel her warmth as she pressed into him harder and closed her arms around him. Their soft kiss grew more passionate as he wove his fingers through her candy apple hair, pulling her head back as his lips traveled down her neck. He felt her melt in his arms.

Sighing, Josephine tried to gain control of her urges. TJ had grown to resemble his father in stature, masculine yet refined. Any control she had was swept away as his hair blew off his broad shoulders in the gentle breeze. She let go and gave in to her desires, running her fingers through his black mane as he opened her blouse and explored one breast with his tongue while caressing the other. They had slipped outside this world and into their own. Later, she wouldn't recall how they ended up in the grass naked, only how much pure joy she felt as they became one again. Josephine dug her nails into his strong back as he took her a second time.

Spent and delirious, they laid side by side staring up into the massive cottonwood branches swaying ever so slightly above them. She felt hypnotized by their motion, feeling like she was floating above the ground as free as the leaves gently waving overhead. When the reality of what just happened sunk in, Josephine turned to TJ already studying her with his deep molasses pools. He smiled and turned on his side to face her as he gently brushed a few damp strands of hair off her face. Then came the words she feared he would say.

"I love you, Jo. I always have and I always will." He gently kissed her on the head. "When can I see you again?"

Josephine panicked. What had she done? She sat up and reached for her clothes.

"You do love me, don't you, Jo?" TJ sprang to a seated position. "You're going to leave him, right?"

She stood up to dress herself, trying to avoid answering. TJ leapt to his feet, standing in front of her, still naked. She took in his gorgeous form, shook her head and turned away, rushing to find her boots.

Grabbing her by the arm, he swung her around. "What is this?"

"It's complicated."

"No, it isn't. You either love me or you don't." He grasped both her arms, holding her still. "You think too much, Jo. What does your heart tell you?"

"I don't know!" she shouted, frozen in fear and unable to move. Her head spun in confusion. Brad, the film, her house in California, her friends, her career.

TJ kissed her forcibly.

"Stop it, TJ!" Josephine pulled away.

TJ gathered his clothes and quickly dressed then stood in front of her, his jaw locked, fists clenched and arms rigid at his sides. His beautiful eyes now raged with anger. Josephine trembled, not sure what he would do next.

"It's now or never, Jo. You leave him now, or I never want to see you again!"

Josephine's mouth opened but no words came. TJ stomped over to King, untied him and swung himself onto the black's back. And without another word, turned and galloped off.

How did this happen? What happened to her apologizing for how she broke it off? What happened to salvaging their friendship? She had ruined it all by giving into her lust. Or was it love? No matter now. It was over forever.

Josephine collapsed to the ground and cried.

11 – The Invitation

Elkhead, Montana

On a chilly November afternoon, Katherine sat in a lawn chair watching Jessie work Major over some gymnastics set up in the middle of the covered arena. It had been a mild fall that year, snow in the high country, but not in the valleys yet. She had another week before her cast came off and couldn't wait to work her boy herself again. Hopefully, the snow would hold off so she could get a few fun gallops in across the back field before it hit.

She decided to stay home through the winter to train for the FEI Show Jumping World Cup Final to be held in Las Vegas that spring. There, they would hopefully qualify to compete in either team or individual show jumping at the 2000 Olympics in Sydney. She often thought about Kayla and Joy and wondered if Erica put the mare up for sale when they returned or if the team would be competing in the spring as well. She chose not to return to the show grounds prior to her flight home from Winnipeg, fearing she'd run into Karen. Katherine had written Kayla twice over the past six weeks with no response.

"Take him through one more time at a trot and let's call it a day," Katherine called to Jessie.

"Will do."

Major looked good, fully enjoying the variety of combinations and striding. So long as he was jumping, he was happy. They kept up with his dressage training, which continued to improve his balance, suppleness and overall condition. Regardless of cross-country now being out of the picture, she had Jessie continue to work him out of the ring on the trails to maintain his endurance and keep him from getting ring sour. Show jumping courses at this level demanded a very conditioned animal to clear the high and challenging obstacles without faults and within the allotted time.

"Good day," said Jessie, as she walked by cooling Major out.

"Yes, he looked great. Thanks, Jess." Just as Katherine stood up, Steven entered the arena and approached her with what appeared to be the mail. He must have picked it up on the way home.

"Did I get a letter from Kayla?"

"Nothing from Florida, but do we know anyone in LA that's getting married?"

"Not that I know of," she said, then considered Roy's youngest daughter. "Maybe Melissa Higgins. Why?"

Steven thumbed through the letters, selecting one and holding it up. "Looks like a wedding invitation to me," he said, handing her the fancy square envelope sealed with a wax stamp.

"Can you open it for me?" She still had a difficult time doing such things with her cast.

Steven carefully opened the envelope and pulled the formal invitation from the glossy interior and handed it to her. When she opened it, she gasped! "What?!" Was she seeing this right? Katherine rushed out the door into the daylight. "Oh my God!"

Earning both Steven's and Jessie's curiosity, her husband chased after her on foot and Jessie quickly dismounted and joined them, Major in hand.

"What's going on?" asked Jessie.

"A wedding invitation," said Steven.

All eyes on the invitation in her hand, they anxiously awaited the news. Katherine finally let out the breath she had been holding since she saw the name on the invitation.

"Well, who's getting married?" demanded Jessie.

"Josephine!"

"What?" Steven seized the invitation from her hand to see for himself. "What the hell? Did she mention anything to you?"

It took Katherine a moment to reply, still in shock. "Not a word."

Steven shook his head, still studying the invitation as if it might be some kind mistake. "We're calling her now," he said, handing the invitation back to her and marching off toward the lodge.

"Brad, I presume," said Jessie.

"Yes. I'm just so stunned. She mentioned considering breaking it off with him in July."

"Why didn't she call? That's not like Jo."

"I better get up to the lodge in case Steven actually gets through to her."

"Please let me know what happens, will you?"

"Sure, Jess. You got Major?"

"Of course. Want him left in or out?"

"You can put him out with his blanket."

"Will do."

Jessie led Major toward the barn as Katherine strode up the drive. Jessie was right, this wasn't like Josephine. She hadn't spoken to her since they returned from wrapping up the film a few weeks ago. She had sounded tired and pressed for time, so their conversation was short.

Katherine glanced at the invitation again. In her surprise, she hadn't even looked at the date or location. Now she was truly concerned. The date read November twentieth at Two Ponies. That was in two weeks!

When she reached the lodge, Steven met her on the porch. "Had to leave a message."

"Something's wrong. Did you see the date?" She handed the invitation to him.

"What? And, at Two Ponies!" he screeched. "You think she would have run it by us first. And, what's the damn hurry?" Suddenly, he turned to her, their eyes locking.

Katherine swallowed hard. "Could she be pregnant?"

"You think?"

She just couldn't imagine Josephine not letting them know about a baby, or the marriage for that matter. Katherine hoped they had a better relationship than that. They seemed so close last visit. "There must be another explanation."

Following a quiet dinner, they waited anxiously by the phone in the library. Katherine sat in a deep, high-winged chair reading, which had a way of calming her, while Steven sat at the desk looking over his calendar. Work was his pacifier.

"Guess I better clear my schedule for that week. There will be plenty to do in preparation. I wonder how many guests are invited."

Katherine glanced up from her book. "I can't imagine too many with this short of notice."

"I'm sure she invited Roy and his family, and who knows how many from his side are coming." Steven shook his head for the hundredth time since they opened the invitation. "I still can't believe she didn't call us first."

Katherine jumped in her seat when the phone rang. She motioned to her husband that she wanted to answer the call. He got up to allow her to sit at the desk and pulled up a chair. Katherine held the phone receiver between them.

"Hi, Jo. Are you okay?"

"Sure, I've been meaning to call you," said Josephine.

"We were a bit shocked by the news."

"What news?"

"We received the wedding invitation today."

"Oh no, I'm so sorry. They weren't supposed to go out until Monday. I had Susan, my aid, helping me. I was going to call you tomorrow. It's okay we hold it at Two Ponies, right?"

"Sure it is, sweetie." Katherine glanced at her husband, his face a scrambled mess. He took the receiver from her. "Hi, honey, of course it's okay, but it would have been helpful to know sooner."

"I know, it's just been so crazy here. You happy for me?"

Katherine leaned in close to the receiver. "Of course we are, just it's all come as such a surprise."

"Brad asked me out of the blue." Silence, waiting for more. "We wanted to get married and go on our honeymoon before we start the next project."

Katherine and Steven gave each other a look of relief. "You hadn't mentioned anything new. What and where is your next film?"

"It's Brad's project, actually. He's going to be a guest on a few TV shows."

"Oh, what about you? Does Roy have another role for you?"

"Not yet. Maybe next year. I could use a little break."

Steven's eyes locked with hers again. Did that mean she is pregnant? Did she dare ask? "I guess that makes sense... anything else you want to tell us?"

"Isn't that enough? I'm getting married!"

Katherine had promised Josephine not to share her doubts about Brad with her father, so she couldn't ask directly. "Are you sure? It's all happening so fast."

"Yes, I'm sure. We'll be the next super couple."

"I thought you already were."

"I have to go, but I'll call you tomorrow to discuss the details."

Steven leaned in. "Can you tell us how many people are invited?"

"I'm not sure. I have to check with Brad, but it won't be many. I can let you know tomorrow."

"Okay, we love you," said Katherine. "We'll look forward to your call."

"Bye Mom, bye Dad."

Katherine set the receiver down and turned to her husband. "She would have told us, right?"

"I hope so." Steven stood up. "I'm going fishing."

"Be back in time for dinner at six," she called after him.

Steven always went fishing when he needed to think or relax. The lake for Steven was like the barn for her. Katherine grabbed a couple carrots, slipped on her coat and exited the side door. Some equine therapy was in order.

Malibu, California

Josephine closed her flip phone and set it down on her nightstand. She felt awful lying to her parents. Was omitting information really lying? It sure felt like it. She had no place she had to go, she just needed to get off the phone before she had to lie any more. Brad insisted they keep her condition a secret from family and friends, ultimately the press, until after the wedding. The thought of talking with them again the next day made her feel ill.

She laid on her side in a prenatal position staring out over the ocean, a view which no longer held the beauty or sense of accomplishment it once did. She had been spending a lot of time in bed lately. Brad was off with friends at some party, again. He tried to convince her to go, but since she learned she was pregnant she stopped drinking and didn't want to expose herself to smoke for the baby's sake. And perhaps more than that, she found herself avoiding Brad at every opportunity. He kept asking how she could have gotten pregnant using her IUD. She stuck to the same answer; it's not guaranteed one hundred percent effective. She was lying to him too, and to Roy… to everyone!

How did she get here? This is not how she envisioned her marriage and first pregnancy. She felt no excitement, no joy. Only fear. What would Brad do once he learned the baby wasn't his? There would be no question once the child was born. Would he choose to raise another man's child or leave her? She must admit it came as a surprise when he offered to marry her. It was a noble and selfless act, so unlike Brad. He must love her more than she realized. But was she capable of reciprocating his devotion? Did she truly love Brad? If so, how could she have cheated on him? Is it possible to love two men at the same time? Had she followed in her mother's footsteps? Did she make the right choice?

Josephine buried her head under her pillow, hoping to drown out the questions battering her conscience. She knew the answers all too well. She never stopped loving TJ. She hoped to come to love Brad as much someday. She had chosen her career and lifestyle over love. Josephine sat up and fished for the picture of TJ she now hid at the back of her nightstand drawer. She studied every detail of his handsome face; strong jaw, high cheek bones and mocha eyes framed by his long onyx hair. But without fail, once again a trail of tears streaked her cheeks as she felt the love and admiration he clearly felt for her as she snapped the image. He had looked at her the same way in Washington with unwavering devotion, even after she had broken his heart years earlier. But that was before it all unraveled. Josephine held the image to her heart. She wished she could tell him she loved him, that she was carrying their baby, that she would leave Brad and California to be with him. But it was too late now. In one weak moment of indecision, she had thrown it all away.

Browning, Montana

The small two-room house smelled of fried chicken. TJ was getting sick of chicken, now the only meat they could afford. Sadie's aunt raised the noisy fowl and she helped them out with all the meat and eggs they wanted. He had gotten a big mule deer buck during bow season but had given all the meat to his mother and grandparents. If he bagged an elk this month, it would fill both their freezers for the winter. But until then, chicken was it. Waiting for dinner, TJ sat staring at a black television screen. The TV set had quit working, and they didn't have the money to fix it either.

All of his portion of the race winnings went into a savings account for his education. Most of what he earned working at the same feed mill as his father had, went into the account as well. Sadie started working part-time at the mill too, to make ends meet in addition to her chores at Two Ponies, which had been cut back since their return from Winnipeg.

Sadie set his meal down in front of him on the coffee table. "Here you go. I don't understand why we can't buy a little beef or pork. You used to love my porkchops."

"You know why. I'm still short funds to return to school this winter." TJ qualified for a few scholarships and grants, which covered a good portion of his tuition, but not any of his housing and meals. He would take out a school loan if necessary. He needed to return to his studies soon to retain and apply what he had already learned.

Sadie returned to the kitchen, which was nothing more than a corner of the living area of the structure. "Well, if you'd swallow your silly pride and let your mom help you again, we wouldn't have to live like this. Maybe we could even move in with her at the ranch."

"There's more to it than that." TJ hadn't told Sadie the Walkers had paid for his education, not his mother. "Will you be getting more hours at Two Ponies? You know the mill will be laying people off for the winter soon."

Sadie sat beside him with her plate and began picking at her meal. "I don't know. I was looking forward to more travel pay, but now that Katherine's not training in California this winter, that's lost." Sadie made a stink face. "I don't understand why I couldn't have taken over Major's training until Kat's arm healed," she added, her voice sounding wounded and laced with jealously.

"You still help with his training like you did before, right?"

"Yeah. But it's mostly grooming and barn work. You'd think after four years, she'd trust me to ride him."

No sense in going there. Katherine and Jessie went way back, and he couldn't imagine Katherine trusting anyone besides Jessie with her horse's training. Best to change the subject. "Have you heard from Sally? Is she going to move back in after I leave for school?"

"Not sure. Depends on how things go with her new boyfriend."

"You should be able to find a roommate if she doesn't, right?"

"I suppose." Sadie drew a deep breath and sighed. "I just can't wait until you graduate and open your own clinic. Then we could get married."

This took TJ by surprise. He set his plate down. Is this the direction Sadie believed their relationship was heading? He had never led her on, never brought up a future together, let alone marriage. He had trouble thinking much past twenty-four hours most days, but it hadn't always been that way. When he and Josephine were together, he often thought about their future together. He envisioned living on his parent's ranch, the one his grandfather built and father worked, with Josephine and a family.

"You have nothing to say?" shrieked Sadie, rising to her feet. "You think I'm putting in all these tough times for nothing? I'm not going to wait forever you know." She stormed out the door without a coat.

Perhaps she had a point. They had been dating, or whatever you want to call it, for three years now. Josephine was gone forever. TJ hesitantly joined her, sitting beside her on the top stair. He put his arm around her shivering shoulders.

"Come inside, you're freezing." She gave him a wounded glance. "I can't look ahead of finishing school right now. I have to stay focused."

Sadie stared off across the prairie. "You are over her, right?"

TJ wasn't about to go another round with Sadie over Josephine. But he supposed he needed to give her something. "Yes, it's over." He could give her that much.

"I'm sorry, I didn't mean to pressure you." She turned with a hopeful expression. Oh boy, here it comes. "But it sure would be nice to hear you say you love me, just once."

Silence.

"You do love me, don't you, TJ?"

Love. TJ didn't know what that was anymore. His heart felt as empty as a dry well, void of any emotion or life-sustaining force.

Josephine had numbed his heart, stolen his dreams and erased his future. TJ gave her a squeeze and kissed her. He chose to be with her, that was all he could give her for now. She seemed to accept that as an answer and led him back into the house to share their bed.

TJ woke to rapping on the front door. He gently slid Sadie's arm from around his chest and slipped out of bed. On the way to the door, he pulled on his jeans. Talon stood on the porch with his hands in his pockets.

"What do you want? It's early, Sunday is my only day off," he said before realizing the sun told him it was closer to noon than daybreak.

"I ran into your old lady this morning at the post office. She said she needs to see you."

"About what?"

"She didn't say. But it sounded important."

TJ hadn't been by the ranch since he returned from Washington, the longest he'd been away from home since he moved out. "Okay, I'll go see her today. Thanks for stopping by. Want some coffee? I can warm up a cup."

Talon shook his head. "No thanks. Me and the guys are heading up to the sacred grounds. Matt and Noot have gotten hooked on sweat lodge ceremonies. You smoke then sweat. Clears the head and cleanses the body, so the old man that performs the ceremony says. It's pretty cool. You want to join us?"

"Not this time. Maybe some other time."

"See ya later."

TJ closed the door and found Sadie awake and studying him while lying on her side in bed.

"Talk to your mom, please. Let her help out."

He needed to end this. "There is no savings or insurance money!"

"Okay, you don't have to get pissy. Why didn't you tell me you spent it all?"

TJ left it at that. Let her think what she wants. It doesn't matter. "Can we drop it now?"

Sadie shrugged her shoulders. "Sure, come back to bed."

"Think I'll head over now."

"Oh, okay," she sulked.

TJ pulled on a shirt and socks and grabbed his boots to put on out on the porch. "See you later."

He wasn't in the mood for any more questions. He needed to find out what his mother so desperately needed to tell him.

TJ found her hanging clothes in the laundry room. She gave him a disapproving look. "Talon said you needed to see me. Are Grandmother and Grandfather okay?"

Sarah hung the last of the garments on hangers. He followed his mother into the living room where she motioned for him to take a seat.

"I have to get something," she said, leaving for the kitchen. A moment later she returned with an envelope, sat beside him and handed it to him.

"What's this?"

His mother just nodded in the direction of the envelope. TJ opened it and pulled out its contents, a card with fancy lettering, another envelope and a smaller card. He glanced over it until his eyes rested on the name Josephine Walker, then he read closer scooting to the edge of his seat. "Wedding? A wedding invitation? Jo's getting married?" He continued to stare at the name Brad Donahue in disbelief.

"Appears that way. I thought you'd want to know."

TJ flung the card on the coffee table. "At least she had the decency not to invite me."

"I'm sorry, son. It was bound to happen sooner or later."

He couldn't say a word, his mind replaying his last words to Josephine. What did he expect? Now more than ever, he needed to hold on to the only other thing he loved, besides Jo and his family. He looked into his mother's painful eyes. "Don't sell. I'm close to having enough money to return next semester. I'll take out a school loan if I have to."

"Too late now anyway with winter coming on. Can't sell a place up here this time of year." She smiled. "I'm glad you're returning."

TJ relaxed back into the couch. "You doing okay?"

"I'm good. My paintings sold well over the summer. We'll get by on the venison and our government checks through the winter. Thanks again for the meat."

"I'll get us an elk soon." TJ offered a sincere smile as he placed a hand on her shoulder. "Just two more years and I'll be able to take care of you and Grandmother and Grandfather."

Sarah clasped his hand and returned his smile. It was good to feel her touch and smile upon him again. It had been a while.

"You need to meet a girl, TJ," she said. "A nice local girl you can share your life with."

He wished she hadn't gone there. TJ hadn't told her about Sadie and didn't intend to for now. His mother still thought he was living with the guys. Besides, there was nothing to tell. He just nodded. "Going to grab a couple things from my room."

"You hungry? I can make you something."

"I'm good, thanks."

TJ left her sitting on the sofa, looking the most content he'd seen her in a long time. He jogged upstairs to his room. His mother hadn't touched a thing since he attended high school. Wrestling trophies collected dust on his shelves, pictures of Josephine lay scattered and pinned to the walls. He picked one up off his dresser. An ache as deep and dark as the densest forest in the dead of winter came over him, his body turning numb. He had to sit on his bed before he fell to the floor. How could this be? His Jo married to someone else. In the back of his head, he had harbored a flicker of hope that they still might make up, put the past behind them and start fresh. Now he could only look forward to returning to school and losing himself in his studies again.

He collected all the photos of Josephine and tossed them in the trash basket, all but the one. He studied the image again, a picture of the two of them ready to set out on what would be their last weekend camping trip into the mountains together. He had suffered through most of the stages of loss with Josephine, just as he had with the death of his father; shock, denial, pain, guilt, anger and now depression. Would he ever find closure and peace?

TJ retrieved his medicine bag from the back of his closet and opened it. The sack contained mementos he'd collected since his father gave him the leather pouch on his tenth birthday. Adorned with beads and feathers, his father had instructed him to fill the bag with objects that represented the important things in life; love, happiness, pride, and honor. He emptied its contents onto the floor; an acorn Josephine gave him when they were toddlers, a tooth knocked out in a fight defending one of his smaller Blackfeet friends as a boy, a lock of tail hair from his first pony, a medal he won in wrestling, and the note his father had written him the night before he died. He picked it up and read it for the umpteenth time.

Dear TJ,
I'm sorry you're having to read this, son. Be strong, and don't be sad. I lived a good life. You were the best part. I know you will take care of your mother. Pursue your dreams and don't be afraid to reach for the stars. I'm so proud of the man you have become and wish you much happiness and peace in your life. Love you, Dad (Get a big buck for me this year.)

TJ folded the note and returned it, along with the photo of Josephine and the other objects, back into the medicine bag. He glanced at the calendar on the wall. Saturday, November twentieth would be a dark day. The day he would lose his "star" forever.

Ever has it been that love knows not its own depth

until the hour of separation.

~ Kahlil Gibran

The weak can never forgive.

Forgiveness is the attribute of the strong.

~ Mahatma Gandhi

A very great vision is needed

and the person who has it must follow it

as the eagle seeks the deepest blue of the sky.

~ Chief Crazy Horse

Sometimes that small glimmer of inner strength

is all that we have to help us press forward through the darkness.

~ Morgan Rhodes

PART TWO

AFTER

12 – Wedding Day

Browning, Montana

A trail of dust followed TJ's truck as he drove up a gravel road to the highest point on the Reservation. Sacred land, he had been told. This would be his first sweat lodge ceremony, but he recalled his father telling him about his experience attending one as a young man. He claimed it helped him through a difficult time in his life. Perhaps that's why he finally gave in to Talon and the guys to attend one. Considering Josephine's wedding that weekend, he could use some spiritual guidance.

When the road ended, he found only one other vehicle, and it wasn't Matt's Dodge truck. An old, rusty paneled station wagon appeared to be packed full of someone's soul possessions; blankets, pots and pans, canned goods, dry goods and clothing strewn about haphazardly. A small mutt barked at the end of a tether tied to a trailer hitch at the back of the vehicle.

TJ checked his watch. He was supposed to meet the guys there twenty minutes ago. A last-minute delivery at the feed store caused him to run late. It seemed unlikely the guys would have given up on him and left so soon after having badgered him for days to join them this Friday. Just as he backed out to leave, an ancient looking Blackfeet man appeared on the trailhead, his face a cavernous map of time. He wore a traditional Blackfeet deerskin outfit adorned with paint and beads, complete with a headdress. A woven blanket rested over his shoulders. TJ pulled back into the same parking spot and stepped out of the cab. The little rat-like dog wiggled like a wet noodle with its tail wagging so fast it looked mechanical, as the man approached. The smell of burning cedar filled his senses. He followed the scent to a spiral of smoke rising above the treetops a short distance away, sparks dancing like stars into the darkening sky.

"You, TJ Black Feather?"

"Yes, that's right. Where are the others?"

"Just you," he said, waving for him to follow. "Come."

Shrugging his shoulders, TJ followed the elder along a path leading to the fire burning in a small open area atop the hill. Not far from the fire sat a domed structure covered with blankets and a tepee. The old man took a seat on a log beside the fire, pulling the blanket more snuggly around his shoulders.

"Sit," he said, pointing to another log across from him.

TJ followed his instructions. The temperature had dropped at least ten degrees since he left Sadie's and the fire felt good. "You know I was supposed to meet…"

"You listen," interrupted the man. "My name Walking Man. I used to walk, now I'm old. I drive. I am leader of ceremony and keeper of sacred pipe. I knew your father. Great warrior, born too late in this world. You look like him. Strong, maybe carry demons like him, too."

Who was this guy? TJ wanted to ask about Matt, Noot and Talon, but sensed he wouldn't get an answer if he tried. Had they arranged all this? Talon had expressed his concern over his apparent blues lately. Had he been set up?

Walking Man focused on the dancing flames, as if they were speaking to him. "Universe, full of good and evil spirits. 'Sun Power' source of all power everywhere," he said, motioning with his arms to include their surroundings. "The mountains, lakes, rivers, birds, wild animals. This power can be given to the people."

Reaching to the sky, he continued. "Creator, 'Nah-doo-si,' comes first. Without Creator, we are nothing. No person, beings, laws above Creator. We pray to Creator now. Words of thanks for beauty of earth, sky, family, health, all life. Then we pray to 'Holy Spirits.' The Grandfathers and Grandmothers, the 'Naahks,' animals, plants, rocks, who work for Creator, so they pity us and answer our prayers."

Walking Man reached behind the log for a drum, rose to his feet and began chanting as he beat the stretched hide with his hands. He danced around the fire, speaking in Algonquian, the native language of the Blackfeet. TJ no longer cared where the guys were, totally captivated by the old man's song of prayer that had survived hundreds of years, passed down from generation to generation by spiritual leaders. It felt somehow comforting to make a connection with his people. TJ joined in, mimicking the old man's steps imagining himself as a young warrior preparing for battle. But instead of fighting for their land, horses and families, he was battling to survive the loss of the love of his life. Suddenly, Walking Man sat down again and replaced the drum with a pipe. TJ once again sat across from him. The elder reached into the fire with a twig until the end caught on fire, then held the flame over the pipe and drew a deep breath until the contents of the pipe smoldered and a thin ribbon of smoke rose into the cold night air. He passed the pipe to TJ, with an exhale.

"Sacred pipe, gift given to people by Creator, holds greatest power. Smoking holy pipe, we find truth."

TJ drew a deep breath, copying the old man's draw. Heat and smoke filled his lungs, making him cough uncontrollably. He noticed the slightest grin deepen the creases of the old man's face. As they passed the sacred pipe between them a few more times, TJ was careful not to drag on the pipe as deep.

Walking Man set the pipe down and nodded in the direction of the hut. "Sweat lodge, another gift from Creator to people. Like our body gets unclean and needs a bath, our spirit needs cleansing too."

"Everything sacred, rocks in fire," he said, pointing to the seven stones within the U-shaped fire pit. Walking Man led him to the opening of the lodge. "Sage for floor, willows for the frame, all sacred." Again, he gestured with his arms in a round, sweeping motion. "Lodge shape of woman with child on her back, gazing up to heavens. Enter womb of Mother Earth," he said.

Inside, it was dark. "Take off clothes," instructed the old man.

After TJ stripped, he motioned for him to sit down on a rug beside a round pit in the earth. Walking Man left and returned with a shovel full of hot rocks. He lit a candle and closed the entryway of the lodge with a flap. TJ watched as the old man sprinkled cedar chips on the rocks and splashed the hot stones with medicine water. As the lodge filled with steam, TJ could feel the pores of his skin open and tingle with life. Walking Man shed his blanket and sat on it. Following more singing and praying to the Creator and Mother Earth, he brought more stones, again dousing them with water. Without a word, he blew out the candle and walked from the lodge, closing the flap behind him. TJ sat naked in total darkness.

He breathed in slowly to keep his lungs from overheating. He felt lightheaded and closed his eyes. What was in that pipe, anyway? In his mind, the dancing flames of the fire outside the lodge came into focus. TJ didn't dare open his eyes for fear of losing the vision. He could hear Walking Man chanting to the rhythmic beat of the drum once again. In the light of the fire, another image appeared, the vision of a man sitting across from him. At first, the man's face was not clear, but slowly it came into focus. It was his father!

"Dad," whispered TJ. "I miss you so much." TJ pressed his eyes shut tighter, holding on to the image of his lost father. "I wish you were here. I need you."

His father's hand made a fist and he drew it to his chest. "Follow your heart, son."

Slowly the vision faded into darkness. Billy Black Feather was gone. TJ felt his heart sink. "Come back… please," he whispered, opening his eyes to the dark, empty space. TJ was shocked to see another image forming right before his eyes, coming in and out of focus like a mirage – the torso of a woman with her back to him. Long red tresses fell between her bare shoulders. He didn't need to see her face, he knew who it was.

"Why, Jo," he asked, "why are you marrying him?"

She turned slowly, tears streaming from her aquamarine eyes. He reached out to the vision as it vaporized.

"Come back, Jo," he begged, sweat burning his eyes, or was it tears? He wiped them away with his hands, searching the darkness for answers.

TJ closed his eyes and lowered his head. He couldn't take any more. This is not what he had hoped to find. No peace, no enlightenment, only the pain of his losses did he find here. Just as he began to rise to his feet, the drumming intensified, and the old man's chanting morphed into what sounded more like cries of a wolf. Visions of lightning flashed about the interior of the lodge like strobe lights. He heard a woman's scream. Josephine! In an instant, all went black and silent.

Disoriented, it took TJ a few minutes to locate his clothes and find the exit in the dark. When he pushed open the flap, he found it dark out and the fire extinguished. Only the light of a half-moon revealed Walking Man was gone. TJ shook his head in disbelief. He had just heard the drum beating! How could the old man have left so soon? Had he imagined it? Was it a part of his vision? He had so many questions for the spiritual leader. Confused, TJ dried the sweat from his body with his shirt and slipped into his jeans and boots. He didn't feel the cold evening air against his bare chest as he ran to the parking area. He found the old station wagon and dog gone. TJ slid behind the wheel of his truck, still feeling not quite himself. He felt drained yet revived. Suddenly, the messages of his visions became clear and new-found purpose pulsated through his veins. His father's words, "follow your heart," echoed through his mind. His heart was Josephine… and Josephine needed him. She was in some sort of danger and he needed to warn her.

Elkhead, Montana

Josephine studied her profile in her mother's full-length mirror that had been moved to Betsy's old room behind the kitchen. She tried to imagine what she would look like in a few months when she could no longer hide her pregnancy. This room had been designated as her preparation room prior to the wedding that afternoon. Her rather simple, white, knee-length and long sleeve sheath dress hung on the door of Betsy's old wardrobe closet. White pumps sat beside the bed and a modest veil lay across the bedspread. Her mother would do her hair later, nothing too fancy, just pulled back to a spree of baby's breath where the veil would attach.

In three hours, the ceremony would be held in the great room where her father had replaced all their furniture with several rows of rented white folding chairs to seat the thirty or so guests. Roy had flown her and his wife, Sandy, to Montana yesterday morning in the Cessna in time to pick up Brad, his parents and his best man, Peter Martin, at the airport that afternoon with a rental van. Lisa and her family arrived two days ago to help with the preparations. Betsy's brothers and their families, Jessie and Dane, their son and parents, Chief, Flo and their kids, as well as Sarah were also invited. Everyone she knew intimately and loved would be there… all but two – Betsy and TJ. Betsy, she felt certain would be there in spirit, but she wondered what TJ would be doing today.

Lisa would be her matron of honor, Lizzy their flower girl, and Jessie's boy, Cole, their ring bearer. The ceremony would take place in front of the stone wall containing the great room fireplace, now adorned with white drapes decorated with wildflowers. Bouquets of more shipped-in out-of-season wildflowers stood on stands flanking the fireplace. Roy offered to bring his camera to take a few photos.

As she ran her fingers over a lace sleeve of her dress, she allowed herself to indulge in a fantasy, imagining it would be TJ exchanging vows with her that day. It would be a very different day, full of joy and anticipation instead of this, whatever this was... settling, avoiding reality, the cliché making lemonade out of lemons came to mind. Yes, she had doubts, but it was too late to back out now. Everything was set in motion and she was along for the ride.

Speaking of a ride, she walked into the kitchen and glanced out the window. She had hoped to go for a spin on Bonanza that morning to help her relax but the weather wasn't cooperating. The rain had stopped, but more was expected soon. The sky continued to darken with thunderstorms in the forecast for that afternoon. Perfect weather for an unperfect wedding. What did her great uncle call it in one of his Westerns? A "shotgun" wedding. That was it. At least any severe winter weather had held off, but today's storm would be ushering in a cold front later that day, turning the rain to snow. She wouldn't get the chance to ride before she left, but she did have time for a short visit with her sweet boy before she had to start getting ready.

Some of their house guests remained in the dining room following a late breakfast, others congregated in the great room and library, including Brad and his parents. Josephine grabbed a couple carrots out of the fridge, slipped on one of her mother's barn jackets and snuck out the door. The moment she exited the lodge, she wished she had chosen a warmer coat, but she wouldn't be out long. She jogged down the stairs and walked briskly to the main barn, bypassing Snickers and Blackjack at the old stable, who were inside finishing their breakfast. The horses in the main barn remained in their stalls in anticipation of the storm. Josephine broke the first carrot in half and gave one section to Major and the other to Dandy. Bonanza stood at his stall door looking betrayed.

"Don't worry, Bo Bo, I have a whole carrot for you." As she approached his stall, she broke the carrot into a few pieces. The gelding raised his head, ears pricked forward.

As soon as the stall door opened enough for Bonanza to fit his handsome head through, he searched her hands, wiggling his lips in anticipation. Josephine fed him one piece at a time. When he finished the last bite, Bonanza nuzzled her hand for more.

"That's all I have for now, big boy."

Once he was certain no more treats were coming his way, he returned to his hay. Josephine stood at his shoulder, grabbed mane and took a quick step and jumped onto her belly over his back. Pushing off his withers and back, she swung her right leg over and around the Quarter Horse's round barrel. Josephine patted his neck. It had been years since she mounted him bareback in his stall like that, but the gentle Buckskin had stood perfectly still like it had been yesterday. He was what her mother called "bombproof." In all the years they owned Bonanza, he had never spooked at anything.

Josephine took a deep breath in through her nose, filling her senses with the smell of hay, shavings and horse. As she slowly exhaled, she could feel her anxiety seep out every pore. It had been a stressful couple of weeks. She scooted back a little, but not so far that she would be sitting on his kidneys, leaned forward and wrapped her arms around his warm, fuzzy neck. Her mother had mentioned they had a lovely fall, by Montana high-country standards, but the horses' winter coats had grown in over the past few days. A sure sign freezing temperatures would soon be upon them. Closing her eyes, she recalled the day her mother had surprised her with the beautiful four-year-old honey-gold gelding for her fourteenth birthday. They had been a great team, winning many barrel races and speed and action events with her high-school gymkhana team. All her friends in California had never heard of gymkhana events. Those who grew up riding, competed on well-bred and expensive Thoroughbreds and warmbloods in Hunter and Jumper classes or Saddle Seat on Arabians, Morgans or Saddlebreds at breed shows. Those that did own Quarter Horses, showed Western Pleasure. Barrel racing had been her favorite event and she still cherished the buckles she had earned, now packed away in her closet at Two Ponies. She had always imagined wearing a pair of fancy cowboy boots to her wedding. She laughed to herself now, picturing what Brad and his parents' reaction would be to that sight.

The temperatures felt like they had already started to drop, but

Bonanza's warmth radiated through her. She continued along her nostalgic journey, recalling some of her favorite times with horses at Two Ponies. Of course, this invited TJ back into her thoughts. Since they were kids, they rode their spunky, and oftentimes naughty ponies, together; playing tag or riding through obstacle courses they designed out of whatever they could get their hands on. Later came their rides together on Bonanza and Cisco, some of her most treasured teenage memories. Their last summer together trail riding and camping in the mountains topped her favorites list.

Suddenly, Bonanza raised his head, alerted to something outside the barn door. Josephine opened her eyes and sat up. In the barn door opening stood a man standing tall, his masculine shape silhouetted in the ambient light. She squinted as her eyes adjusted. The shape moved toward her.

"Hi, Jo," he said. She recognized the voice immediately. TJ!

She slid off Bonanza's back and slipped out of the stall. After latching the door, she turned and was shocked to find him standing within inches of her face. She stepped back.

"TJ, what a surprise…" This was the last person she expected to see today. She couldn't think of another word to say. He wore his hair tied back and a tight shirt clung to his well-defined chest. She didn't dare look any lower. Instead, she fumbled with Bonanza's halter hanging on the front of his stall, pretending to straighten it.

"I needed to see you," he said.

"Did you go to the lodge?"

"No. I thought I might find you here."

Thank goodness. That might have gotten complicated depending on who answered the door. Josephine swallowed hard. "You shouldn't be here," she mumbled, TJ's deep gaze caught in her throat. The tension building between them felt like a thunderhead about to burst recalling their romp in the grass at the lake, but she managed to squeak out, "I'm getting married today."

"I know."

"I couldn't invite you," she added, a few octaves lower.

"I know."

Was that all he could say? "You said you needed to see me?"

"Can we sit a moment?"

Her curiosity built as she led them through the tack room and into the barn office where she sat at one end of the couch, perched on the edge of her seat. TJ sat at the other end, facing her. Josephine avoided making eye contact, afraid those bottomless brown pools of his would pull her in again.

TJ started quiet and slow. "I had a vision."

This piqued her interest and she gave him a glance.

"I saw my dad. He spoke to me."

Okay, he had her. She turned toward him, making eye contact. "What did he say?"

"He told me to follow my heart."

An inner battle began, she fought to maintain control of her emotions. She knew where he was going, but perhaps she could derail him. "You are, TJ. You're well on your way to becoming a vet."

"My heart is here with you, Jo." And before she could object, TJ rambled on, his words coming faster and faster as if racing toward a finish line. "Jo, don't marry this guy. Don't rush into something. I'm sorry about what I said – all that now or never bullshit. I'll wait, no matter how long it takes. We need to give us another chance. We were meant to be together." TJ finally took a breath. "You can't tell me what happened in Washington didn't mean something. I haven't been able to put you out of my mind and I have a feeling it's been the same for you. Tell me I'm wrong."

Josephine squirmed in her seat, turning her focus to her hands in her lap. "It's too late, TJ."

"You look me in the eyes and tell me you don't love me."

She slowly raised her focus to meet his intense gaze. She couldn't say it and she wouldn't lie, not to TJ. "I can't."

TJ scooted closer and took her hand, studying her engagement ring. "He doesn't love you as much as I do. No man ever will."

Josephine took a deep breath and rose to her feet. "I'm getting married in three hours," she said, trying to conceal the panic growing within her with a firm tone, but the quiver in her voice said otherwise. "You need to leave."

In an instant, TJ was holding her by the arms, her body shook uncontrollably attempting to resist the heat building between them. It was like fighting the gravitational pull of the universe.

"Call it off. Please," he pled.

Before she could find her voice, TJ kissed her. She tried to pull away, but he held her fast. Just as she began to melt into his arms, a male voice startled them both.

"Jo, you out here?"

TJ broke off their kiss, but still held her firmly, his eyes fixed on hers, begging.

Josephine wiggled free and stepped into the tack room. TJ followed her. Suddenly, Brad stood at the tack room door. Josephine froze as TJ and Brad surveyed each other.

"Mother warned it was bad luck to speak to the bride the day of the wedding. But we need to make some decisions about the honeymoon. It can't wait."

"Jo?" said TJ, desperately.

Her silence was answer enough. TJ brushed past them both. She wanted to chase after him, but her legs wouldn't move. She watched him stride by the office window and heard gravel fly against the exterior of the barn.

"Pretty disrespectful, if you ask me," said Brad. She had almost forgotten he was standing there. "My family always demanded the utmost respect from their staff."

Josephine turned and studied Brad. Anger rose is her throat, nearly choking her. "He's not an employee!"

"Okay, I get it, your help is like family… like the Indian woman."

"Betsy!"

"Right. C'mon, we need to figure out which Hawaiian Islands we want to hop. Mother says Maui, Kauai and Oahu are a must." Brad stepped closer and took her hand. "You're shaking." Brad's eyes narrowed. "Who was that guy?"

Josephine stood frozen, trying to answer that question for herself; an old friend, once her best friend, her first love? It didn't take Brad long to figure it out for himself. "Oh, I see. That was that old boyfriend of yours, wasn't it? What is he doing here? Today of all days!" Brad's voice escalated. "I can't believe you were ever with that guy! What is it about you and your family? Don't you know you're above the likes of that trash?"

"Trash?!"

"Damn straight."

Josephine pushed past him, stomped straight to Bonanza's stall, grabbed his halter, slipped it on, and once again jumped onto his back.

Brad blocked the opening. "What are you doing?" A look of panic replaced his cocky expression. "I'm sorry, baby. I didn't mean…"

"Move!" she screamed. When he reached for the halter, she kicked Bonanza hard, pushing Brad out of the way and nearly to the floor as they leapt from the stall. All she could think was she needed to get away; away from Brad, away from the wedding, away from her ridiculous future with such a man! What was she thinking? That was it, she had been thinking too much and not feeling enough. She must find TJ. Now hysterical, tears running down her face, she galloped past the lodge and onto the trail leading to the creek without looking back. The creek led to TJ's ranch. Hopefully, he would be there.

Brad stomped back to the lodge. What the hell was going on? Why was that guy here? Why did Josephine get so upset over nothing? By the time he reached the stairs he had convinced himself that his bride would come to her senses, return and the wedding would proceed as planned. It had to! All the press they had received announcing their marriage had put them in the headlines and on the covers of all the prominent celebrity magazines. They would be the hottest couple in Hollywood. There was no way he would allow her to ruin everything. Besides, she didn't have a choice with the baby and all. She would be back; the wedding would take place.

Before he could open the side door, Mrs. Walker exited the lodge. "What's going on? We saw Jo ride by. What is she doing? The wedding is in less than three hours."

"We had a little spat, nothing really. I'm sure she'll be back soon."

"I don't think you know Jo as well as you think you do. I'm going to see if I can find her."

"Don't say anything to my parents, okay? No need upsetting them for no reason. She'll be back soon. I'm sure of it."

She just turned and reentered the lodge, he guessed to change clothes. Brad took a seat at the picnic table where he could keep an eye on the trailhead. It had started to rain again. Moments later, Mrs. Walker reappeared dressed to ride, wearing a slicker, and strode past him without a word. Brad checked his watch. It read ten-thirty.

A fine drizzle turned to a heavy rain as Josephine rode toward a darkening sky. Thankfully, Bonanza handled effortlessly with just a halter and lead rope, having been trained to neck rein and move off her leg. Nearly blinded by the downpour, she strained to navigate her mount around low branches and bends in the trail. Soaked to the skin, Bonanza's body kept her lower torso warm, but her upper body ached from the cold, her hands especially, so cold she could hardly feel the lead in one hand and mane in the other. She didn't contemplate turning back, having abandoned all reason. All that registered was the need to find TJ.

It didn't take long at a gallop to reach the creek. Bonanza followed her direction through the shallow stream, around boulders and over small fallen trees, but the further she went, the more the forest closed in on the tributary. It had been years since she last rode the creek to the Black Feather's ranch and some large unpassable trees had fallen, forcing her to ride inland around the obstacles. The going was slow as the storm intensified with gusts topping thirty miles an hour, she estimated. Looming pine trees swayed above her. In the distance, she could hear thunder and see lightning strikes. Josephine pushed Bonanza on faster, praying the electrical storm would miss them.

TJ arrived at the family ranch just as the storm hit. His mother convinced him to stay until it passed. While he waited, he went upstairs to collect more of his clothing. Out of frustration, he threw items on the bed, slammed drawers and kicked his closet door shut. He never even got the chance to warn Josephine about his other vision. He tried to convince himself she was no longer his concern. She belonged to another now.

When he returned downstairs, Sarah sat waiting for him. "What happened?"

She must have heard him banging things around upstairs. "I went to see Jo."

"Oh," she said.

"I shouldn't have gone."

"You did what you felt you needed to do. Perhaps now you can get on with your life." Just hearing her say those words, brought tears to his eyes.

"I don't know how to, Mom!" He hated it when he cried. He wiped his face. "I still love her. I thought she still loved me. I didn't tell you, but when we raced in Browning, she came to watch me. And when we were in Washington, I arranged to see her. We…" His mother's eyes widened, fully understanding. "I thought she'd leave him. I told her she must, that it was now or never."

"I'm so sorry, TJ," she whispered, reaching for his hand.

"I pushed her into his arms."

"No, Son. She had already made her choice."

"But why would she fly back to see me? How could she be with me if she loved him?"

"Love can be complicated. Life can be too."

"It isn't for me. I know what I want. I know who I love."

"That's what makes you special. That's how it should be, but some people want too much and when you want too much, you end up having to sacrifice something."

"Like me."

Katherine rode the lake trail to the old hunting cabin where she hoped Josephine might have sought shelter. Finding it empty, she returned to the lodge where she found the parking area full of vehicles, and her husband sitting at the picnic table in place of the groom. Josephine had not returned. When they closed the side door behind them, several voices emanating from the great room hushed. She slipped off her boots and peeked in at the kitchen clock. It read eleven-thirty. It was time to inform their guests the wedding would be delayed. Laddy trotted to meet her in the dining room, followed by Brad.

"I didn't find her. Let's step into the kitchen," said Katherine. Brad hesitantly followed her and Steven. "You need to tell us exactly what happened."

Rather cavalier, he said, "We had a disagreement, that's all." Then going on the defensive, added, "I can't imagine what got into her, riding off like that on our wedding day, in a storm no less and for no reason."

Steven stepped in front of Brad, inches from his face. "Jo wouldn't have done this for no reason. What did you do?"

Katherine wedged herself between the two men, facing Brad. "How was she dressed?"

"She had a jacket on, jeans, tennis shoes."

"We'll have to postpone the wedding and pray she returns soon," she said. "Until then, we need to inform our guests."

"I'm going to join my parents and Peter upstairs. I'll let them know," said Brad. The groom calmly headed for the stairs, then turned and added. "Please keep us posted," before disappearing around the corner.

Steven was steaming. "He didn't even offer to help search for her!"

Katherine rested her hand on his arm. "C'mon, let's get this over with." She hung her slicker on the coat rack by the door and followed her husband into the great room. The whispering which had resumed, ceased once again. The concern written across their friends' and family's faces said volumes.

"I'm sorry to inform you, the wedding will be delayed," said Katherine. "Josephine got upset and went for a ride and hasn't returned."

The room filled with gasps and murmuring between the guests. Roy and Mike sprang up from their seats to join them at the front of the room.

"In this weather?" Roy said under his breath. "What's going on?" He directed his questions to them both, but Steven answered.

"Lovers' quarrel. Kat already rode out to the cabin. She wasn't there. If she's not back soon, we'll split up and search the rest of the property."

"Should I call my squad?" said Mike. Dane joined them.

"Let's give her another thirty minutes," said Katherine.

"It's pretty nasty out there," said Dane. "And temps are dropping."

"Thirty minutes," reiterated Steven.

The three men glanced at the grandfather clock and returned to their seats.

"I'll put some food out in the dining room," said Katherine to Steven. "Let everyone know."

Katherine rushed to the kitchen, glancing out every window on the way, hoping to see Josephine ride up. She pulled the sandwich plates out of the refrigerator and set some more sodas out.

Lisa joined her. "I'm so worried, Mom. It's awful out there. She'll come down with something for sure. Did they have a fight?"

Katherine turned toward her. "Yes."

"About what?"

"Brad isn't saying." Katherine reached into the refrigerator.

"I think I know."

Katherine stopped what she was doing, giving Lisa her full attention.

"When I was in the kitchen earlier, I saw a truck parked out by the barn."

"What make, what color?"

"It was a Chevy, I think. Red."

"Oh my God. TJ was here!"

"I thought, maybe."

Now things were starting to make sense. "Take these out," she said to Lisa, handing her some condiments. "I'm getting to the bottom of this."

Guests were already filing into the dining room as Katherine swept around them and up the stairs. She found Brad and his guests seated in the loft sitting room overlooking the great room.

"Excuse me," she said to Mr. and Mrs. Donahue, "I need to speak with Brad." They just shook their heads. She led him into Josephine's room and closed the door.

"Okay, I know TJ was here, Lisa saw his truck. What happened? I want to know everything this time."

"I went to the barn looking for Jo. She was in the tack room with this Indian guy. I didn't know it was her old boyfriend at first. I thought he was some ranch hand."

"Did you hear anything they said to one another?"

"He said her name… like a question, expecting an answer. When she didn't answer, he left. I said some things… I probably shouldn't have. But do you blame me, meeting with him on our wedding day? She got upset and rode off. I tried to stop her but she damn near ran me over."

Without another word, Katherine turned and left him standing there. She could only guess what was said between TJ, Josephine and Brad, but it was enough to cause her daughter to abandon their wedding and ride off into a storm. She could just imagine how upset and scared she must be, running out on everyone and afraid to come back. As she passed Brad's parents, she informed them the wedding was cancelled. They didn't look too surprised as they looked down their noses at her with superiority.

When she returned to the dining room, all eyes and ears were on her. "I'm afraid the wedding is off," she said, raising many questions from their guests. Katherine raised her index finger, asking everyone to be silent. She took a deep breath while she gathered her thoughts. "As you may have already guessed, there was a lovers' quarrel. But our biggest concern at the moment is finding Josephine and returning her home safe. We will form a search party and inform you all as soon as we find her.

Steven joined her and rested his hand on her shoulder and added, "We're so sorry."

Katherine placed her hand over his with a squeeze. "We love you all. Please drive carefully. House guests, please make yourselves comfortable. Volunteers and suggestions are welcome."

Mike stepped up first. "I'll have my men cruise the surrounding roads. I'll head out myself. Should we reach out to Search and Rescue?"

"Thanks, Mike, not yet," said Steven patting him on the back.

"I'm going to drive to the station and get the dogs," said Dane. "Hopefully, we won't need them by the time I get back." Dane grabbed his coat and rushed out the door.

Jessie stepped up holding little Cole's hand. "I'd ride with you if

I could."

Lisa squeezed in between the men. "You go, Jess. Daniel and I can watch the kids."

"Have something I can change into? A coat, boots, slicker?" questioned Jessie.

"Sure," said Katherine.

"You still have the four-wheeler?" asked Roy.

"Sure do. I can outfit you as well," said Steven.

Chief limped up. "I'm afraid I won't be much help." They had just learned he was scheduled for hip replacement surgery next month.

"Get Flo and the kids home before this the rain turns to ice or snow," said Steven. "We've got it covered. We'll let you know when we find her."

Chief shook Steven's hand and patted Katherine on the back. "Good luck. We'll be praying for her safe return."

Steven turned to the volunteers. "Ok, here's the plan. I'll ride the lake trail to the south, Roy, you cover the north side. Jessie, you check out the front and back pastures on Black Jack. Kat, how about you search the hunting cabin again and the old girls' cabins."

"Sounds good," said Katherine. While she outfitted Jessie, Steven did the same for himself and Roy. When everyone met back at the side door, their day guests had left. She could hear Lisa, Daniel and the kids playing in the library. Roy's wife, Flo, and their family were still seated in the dining room. She guessed that Brad and his guests took their meals upstairs to eat. Katherine handed everyone a slicker, a blanket and an extra coat and slicker for Josephine.

"Let's meet back here as close to two o'clock as possible," said Steven. Everyone checked their watches and nodded.

Katherine prayed they would find Josephine hunkered down someplace, or better yet, waiting for them when they returned.

Roy opened the door. "Let's get moving! It's not getting any better out there."

13 – The Storm

Lightning crashed nearby. Josephine counted, one thousand, two thousand… it was only two miles away! Her hands ached from the cold as the increasing wind whipped her hair across her face. The Black Feather's ranch couldn't be much further.

Between feeling numb, her saturated garments and Bonanza's slick wet back, she would catch herself slipping to one side or the other as they trotted along. The deafening wind howled, bringing a shower of dead branches down around her. Abruptly, her mount halted, nearly unseating her. At the top of a hill, a huge dead tree fell across their path only seconds before she would have passed through that very spot. Again, she entered the dense forest, so dark it turned day to night, to find a route around the obstacle. As multiple lightning strikes surrounded her, she recalled her reoccurring dream. It was coming to fruition!

Suddenly, she stopped. Something felt wrong. Within seconds, the aspen leaves turned upside down and a tingling sensation radiated through her body. Fear gripping her, she couldn't swallow or breath. The air smelled of sulfur… then crash!

Josephine screamed! Bonanza reared and spun away from the bright flash of light. She blindly reached for mane with her free hand, grasping only air, as the lead slid through her numb fingers. The next thing she knew she fell hard onto her back. Her head and chest ached; she couldn't breathe! Everything was a blur. Then the green ceiling of the woods crashed down on her. Pain like she had never felt in her life, ripped at her face and the right side of her body. Everything went black.

When Josephine tried to open her eyes, a sharp pain stabbed her right eye. How long had she been unconscious? She strained to see out of her left eye, but something blurred her vision. A metallic taste filled her mouth.

Where was Bonanza? "Bo Bo! Where are you?" she tried to call out, but only a weak squeal emerged.

The right side of her face screamed in agony and what little voice she could find was muffled by pine branches across her face and in her mouth. When she tried to move to see her horse, she nearly passed out from the pain in her right arm and leg which were pinned to the forest floor. Her mind clouded by fear, it took a moment for her head to clear. Her first cognitive thought — her pregnancy! After a few moments of panic, she chose to believe there was little risk of losing the baby since she was only a couple months along. She wouldn't allow herself to acknowledge the possibility she could lose all she had left of TJ.

Josephine's thoughts reverted to Bonanza. Was her horse in pain, trapped by the tree as well? Closing her eyes, she quieted her mind so she could focus on any sounds. To her relief, above the roar of the storm, she could hear Bonanza pawing through leaves to her left.

He was on his feet!

Using her left arm, Josephine managed to wipe her left eye free of a sticky substance and pulled the branches from her face the best she could. Every movement brought excruciating pain down her right side. Pushing through her anguish, she held the branches from her view and strained to see Bonanza. Out of the corner of her left eye and between pine boughs, she could make out a gold mass. She repeated the procedure until she had a better view. Bonanza stood about twenty feet away, his head held low and set back on his haunches, the lead pulled taut. It must be tangled in the tree. Bonanza shook his head, trying to pull free of the constant pressure on his halter.

"Easy, Bo Bo," she managed to call out. Bonanza's ears pricked forward, his eye rolling back to focus on her. She couldn't bring him totally into focus to see if he had any injuries.

Hearing only distant thunder now, she guessed the worst of the storm had passed. A freezing rain penetrated the forest canopy, blasting her face like a sandstorm. As the adrenaline stopped pumping through her veins, a chill gripped her. Shaking uncontrollably, she tried to assess her injuries. She could wiggle her right toes and move her left leg. It was too painful to move her right leg, arm or fingers. With her left hand she tenderly felt her head. Panic set in when she felt an abundance of a pasty substance. Blood! And it was still warm in these temperatures. She was still bleeding! Her head and back still ached and she felt pressure on her abdomen. Again, her pregnancy and the thought of losing the baby crept into her mind. Josephine closed her eyes and shook her head in denial.

As time passed, the rain slowed to a drizzle and what little light penetrated the dense woods disappeared. Not a branch stirred, as if the whole forest had frozen in place. Her body told her to just close her eyes and drift off into a peaceful and stress-free silence. Her mind screamed, "No!" She must fight to stay awake, fearing if she fell asleep, she'd never wake up again. She no longer had the strength to pull the branches away, but she continued to talk to her horse. It helped her stay conscious and was somehow comforting.

"Hey boy, you doing okay? I know it's scary, but you'll be okay. Someone will find us." This mantra she repeated until she no longer had the energy.

Lying silently in the cold and dark, Josephine engaged her mind to keep from drifting away. Her thoughts were fuzzy and unclear, but she recalled the night she and TJ nearly froze to death in the mountains when they rode off to find their parents. She pictured them making love for the first time, trying to recapture the heat of that moment. Soon the images turned dark. This time, TJ wasn't there to build a shelter, make a fire or keep her warm. No one knew where to find her. Again, she tried to move her right limbs. Numbness had begun to replace the pain. She would die here… all alone. Josephine would have cried if she had the strength. Her thoughts became scrambled. Closer and closer, she drifted toward the edge of the unknown.

Shocking her awake, another tree crashed to the ground not far from her. Would more fall under the weight of the freezing rain? She mustered up the energy to pull the branches away one more time so she could see her horse. Again, the Buckskin had set back onto his haunches, shaking his head violently. Within seconds, the leather piece of the breakaway halter broke under the pressure, sending the gelding onto his rump, nearly flipping over backward. Stunned, Bonanza stood for a second, but once he realized he was no longer restrained, he walked toward her. A sudden pang of affection filled her heart. Bonanza had chosen to stay with her rather than flee; a horse's instinctive reaction to any frightening situation. But she needed him to flee.

Bonanza had to run home for help! Her family would be searching for her by now, but probably just on Two Ponies. How would they know to look for her down the creek? If Bonanza turned up without her, they might be able to see his tracks along the lake trail ending at the stream. She knew horses always trace their tracks back home especially near feed time. It was worth a try. Bonanza might be her only hope.

"Go, Bo Bo! You have to go home. Go boy, go home!" she tried to yell, but her strained voice wasn't too convincing. She waved her free arm, but the gelding only took a few steps closer. She hated to do it, but she felt the ground around her for anything she could throw. She began tossing rocks and pinecones at her poor confused boy. He stepped back and snorted. When a rock hit him squarely on the chest, he spun around and trotted off. Josephine sighed. It hurt scaring him like that, but her life might depend on him reaching home. It gave her some hope. She knew between the loss of blood and possibility of hypothermia setting in, if it hadn't already, she didn't have much time.

Josephine listened as his hoof beats faded. She closed her eyes and prayed for the fourth time in her life. She had prayed when her and TJ nearly froze to death, when TJ was shot, when her captures hauled her mother from the cellar to be raped and killed… and now. It occurred to her, that perhaps if she had prayed more often, God would have spared her from this ludicrous situation. Then, maybe she got what she deserved. Dumping the man she loved, marrying a man she couldn't say she truly loved, all in the name of fame and fortune and out of convenience and fear.

Betsy was wrong. She was not as strong as her mother. She suddenly hated herself. "You stupid, weak bitch!" she spat.

When Katherine returned, Jessie sat waiting on the front porch. The men had not come back yet. "No luck?"

"I'm sorry, Kat. Dane is ready with the dogs."

Katherine checked her watch. It read five to two. "I'll get something of Jo's to give him for her scent." She left for her room. As she passed through the great room, she found all their house guests sitting around a fire.

"Jessie and I didn't find her. The men should return soon," was all she said on her way up the stairs.

As she passed by the Donahues, now reading books they must have borrowed from the library, Brad followed her into Josephine's room. "We need to call the authorities. Report her missing."

"The authorities are here." Katherine picked a shirt up off the floor Josephine had worn yesterday. "We'll find her."

"My parents will be flying out tomorrow as planned."

"That's understandable. You staying?"

"Of course, I'm staying. We'll work things out, reschedule the wedding."

Katherine didn't feel as confident, but no use in sharing her thoughts with him at this point. "We'll let you know the moment we find her."

She found Lisa waiting at the base of the stairs. "Is there anything I can do?"

"If we're not back by dinner time, pull out the leftovers from last night."

"Okay." Lisa gave her a hug. "I hope you find her soon."

"Me too." Katherine smiled at Lizzy and Cole playing with Daniel on the floor with Legos. A rap on the window got her attention. Jessie waved her outside.

The men had returned without Josephine. Her heart sunk. Her daughter had been in the cold and rain for nearly three hours with only a medium-weight jacket and no rain gear. Where could she be?

Dane had the dogs ready and she met them at the trailhead with Josephine's shirt. The German Shepard and Bloodhound smelled the shirt but could not pick up her scent on the trail. "I'm afraid as long as she's mounted, this isn't going to work."

"I'll be right back." Katherine raced to the barn and grabbed Bonanza's blanket. "Will this work?"

"I'm not sure if they'll follow a horse's scent. We've never tried it before."

The dogs dug their noses deep into the horse rug and pawed at it, but stood over it, looking confused.

"The rain too, it's not helping. I'm sorry, Kat." Dane took the dogs back to his truck.

"Jess, you need to get Cole home before the roads get any worse."

"No, I won't leave."

"Yes, you will. There's nothing more you can do. We'll contact Search and Rescue and let you know as soon as we find her. But could you feed and water the horses before you leave?"

"Of course."

Katherine turned to Roy, who was nearly as old as Chief. "Roy, Steven and I are going back out. Tell Mike to call Search and Rescue and fill them in on the situation. We could use you to man the house phone."

"Will do. Too bad the cell phones are no use out here," said Roy. "Good luck."

She turned to Steven. "I have an idea." Katherine ran to the lodge, returning with her faithful companion. "Laddy might be better at tracking an animal."

Sure enough, Laddy smelled the blanket and headed down the trail. When they reached the creek, the wolfdog stopped, waded across, smelled the opposite bank and returned to her and Major's side.

"He lost the scent," she said, stating the obvious.

Steven shook his head. "Now what?"

Katherine glanced downstream. Why hadn't she thought of that sooner. "She's riding the creek to the Black Feather's!"

"Of course, she wants to find TJ," said Steven.

"You need to ride back and call Sarah. Jo might already be there. I'm going to start down the creek with Laddy just in case.

Steven hesitated, no doubt considering switching with her, but he knew Laddy wouldn't leave her and he might prove useful. "Okay, be careful."

Katherine directed Major down the tributary with Laddy keeping pace onshore. Thankfully, the rain and wind had let up, but she could feel the temperatures dropping every minute. About a mile down the creek, Laddy stopped, focusing downstream. A wave of hope washed over her hearing plopping sounds in the water coming their way. From around a curve in the stream came Bonanza trotting briskly toward her, rider-less! She couldn't breathe from the fear building in her chest.

Josephine had taken a fall!

Bonanza stopped beside Major, his turnout buddy, and Katherine latched onto the dangling lead rope.

"Jo! Josephine!" she screamed repeatedly. No response.

The Buckskin was hot having traveled a good distance at a brisk pace. She estimated the Black Feather's was another two to three miles northeast. Her daughter could be lying injured anywhere along that stretch. She would send Bonanza home to notify Steven of their daughter's situation. If Search and Rescue were hesitant to send out a chopper, they would now. In her saddlebag, she carried a pocketknife. Recalling, how Billy had written his phone number on a piece of bark the first day she met him, she dismounted and cut off a piece of aspen bark. Using the knife, she etched "Jo fell, not found, send help."

She removed the extra jacket and tied it around Bonanza's neck with a tight knot and slipped the note in one of the zippered pockets. Steven would know she sent Bonanza and the jacket for a reason. He would search the pockets. Next, she looped the lead rope around Bonanza's neck, securing it back to the halter to keep it from dragging the ground and possibly getting snagged. Now to send the message. Katherine broke off a branch and smacked Bonanza on the rump, sending the gelding down the creek toward home.

The rain had begun to freeze. With new-found urgency, she navigated the stream at a brisker pace, studying the banks for any sign of tracks or Josephine as she yelled her daughter's name. Laddy continued to keep pace along shore, periodically changing sides. Soon she came across a large fallen tree and easily found Bonanza's tracks running each direction. Josephine was still mounted and heading for the Black Feather's at this point. As she began traversing the creek once again, her heart sank as it began to snow.

Josephine opened her eyes, awakened by something cold and damp on her face. Snow! She wiped her left eye free of it, her hand shaking uncontrollably from the cold. How long had she slept? At least she had woken up, but she felt so alone and scared. Had Bonanza reached home? Was help on the way? They had to be coming soon to rescue her, she told herself. She tried to stay positive as she lay motionless in the cold, bleak forest.

Just as her eyelids began to get heavy again, her eyes opened wide. Nearby, branches snapped under the weight of someone or something moving toward her. See couldn't see a thing.

"Help! I'm over here. Please help me!" she called out. "Mom, Dad?" but with no response.

Then she heard the same sound from two other directions, then again from the same direction. Two, maybe three somethings were circling her!

Wolves!

They must have smelled her blood. Again, she rooted around with her left hand, grasping whatever she could to defend herself with. She collected a pile of rocks by her side and broke off a branch from the tree. She strained to turn her head both directions but could only see to the left. There in the shadows, she saw a pair of yellow eyes fixed on her. Slowly the wolf approached from the left, evaluating his prey. Josephine gripped a rock and threw it. A yelp and the yellow eyes disappeared. Then she heard another, this time from the right. Her blind side! She grabbed the branch and shook it wildly as she screamed at the top of her strained voice. Then, silence.

Her shriek split the stillness of the frozen forest as sharp canine teeth broke the skin of her left ankle. She kicked violently, warding off the wolf for the moment, but she lost her shoe. Her foot throbbed, but quickly became cold and numb. If they attacked her right side, she wouldn't be able to defend herself. And she knew she didn't stand a chance if they attacked her all at once. The idea three carnivorous beasts were out there, hungry for her flesh, terrified her. She quietly listened for the next attack.

When Katherine reached a tree that had recently fallen across the creek, she called for Josephine with more urgency. Could this be the tree that caused her daughter's fall? She watched Laddy to see if he sensed anything, but he only looked up at her with a questioning expression. Since the snow cover, she could no longer follow any tracks, so she turned into the woods in the direction which appeared the shorter and clearer route around the fallen tree. Not far into the forest, Laddy stopped ahead of her with his hackles raised. Her first thought was a bear and she cussed at herself for not thinking to bring Steven's shotgun with her. Slowly, Laddy advanced. Major hesitated, then followed at full attention as well, head raised, ears pricked forward. Again, Laddy stopped, a growl emanating from deep within.

A scream cut the still night air. Josephine!!

Laddy charged into the forest and without a thought, Katherine kicked Major and bolted after him. The scene unfolded within seconds. Three wolves circled her daughter trapped under a fallen tree, one nipping at her right hand which appeared immobile. Josephine tried to fight it off with a branch in her other hand. The attacking wolf didn't see Laddy coming, and her wolfdog caught him by the scruff of the neck and shook him, digging his incisors deep and drawing blood. The other two wolves jumped on Laddy. The sound of their snarls and cries were deafening. Katherine leapt off Major, screaming, and lunged toward the fighting canines with her arms flailing. Josephine screamed one last time before she went limp. Katherine ran to her daughter, watching in horror as one wolf had Laddy by the neck while the other had a rear leg.

"No!" she shrieked.

Suddenly, the wolf at Laddy's head fell away, lifeless. TJ appeared from nowhere and the other two wolves disappeared into the forest. Once again, Laddy had saved a life, this time her daughter's. He limped toward her as TJ, unaware of Josephine hidden beneath the tree, retrieved his knife.

"Are you and Laddy okay?" asked TJ as he wiped his knife clean on the dead carcass.

"It's Jo, she's trapped!"

TJ ran to Josephine's side. "How long has she been out here!" The panic in his voice reflected her own horror.

"I don't know, but help is coming," she said.

TJ tested the weight of the tree, unable to budge it. "I came as quick as I could after Jessie called."

"Thank God you came when you did. I sent Bonanza home with a note. Search and Rescue should be on their way."

TJ felt Josephine's pulse. "It feels weak and she's not shivering." Next, he lowered his head to her chest. "Her breathing is shallow. All signs of hypothermia, advanced most likely since she's unconscious."

"She was conscious just moments ago," said Katherine. "But I fear she's lost a lot of blood."

"We need to warm her up fast." TJ striped off his coat and laid it over her the best he could then began cutting the branches away from Josephine's face.

"Between the shadows and the tree branches, it's impossible to determine the extent of her injuries." Katherine turned toward the stream. "Did you see Major?"

"Yes, he's with Cisco."

"Stay with her, I think I have some matches in my saddlebag." Katherine hurried, slipping and sliding through the wet snow, to where she found the horses standing quietly. She tied Major and rifled through her saddlebag until she latched onto the pack. She also grabbed the blanket and hurried back to Josephine. She was still unconscious. TJ had cleared most of the branches from her face. When she lit a match, both she and TJ gasped at what they saw. The right side of Josephine's face had been torn away. Her eye was swollen shut and the snow was blood-soaked around her head.

"She needs help fast!" cried TJ.

Katherine could not find her voice. She just nodded as warm tears streamed down her face. How could this have happened to her beautiful little girl?

When she turned to TJ, his face was a snarled mess of fear. "We have to free her from this tree." He sprang to his feet and disappeared into the woods. He returned moments later with a dead, but well dried and hard, large branch.

"Thankfully, just the top half of the tree broke off. I'm going to try to pry this end of the treetop up enough for you to slide Jo out," he said as he positioned the branch. "Looks like a lightning strike," he added, nodding in the direction of the stump still smoldering. "It's a miracle Major and Jo survived the strike and if it wasn't for the rain and snow, it might have started a fire."

Stifled by the terror of the situation, Katherine silently watched as TJ placed a large rock near the fallen trunk just below Josephine's feet. He worked the end of the branch as far under the tree as he could then rested it over the rock. Katherine prayed TJ was strong enough and the branch would hold to lever the trunk off Josephine's arm and leg.

"On the count of three," said TJ.

Katherine slid under the remaining branches, lifting them with her back as she gripped her daughter's left arm.

"One, two, three!"

TJ grunted, putting all his weight and strength into the effort as she tenderly pulled on Josephine's left arm until she felt it give, then pulled as hard and fast as she could, scooting backward along the ground.

"She's free!" screamed Katherine, still pulling her clear of the tree branches, and none too soon, as the branch slid from the rock and the treetop fell back to the ground with a thump.

More panic set in when she noticed the trail of blood in the snow following her daughter's body.

TJ rushed to Josephine and gently examined her. "Her leg is broken, but I don't think her arm is. She's just so cold." TJ softly caressed Josephine's left cheek then turned to her. "She's in bad shape, Kat. We need to warm her up soon."

"Let's clear this area and start a fire," said Katherine. "It'll warm Jo up and let them know where to find us. There's a surface rock opening upstream a bit that should be big enough to set a helicopter down on." She checked her watch and was thankful it had been less than an hour since she found Josephine. Bonanza should have reached Two Ponies by now. Search and Rescue must be on their way.

TJ rushed off to collect wood, most of it wet. Thankfully, they found some dry pine needles and pinecones so they could get the damp branches to burn. The fire produced a lot of smoke to signal the chopper from above. Katherine held her daughter close, sharing her warmth as she held her hand and prayed.

TJ examined Laddy. "Just a couple puncture wounds, nothing serious," he told Katherine. "Couple stitches and he'll be fine."

He continued to throw wet branches onto the fire to produce as much smoke as possible. Darkness would soon be upon them. Even though he might not be a human medical student, he knew enough that if help didn't come soon, Josephine might not make it. His throat tightened and stomach wrenched at the thought of the possibility. How could this be happening? Josephine had run out on Brad and their wedding and was coming to find him. She had chosen him after all. He couldn't lose her now!

Soon the rumble of an aircraft could be heard followed by a spotlight searching the forest. TJ ran to the opening and waved his arms. The searchlight found him, and he backed away. The tops of the surrounding trees blew violently as the helicipter turned to position itself to land in the tight opening. The moment it sat squarely on the ground, the doors flew open and Dr. Walker jumped out and ran to him.

"She's hurt bad," yelled TJ above the roar of the chopper.

Steven ran back to the aircraft and two medics followed, one pulling a rescue board, the other carrying a first aid bag. TJ waved them on to follow him. Immediately, the medics went to work on Josephine, checking her vitals and assessing her condition. Dr.

Walker looked nearly as white as Josephine, clearly in shock. It was a lot to take in, seeing someone you love in that state – barely recognizable. Within minutes, they had her loaded.

TJ offered to return Major and Laddy to Two Ponies so Steven and Katherine could both ride with their daughter to the hospital. As he watched the helicopter lift off, his heart split in two – half full of promise, the other half terrified he would never get the opportunity to hold his Jo again.

It was dark by the time TJ trotted Cisco and Major into the parking area beside the lodge at Two Ponies. He guessed Josephine would have arrived at the hospital by then. The moment he entered the glow of the flood light, the side door flung open. Out stepped Roy.

TJ rode up to the stairs. "Is she okay?"

"She's in ICU, but stable."

"Thank God."

"Jessie left. Need any help?" said Roy, motioning toward the horses.

"I can handle them, but I will need some help treating Laddy."

"I heard about the wolves. Steve told me where to find what you'll need."

"Great, thanks. Then could you drive me to the hospital?"

"Sure," said Roy.

"Great. Give me about fifteen minutes." TJ gave Cisco a kick and trotted off toward the barn, Major in tow.

Having dried the horses the best he could, he blanketed the Thoroughbred and stalled and fed both horses. He called his mother on the tack room phone and promised to keep her updated. After treating Laddy, TJ quickly cleaned up the best he could.

On the ride to Great Falls, Roy filled TJ in on Josephine's overall condition. "She suffered a concussion and lost a lot of blood. They're slowly bringing her body temperature up but can't say if there will be any permanent damage. The cold probably saved her from bleeding out, but the hypothermia cut oxygen to her brain and organs. Her leg has a clean break and should heal fine."

"What about her face?"

"She will require reconstructive surgery, but she needs to recover from her pneumonia before it can be performed."

"Pneumonia?"

"I understand it's common with hypothermia." Roy took a deep breath.

TJ held his breath not knowing what else could possibly be wrong.

"And… she could lose sight in one eye," continued Roy.

TJ glared at Roy. "Has she regained consciousness?"

"Not yet."

"Is she in a coma?"

"I'm not sure. But I must let you know, Brad is already there."

TJ nodded then turned and stared aimlessly out the passenger window in silence the rest of the drive. In the darkness, memories of his beautiful Josephine battled with the images of her frightening injuries. Suddenly, guilt ravaged his body and soul. Had he caused this catastrophe? Running on adrenaline up to that point, he hadn't considered the ramifications of his actions. If he hadn't driven over to see Josephine that morning, none of this would have happened.

14 – Darkness

Great Falls, Montana

Katherine held Josephine's pale hand, willing her daughter to regain consciousness. Tubes and wires crisscrossed around her like she was caught in a spider web as various machines beeped and groaned. In the two hours since they arrived at the hospital, multiple teams scrambled to examine and handle her long list of injuries and conditions. To treat the advanced hypothermia, they rewarmed her core temperature gradually with warmed IV fluids, heated and humidified oxygen, performed peritoneal lavage (internal "washing" of the abdominal cavity) and extracorporeal blood warming. So far, no other complications had occurred resulting from the hypothermia beyond her pneumonia and coma. They were waiting on the results of her blood draw, x-rays and scans.

She could hardly recognize her beautiful girl. Half her face, her nose and most of her scalp were bandaged, the bruising now spreading to the unbandaged portion of her face. They had set and applied a cast to her right leg and a deep bone bruise on her right arm seemed to grow deeper in color by the minute. Yet, she was grateful. Katherine knew if that tree had fallen a few inches over, she would be visiting with her daughter's corpse instead.

Katherine leaned over and kissed Josephine on the only exposed area of her head that wasn't bandaged or bruised, a two-by-two-inch square of red hair. Steven had left to get them sandwiches. She wasn't hungry even though she hadn't eaten since breakfast. She imagined neither was her husband, but Steven needed to do something. Brad left to call his parents again, seeming to look for any excuse to leave Josephine's side. He could barely stand to look at her and Katherine hadn't seen him touch her once. He seemed more upset that he couldn't get through to his folks at Two Ponies on his cell phone. Perhaps he might just be in shock, having lived such a sheltered life. How all this would play out between Josephine and Brad remained to be seen, not to mention between her and TJ. Deep down, she hoped the wedding would be called off altogether. She just didn't see the connection between the couple, and it all had come as such a surprise following Josephine's comments about Brad and their relationship over the summer. And the big hurry. What was that all about?

A tap on the glass pulled her from her thoughts. Steven waved a sack in one hand and a drink in the other. Only one visitor was allowed at a time in the airtight room to minimize the chance of infection. Katherine gently set Josephine's hand down, exited the room, and followed her husband into a private waiting room just outside the ICU. She pulled her mask down, almost having forgotten she was wearing one, and took a bite of the club sandwich. It tasted like cardboard, but Betsy's voice whispered in her head that she needed to eat something to keep up her strength. Josephine had a long road of procedures and treatments ahead of her.

Just as she managed to finish half the club, one of the doctors treating their daughter approached them. It was the young one that had been so attentive when they first arrived, but she couldn't remember his name.

"Oh, I'm glad I caught you both," he said, taking a seat across from them. "I have some results from her blood work and tests."

Katherine detected some hesitance in his voice. Not more bad news, please, she prayed.

"Some good, some bad. The good news, all her organs seem to be functioning normally, which is huge. We won't know about her eye until the swelling goes down." Steven gave her hand a squeeze as the doctor continued. "Unfortunately, your daughter suffered a miscarriage."

Katherine dropped her sandwich in her lap, her eyes connecting with Steven's before returning to the doctor. "We weren't aware."

"Sorry. I felt you should know."

"Of course. How far along?"

"About two months. She'll be fine, but there was some bleeding and infection set in. We won't know the extent of the damage, if any, right away."

"Damage to what?"

"Her uterus."

"What are you saying? That she might not be able to have children?"

"We won't know until after she heals. Our priority now is getting her over the pneumonia and for her to regain consciousness. She's remaining stable, so we'll be moving her to a room upstairs shortly."

"Thank you, doctor," said Steven.

The moment he left the room, Steven turned to her. "We were right, but why didn't she tell us?"

"Well, we can guess it wasn't planned," she said. But still, it didn't seem like something she would keep from them. "Maybe she was afraid to tell us, or Brad didn't want her to."

"Where is he anyway?"

"Off to call his folks again."

"Something is way off with that guy," said Steven. "I hope she breaks it off."

"I don't think she'll have to. This accident is going to be life altering for Jo. She may not be able to continue with her career. I think Brad is all about being married to Josie Walker the famous actress, not to mention the loss of the baby."

"I'm finding him," said Steven. "He needs to know." He didn't wait for a response and strode out of the room.

Her husband probably wasn't the best choice to notify Brad of such a sensitive matter, but at that point she didn't care and only wanted to be with her daughter. As she headed back to Josephine's room, a gurney was heading toward the elevator. She recognized the bandaged head and leg. They weren't wasting any time moving

Josephine upstairs with a full ICU ward. She rushed to catch up and walk alongside her daughter.

"Please let my husband know. He'll be returning to ICU," she said to one of the two nurses transporting Josephine.

"Will do."

"Thank you."

Katherine settled in beside Josephine, once again hooked up to several monitors while she was fed and sedated intravenously. She wanted to be there when she awoke. As much as she anticipated her daughter coming out of her coma, she also dreaded it. It would be a lot for Josephine to absorb and accept. How would she react to her frightening appearance, perhaps the loss of an eye, not to mention the loss of the baby? All Katherine knew for certain was Josephine would need her and the support of everyone she loved to pull her from the darkness that now hung over her. Katherine had experienced the black pit a person can sink into, overshadowing all that is bright and good. Josephine will surely need the strength and courage of her Irish ancestors, who braved a famine, faced angry seas, and overcame the bigotry that greeted them on foreign soil, to find her place in what will surely be a new and strange world for her.

Steven found Brad alright, but not before TJ did. The two men stood beside a pay phone in the lobby. Neither of them noticed him, but he was close enough to hear their discussion.

"What are you doing here?" said Brad, his words laced with contempt. "Haven't you done enough damage already?"

"How is Jo?" TJ asked Brad, disregarding his comments.

"She's alive, but she's going to wish she was dead. Why couldn't you just leave us alone. If you hadn't shown up… you ruined everything. You ruined her career and our future!" he said dramatically, in Academy Award winning fashion.

TJ stood stunned by his cruel words for a moment then boldly stepped up to Brad. "I want to know what you said to her or did after I left!"

A few people had stopped in the hall, taking notice of their escalating voices. The woman at the information desk got on the phone. Steven stepped forward. "TJ, please take a seat! I'll fill you in in a moment. Brad I need to speak to you… now!"

Steven didn't mean to snap at them, but he didn't care for the direction this conversation was heading. He didn't need the drama of a brawl in the hospital lobby on top of the day's events so far. But neither of them seemed to hear him.

TJ got in Brad's face. "What happened to cause her to ride off like that?"

Brad backed away, nearly tripping over himself. "That's none of your business! Who do you think you are anyway? You're a nobody. You were never good enough for Josephine…"

That did it. TJ was Billy's son after all. TJ clenched his fists. "Let's take this outside!"

Brad suddenly took notice of Steven and inched his way toward him without turning his back on TJ. Steven guessed he wasn't accustomed to anyone challenging him, especially someone he believed was inferior.

"You're crazy!" said Brad, feeling a little braver standing beside Steven, no doubt thinking he would naturally take his side against the crazy Redskin.

"I'll show you crazy!" Again, TJ got in his face.

"That's enough!" Seven stepped between them, resting one hand on TJ's chest and motioning Brad away with the other.

Brad snickered. "You know what? You can have her. Nothing but damaged goods now anyway, thanks to you."

TJ approached Brad again, rising onto the balls of his feet. Steven had watched Billy fight enough times to know what would come next, a roundhouse kick or punch to the solar plexus. He quickly grabbed TJ by the arm.

"Let me handle it," said Steven. TJ stepped down.

Steven pulled Brad toward the door. About that time, he would have liked a piece of Brad himself. "You need to leave, but before you do, you should know Josephine had a miscarriage," he whispered.

"Perfect!" he said, then wrestled his arm free and fled the building, hopefully out of their lives forever.

A guard appeared from down the hall. "What's the problem?"

"The problem just left. We're good," said Steven, motioning for TJ to follow him. "I'm sorry you had to hear that," he said directing TJ down the hall toward ICU. "He's the one that never deserved Jo."

"How is she?"

"Stable."

"That's what Roy said. He drove me. He's parking the car. I want to know everything."

Steven led TJ into the same private waiting room where he had left Katherine. "Have a seat."

First, he thanked TJ for his part in rescuing his daughter. Then he explained her condition the best he could, all but the fact she had been pregnant. That was something he would leave to Josephine to divulge, if and when she chose to.

"Can I see her?"

Just then a nurse entered the room. "We've moved Miss Walker upstairs to the fourth floor, Room 420."

"Thank you," said Steven.

When they reached the fourth floor, Steven took it upon himself to embellish a bit with the nurses who hadn't met Brad, introducing TJ as Josephine's fiancé so he could visit her. Steven motioned with his hand for TJ to wait outside the room for a moment.

Katherine looked exhausted, yet she welcomed him with a smile. "Hi, honey. Did you find Brad?"

"Yes. He left. He walked out on Josephine before he even learned about the miscarriage. You were right earlier. He was only in love with the celebrity, not our daughter."

"No surprise. He was gone before he left."

"You got that right." Steven turned toward the door. "TJ's here. He wants to see Jo. I got permission from the floor desk."

Katherine stood up and accompanied him out of the room to where TJ stood waiting in the hall. "Hi, TJ." She gave him a hug. "Thank you for everything."

"Major is tucked in for the night. I hope you don't mind, I put Cisco in an empty stall."

"Of course not. Roy drive you?"

"Yes. He's parking. I just had to see her."

"She's still unconscious."

"Dr. Walker got me up to speed." TJ turned to Steven. "I'm sorry about that business downstairs. Josephine was fine when I left, I promise."

"We believe you, TJ," said Steven.

"It was just an accident," Katherine added. "Accidents happen. No one is to blame."

Steven patted him on the back. He was glad TJ came. Perhaps he's just what Josephine needed to bring her out of the coma. "Go visit Jo. We'll be down the hall in the chapel."

TJ nodded and quietly entered her room. It was dark except for a small opening in the vertical blinds where he could see a gentle snow still falling. All the typical hospital smells brought back unpleasant memories, recalling his stay years ago following his shooting. TJ stood and stared at Josephine in disbelief for the longest time. Eventually, he pulled up a chair on Josephine's good side, took her hand and cried.

His tears eventually turned to prayers. This was the second time he'd cried that day. He felt in a fog, as if back in the sweat lodge. It all seemed so surreal. As he held Josephine's hand, he wondered if she could feel his tender grasp, feel the undeniable connection he had always felt when they touched. This was his first experience with anyone in a coma and he wondered if she could hear him.

"Hey, Jo, it's me, TJ. Can you hear me?" He stroked her soft hand with his thumb as he tenderly cradled it. "It's okay. You need to rest so you can heal." TJ gave her delicate long fingers a gentle squeeze. "I'm right here. Right where I belong, beside you. I'm going to stay with you as long and as often as they'll let me. Until you wake up. Then you can decide if you want me here. I hope you will… want me here… want me forever. You were coming to find me, weren't you, Jo? I'm so sorry this all happened. I hope you won't blame me, because I sort of blame myself already. But I'm glad you didn't marry that Brad guy. Am I talking too much? I'm sorry."

The door creaked open and a plump nurse with rosy cheeks entered and began checking Josephine's vitals. "One of the doctors will be in soon to check on her," she said, with a caring smile. "I can see you love her very much. She's going to need a lot of that."

TJ studied Josephine's bandaged face, understanding her meaning. "She was beautiful," he said. "And she always will be in my eyes."

She gave him a pat on the shoulder and broadened her smile. "Good boy."

Katherine and Steven peeked in the doorway. "Do you want me to leave?" he asked, considering there were only two chairs in the room.

The nurse quickly spoke up. "We can bring in another chair, no problem," she said. TJ focused on her name tag. "Thank you, Rita. That is, if it's okay with you," he added, directed to Dr. and Mrs. Walker.

"Sure," said Katherine.

Not long after they got seated, Roy sauntered into the room still looking every bit the Western hero he once portrayed in his films, in his oilskin coat, cowboy boots and Stetson in hand. "Hi, Kat, Steve. Sorry it took me so long. They sent me to the wrong floor." He stood focused on the patient. TJ could see he was struggling to hold in his emotions. "My Lord, our poor, sweet Jo. I'm so sorry."

Once they filled Roy in on her condition, he mentioned he ran into Brad in the parking lot. "Now I know why he wanted to drive his own vehicle. The man has no spine." Roy shook his head, his face reddening. "Coward!" Silence filled the room, apparently no one objected to Roy's analysis. Once his face lightened a few shades, he added, "Brad said they'll be flying out on an earlier flight in the morning. Good riddance. I'm afraid we need to get back tomorrow too. Is there anything we can do before we leave?"

"No, but thanks for offering. Jessie can handle Laddy and the horses. Dane offered to clear the drive in the morning so everyone can get out to make their flights," said Katherine. "Lisa plans to visit before dark. How are the roads?"

"Not bad now, but they'll probably freeze overnight. I wish there was more we could do, but you all will be in our prayers."

"Thank you and thanks for helping out earlier," said Steven.

Roy gave Katherine a hug. "Please keep us posted."

"Will do."

Steven stood and shook Roy's hand.

TJ followed Steven's lead. "Thanks for the ride." Roy nodded and left.

Katherine turned to TJ. "Since you're here. I could use a hot meal,"

"Me too," said Steven. "Can we bring you something?"

"Not now, thanks."

Once the Walkers left, TJ resumed his vigil beside Josephine. Again, his heart ached for her.

"Please Jo, come back to us."

It was Katherine's turn to sit with TJ over Josephine. He refused to leave her side for more than a few minutes to grab something to eat or use the restroom. All through the night, she and Steven had taken turns stretching out on the booth seats in the chapel to get a little sleep. Rita had supplied them with pillows and blankets before her shift ended. Lisa had brought some reading material with her. It had been an emotional visit for her overly sensitive eldest daughter, bringing all of Katherine's fears to the surface again. They had sat and cried together. Lisa hated to return to New York the next day, but Daniel had to return to work and Lizzy to school on Monday.

TJ sat across the bed from her, his hand resting on the pillow behind Josephine's head with his thumb softly stroking the lone patch of hair. His devotion astonished them and the staff.

As she looked upon her daughter, the image of her face illuminated by the matchlight in the forest continued to haunt her. Now only a portion of her swollen, bruised and distorted face was visible. Most of her ruby red hair had been shaved off so they could clean and suture her wounds. Hidden under the bandages, her right jaw, cheek bone and nose were broken and would require reconstructive surgery. If that wasn't frightening enough, the possibility remained she might lose sight in the one eye. She sustained a clean break of her fibula and it would heal quickly. Later would come the skin grafts to put her baby girl back together. But that would be only physically, how she would heal psychologically remained a question.

When Katherine pulled her eyes away from Josephine, she noticed TJ studying her. "You're scared," he said. "Me too."

"I'm glad you're here, TJ. We've missed you." She glanced out the window. "Did you call your mother? I should have called her."

"I did. She knows and she's praying to the healing spirits for Jo."

After a long silence, Katherine hoped changing the subject from Josephine might help them both. "We heard you were taking some time off from school."

"Did my mom tell you why?"

"No. But, she's worried you won't go back."

"She told me…" said TJ.

"What?"

"That you were paying for my education."

"Oh, I see." Now it all made sense. Silly men's pride.

"That was very generous of you," he said. "Thank you. I'll find a way to repay you."

"No need, TJ. We wanted to help any way we could."

"I'll pay my own way from here. I plan to return in January."

"I'm glad. But please, if you run short, let us know. It can be a loan if you insist."

"Thank you, but I can get a school loan if I need to."

Katherine nodded. "I understand. I'm very pleased you're planning on finishing. We need another good vet in the area. I've been trying to get Steven to retire, but he's not ready. He may never be. He loves his work so."

"I love working with animals too. Especially horses."

"Yeah, me too," she chuckled.

They shared a warm smile. "Perhaps you'll consider assisting Steven again this summer. You have two more years left, right?"

"Yes. A little less actually. I attended a couple summers before I started racing."

"Right, the Indian Races. I heard you won the Championship this year. Congratulations."

"Thanks, and we'll win again next year," he said confidently, sounding so much like his father, it hurt. He had grown into a strong young man, with Billy's build, jaw and nose but with his mother's kind eyes. He had the same dark mahogany irises, but void of the wildfire that burned in his father's. TJ would make a good husband and father; loyal, loving and giving. Katherine glanced at the young Blackfeet, once again totally absorbed in her daughter. She prayed Josephine would give their relationship another chance.

TJ stretched. He had been sitting for days, spending most of his time reading the books and magazines Jessie dropped off. She tried to bring a variety that might interest each of them, but he found himself reading everything from romance novels to fishing magazines to pass the time. When he wasn't reading, he held Josephine's hand as he dozed off for short periods of time but always attuned to monitoring any movement or sound from her. He imagined this was how parents slept after bringing home a newborn. He dreamed of sharing that experience with Josephine someday.

Slanted rays of early morning sunlight cut across the room. Steven and Katherine had gone for breakfast in the cafeteria. They would bring back a plate for him, like they always did. Even though his appetite had not yet returned, he would force himself to eat to silent Katherine's concern over his well-being. Ever since he and Josephine played together as kids, Mrs. Walker had always treated him like one of her own, even now as an adult, she mothered him. The waiting for Josephine to wake up was stressful on all of them, including the doctors. All the staff tried to shield them from their concerns, but their intensified schedule of visits and tests said otherwise. Once the antibiotics handled the pneumonia, her doctors were anxious to begin work on her face. The longer they had to wait, the chance of good results from the surgery lessened.

The words of the mystery he was reading began to run together. TJ closed his eyes, clasped Josephine's hand and once again began to play his and Josephine's best hits over in his mind; playing as kids, sharing their love of horses and the outdoors, making each other laugh, passionate kisses and making love like there was no tomorrow. Nineteen years of happy memories to pick from. Would he get the opportunity to make more? The future was so uncertain, it killed him not knowing. He had to refocus on pleasant memories to get some rest.

Groggily, Josephine licked her dry, chapped lips. The pain in this simple task astonished her. Fear consumed her. When she tried to open her eyes, only a sliver of sight took shape before her left eye.

Everything was a blur. Her right eye would not open and it was painful trying. Her fuzzy head could not comprehend why. Where was she? What was wrong with her? Her body felt heavy and nonresponsive. Slowly, her surroundings began to take shape. She was lying in a bed, not her bed at Two Ponies, a strange bed with no bed frame. Only the shape of her two feet under the covers lay before her. She could not will her toes to wiggle. When she tried to move her right hand to free her eye of whatever was obstructing her vision, she almost passed out in agony. She glanced at her right arm to find it a swollen rainbow of colors. Then she felt something warm gently embracing her left hand. She squeezed it.

"Jo, you're awake! It's me, TJ."

"TJ? Where am I?" she whispered. Again, Josephine tried to turn her head, but it was too painful. She wanted to see TJ.

"You're in the hospital," he said.

"Were we in a car accident?"

"You took a fall and a tree fell on you. Don't you remember?"

"Fall? Tree?" TJ moved center so she could see him. His hair was long again. "I like your hair long." Josephine had hated it when he had cut it short the summer following graduation.

TJ leaned over her and pushed a button. Within seconds the room filled with white blobs moving about her, touching her and the maze of tubes and wires restricting her movement.

While a bright light pierced her eye, someone felt her pulse.

One nurse leaned over her. "Hi, dear welcome back. Someone is getting your parents. They'll be here soon."

Next, they took her temperature and blood pressure. A male nurse spoke to her next. "How are you feeling?"

"Sore, pain… arm, head, leg…" was all she could get out.

"I'm sure the doctor will up your meds," said the man. "You'll feel better in no time. He should be here soon."

Several voices hummed around her, making her head spin. She panicked. "TJ, where are you?"

"I'm right over here, Jo."

He sounded so far away. Slowly, things began to come into focus. Nurses and doctors continued to move in and out of view as they examined her and the machines, but now she could make out their faces.

One doctor moved into her narrow line of vision. "Hello, Josephine. I'm Dr. Molloy. You were in an accident and got banged up a bit, but you're in good hands. We'll take good care of you." Where was the part about "you'll be just fine," she wondered?

"TJ," she called, reaching out her left hand, grasping the thin air for him.

"Is it okay?" asked TJ.

"Yes, dear," said one of the nurses. TJ clasped her hand. It was comforting feeling his contact once again. She squeezed it tight.

The room quieted. Only Dr. Molloy remained, appearing to wait by the door. Perhaps waiting for her parents.

She glanced as far as she could toward TJ. "Did I take a fall off a horse?"

TJ spoke, but not to her. "I don't think she can remember," he said to the doctor.

"That's normal," he said to TJ. Then he leaned over her. "Don't worry, Ms. Walker, it's normal for things to be a little fuzzy following a head injury."

Head injury? Suddenly, TJ let go of her hand.

"Oh, Jo, sweetheart, you're awake." It was her mother, sounding on the verge of tears. She leaned over her and softly brushed the top of her head with the tips of her fingers. She heard TJ rise to his feet.

"I'm here too, Jo," said her father, taking TJ's seat.

"Mom, Dad," she said, barely above a whisper. It hurt to speak, to move. The fear returned. How messed up was she? "Am I okay?"

"Sure, honey," she said. "You'll be fine. You just have some healing to do first."

She felt somewhat reassured, but she'd rather have heard it from the doctor. What was his name? He did tell her. How could she have forgotten it already.

As if reading her mind, the doctor stepped up. "You injured your head and right arm and broke your right leg. You suffered a nasty concussion and have been in a coma for four days. Do you recall anything about your accident?"

Josephine slowly shook her head. She couldn't remember a thing. Her head was in a fog, and the harder she tried to remember, the more it hurt.

The doctor turned toward her mother. "It's okay, it'll take time." Again, he focused on her. "Jo, is it okay I call you Jo?"

Josephine nodded again.

"Try to get some rest. Some stronger pain medication is on the way. I'll come and check on you in a little bit." She heard him leave, then another older doctor stuck his head in the room.

"We're going to step out for a moment, sweetie," said her mother. "We'll be right back. Like the doctor said, try to get some rest."

TJ resumed his spot beside her. Again, she reached for him and he clasped her hand.

Josephine did feel exhausted. How could she be so tired after sleeping for four days? As she drifted off, she could hear muffled voices in the hall. She fought to stay awake so she might decipher what they were saying, but it was useless and within seconds, she fell asleep.

Katherine, followed by her husband, joined the plastic surgeon in the hallway. Dr. Wilkes explained their course of action, step by step, assuring them of his team's success with similar cases. Yet he finished with a disclaimer.

"Of course, we can't guarantee anything. Only that we'll do our best. It will be a long process."

Again, her fears about how Josephine would handle all of this, surfaced. "How do we tell her about her injuries," asked Katherine.

"Don't offer any more information. I deliberately did not mention her sight, because we really don't know at this point. If she asks about her face, and she will, try to be as vague as possible," said the doctor. "Let's try to get her through the first surgery without her knowing the extent of the damage."

"I understand," said Katherine.

"She may be our little girl, but she's also an adult," said Steven. "I don't know if I feel right about concealing information from her if she asks."

"It'll be for her own good, honey," said Katherine.

"Your wife's right. If Josephine were to become upset or in the worst case, clinically depressed, it could affect her recovery and the healing process. The mind is a powerful thing."

Steven nodded, and turned to her. "Okay."

"Hopefully, after the first reconstructive surgery, we'll see a significant improvement," said Dr. Wilkes. "The bandages will conceal things for a while, but eventually they're going to have to come off for her to heal. That's when we'll know more about her eye. But regardless, she's going to need all the love and support you can give her. As I mentioned before, the reconstruction of her face will be a long road requiring several surgeries."

Katherine couldn't help it, she had to know. "What are the chances she'll look like she used to?"

He gave a canned answer she should have expected. "Reconstructive and plastic surgery has come a long way and we're discovering new techniques and improving procedures every day. I've worked on worse cases with very good results."

"When will the first surgery take place?" questioned Steven. "What will be done?"

"Very soon. First, we will work on the foundation; her fractured eye socket, cheek bone and broken nose. It was a miracle her jaw wasn't broken too. The ophthalmologist will do an evaluation of her right eye at that time and you'll be the first to know her findings. Then the skin grafts will begin. There are no guarantees they will take, but we've had great success on hundreds of cases just like Josephine's."

He still didn't really answer her original question, but she guessed she already knew the answer. Most likely no. It all sounded so overwhelming. Her poor baby. Katherine took a deep breath. "We understand," she exhaled.

"I'll be back after lunch. I'll let you know then when her first surgery will be scheduled." The good doctor left them for lunch, she presumed. Steven put his arm around her and led her back into the room. There sat TJ, sound asleep cradling Josephine's hand as always, while her daughter rested quietly. She feared the next few days as Josephine's head cleared. Surely, the questions would come.

Every day, Josephine recalled bits and pieces of her memory, mostly long-term memories like her childhood, school days through high school, but not much after that. Somehow, her head injury had affected her short-term memory. Following her first surgery earlier that week, she woke up recalling everything leading up to and during her abduction, which had come as quite a shock to her. The memory of seeing Mr. Black Feather lying lifeless in a pool of blood she would rather have forgotten forever. Most surprising were the developments between her and TJ after that. She had blushed remembering them together. She guessed she had always loved him but was afraid to admit it to herself, her friends and her parents.

That evening was the first time they had left her alone since she woke up in the hospital. Her parents went to pick up some takeout dinner. They were all getting pretty sick of the cafeteria food. And only after she assured TJ she'd be okay, did he leave to make a few calls.

Josephine raised the bed and sat up, then gingerly felt her face. Bandages still covered most of her head, including her right eye. She had undergone surgery earlier in the week. They said the procedure had gone well, but the bandages wouldn't come off for a few more days.

She could hear the muffled sound of dinner trays clanging down the hall. They would be bringing her meal soon. Yuck, she thought. More dribble she had to suck with a straw. Thankfully, her parents and TJ had gotten in the habit of eating outside her room. The smell of real food drove her insane. The only other sound was the beeping of the monitor beside her bed. She didn't care for the silence. It gave her too much time to think. Trying to remember the past few years hurt her head. She turned on the television and began flipping through the channels. All she could find were news programs during the dinner hours. Following the national news, local news and sports, came entertainment.

Unexpectedly, the image of herself on a horse she didn't recognize appeared on the screen. Josephine froze. What the hell! Why am I on television? Why is my hair bright red? She turned the volume up.

"Best supporting role nominee, Josie Walker, remains in the hospital following a freak riding accident in Montana two weeks ago. A spokesperson for the actress said her wedding, which was scheduled to take place earlier this month to co-actor Brad Donahue, has been postponed indefinitely. Little information is available on the actress's injuries or her condition at this time, only that she sustained a serious head and face injury that could end her career. Her latest film, *Secrets*, opens next week."

Josephine couldn't breathe! Her mind felt like it might explode as it struggled to register this information. Suddenly, it all came back; attending UCLA, breaking up with TJ, Roy, her acting career, Brad, the wedding, the storm… the baby! "Oh my God!"

She felt her abdomen – no bump! But she wasn't that far along… she wouldn't be showing yet, right? The injury to her head and face — serious enough to end her acting career? What did that mean?

Josephine had only been out of bed with supervision to use the restroom, but now she had to know. Slowly, she swung her legs over the side of the bed and limped to the bathroom with one crutch.

Sheer panic crushed her chest. Why had the mirror been removed? She hadn't noticed it missing until now. She felt the remaining screw holes in the wall with her fingertip. What were they hiding from her? She searched the small clothes closet for her purse but found her mother's instead. She grabbed it and began rifling through it, finally locating a round, pressed powder compact. Awkwardly, she managed to flip it open with one hand.

Josephine gasped! Most of her hair was gone. What little she could see of her face was bruised and swollen. She looked hideous! A brace supported her nose and bandages concealed the rest. She set the compact down and carefully began unwrapping the long strands of gauze until she reached a large square bandage pad covering the right side of her face and eye. Just as the nurses had changed her dressings all week, she slowly lifted it from one corner and gently pulled it free. She still couldn't see out of her right eye, but they had told her it was because her face was so swollen. Josephine lifted the mirror.

"No!" she screamed. This can't be happening. She was a monster!

All she would remember was her crutch crashing to the floor as she collapsed over the toilet.

When Katherine returned with Steven, they found the room full of nurses and doctors. Dr. Wilkes was among them, examining Josephine's face. TJ sat in the corner with his head in his hands. "What happened, TJ?"

"I'm sorry," said TJ. "I left her for just a few minutes. She found a mirror. She was found passed out in the bathroom when they brought her dinner tray. Don't worry, she's okay. She didn't hit her head or face. But she knows."

He didn't have to elaborate. Josephine had seen her face.

Katherine squeezed in and sat beside her daughter, still unconscious. Fewer bandages now covered her face. No need to hide it any longer.

"The air will help her face heal," said Dr. Wilkes. "But, emotionally? Try to have someone with her at all times."

Katherine nodded. Steven stood at the door, his face reflecting her own sheer panic. After the doctor and nurses left, Steven sat opposite her.

TJ approached; his hands clasped in front of him. "I'm sorry. I shouldn't have left her. This is my fault."

"She was bound to find out sooner or later, TJ. We couldn't avoid the inevitable forever."

TJ wiped away a tear running down his cheek. "I'm going to take a walk. I'll be back in a bit."

"Sure, TJ."

Shortly after TJ left the room, Josephine stirred. Her free eye gradually opened. Her daughter turned to her but didn't say a word. She didn't have to. The light which had always burned bright in her beautiful jade eyes, had dulled to a blank, milky stare. Katherine shuttered to her core, her fears realized. She took her daughter's limp hand and held it tight as though it might disappear within her grasp. Josephine turned to Steven with the same defeated expression, bringing her husband to tears. Suddenly, it had all become more real for all of them.

Josephine closed her eye and drifted off to a restless sleep, her hands and eye twitching periodically as she fought her inner demons. TJ eventually joined them again, resigned to sitting in the corner. Katherine couldn't imagine the turmoil TJ must be experiencing, not knowing what their future might hold. So much uncertainty for all of them.

Two hours later, Josephine woke up. Her first words since the bathroom incident were shocking. "I want him to leave," she demanded, focusing on TJ. His heart could be seen shattering across his face. "I don't want his pity. No one in their right mind would want me now. I see Brad isn't here. At least he's being honest."

TJ didn't say a word. As he got up to leave, Katherine reached for his hand. She could feel him trembling.

Katherine turned back to Josephine. "You remember everything now?"

"Yes, everything. Leave!" she shouted at TJ.

TJ's brows drew tight, his jaw locked. Katherine could see the pain glistening in his eyes. TJ let go of her hand and left the room, followed by Steven.

"Sweetie, I can understand how upset you are. It must have been quite a shock, but this week's surgery is just the first. The doctors say once the swelling goes down it will make a big difference. And with time…"

"I'll look better than ever?"

Katherine drew in a deep breath. What could she say, what should she say? Nothing came out in time.

"Yeah, that's what I thought."

"Reconstructive and plastic surgery have come a long way and they're discovering new techniques and improving procedures every day." She couldn't believe that was the best she could do, regurgitating the doctor's hollow words. Katherine took another deep breath. "You have a tough road ahead of you. There are going to be several more surgeries. The doctor said they've had great results with hundreds of cases just like yours. You need to be strong and stay positive."

"That's easy for you to say. You haven't lost your beauty, your career… your future." Her scorn abruptly dissolved, replaced by a sadness she recognized all too well. "The baby?" Josephine quickly read her forlorn expression. "See. I've lost everything!"

"I'm so sorry, Jo." Katherine reached for her hand, but she pulled it away. "You're wrong, that's not true. You have our love, and the love of everyone that has been praying for you. TJ's been here the whole time."

"Please, just leave me alone."

"You're a strong, talented, intelligent young woman with so much to offer."

"I said to leave me alone!"

Katherine didn't want her to get any more upset. Perhaps it was for the best, for a short while anyway. Josephine needed time to sort it all out. Katherine prayed her daughter would find her inner strength and tackle this affliction with the courage and fight she knew lied within her. Katherine exited the room.

She found Steven and TJ leaning against the wall next to each other, silently waiting for her. Both men stepped toward her as she closed the door behind her.

"Has she settled down?" questioned Steven.

"No, she asked to be alone. I'm not sure what more we can say or do at this point. She needs us but she just doesn't know it yet. We need to have patience."

"What should I do?" said TJ.

"Might be best to give her some time. I don't want her getting so upset again. I know you need to return to work. The mill hasn't let you go, have they?"

"No, not yet. They threatened to."

"I'm sorry, TJ. Thank you for all you've done." Katherine gave him a hug. Let's give her a few days. We'll keep you posted."

TJ just nodded and started for the elevator with his head hung low. It broke her heart to see him so crushed. She turned to Steven. "This is heartbreaking. He loves her so much. What else could we do?"

"Nothing. Jo will come to her senses."

"I hope so. She asked about her pregnancy. She knows."

"How did she take it?"

"Harder than I imagined."

"I thought she might even be a little relieved."

"It's hard once you envision having the baby."

"I'm sorry, hon. I didn't mean to be harsh. Just under the circumstances…"

"I know."

Steven slid his hands in his pockets. "I'm just so worried about our little girl, Kat."

"Me too."

Katherine slipped her arm around Steven's and together they walked to the chapel to pray.

15 – The Healing

Two Ponies
December

Katherine chased after an elusive road apple as she picked Major's stall. Cleaning stalls had always been something she enjoyed, even in the freezing dead of winter. She relished the quiet time to reflect or just focus on nothing at all as she performed the mindless task. Lately, it had become her only opportunity to escape the negativity surrounding her. It was the week before Christmas and from the outside, things might appear back to normal with her returning to conditioning and schooling Major, Steven returning to work at the clinic, and TJ back to work at the feed store. But that was as far as it went.

Josephine was home and doing well physically, out of her cast, her arm healed, but she had not regained her vision in her right eye. The trauma had caused severe optic nerve damage. Known to sometimes reverse itself in one third of cases within two to four weeks, but all hope had been lost at her last ophthalmologist appointment, confirming she had permanently lost sight in that eye.

The plastic surgery team made great progress on her second reconstructive surgery, but she continued to describe herself as "Two Face" from the *Batman* comic books and films. Katherine had caught her looking in the mirror with the injured side of her face covered with a magazine. Her shaved hair had begun to grow out her natural color, giving her a cartoonish look with multi-colored, spiked hair. But Josephine couldn't see how much worst it might have been, that she was lucky to have survived. She just couldn't seem to see the glass half full. Josephine seemed lost in some sort of limbo between the living and the dead.

Steven had a difficult time being around her. Every effort to cheer her up seemed to explode into an argument or silence between them for days. He just couldn't understand or accept her negative attitude. TJ tried to visit once after her return home, but she refused to see him. He had moved back home, which pleased Sarah, and called daily to check in on Josephine. The call always ended the same, Katherine promising to let him know the moment she asked for him. He was so certain she would, eventually. And for Katherine, she fell someplace in between. Sometimes angry and frustrated like Steven and other days, just sad and heartbroken like TJ. Some days, it was almost more than she cold bare; still mourning the loss of Betsy and her leg getting progressively worse on top of everything else. Of course, the animals picked up on the dire vibe. Laddy moped around the lodge and Major started acting out; not wanting to be caught and throwing in a few uncharacteristic bucks in at the canter and following jumps. Even she and Steven were at odds about how to handle their daughter's behavior. Josephine's despair was contagious, and a dark cloud now hung over Two Ponies.

Jessie and Dane, Chief and Flo, Sarah, Betsy's family, and Mike and his family all asked to visit her, but she turned everyone down, saying she wasn't up to any company yet. She heard from no one in California besides Roy and Sandy, which only dampened her spirits more. Apparently, once the word got out about her disfigurement, all the pretty people didn't want anything to do with her. She had nothing to offer them any longer. The beach house was up for sale and Roy had flown home all her personal belongings. After a month, people had given up on trying to visit her, all except TJ. Bless his heart.

Josephine spent her days sitting in her room with the drapes drawn and sulking. Katherine had tried every way possible to get Josephine out of her room and out of the house. But she had no interest in seeing Bonanza or watching television or reading outside her room. When she claimed the bright light hurt her eye, they bought her some big dark sunglasses, the kind the movie stars wear to conceal their identities. She still wouldn't leave her room, not even to join them for dinner downstairs.

Once again, the barn had become Katherine's refuge. After dumping the last load of manure, she hung up her picking fork and brought the horses in for the night. They all wore heavy winter blankets, Major to keep his coat from getting too heavy while being worked through the winter, and for the older horses, to maintain their body heat so they didn't have to burn so many calories to keep warm. Katherine closed the barn doors and trudged through the snow back to the lodge. Rather than joyfully leading the way as usual, Laddy sulked beside her, head hung low. The white winter wonderland resembled a Christmas card, but this year, the holidays held little joy.

Normally, the week before Christmas she would be merrily preparing for their huge feast and party with family and friends at Two Ponies. This year she considered cancelling Christmas. In her last weekly letter to Lisa, she let her know they were at their wit's end with Josephine and considered not having the big annual gathering this year. She had asked for her thoughts on the issue but hadn't heard back from her yet.

Just as she reached the top of the stairs, Steven pulled into his usual parking spot beside the side door. He was home early. This came as a surprise since he'd gotten in the habit of staying at the clinic later and later recently. Steven met her at the door. "Let's talk."

When she gripped the doorknob, he added, "Outside."

She followed him around the covered porch to the seating out front where she brushed off the corner glider. Laddy lay at her feet. Steven sat beside her, but he just stared out over the frozen, snow-covered lake in silence. She waited.

He finally turned toward her. "We have to do something. We can't go on like this. It's not healthy for any of us."

She couldn't agree with him more. "What do you have in mind?" She hoped he had some ideas, because she had already tried everything she could think of to break through Josephine's wall of self-pity.

"What would Betsy do?"

That was it? Okay, maybe it wasn't so lame, she considered. "Let me think." Katherine recalled when she had holed up in her room following Billy's presumed drowning. "I believe she would dish out some tough love."

"Exactly. We've been handling Jo with kid gloves for too long. Look where it's gotten us."

"It's going to be me, isn't it?"

"It'll be better coming from you, don't you think?"

"Okay, I guess things can't get any worse. It's worth a try."

That evening, Katherine set the table for the three of them. She cooked one of Josephine's favorite winter meals, beef stew, and made some homemade sourdough bread. Steven gave her a thumbs up as she climbed the stairs. She knocked on Josephine's door. "Dinner is ready."

The door opened a sliver. A hand reached out for the tray.

"Dinner will be served in the dining room this evening. I made your favorite. Beef stew."

The door closed. Katherine turned on her heels and returned to the kitchen passing Steven already seated at the table. She gave him a thumbs down.

Josephine never did come downstairs to eat. As they placed their bowls in the dishwasher, Steven turned to her. "I thought for sure that was going to work."

"Yeah, me too. I don't want her to starve."

"Let's give it more time. Maybe by breakfast she'll be hungry enough to come down."

Sunday morning the outcome remained the same. No Josephine for breakfast and she even made pancakes and sausage. When Katherine pulled out the leftover stew for lunch, she discovered a portion missing. She found Steven in the library.

"She snuck down and ate her dinner after we went to bed last night."

"Really? Well, now what?"

"I don't know." Katherine plunked down in a chair across from where he was seated at the desk. "Should we even try to have our traditional Christmas dinner this year? Maybe just Lisa, Daniel and Lizzy."

"Oh, I forgot. I picked up the mail on the way home yesterday." Steven reached across the desk and pulled an envelope from a small stack of mail. "There's a letter from Lisa." He handed her the envelope.

She quickly opened it and began reading it to herself while sharing the highlights with Steven. "Lisa agrees we should not have the big get-together this year. And she wants to come alone… without Daniel and Lizzy. And she can stay a whole week. Daniel is taking the time off."

"Hmm, guess it will be just the four of us then."

"I'll let everyone else know tomorrow."

"When is she arriving?"

Katherine read on. "This Friday, staying through New Year's weekend."

"Under different circumstances, I'd be looking forward to having both girls home again for the holidays." Steven focused in on her. "But this could really go sideways, you know."

"Sure could." Katherine stood up. "See you for lunch. Sadie just pulled in. I'll be at the barn if you need me."

When Sadie pulled up to the barn, she studied the upstairs windows from her seat. She wondered which room Josephine was holed up in. Dumb bitch, riding off into a thunderstorm. She got what she deserved. At least she had sense enough not to drag TJ along on her pity parade. All that time he spent at the hospital and she just blew him off. He got what he deserved too.

Sadie felt certain with a little more time, TJ would give up on Josephine for good, move back in with her and they would pick up where they left off. She hadn't seen him since he moved out following Josephine's accident, having only spoken over the phone. She would play it cool and wait for him to come back to her, licking his wounds. Until then, she found a roommate since Sally didn't move back in, and one with privileges. Sadie smiled, hoping TJ would be jealous when he learned Matt had moved in with her.

When she saw Katherine come down the stairs, she exited her car. "Good morning," she said, cheerfully as she approached.

Katherine met her at the barn door. "Hi, Sadie, have any trouble coming down the drive?"

"No, it was fine."

"Great. Let's strip the stalls today. They need it with the horses being in every night this week. Nice we have a clear day."

Sadie slid open one barn door while Katherine pushed open the other. "Not supposed to snow again until Wednesday."

"Ha, so they say," said Katherine.

"Right." Sadie shared a laugh with Katherine knowing how unpredictable the weather could be at this elevation in the mountains. "How's your leg doing?"

"About the same, some days worse than others."

"I'd be happy to ride Major for you anytime," said Sadie, quickly adding, "If Jessie isn't available."

"Thanks, I might take you up on that."

This made her day. Katherine trusting her with Major would be huge. A big step in solidifying their relationship. Sadie gleefully dug into Dandy's stall. She enjoyed their time together, just the two of them, but she was curious to hear any news about her competition. When Katherine began cleaning Major's stall beside her, she had to ask, "How is Jo doing?"

"The same," she said flatly, not offering to elaborate. Sadie knew the situation with Josephine had become a strain on the whole family.

Rumor had it that Josephine lost half her face. Ha, not so "perfect" anymore. It pleased Sadie guessing she would most likely not act again, yet she feared Josephine might end up staying at Two Ponies. Hopefully, she wouldn't, and she'd go and be ugly by herself someplace else or get so depressed… Sadie stopped there. Did she really wish Josephine would harm herself? Maybe. Her accident and having her home again did disrupt her plans with TJ and Katherine. But she would be the one traveling to Las Vegas with Katherine this spring, not her damaged daughter. That thought put a smile back on her face as she scraped the last of the manure and shavings from Dandy's stall.

"Say Sadie, we haven't had much of an opportunity to chat lately. How is it going with that special fella?" inquired Katherine from the neighboring stall.

"I don't remember telling you about him."

"Ha, you didn't. But there is someone, isn't there?"

"Okay, you got me," she said, trying to sound amused. "It's going slow."

"Good. That's the best way. But if things get serious, I'd love to meet him sometime."

"Sure," she said. Hopefully sooner than later!

TJ sat studying his last semester's books and exams in preparation for returning to classes next month. Luckily, he didn't lose his job at the mill, but he figured Dr. Walker may have had a hand in it. He'd been putting in extra hours at the feed store whenever possible, doing the difficult deliveries the other guys didn't want to do. Living at home again had helped financially, yet he still came up short for his housing and had to secure a school loan.

He felt bad about leaving Sadie so unexpectedly and paid the rent until she found a roommate. When he first left, Sadie was livid, but the last few times they spoke over the phone, her demeanor had drastically improved, even sounding sympathetic about Josephine's condition. Where he stood with Josephine remained a question. He hoped she only needed more time. Time to heal and feel better about herself. Perhaps then she would allow him back in her life.

TJ put his books down when his mother called him to supper. His grandparents already sat at the table. He helped put the food on the table and took a seat across from his mother.

"I spoke to Kat today," she said, earning his full attention. Sarah took a bite of her cornbread, keeping TJ in suspense.

"Well, what did she say? How is Jo doing?"

"Worse, if you can imagine that." Both his grandparents just shook their heads. They had always been people of few words. "I feel so sorry for them," continued Sarah. "They can't even get her to come downstairs for a meal now."

TJ suddenly lost his appetite. "Wish she would let me help her."

"They cancelled Christmas dinner."

That news didn't come as a surprise. "That's understandable," he said. "It would be difficult and awkward for everyone."

"Lisa is coming, though, for a week."

"That's good," thought TJ out loud. They were close as kids. "Maybe Lisa can break through to her."

"I hope so," said Sarah.

TJ picked at a piece of salmon. "I was hoping to see Jo before I leave."

"I wouldn't count on it. Eat your meal. Starving yourself isn't going to help anyone, least of all Josephine."

Josephine pulled the covers over her head. She wished she could just shrivel up and disappear. No, she wished she could go back in time… to the summer of 1995. Why didn't she have the guts to stay with TJ? Why did she care so much about what others thought? They could have made it work somehow. Now everything is ruined. TJ just feels sorry for her. How long could he stand looking at her ugly, distorted face before he'd leave her? She couldn't look at her own reflection for more than a few seconds. It made her almost puke every time she did.

All her life, she had been proud of her pretty face, getting looks from every boy or man that passed by. Now people would stare at her for a different reason. The doctors kept saying with each surgery she would look better, getting her hopes up. She was tired of the surgeries, tired of the disappointment, not to mention the pain. Before each surgery, she imagined looking normal afterward, like her old self. But that had not been the case and probably never would be. Yeah, there were improvements, but her eyebrow would never grow back, her nose and face were no longer symmetrical, she had lost sight in her right eye, and she was told they weren't sure how much scarring would remain. The next surgery wasn't scheduled until after the holidays.

Peeking out from under her quilt, she found the room brighter than usual. The blanket she had hung over her window to block out the light had slipped off one side. Sunlight now cut across the room, blinding her. She walked to the window, shielding her right eye, and peered out over the parking area. Her father had left to pick up Lisa from the airport a while ago. They would be pulling in soon. Josephine dreaded her visit. Lisa would insist on seeing her. The thought of her sister staying in her old room right next door threatened her privacy, something she had come to cherish. Wait. She would just refuse to see her too. Nothing had to change. After all, she didn't invite her!

Lisa didn't know what the outcome of her visit would be, but she felt she had to try. Try to break through to the brave, stubborn and determined Josephine she knew was hiding from the world and herself. She had prayed to Betsy for some spiritual guidance and felt she had come up with a good plan.

The few words her father had to say when he picked her up, she had already heard from her mother via her letters, the self-pity, denial, isolation and self-deprecation. They were concerned where this might lead, perhaps even to Josephine harming herself. They tried to get her to see a psychologist with no success. She was a grown woman. They couldn't force her to go. She had never seen her father so distraught. It hurt to see him hurting so.

They drove in silence and when they arrived at Two Ponies and entered the lodge, she was shocked by her mother's appearance. She looked drained and exhausted. When she pulled her in for a hug, she could feel her pain exuding from every pore.

Katherine held her at arm's length. "I'm so glad you're here."

"I hope I can help."

Her father fetched her bag and left it at the base of the stairs. They followed him and all took a seat in the great room. Her mother filled her in with more details about Josephine's condition. Wishing each other a Merry Christmas never entered the conversation.

"She knows I'm coming, right?"

"Yes, I told her just this morning," said Katherine.

"Did she say anything?"

"No. She just took her breakfast tray and closed the door as usual."

"I'm not going to force myself on her."

Her father just shook his head. She guessed her mother spoke for both of them. "I'm afraid she won't make an effort to see you."

"Guess time will tell, then. Regardless, let's enjoy Christmas together. I want to go for a sleigh ride and cut a tree like we do every year."

Both her parents' eyes narrowed as they tried to comprehend her disregard for Josephine wasting away upstairs in her room. Suddenly, they both smiled at each other, nodding.

"Okay. We see where you're going here," said her father. "It's worth a try."

Lisa grinned. "Play Christmas music and watch holiday movies so Jo can hear them."

When Steven picked up her suitcase to carry it upstairs, Lisa stepped in.

"I'll take it."

"Okay, be careful going up those stairs."

"I will."

Just before she reached the landing, she felt the vibration of a door closing down the hall. Lisa smiled, walked right past Josephine's room and set her bag down on her old bed, then returned downstairs without so much as a pause at her sister's door.

When it was dinner time, Lisa offered to carry her tray up to Josephine's room. She tapped the door. "I have your dinner," she said. There was no way of her knowing if Josephine responded. So, she tapped the door again. "It's Lisa. I'm deaf, remember."

The door opened a crack and a hand pointed to the floor.

"Okay, Jo. I'll leave it here on the floor for you. We're going to watch *A Christmas Story* after dinner. We'd love to have you join us. It used to be one of your favorites, remember?"

Lisa wasn't surprised Josephine did not join them downstairs that evening, but she kept peeking up at the open loft landing at the top of the stairs and swore she saw some movement at one point. After the movie, she retired early. The long travel day always left her exhausted. She must have surprised Josephine heading upstairs so early, because when she reached the landing, a blanket lay on the floor near the railing. Josephine wouldn't have been able to see the television from there, but she must have sat and listened to the film. It broke her heart picturing her sister so afraid and alone. Lisa knew what that felt like all too well; growing up unloved, teased and bullied. She knew what it was like to be different and to have to make the most of what she was dealt in life. As she lay in bed, she wondered what Josephine was doing and thinking just on the other side of the wall dividing their rooms. She began to read one of

Joseph O'Reilly's books she picked out from the library. It didn't take long for her to doze off.

The next day, Lisa took Josephine her breakfast. Again, she tapped on the door, getting the same result. Lisa set the tray down on the floor. At lunch time, she tried again.

"Mom and I are riding in the arena after lunch. I haven't ridden Blackjack in years. Wish you would join us." Again, she left the tray with no response.

She planned to try this strategy for a few days. Dr. Hanley, Dad's associate, would be covering Christmas Eve and Christmas Day, but her father would be working each day that week. So, the house would be empty while they were out riding. Lisa didn't expect Josephine to join them right away, but she wondered if her sister would venture downstairs to try to watch them. The far kitchen window offered a view of the barn aisle, the trail down to the ring and a portion of the indoor arena if the doors were left open. They were expecting a clear and sunny day so having the doors open wouldn't be an issue. Lisa recalled a pair of binoculars hanging in the coat closet and left them auspiciously hanging on the coat closet doorknob, right in Josephine's line of sight as she passed by to enter the kitchen.

Josephine did not join them that day, but Lisa felt the ride did her and her mother some good. Like her mother always said, nothing like fresh air and the scent and feel of horse to heal the soul. With their spirits lifted and feeling encouraged by Josephine having left her room last night, they were anxious to see if she came downstairs to watch them ride.

"Yes! She was here," said Lisa, as enthusiastically as possible while keeping to a whisper. She showed her mother how the binoculars were returned differently than how she had left them.

Mother and daughter shared a warm smile. Katherine placed her hand on Lisa's shoulder.

"It's a start!"

Josephine didn't think it was possible to feel any more miserable or sorry for herself, but she did as Bing Crosby's famous rendition of "White Christmas" carried throughout the lodge. How could they all be going about being so jolly without her? Their laughs during the movie and smiles while riding taunted her. That evening, when her sister brought up her dinner, Lisa informed her they would be going out to cut a tree in the morning. Again, she said they hoped she would join them. Would they really follow through with their family Christmas tradition without her?

That evening, just as Josephine was about to turn off the nightstand light, a knock on her bedroom door startled her.

"You awake, Jo?"

It was Lisa! Josephine panicked, gripped by fear. She shot up off her bed, and just as quickly, sat back down. What was she afraid of? Rejection? Not with Lisa. Embarrassment? Again, not with Lisa. What exactly was it she was hiding from? Could it be her vanity? She had always been the pretty and confident sister, the one who made boys heads turn growing up. Now, who had she become? She had lost more than just half her face. Where was the confidence now that she couldn't hide behind her good looks? Perhaps she had been a coward all along.

Turning off the bright reading light, Josephine left a dim nightlight on in the corner. She ran her fingers through her hair, pulling it down over the right side of her face. Another tap on the door. Slowly she turned the handle and cracked it open.

"Can I come in?"

Josephine opened the door with her back to Lisa and sat on the bed with her back to the nightlight.

Lisa stepped into the room. Her sweet smile warmed Josephine's insides and for a moment, she almost forgot... and wanted to rush to her with a hug. She turned away and lowered her focus. Her sister sat on the end of the bed within reach and gently pulled her hair away. Josephine could feel her eyes begin to well.

"Let me see you, Jo."

She raised her chin and faced her big sister. Lisa's eyes were full of love and compassion. "You'll always be beautiful, Jo, where it matters."

That was it. She collapsed into Lisa's arms, her head resting on her sister's frail shoulder as she sobbed. Lisa patted her back, consoling her. She couldn't recall how long she cried, but she felt exhausted afterward, yet lighter.

Josephine sat up and managed a weak smile.

Lisa sprang off the bed. "I'll be right back. I have something for you." She left and returned with a folded piece of drawing paper. "It's from Lizzy."

Without a thought, Josephine turned the overhead light on and opened the drawing. She could make out a person with red hair on a yellow four-legged something.

Lisa resumed her spot on the bed. "It's you riding Bonanza," she pointed out.

"Yes, I see it now." As she deciphered the child's writing, she pointed and read it out loud, "I love you, Aunty Jo." Her finger affectionately grazed over the several red hearts adorning the drawing. "It's so sweet. Is there a way I can call her to thank her tomorrow?"

"Sure. Just text Daniel first. She'd like that. We'd all like that."

Her meaning was clear. It was time for her to return to the living.

"Will we see you for breakfast?"

Again, the panic took hold. "I don't know."

"When you're ready," she said, giving her a pat on the back. "Love you. Maybe we can talk more tomorrow night, my room, like old times and I'll bring the chocolate." Without expecting an answer, Lisa hugged her and said goodnight.

Josephine sat awake on her bed. Lisa's visit had brought things into focus, or perhaps it was the good cry that cleared her head. For the first time since she came out of her coma, she considered someone else's feelings. She had been self-absorbed and thoughtlessly putting her family through hell. Sure, she had been dealt a bum deal, but so had her sister, who had to adjust to slowly becoming deaf as a child. How frightening that must have been. And she had always considered herself the brave one. Josephine tried to imagine living in a silent world without music or ever hearing a voice whisper in your ear, "I love you." Lisa was the brave one, not her.

Again, she pondered what she was so afraid of? Suddenly, something clicked. My God, she was living her most recent role. Like the ballerina who could no longer dance, she could no longer act, and couldn't stand the looks of pity from her family and friends. Her character had run away, hiding from all who loved her until someone, crippled far worse, made her see the light. The pity she thought she felt from others, turned out to be only a manifestation of what she felt about herself. Only when her character learned to love herself again, did she feel she deserved the love of others. Perhaps with time, she could learn to love herself again too.

The next morning, Josephine pulled on some jeans and a sweatshirt. She hadn't gotten dressed in street clothes since returning from her last surgery weeks ago. Dang! She had to lie on her back on the bed to zip up her jeans. Great, now she was fat and ugly! She slipped into her hooded jersey jacket and found her dark glasses. Stopping at the bathroom down the hall, she froze when she turned on the light. She kept expecting to recognize the stranger in the mirror. It was easy to forget how she looked alone in her room. Josephine flipped up the hood, slid on her glasses, took a deep breath and started for the stairs.

Halfway down the stairs, she paused. Snowflakes the size of coat buttons floated past the great room window giving the world a fresh, clean start to the new day. It was almost Christmas, a time of rebirth, a time to celebrate the gift of life. She had felt cursed. If the lightning hadn't struck, if Bonanza hadn't reared, if the tree hadn't fallen… but if the tree had fallen just a few inches to the left, if her mother and TJ hadn't found her, or if Search and Rescue hadn't arrived when they did, she wouldn't be feeling sorry for herself, she wouldn't be feeling anything at all. All of a sudden, she felt grateful to have survived her ordeal and ready to face her new world.

Josephine could hear her mother and Lisa down the hall in the kitchen, giggling as they prepared breakfast. When she entered the room, all clanging of dishes and silverware stopped. Their expressions were almost comical as their demeanor turned from one of surprise to "nothing to see here" like it was normal for her to show up for breakfast, let alone in a hoodie and dark sunglasses.

"Good morning," they said in unison, followed by "jinx." The once personal joke between her parents, which had been some old kid's game, had become a family tradition over the years.

"Hi," said Josephine. "What can I do?"

"You can pour the orange juice. The glasses are…"

"I know where the juice glasses are, Mom."

"Right. Thanks!"

Lisa snuck her a sly grin before heading for the dining room with the place settings. Josephine recognized the tray they had been using to serve her meals sitting on the counter. She set the full glasses on it and followed Lisa to the table.

"Coming with us to cut the tree?" asked Lisa. Her energy was contagious.

"Sure, why not. Where's Dad?"

"He's clearing the drive. He'll be thrilled."

After a couple more trips to the dining room, the buffet style breakfast was ready. Josephine sat down beside Lisa as Katherine made one more trip with a platter of hot scrambled eggs. Just as they were all seated, on cue at exactly eight o'clock, she heard her father enter the side door and slip out of his Carhartt overalls and boots. Mom had trained him well. His face lit up when he entered the room.

"Well, howdy stranger," he said. Her father never was one to sugar coat anything.

Josephine peeked from under her hood. "Hi, Dad."

Steven took his seat at the head of the table across from Katherine. "Isn't this great? The four of us."

"Sure is," said her mother. Even Laddy seemed pleased, acting more himself, making the rounds around the table for handouts.

Halfway through the meal, Josephine pushed her hood back and took off her glasses, earning a grin from all present. She did put the glasses back on before venturing outdoors to shield her bad eye from the sun. She breathed deep, the cool fresh air lifting her spirits.

In the past they would utilize the tractor and wagon, sleigh and snow mobile for large tree-cutting parties, but this year they would only take the cutter pulled by Major and the snowmobile. While Steven filled the Ski-Doo with gas and collected what he needed to cut and pull the tree home, the women worked as a team to harness Major.

Before they ventured out to find the perfect tree, Josephine visited with Bonanza. She had avoided him since her accident. Did she somehow blame her boy? She knew that was unfair. Any horse would have spooked in that situation, but she couldn't help feeling disappointed in her bombproof horse. She had never taken a fall in all her years of riding and the one time she did, it nearly took her life. The thought of mounting any horse raised her heartrate. Even anticipating the sleigh ride made her nervous. This was so unlike her old self, the one she believed she knew.

It was a tight fit, but the three of them crammed into the single bench seat of the cutter. Her mother sat center manning the lines, as Steven let go of Major and he trotted down the drive toward the back field. For years now, they only needed to cut the top off one of the few remaining blue spruce they had planted years ago for this very purpose. Now ranging ten to fifteen feet tall, they could still fit in the high, open beam ceiling of the great room, but as they learned a few years back, the base would no longer fit in their tree stand.

A light snow fell as they laid tracks down the two-track through the woods. The beauty was invigorating and helped Josephine to relax and enjoy the ride. Their voices joined in a chorus of "Jingle Bells" scattering jays and crows while squirrels chattered an alarm. Laddy uncovered a rabbit and took off after it.

Unexpectedly, a resting mule deer bolted from its bed under a stand of dense pine. Major shied a little, raising one runner of the sleigh onto the rim of the trail off-kilter, pushing Josephine's panic button. She took a white-knuckle grip of the side of the cutter. Her mother centered the sleigh again, then took the lines in one hand while giving her a few reassuring pats on the leg with her free hand.

The remainder of the excursion was uneventful, resulting in a lovely Christmas tree standing tall in the great room, infusing the scent of evergreen throughout the lodge. Josephine joined Lisa and her parents in decorating the tree that afternoon and for dinner that evening, along with all their family holiday traditions the remainder of her sister's visit. Her mother had even convinced her to leave Two Ponies to do some Christmas shopping in Great Falls under the cover of a scarf and dark glasses. Thankfully, no one recognized her.

The final night of Lisa's stay, Josephine visited with her in her room one last time, running late into the early morning hours. They reminisced good times together as kids, sometimes laughing so hard they cried. Following some eggnog and chocolate Kisses, Lisa dared to mention TJ.

"I heard TJ stayed with you the whole time you were in a coma."

Josephine squirmed in her seat. "Yeah, that's what Mom said."

"I don't understand, Jo. If you ran out on Brad and the wedding and were trying to find TJ, why did you send him away and refuse to see him?"

Josephine's brows pinched together as she bit her lip.

"I'm sorry, Jo, maybe it's too soon."

"Everything changed."

"Not everything, Jo. TJ hasn't changed. We hoped once you came out of your room last week, you'd see him."

"It's different. You, Mom and Dad… I feel safe. With TJ... I… what if…?"

"What if he couldn't love you anymore?"

Josephine nodded. She stood up and walked to the window and gazed out across Pine Island Lake, then turned toward Lisa. "There," she pointed. "Across the lake at the cabin, we promised to love each other forever, that nothing would ever come between us. I broke my promise. And now, I don't want him to feel he needs to keep his."

"What makes you think anything has changed for TJ? Isn't it obvious he never stopped loving you? He wouldn't leave your side, Jo. What more does he have to do to prove that to you?"

"Whenever he told me he loved me, it always came before or after him saying how beautiful I was."

Lisa patted a spot beside her, and Josephine returned to the bed. "You need to give TJ more credit. TJ saw what happened to you and he didn't run like Brad did. He stayed. TJ loves all of you, not just your face. See him."

Josephine nodded. "Okay, I'll see him soon, I promise."

"Good, that's settled. Guess we should get some sleep. I have an early flight in the morning."

"I'll get up to see you off."

"You better," teased Lisa, sharing a warm embrace with her sister.

Josephine got up to leave, then turned. "Thanks for coming."

"It was Christmas. Where else would I be?" said Lisa. "Good night, Little Bit."

"Good night, Lisa."

Lisa hated to leave, but her mission was accomplished.

The healing had begun.

16 – Reborn

New Year's Day, the wind howled outside the arena, making the metal roof shudder and creak. Major had become accustomed to the noise and traveled along the back wall at shoulder-in without a hitch. Katherine glanced over at Josephine bundled up in front of the space heater.

"How did that one look?"

"Good. Better than the last one, more consistent." Josephine left her cozy seat and approached her and Major at the center of the ring. "Ready to do some jumping?"

"Sure. Can you lower that two-stride combination for us to warm up over?"

"Coming right up."

Katherine dismounted to replace her dressage saddle with her jumping saddle that Josephine had carried out for her. After a few warm-up passes through the combination, she asked her daughter to raise all the jumps to three feet. Following a few courses, she had her add an oxer to a couple of the fences. Josephine watched intently. She had started joining her schooling sessions with Major about a week ago, taking an interest in their jumping, primarily. She enjoyed helping with the jumps and coming up with new gymnastic combinations and courses with challenging turns and striding. Katherine had hoped Josephine might join her on Bonanza at some point, but she still hadn't gotten back in the saddle.

Following a course of four-foot jumps, Katherine brought Major to an abrupt halt. "We're good for today," she said, rubbing her leg. Due to the discomfort and weakness in the leg she had broken, Katherine found herself jumping less each week. Luckily, Major didn't need much work over fences, but she needed to stay in shape. She feared if anything went wrong, like a bad spot or landing, her leg might give out, especially over the higher and wider spread jumps. Katherine decided on the spot to make herself an appointment with Josephine's osteopathic doctor their next visit. Perhaps some physical therapy would help.

Katherine circled Major around Josephine at a walk. "We'll just do some flat work tomorrow."

"Okay," she said, sounding disappointed. "I could watch him jump all day long. He sure looks fun to jump."

"He is." That gave Katherine an idea. "You know Bonanza jumps now. Jessie's been using him with beginners over some low fences. He does great."

"Really?"

"Why don't you tack him up tomorrow and ride with me?"

"You mean jump him?"

"Not right away. You need to get your balance, seat and leg back first. You do remember how to tack and ride English, right?"

"How could I forget," Josephine replied, sarcastically.

Katherine guessed she had that coming. Her daughter had grown up in an English saddle, from age three until high school. Katherine insisted her daughter take a lesson with her every afternoon during the school year and join student classes daily throughout the summer. Thinking back, she was pretty tough on her, expecting more from her than any of her students. And it must have been difficult having her mother as her instructor. No wonder Josephine got burned out and switched to Western. It was such a shame. She had been a natural, especially over fences.

"Well?"

"I don't know."

Katherine knew she had developed a fear of riding after her horrific accident, which could only be expected. But now with her leg healed, she felt positive some riding would do her good. It always picked her up when she was feeling down.

"You can ride at your pace. Western or English. It won't be a lesson or anything. Just get on and have some fun." She could see the wheels turning as Josephine worked up the courage.

"Sure, why not," she finally replied, trying her best to sound like it was no big deal.

Katherine smiled. Baby steps.

Over the course of that week, Josephine graduated from a walk to a trot and then to a lope, riding Western. That afternoon, Josephine surprised her by tacking up English. Katherine had to admit it warmed her heart seeing her daughter back in an English saddle. And Josephine looked damn proud of herself too, not missing a beat with her diagonals or leads. Bonanza looked the best she had ever seen him go, trying so hard to please Josephine. Toward the end of their ride, Katherine sat center full of pride as her daughter circled her at a lovely, stretchy trot. She had the softest hands and most beautiful posture. She had always felt Josephine could have competed successfully at the national level in equitation. But then and now, if she was going to ride English, jumping was her game.

Within days, Josephine was jumping Bonanza, but her daughter found she had issues with her depth perception, seeing with only one eye. They called her doctor who told her she would need to relearn how to see in depth, especially when driving, but in time her remaining eye would adjust. Josephine was a quick learner and within days she was jumping low courses without any problem.

Katherine could see Josephine's confidence growing and not only in the saddle. The sense of accomplishment she felt conquering one goal at a time with her riding, began to parallel her progress at overcoming her insecurities about her appearance. Josephine hadn't yet agreed to see TJ, but she had agreed to join her on a trip into Elkhead that afternoon. This would be her first visit into their hometown since her accident, knowing there was a good chance of running into someone they knew or getting stares from strangers who may or may not recognize her as the famous actress. Katherine was very pleased. Now more than ever, she believed in the power of horses to heal the heart and soul.

Thankfully, it was a cold and sunny day, giving Josephine the excuse to wrap her head and neck with a scarf and to wear her dark sunglasses. They made the rounds from the post office to the grocery store, then to their last stop at the feed store. Her mother parked in the designated spot for pickup and went inside to pay for their order. Josephine felt relieved Elkhead was quiet with little traffic that afternoon. Only the checkout lady at the Food Lion recognized her and went out of her way not to stare. That was nice, she thought. Josephine was sure everyone in town was now aware of who she was and knew about her accident. News traveled fast in the small town.

Her mother returned and tapped on the window. "I forgot to pick up something. I'm going to run over to the drug store. I'll be right back."

With their truck backed into the loading dock, Josephine faced the street, watching her mother carefully maneuver across the icy road. Suddenly, the back of the truck jumped as sacks of grain were tossed in the bed. Josephine turned around and was shocked to see TJ loading their feed. He caught her glance and quickly focused back on his task. She turned away in a panic. It would be rude not to at least acknowledge him. Should she just wave? No, she must say something. After all, he might have very well saved her life, not to mention the days he spent at the hospital sitting with her. She owed him at least a hello after having been so cruel to him.

Josephine exited the passenger door and walked to the back of the truck. TJ had his back to her as he picked up another fifty-pound bag of feed off the handcart. When he spun around with it, he froze with the sack resting on his broad shoulder, looking down at her from under his cowboy hat. When their eyes met, Josephine drew a deep breath.

"Hi, TJ," she said, pulling the scarf a little further over the right side of her face.

"Hi, Jo." TJ set the bag down and in one fluid motion, vaulted from the loading dock off the back of the truck bed, softly landing on the parking lot just inches from her. A breath caught in her throat. She stepped back to escape TJ's intense gaze, stripping her of her defenses. She wondered if he could see her through the dark glasses. Sensing she felt uncomfortable, he broke eye contact and stepped away too, his hands finding his pockets.

"I wanted to thank you for everything," she said. "I'm sorry about how I treated you at the hospital." Again, their eyes locked. Josephine must have been holding her breath because she began to feel a little faint. Breathe. It's only TJ, she told herself.

"No big deal." TJ removed his hat. "Glad you're out of the cast and it's nice to see you out and about. Your mom told me you're riding again."

"Oh."

"I've been calling to check in on you."

"Did she mention I'm riding English and jumping Bo?"

"No, that's great!" After fidgeting with his hat for a few moments in silence, TJ flipped it back on, leapt effortlessly back onto the loading dock and finished lobbing the last few bags. He closed the tailgate and jumped back down, leaving a little more space between them this time. "Maybe I could come over and we could ride together. I've never ridden in an indoor riding ring."

Suddenly, it felt like old times. Josephine smiled. "I'd like that."

Her mother approached the truck. "Oh, hi, TJ."

"Hi, Mrs. Walker." TJ turned to Josephine. "Call me. I'll be at the ranch, when I'm not working that is, until I return to school next week."

"Okay," she said, bringing a broad smile to TJ's face. She returned a warm glance and turned toward the cab.

"Bye, Jo."

She turned and waved. "Bye, TJ."

As soon as they closed their doors, Josephine had to call her mother out. "Why didn't you tell me TJ's been checking in on me? Did you know he was back working at the mill?"

Her mother started the truck and put it in gear, turned toward her and replied with only a silly grin. As she suspected, her mother had planned this meeting all along. Josephine wasn't mad at her. She was glad she did it, relieved even. She and TJ had taken the first step in rebuilding their friendship. She wouldn't allow herself to think beyond that, not yet.

All Josephine could think about the rest of the day was getting to see TJ again. She found herself even forgetting about her face and eye for brief instances and only about how much fun it would be riding together. She really did feel like a kid again. Reborn. She couldn't wait and called him the next morning with an invitation to ride that afternoon.

Wearing her glasses and scarf, Josephine had Bonanza tacked and waiting a half hour before TJ was scheduled to arrive, just inside the arena door. She felt as giddy as a schoolgirl when she heard his truck and trailer pull in the gravel drive. Josephine left Bonanza tied and met him at the trailer. Cisco whinnied; Bonanza answered. The War Bonnet Paint jumped off the trailer and TJ slid a bridle over his halter and followed her into the covered arena. The horses greeted each other with deep vibrating nickers.

"They remember each other," said Josephine.

"I think you're right." TJ flung himself onto Cisco's bare back. "You should ditch the saddle. It's a lot warmer this way."

"I want to show you something first." Josephine planned to show off a little, plus she hadn't ridden bareback since her accident.

As TJ introduced Cisco to the arena, the Paint came to a screeching halt and snorted at his reflection in the dressage mirrors. They laughed as the gelding cautiously approached the strange horse that had suddenly appeared as they rounded the corner.

After she warmed up Bonanza, Josephine took him through the jumping course she had set up. TJ clapped and cheered and took Cisco over a couple jumps himself to Josephine's delight.

Following a couple tracks circling the arena, TJ looked around and halted center. "Say, let's have some fun like when we were kids."

Josephine paused, not sure what he had in mind.

"Let's set up an obstacle course."

"Sure. Great idea!" They dismounted, tied their horses and went to work. Twenty minutes later they were taking turns maneuvering through a maze of obstacles they constructed from the jumps and whatever was laying around; side passing over a pole, changing leads as they weaved through a line of schooling standards, walking over a blue tarp and piece of plywood, and backing through a ninety-degree turn of poles on the ground. Soon they were timing each other through the course.

Josephine was having so much fun, she didn't notice her scarf had slipped off. As she raced through the course one more time, she happened to catch her reflection in the mirrors and brought Bonanza to a sliding halt.

"Say, that's a great addition. Good end to the course," shouted TJ from across the ring.

Josephine slid off her horse and searched hysterically for her scarf. It took TJ a moment to figure out what was happening. He found her scarf on the ground along the rail, dismounted and ran it to her. Josephine turned toward the wall, with one arm across her face, the other reaching for the scarf.

TJ tenderly took her arm and turned her toward him. And removed her glasses. Cradling her face in his hands, his gentle gaze held her captive. "Jo, you don't need to cover your face. I see you as I've always seen you. Beautiful." He brushed a single tear from her cheek with his thumb. "Scars are signs of courage. Warriors once displayed their wounds proudly. You endured freezing temperatures and broken bones for hours. You're a warrior too, Jo. You fought to survive. Don't be ashamed. Let them be a reminder of your strength and courage."

Josephine closed her eyes as TJ kissed each of her scars then brushed his lips over her trembling lips. How could this be? How could he still find her beautiful? Could he still love her?

She stepped away. "I couldn't stand to be with you out of pity."

Shocking her, TJ smiled and shook his head. "Oh, Jo, I've never pitied you or said anything just because I thought that's what you wanted to hear. I've always been straight with you. Did I ever let you win at our game of tag at the creek or at any other game? No. If you won, you won fair and square. Now, hop back on your horse and try to beat my record time through the course."

"No."

"No?"

"Not yet." Josephine leaned in and kissed TJ. It must have taken him by surprise because it took a moment for him to respond and deepen their kiss. For an instant, Josephine couldn't feel the earth beneath her feet. Again, she shed a tear, but this time a happy one. She couldn't describe the feeling of overwhelming joy she felt back in TJ's arms.

The day before TJ left for Fort Collins, he suggested they ride out on the trails bareback. It took Josephine a moment to work up the courage to venture out of the security of the riding arena.

"Not too far though, okay?"

"Whatever you feel comfortable with."

Josephine knew exactly where she wanted to go and led the way onto the lake trail. Even though it was the warmest part of the day, the snow still crunched beneath the horse's feet, telling her it remained below freezing. Her face burned from the cold as they trotted through the aspen grove to the top of the hill overlooking the lake, but it felt good. She felt alive.

The view was remarkable. The frozen lake, forest and mountains lost all definition, covered by a blanket of snow. She was glad she wore her sunglasses, though. Her right eye remained sensitive to bright light. Josephine glanced over and smiled at her riding partner. The joy in his face matched her own. She was happy, genuinely happy. Not long ago, she didn't think that would ever be possible again.

When they reached the creek, Josephine halted, staring downstream. Not two miles away, she almost lost her life. She had survived, but their baby had not. Not only had she lost this pregnancy, but perhaps any chance of conceiving a child again. When the time was right, she would need to tell TJ.

Josephine pushed those dark thoughts into the shadows where they belonged on this bright and joyous day. She guided Bonanza across the stream and picked up a canter. TJ joined her. Here, the path was wide enough for them to ride side by side, smile to smile. This was perfection, Bonanza cutting a path through two feet of virgin snow beneath her, puffs of his breath breaking the silence of the frozen forest as she gazed into the eyes of the man she loved. How had she thought she could ever be happy with anyone else, perched on a cliff in a glass house surrounded by strangers. This was where she belonged.

TJ didn't look surprised when she slipped off her Buckskin out front of the cabin. Quickly, they tied their horses to the hitching post. TJ didn't waste any time collecting wood from under the porch to start a fire in the wood-burning stove. Josephine did her part, producing an armful of dry pinecones she harvested from under low hanging branches. Leaving their snow pants and boots at the door, they soon sat snuggling under the quilt on the lumpy old couch in the warm glow of a crackling fire. The flames were hypnotic, bringing back fond memories of past visits to the cabin.

Josephine leaned onto his shoulder and asked, "Remember our last visit here?"

"How could I forget. I relived it a thousand times over the past three years." TJ clasped her hand and gave it a squeeze.

Josephine sat up and turned toward him with a smile. "We were so much in love." Suddenly, her smile faded recalling her broken promise. "We made a pact that day before I returned to school. I'm sorry I didn't hold up my end."

TJ studied the firelight dancing across her solemn face. "What happened, Jo? Why did you give up on us?"

Josephine stared into the fire. "I was all caught up in my work, my new friends."

"You were ashamed of me…"

"No… maybe. I don't know. It's a whole different world out there. I couldn't see you fitting in."

"You didn't give me a chance to."

"You're right. I should have. I owed us that much."

"Do you miss it? The fame, the money, your fancy house and friends?"

"No. They weren't my friends any more than Brad loved me. Haven't heard a word from any of them." She paused, shaking her head. Everything seemed so clear to her now. "They weren't real. I think the truth becomes fuzzy with people in the film industry over time. They get so good at fooling others and themselves, they're unable to separate what's real from what's fiction anymore." They laid silently for a moment as Josephine reflected on her past life. "It's all about what you have and who you know out there. I don't think many of them are truly happy. Roy and Sandy are the exception. I do miss my work, though. But that's it." When she turned to find his russet pools, she caught him studying her through a curtain of black tresses. She swept them behind his ear and stroked his bronze cheek. "I'm so sorry for what I put you through. But never, not once, did I stop loving you. That promise I kept. Do you forgive me, TJ?"

"I forgave you the moment I saw you in the stands at the race. And again, when I learned you were on your way to find me in the freezing rain and snow."

Josephine searched his eyes. "Can we really pick up where we left off, TJ, after all that's happened? Can you love me again?"

"Jo, don't you know, I never stopped."

He leaned in and kissed her passionately. Josephine laid down and guided him over her. Immediately, she felt him become aroused, triggering the kind of desire she felt only for him.

Suddenly, Josephine jumped. "Ouch! That spring again!" They shared a good laugh and rolled onto the floor taking the old quilt with them. Patiently, they undressed each other. Josephine savored every reveal as if it was their first. Unlike at the lake when they ravaged each other, they took their time. TJ slowly covered every inch of her body with kisses before hovering over her, his chest brushing against her erect nipples. Josephine purred in anticipation, then when she couldn't stand it any longer, she reached her hands around his buttocks and pulled him to her. Josephine moaned as TJ brought her to a climax, then pulled out. Again, neither of them had come prepared. Josephine had imagined cuddling by the fire, but she should have known it might lead to more, it always had in the past. But the thought of carrying her IUD in her pocket on their trail ride brought on an inner grin, which quickly fell away, sadly recalling she might not need one any longer.

Not in TJ's wildest dreams did he think today's ride would lead to this. As they spooned in front of the fire, his mind drifted to the future. Again, he could see beyond tomorrow, picturing them living together on his ranch with a beautiful family. Perhaps it was their sweet lovemaking reunion, or the wonderful week they had spent together, but unexpectantly, TJ found the confidence and courage to pursue his lifelong dream. He rolled over to face her.

"Let's get married, Jo. Not now, but after I graduate next year."

She sprang up into a seated position. "Are you proposing to me?"

"Yes, I suppose I am." TJ took her by the shoulders and sat her down on the sofa wrapped in the quilt. He slipped into his jeans and frantically searched for something to use as a ring. Pulling a lose fiber from the quilt, TJ knelt in front of her and took her left hand.

"Will you marry me, Josephine Mary Walker?"

Josephine's eyes grew large and she took a deep breath. Her answer poured slowly from her lips like honey as she exhaled. "Yes. I will marry you, Theodore James Black Feather."

The couple sealed the engagement with a kiss. Was this real? Could he have finally caught his shooting star? TJ tied the thread around her ring finger. "Of course, I'll give you a real ring. I have something special in mind, but if you'd rather pick one out yourself, that's fine."

"Something special?"

"My grandmother's wedding band. My Dad's mom."

"That would be perfect, TJ."

Again, as they cuddled on the couch watching the fire, he looked to their future. "I want a big family, lots of rug rats," said TJ, thinking out loud. He felt Josephine immediately stiffen. This was not the reaction he expected. "Don't you want children? Or just not that many?"

It was time. She must let him know before this went any further. She searched his questioning eyes, hoping he could still love her if they couldn't have a family. "I lost more than my face in the accident," she whispered.

TJ's face became a scrambled puzzle. "What are you talking about?"

"I was pregnant. The accident… it caused a miscarriage."

She wasn't surprised it took a moment for TJ to overcome his shock. "I'm so sorry, Jo." He closed his arm around her. "But you're young and…"

"But there was damage," she interrupted, then rambled on before she lost her nerve. "The doctors said I might not be able to get pregnant again or go full-term. I'd understand if you want to call off the engagement. I should have told you sooner. I know how much you want a family…"

TJ pressed his finger to her lips. She could see the sincerity in his eyes. "Don't. Nothing matters but us… being together." He held her hands. "If you can't have children, we can adopt if you want or I'd be perfectly happy, just the two of us."

Josephine swallowed hard. "There's something else I need to tell you, TJ." She hesitated, trying to build up the courage. Now, it seemed so obvious she should have told him the baby was his right away.

"What, Jo? Your hands are trembling."

Everything was so perfect now between them, she was terrified he'd be angry with her for not telling him and ruin their special moment.

"After all we've been through together. You don't need to be afraid to tell me anything," said TJ, his intense gaze begging for her to confide in him.

"The baby… was yours."

The painful look in his eyes nearly gutted her. "I'm so sorry, TJ," she managed, her eyes welling.

When he pulled her close and she rested her head on his shoulder, she could no longer hold back the tears.

"Oh, Jo. Why didn't you tell me?"

"I thought you hated me," she sobbed.

"Never, Jo. I was hurt, feeling rejected. Like I said at the barn that day. I didn't mean it. Did Brad know?"

Josephine shook her head. "He wanted me to get an abortion regardless, but I wanted the baby. It was all I had left of us." Now TJ was crying too. "When I learned I'd lost it, I just wanted to shrivel up and die."

TJ gently clasped her arms. "It was an accident. We can try again.

If it's meant to be, fine, if not, fine. I love you, Jo. You're all that matters."

Josephine nodded and smiled. With all her secrets revealed, a huge burden had lifted off her shoulders. "Let's head back. I don't want to worry Mom."

"Can we tell your folks we're engaged?"

"Of course. Come for dinner tonight, bring your mom and the ring. We'll make an official announcement."

"Perfect! I can't wait to see their faces."

"Me neither!"

Katherine rushed about, cleaning house and preparing a special meal with Josephine's help. The last-minute invitation for TJ and Sarah to join them for dinner came as a surprise, but a pleasant one. She and Steven couldn't be more pleased seeing the kids back together. This was the happiest they'd seen Josephine since her accident, and if possible, she seemed to glow even a little brighter that afternoon.

It was sad TJ would be leaving for school soon, but at the same time, they were pleased he was returning to his classes, Steven especially. Josephine planned to continue her daily rides and mentioned she had an idea for a screenplay to help pass the time until TJ's return. This idea thrilled Katherine. Josephine needed something to delve into. Her writing would give her purpose and something else to give her a sense of accomplishment and pride, along with her riding.

When their guests arrived, Katherine was surprised to see Josephine come down the stairs in a lovely dress and a little extra makeup. She looked beautiful. Her daughter had given up the dark glasses, hoodie and scarves last week. All TJ's work.

Sarah gave her a hug and TJ shook Steven's hand. Steven poured apple martinis while they congregated in the great room until dinner was ready. Everyone seemed to be in a festive mood, laughter once again ringing throughout the halls of the Two Ponies lodge.

Katherine's heart sang.

During dinner, TJ filled them in on his classes that semester, Josephine gave a short synopsis of her screenplay, while Steven shared the recovery of a horse that had miraculously healed from a severe leg injury. Katherine and Sarah just sat and shared smiles.

Following dessert, a fruit Jell-O mold she threw together at the last minute, Katherine served coffee. She noticed TJ and Josephine smiling at each other in a goofy kind of way, then Josephine nodded to TJ. He walked around the table to Steven.

"If it's okay with you sir, I'd like to marry your daughter."

Steven nearly dropped his cup of java. Katherine sort of saw it coming and wasn't as surprised. "Well, of course. What wonderful news. Congratulations!" said Steven, shaking TJ's hand like a well pump.

Katherine was already on her feet, giving Josephine a hug. "I'm so happy for you both."

Sarah didn't look too surprised either. After everyone congratulated the couple, TJ placed a beautiful antique silver and sapphire ring on Josephine's finger.

"It was my grandmother's wedding ring," he said. Katherine remembered Beth's ring fondly. TJ went on to share the story of his grandparents with Josephine as told by his father. "My grandfather, Teddy Black Feather, who I was named after, was a prize fighter competing up and down the Pacific Coast. He earned enough money to purchase their ranch back when few Blackfeet owned property off the Reservation. Sadly, I never got to meet him. He met my grandmother at a horse auction in Alberta."

"Aunt Beth was a special lady," said Josephine. "I was little but I remember her fondly."

"And I guess the rest is history," said TJ. "I'm looking forward to the day Jo and I will share a life together on their ranch."

Before Sarah and TJ left, the kids bundled up and sat out on the porch together, presumably to say their goodbyes. The three months apart would go faster for TJ at school, but at least Josephine now had something to look forward to, a future with TJ.

Snuggled on the front porch loveseat glider, Josephine quietly watched a light snow fall past the parking area flood light.

"I'll miss you," said TJ, breaking the silence.

"Me too," said Josephine.

TJ squeezed her hand. "I'm sorry I won't be here for your next surgery."

"I'll be fine."

"Keep me posted and I'll be home before you know it for spring break."

"I'm already counting the days."

They sat for a while longer cuddling, before Sarah came looking for them. She cracked open the front door. "TJ, you have a long drive ahead of you in the morning. You need your rest."

"Okay, Mom. We'll be right in."

Sarah stepped back inside and closed the door behind her.

Josephine slipped off her glove and admired her ring one more time. "I love it."

"I love you," said TJ, turning to kiss her goodbye.

As the harsh Montana winter intensified in January, Josephine did all of her riding in the arena. She began noticing Katherine jumping less and shortening her rides on Major. One day as they wrapped up their schooling session and approached the exit, her mother nearly fell to the ground as she dismounted. Josephine quickly slid off Bonanza as Katherine reached for her bad leg in pain.

"What happened? Are you okay?"

"This damn leg of mine. It's been acting up lately. It's all this damp, cold weather. I'll take an Advil. It'll be fine."

Josephine dismissed it as her mother had, until a week later when she pulled Major up after taking only a couple of jumps. "C'mon.

How about you take him over a few?"

"I'm worried about you, Mom."

Her mother casually explained she had an appointment with Josephine's doctor that week to take a look at her leg. "Probably just need some physical therapy."

She felt relieved. "I'm glad you're getting it checked out."

"Well, you want to give the big guy a whirl, or not?"

"You want me to jump Major?"

"Sure, you're looking great and you'll do just fine."

"Okay!" Ever since she started jumping again, she dreamed of taking Major over some fences. She couldn't wipe the zealous smile from her face if she tried. She left Bonanza standing in the corner with his reins pulled over the stirrups of her saddle.

"We should still share the same stirrup length," said Katherine, motioning for her to mount with her hands clasped, ready to give her a leg up.

Accustomed to mounting from the ground on her fifteen-two-hand stout Quarter Horse, Major stood five inches taller, requiring some measure of assistance. Josephine would have preferred using the mounting block by the door, but mother ruled in the ring.

Once seated, she gathered her reins and surveyed the course. "The jumps look a lot smaller from up here!"

"Ha, wait until you feel him jump. He just floats over them. Take him around the ring at a trot and canter first, so you get a feel for each other."

Josephine trotted the big Thoroughbred on the rail, amazed by how much ground he covered so effortlessly. When she picked up a canter, she felt like she was sitting in an uphill rocking chair. When she passed her mother, Josephine was relieved to see her smiling. "He's amazing!"

"You look amazing on him. He likes you."

"Good," she called back.

"Start with the high cross-rail to the five-stride line from a trot."

Josephine's heart was beating like a bird's up to the first jump. Oh my! They glided over it like it wasn't even there. She was pleased with their good spots and their even five strides between the jumps.

"Great, take him through again, this time at a canter for four strides."

This time she could feel him pulling her to the fences, and she had to work a little harder to get their striding.

"He was testing you," said Katherine. "You did good. Go ahead and take the course now at a steady pace, well into the corners."

Josephine had never had so much fun jumping. None of their school horses she rode growing up jumped so effortlessly. Of course, she had to remind herself this was only a three-foot course with no spreads, but she was dying to do more. She imagined the thrill of taking Major through a Grand Prix course.

Bonanza stood in the corner, one back leg cocked, eyes nearly closed as Katherine approached him. "I'll take him up while you cool out Major."

Josephine nodded and waved from the opposite side of the arena.

"You two looked great. Would you mind jumping him while I'm on the mend?"

"Mind? Are you crazy? I'd love to."

"I thought you might," she grinned.

"Was it that obvious?"

"Yes. I haven't seen you that happy on a horse in a long time."

"Who knew — riding English no less!"

17 – Jealousy

Two Ponies

Sadie arrived at Two Ponies early that morning so she could fill in for a sick employee at the feedstore later that day. Normally, Katherine would have the horses fed and turned out before she arrived, but when she opened the barn doors, her boss had just finished dispensing their grain.

"Good morning! You're early," said Katherine, returning the feed can to the grain bin.

"They gave me some extra hours at the mill today."

"Great. You can turn the horses out when they're done with their grain. For now, I could use some help with the laundry."

Katherine disappeared into the restroom, which also housed a washer and dryer, and reappeared carrying an armful of towels and leg wraps. Sadie followed her into the office where she set the pile down on the center of the couch. Katherine sat on one end of the sofa, she sat on the other. They started in on rolling the polo wraps which was a tedious chore, starting Velcro to Velcro and rolling them tight.

"How was your drive over this morning?"

"Okay," said Sadie. "Hit a little ice on eighty-nine, especially on the bridges."

"Thanks, I'll take it slow. Leaving for a PT appointment soon."

Sadie finished one set and moved on to another. "How is the leg?"

"About the same. I've stopped jumping for now."

"Bummer. Sorry to hear that. I can't today, but I'd be happy to work Major over some jumps for you tomorrow after chores," she said, enthusiastically, hoping she might finally get to ride the big Thoroughbred.

Katherine started in on the towels. "No need. Josephine's jumping him. They're doing great together."

The wrap Sadie had just finished rolling fell from her hands and rolled across the office floor. Anger built in her like hot lava ready to erupt. That bitch! She didn't dare speak for fear of what might come out.

"You'll have to stay and see them go one afternoon."

Sadie tapped down her emotions and managed a respectful, "Sure." Moments later, she couldn't sit any longer. She needed to work off her anger, escalating once again. "The horses should be done. I'll put them out and start in on the stalls."

"Okay, thanks! Be sure to get all of Major's wet spot. I've never seen a horse drink so much."

She just nodded and scooted out of the room. Josephine's jumping Major and what do I get – his wet spot! She was so furious she could feel her heartbeat in her temples. Great, another migraine! She seemed to be having a lot of them lately. Ever since she learned TJ and Josephine were engaged, she could hardly think straight. How could TJ pick that mangled brat over her? How much more could she take? All her plans were coming unraveled. As she cleaned stalls, she schemed on how she could get TJ back and get even with Josephine, even if it ruined her relationship with Katherine. She would do anything to have TJ.

Within weeks, Josephine was jumping Major over four-foot courses with oxers. Turns out, one of the pins in her mother's leg must have gotten jammed during her fall at the Pan American Games over the summer. Using her legs when jumping somehow caused a deep bone bruise from the displaced pin. It could take months to heal or might require corrective surgery if her physical therapy didn't work. Her mother still conditioned Major on the flat while Josephine schooled him and herself over fences.

Josephine was scheduled to check into the hospital for her next reconstructive surgery that afternoon. She had another scheduled for the spring, hopefully her last. She hated the thought of interrupting her riding, and almost cancelled the procedure when she learned they planned to use her inner thigh as a donor site. If that was the case, in addition to her week-long hospital stay and home recovery, she wouldn't be able to ride for another week, possibly two. Eventually, they agreed on using skin from under her arm. That she could manage.

Normally, she rode Major in the afternoon when it was warmer, but she wanted to squeeze one more ride in before she left for the hospital. Her mother had a doctor appointment that morning but arranged for Sadie to be there so she wouldn't be riding alone. Josephine had left a note for Sadie on Major's stall the night before, asking her to leave him in that morning. But when she entered the barn, she found his stall empty and Sadie cleaning it.

"Hi, Sadie. Didn't you see my note to leave Major in? I'm riding him this morning."

Without so much as a glance in her direction, Sadie continued working on the stall. "Must have fallen off."

Josephine searched the floor. No sign of it. "Okay, then," she said to Sadie's back. "Guess I have a horse to catch. He's not going to be very happy about leaving the hay and coming back in so soon."

"Good luck!"

Josephine detected a tinge of sarcasm. They never had hit it off, but she never recalled Sadie being rude. She collected Major's halter and lead and started for the front pasture. She looked down at her leather high boots. She hadn't planned on trudging through the snow to chase a horse down. Before entering the pasture, she returned to the barn for the grain can. The sound of grain normally caught any horse's attention and might save her boots from getting too wet. When she entered the door, she heard Sadie cussing about something. She thought she might have heard her name.

"Everything okay?"

"Perfect!" she spat from the stall.

Josephine didn't have time to deal with moody Sadie. She didn't take it any further and exited the barn with enough grain in the can to entice Major. A few shakes and she had all three horses at the gate, Major front and center. She brought Major into the barn, closing the sliding door behind them. After putting him in the crossties and removing his blanket, she left for the tack room to collect what she needed for her ride. When she returned, Major was prancing in place, his eyes rimmed with white. Something had spooked him.

Rushing to Major, she stroked his neck while speaking to him in a soothing voice. "What happened?" she called out to Sadie who had moved on to Bonanza's stall.

"What are you talking about?"

"Major. Something upset him."

"Didn't see or hear anything."

This was getting weird, if not annoying. Josephine approached Bonanza's door. The wheelbarrow was parked in front of the stall door. Just then, Sadie spun around with a fork full of urine-soaked bedding, tossing it in the general direction of the wheelbarrow, but missing, it landed on her breeches and boots.

"Oops, sorry about that." A fraction of a smile slid across Sadie's face.

"Okay, what's going on? You pissed at me about something?"

Sadie set down the fork and strode around the wheelbarrow and stood with her arms crossed only a few feet from her face. "So, I heard you and TJ are engaged."

"Yes, we are." Josephine couldn't imagine where she was going with this.

Sadie cocked her head and smirked. "He asked me first, you know."

"What are you talking about?"

"We were together for over two years. I suppose he didn't tell you about that, did he? He said he loved me. We were living together when you had your accident."

Josephine couldn't breathe. "I had broken it off between us. He had every right to move on with his life."

"He didn't tell you about us though, did he?"

Turning away, Josephine began to tack Major. Why hadn't her mother told her? Could this be true? Sadie resumed her work without another word. Josephine tried to steady her shaking hands as she tightened the girth. Maybe this wasn't such a good idea. Her mother had told her how sensitive Major could be, picking up on any negativity and there was plenty of that exuding from both her and Sadie. She stood for a moment, her mind racing in a million directions. Was she lying? If not, why hadn't TJ told her about Sadie? Was it really any of her business? But wouldn't he have told her if it didn't mean anything? Does he still love her? His mother's words last summer came to mind. How much had TJ changed? As she patted Major's shoulder, he shuddered. That was it. She removed the saddle, returned his tack and put his blanket back on. As she led Major out of the barn, Sadie stood at the door of Bonanza's stall wearing a sinister grin.

As she stormed up the drive toward the lodge, she couldn't wait to tell her mother about Sadie's behavior when her and TJ when she got home. Josephine wanted her fired. As she waited in the library, she had time to think and cool off. Perhaps she shouldn't say anything recalling how pleased her mother was with Sadie and grateful she had her as an assistant and workhand. Hopefully, if her mother's leg improved, they would be leaving for Las Vegas in a few short months and her mother would need Sadie to assist her on the trip. If she were fired, her mother might not be able to find a qualified replacement in time, and even if she could, she wouldn't have time to adequately train them. Josephine could accompany her mother if she wasn't scheduled for another surgery the week before the World Cup. She would remain silent and not jeopardize her mother's trip.

And for TJ, maybe he just didn't have an opportunity to tell her about Sadie yet. Everything did happen so fast before he left. Regardless, the news was certainly disturbing. Imagining TJ with Sadie made her skin crawl. Now she knew how TJ had felt when she was with Brad. She guessed she had this coming. Strange, though, that she had never thought about what TJ was doing and with whom for those three years. Did she really think he was pining away for her the whole time, incapable of loving another? Grow up! The past was the past for them both. She needed to focus on their bright future together, nothing more.

When her mother returned, Josephine stood at the counter in the kitchen making sandwiches for them.

"How did your ride go?" asked Katherine.

Josephine turned. "It didn't. Had a bad headache, better now."

Her mother looked concerned.

"Really, I'm fine."

"Need some help?"

"No, sit. Almost done."

Katherine slid onto the bench of the kitchen nook as Josephine set their plates down and took a seat across from her. "How did your appointment go? Is your leg getting better?" She took a bite of her BLT.

Her mother stared at her sandwich. "I'm not going."

"Not going to PT anymore?"

She shook her head. "Not going to compete in Vegas."

Josephine's sandwich crumbled to her plate. "What? Why? After all you've been through?"

"I'm going to need surgery."

Josephine got up and slid in next to her, giving her a big hug. "Oh, Mom, I'm so sorry. All the work for all those years."

Katherine turned to her. "I want you to take Major. This will be his only chance."

Josephine's jaw dropped as she moved far enough away to make eye contact. She stared at her mother in disbelief. She couldn't speak as her mind tried to register her words.

"Only if you want to, of course."

"Me, Major, the World Cup? You really think I'm ready? I've never shown at that level. What am I saying, I've never competed in show jumping, period."

"We have two months. I already registered you with the North American FEI World Cup League, just in case."

"You what?"

Her mother continued, her voice building with excitement. "We'll hit the road as soon as you're healed. There's a couple recognized shows on the West Coast we can attend to build your confidence at competing at this level. Major's been there and done that."

"So, I just hang on for the ride?"

"Very funny!" said her mother, dismissing her comment. They both knew no matter how talented and experienced a horse was, it took the right touch, control and aids to be successful. "You'll have to compete and do well at one qualifying event. And it just so happens, there's one outside Sacramento at the Murieta Equestrian Center the end of March. Then we wait to see if you're selected for the finals. Major's reputation will help. If so, we head to Vegas for a chance at the Olympics."

"Oh, is that all?" Josephine shook her head. "The World Cup? The Olympics! I don't know, Mom. This is insane! And, what about sponsors? I don't have any and you said you needed them."

"You will. Think about it, Jo. Josie Walker reaching for a gold medal instead of a gold Oscar."

"But do I really need sponsors? How much are we looking at?"

"It'll cost tens of thousands to get us to Sydney. Your father and I could come up with part of it."

"No, I'll cover any difference. It won't be a problem. The house should sell by then. Oh my God, you have me actually considering this!" Josephine shook her head and smiled.

"I'm sure the sponsors I have will switch their backing to you and I know you won't have any trouble securing a few more. But it would put you back in the spotlight. Are you ready for that?"

Josephine felt the scars on her face. "I think so. But what about my blind eye? Will that be an issue?"

"It'll be a little more challenging. You'll have limited vision taking corners to the right, but so long as you know your course, you'll be fine."

"Okay. Then what about my surgery tomorrow? I won't be able to ride for a week or so."

"Jessie will be happy to work Major a few times next week. He's ready to go. I've only had him jumping to get you up to speed."

"Listen to you. And you said Betsy was the schemer."

"Guess I learned well. So, what do you think?"

"I love jumping Major. I've even dreamt of taking him over a Grand Prix course, just not so soon and on such a big stage."

"You're an internationally known actress!"

"I was. Besides this is different."

"Think on it. Talk it over with TJ. But I need to know soon so we can get your entries in."

Josephine smiled. "I know now. TJ will be onboard. Let's do it!"

That evening, Josephine had to call TJ to share the news. Some male student answered the house phone and said he'd try to find him. About five minutes later, TJ came on the line.

"Jo, is everything okay?"

"Yes, it's great! I have some news." She kept him waiting to build the suspense.

"What Jo? What's the news?"

"Mom isn't taking Major to the World Cup. I am! Well, if we qualify!"

"What? Why?"

"She's going to need surgery on her leg, and she wants me to see how far we can go. She thinks I'm ready. We'll compete at a few shows in California and hopefully be selected. But, I'm so sorry TJ, if we make it to the World Cup, I'll be in Vegas during your spring break."

"It's okay. I'm sorry to hear about your mom, but I'm so happy for you, Jo. This is such a great opportunity for you. I love hearing you so excited. You need this."

Even though TJ tried to hide it, Josephine could hear the disappointment in his voice. She knew he'd drive or fly out to Las Vegas if he had the money. She also knew if she offered to pay his way, he wouldn't accept it. "Hey, I know. I'll come visit you in Fort Collins after we get back."

"That would be awesome. Say, does this mean you could qualify for the Olympics?"

"Yes, isn't it crazy!"

"Wow, huge."

"I know. I'll be back in the news, though."

"You okay with that?"

"I'll have to be."

"Sorry, Jo. I've got to go. Have a line forming at the phone here. I'll call you at the hospital tomorrow evening."

"Okay. I love you."

"Love you too."

Josephine sat a moment with the phone in her hand reflecting on their call. She didn't bring up the Sadie thing. It still niggled at her brain now and then, but she chose to put it behind them where it belonged. He would tell her when the time was right.

Katherine was pleasantly surprised when changing bandages at home after Josephine's surgery. Even though the area was still swollen and bruised, there was significant improvement. Josephine rushed to the bathroom to look for herself.

"Now I'm really ready to return to the spotlight."

Her daughter's jubilation was contagious. Mother and daughter held hands and jumped up and down in front of the mirror. "Ouch, I better slow down," giggled Josephine. "I need to heal ASAP!" She studied her face again, turning and leaning into the mirror to get a better look.

Katherine took a closer look too. "And just think if you have the same results after your last surgery this spring."

"I might make a beautiful bride after all."

"Oh, sweetie, you would always make a beautiful bride."

"I can't wait to tell TJ, or maybe I should surprise him?"

"That sounds like fun."

"I'll wait, then."

"Let's get you bandaged back up. You can show Dad later when he gets home."

"He'll be thrilled."

Katherine's heart sang seeing her daughter's sprits soar. Between her and TJ back together, looking forward to showing Major and now such positive results from her surgery, Josephine looked the happiest she'd seen her in years. She had come to the light at the end of a very long, dark tunnel.

Sadie sulked as she swept the aisleway of the barn while Jessie schooled Major in the covered arena. Just when she thought things couldn't get any worse, she learned Josephine would be competing with Major and could possibly qualify for the World Cup. On top of that, Katherine would need her here at Two Ponies to man the barn while they were gone. Not that she'd want to spend that much time around Josephine anyway, but she sure was looking forward to experiencing the event. Disappointing, indeed. She'd never been to Las Vegas and she loved mingling with all the international riders and trainers, not to mention the loss of the additional pay on the road.

As she was finisheing sweeping, Jessie led Major, followed by Katherine, into the barn.

"I can ride a little later on Sunday," said Jessie to Katherine, slipping off Major's bridle. "Dane will be home to watch Cole."

Katherine began removing the saddle. "Great! My hands and feet are frozen. I can barely feel the billets. This morning training in the winter is for the birds."

"I'm sweating," teased Jessie.

Katherine chuckled. "It was a good workout for both of you. Sunday should do it. Jo plans to ride Tuesday. She would have watched your ride, but she has strict orders from the doctor to stay out of the barn for at least a week."

"That was great to hear her surgery went so well."

"But don't say anything to TJ about it if you see him at the mill. Jo's going to surprise him."

"Sure. Think she'll return to California and acting now?"

"I don't know. She hasn't mentioned anything. It wouldn't happen until after her last surgery this spring and depending on how far she gets with Major. Not sure how TJ would feel about it."

Sadie's face lit up. This was her chance. "I'm finished. Taking off."

"Thanks, Sadie."

Wow, that was some piece of news! She'd been hoping to find some way to come between Josephine and TJ, and this little tidbit might just do the trick. She heard from Matt that TJ planned to return home during spring break even if Josephine was in Las Vegas. Matt mentioned visiting his uncle in Bozeman, Montana for his birthday, which just so happened to be the day TJ would be returning home. Now Sadie prayed Josephine qualified for the World Cup. The timing couldn't be more perfect for her scheme!

Sacramento, California

One month later

Josephine had gone unrecognized at their first two shows. She had blended in with all the other women in riding garb, helmets, boots and smelling of horses. It took some pressure off knowing she could fail and not make headlines. Josephine was thrilled with placing third at the first show and winning it all at the second. She had felt prepared having jumped the big bay over five-foot obstacles at home, but she found maneuvering these challenging courses in front of an audience raised the bar to a whole new level, literally and figuratively. Just as her mother had assured her, Major didn't look at any of the jumps. Their only faults were her doing; taking a corner too tight, not gathering him well enough between combinations, and allowing the overzealous Thoroughbred to come in too hot to a fence or two.

Today was different. A writer from an equestrian publication had recognized her earlier that week and it didn't take long to make national entertainment news. Now as she dressed for the qualifying course at the Murieta Equestrian Center, a group of reporters had gathered outside their trailer. Now, not only did she have to run over every detail of the course in her head, she had to prepare a statement to the press.

Her mother slid in the trailer door. "You ready? Just keep it short?"

"I'm good. This I have plenty of experience with."

Her mother smiled and patted her on the back.

Josephine glanced in the mirror one more time, checking her makeup. "How do I look?"

"You look beautiful. Let's go. Major is tied in his stall. He's ready except for his bridle."

"Thanks, Mom." The moment she stepped out the door, she was bombarded with questions. "I have to warm up, so I have just one statement for you all. I'm thrilled to have this opportunity to ride such a special horse and to compete with so many wonderfully talented riders and horses. No, I don't have any plans to return to acting. At the moment, anyway. Wish me luck!"

A barrage of well wishes followed her to the barn where her mother intervened and sent them all packing to the stadium.

Once Josephine bridled Major, she mounted outside the barn and headed for the warm-up area. A couple diehard reporters followed them from a distance.

"Light and easy warmup, then take just a couple jumps," said Katherine. "Get to the gate in time to watch the previous rider go. Always helps to see the horse before you go navigate the course."

"Will do."

"Remember, you can't turn your head too sharply to the right to compensate for your blind side. Major might overreact."

"I understand. Thankfully, it's a big open course."

Standing at the gate, she tried to focus on the horse and rider on course, but the crowd drew her in. This was the largest venue she'd competed in so far and she found it daunting. Josephine took a deep breath and returned her focus to the big gray on course. There was a tricky three-jump combination following a sharp turn that worried her. Several of the horses they watched earlier had difficulty focusing on the B and C components of the combination, their attention drawn to the huge and brightly colored oxer on the same line.

When she was announced, the stands erupted setting Major onto his haunches for a moment. She heard the rider behind her ask, "Who is that anyway? I've never heard of her."

A man answered. "That's the actress Josie Walker on that off-the-track Thoroughbred from Montana."

When the gate opened, her mother gave her a pat on the leg. "Good luck, Jo. Have fun!"

Josephine refocused as the gray completed the course with one dropped rail; four faults. Again, the crowd recognized her with cheers and applause. She rode center, saluted the judge, circled and crossed the starting line. They were on course and under the clock!

The Grand Prix course consisted of fourteen obstacles, with heights up to five feet, three inches and with spreads of up to six feet, seven inches with an optimum time of eighty-one seconds. Most of the course was pretty straightforward; verticals, oxers, a one-stride combination, a broke line, the triple combination and a Liverpool jump with a vertical fence set up over a span of water. The latter, her mother had warned her of early on. Major had a habit of wanting to take off early and jump long over these jumps, having always been leery of water. He had knocked the top pole down in the past.

Major sailed clean over each jump, including the triple combination, coming up to the Liverpool. For some unknown reason, Josephine glanced down at the water just for an instant, losing her focus, then felt the big bay launch ahead of her a couple feet early, leaving her behind in her body position. Josephine grabbed mane and prayed they'd clear the top pole. The next five seconds played out in slow motion. She gasped as she heard the knock of one of Major's back hooves hitting the top wood pole. She could hear it vibrate within the jump cups. Had it fallen? She listened for the thump of the rail hitting the ground or the clamor as it hit the Liverpool enclosure. Silence. Would they clear the pool of water? They landed awkward but she heard no splash. Immediately, she turned. The pole was still in place! They made it! The pair cleared the remaining jumps and finished with a nearly perfect time, just a couple seconds too fast.

It turned out five other horse and rider teams also went clean. The winner and subsequent places ended up being determined by ride times. One pair had finished a few seconds closer to the optimum time, to take first place. Josephine and Major finished second, but more importantly, they stood a good chance of being selected to attend the World Cup!

Elkhead, Montana

TJ almost decided not to return home for spring break since he wouldn't get to see Josephine. But his mother was looking forward to having him home and he didn't like to go too long without seeing his grandmother and grandfather at their age. He wouldn't have the opportunity to see them again until summer break.

No sooner than he tossed his overnight bag on his bed upstairs, his mother called him down to the kitchen to take a call.

"Is it Jo?"

"No, some girl though," said his mother.

TJ's gut tightened. "Hello?" His fears were realized. It was Sadie asking him to join a group of friends at Rudy's that evening. "I don't think so," he told her, then she mentioned Talon would be there. He wouldn't mind hanging with Talon. His mother gave him a curious glance from the stove. "What time? Okay. Tell Talon I'll be there. Bye."

"Going out?"

"Yeah, later. That was a friend of Talon's."

'Oh," she said, seeming satisfied. She never had asked if he was seeing other girls while he was living on the Reservation or in Fort Collins and he never volunteered.

When TJ arrived at Rudy's around eight, he searched the bar and grill for Talon. There was a good Saturday night crowd with a live band doing a sound check against the back wall. He found Sadie sitting at a table in the corner, alone.

Sadie waved him over. He looked as gorgeous as ever, his jeans fitting snug in all the right places. "Hi, TJ."

"Hi, Sadie. Where is everyone?"

"They must be running a little late. Have a seat."

TJ sat down and ordered a beer for them both, keeping an eye on the entrance.

"How are you TJ?"

"Good."

"Classes going well?"

TJ nodded. "I heard you're still working at Two Ponies."

"Yes, I'm taking care of things while they're on the road. Pretty cool Jo is showing Major now," she said, cheerfully.

TJ's glance showed his surprise at her mentioning Josephine. "Yeah, she's pretty excited they were selected to attend the World Cup. They're on the road now to arrive in Las Vegas late tonight. Her first round is Wednesday. She's really excited."

"Right." Bring up Josephine and all of sudden he turns into Chatty Cathy. Now time to set the hook. "It was great to hear Josephine's last surgery went so well and that she's planning to return to her acting career in California." TJ swiveled in his seat toward her like a top. Yep, that got his attention.

"What? Who told you that?"

"Jessie mentioned it when she was riding last week. And I saw it on TV this week."

TJ fidgeted in his seat and downed the last of his beer. "You know we're engaged, right?"

"Sure. Congrats!" Now to eliminate the suspicion. "I'm seeing Matt. He's always been crazy about me, you know?"

"Why isn't he here tonight?"

"He's in Bozeman with Noot visiting some uncle. Hey, let's celebrate your engagement. The others will be here soon." Sadie flagged their waitress down and ordered four shots of tequila.

When the shots arrived, TJ turned to her. "Who's that for? You?" His voice had turned harsh. "If I remember correctly, you're a bit of a lightweight."

"Really, look who's talking? I'll bet any guy in here could drink you under the table, even Josephine's prissy ex-fiancé, Brad? Maybe even me!" she laughed.

She could almost see the steam rising from TJ's flushed face with the mention of Brad's name. Sadie downed the first shot. TJ followed. Within seconds, she drank the second one, again followed by TJ throwing back his second shot.

Much to Sadie's surprise, TJ ordered four more shots. "We'll see who's the lightweight. Where's Talon, anyway?"

While TJ turned to search the room, Sadie dumped her shots in her water glass. "He was supposed to come along with Cindy and some of the others."

The local country band started playing their rendition of Lonestar's "Amazed" and couples flooded the dance floor. Sadie began swaying to the music in her seat. "I want to dance. C'mon TJ, one little dance, please. For old times' sake."

TJ turned to her with a scowl. "Did Kat say anything about Josephine moving back to California?"

Sadie smiled. Her plan was working. This was tearing him up. "Yeah, something about her returning to her acting. Geez, don't you two talk? You'd think she'd tell her fiancé her plans before she told the world. I'll bet she told Brad."

"Shut up. You don't know anything."

"Apparently, more than you do."

TJ ordered four more shots, drinking his two in quick succession. Sadie had never seen TJ drink more than a beer or two. She pointed across the dance floor. "Isn't that Talon and Cindy at the back?" TJ rose from his seat to get a better look, almost toppling his chair over. Again she dumped her shots in her water. Now time to reel him in.

"Let's dance. I love this song. You'll have a better view of the place and maybe Talon will see us. I'll bet they're here someplace."

TJ took her by the hand and staggered to the dance floor where they awkwardly slow danced, his hands lightly resting on her hips. As he continued to search for Talon, Sadie laced her arms around his neck and pulled him close, pressing against his belt buckle. TJ stiffened and stumbled as he backed away from her. "I don't see Talon. I'm leaving."

"You can't drive like this."

"Like what?"

"You're drunk."

TJ appeared to be trying to bring her into focus. When he started for the door, he ended up with his arm around her neck to steady himself. "Ha, maybe you're right."

"You wait right here. I'll get my car."

TJ passed out on the way home, but Sadie didn't care. She had all she needed to raise suspicion and doubt between the couple. She managed to wake him enough to help her get him to the couch. The next morning, Sadie let TJ sleep it off while she worked at the Walkers. During her morning call from Katherine on the barn office phone to check in on the horses, she asked to speak to Josephine.

"Hi, Jo. Just thought you should know, one woman to another, that TJ showed up at my place yesterday and spent the night. You need to take better care of your man if you know what I mean. Good luck this week!"

Sadie hung up, not giving Josephine the opportunity to respond. There, that should do it! Joyfully, she returned home and drove TJ to Rudy's to get his truck. He didn't say much, just thanked her for the ride. Sadie was very pleased with herself. Her plan was set in motion.

Las Vegas, Nevada
Tuesday

Josephine set the hotel phone down. She certainly would have slammed the receiver down if her mother wasn't in the room. Could this be true? Had TJ really slept with Sadie again? No, he wouldn't do that, not now. Lies, all lies.

"What was that all about?"

"She just wanted to wish me luck."

"Well, that's a first. She sure is a strange one." Her mother checked her watch. "We overslept. Let's get dressed. We need to grab some breakfast to go and get to the barn pronto. Major is probably putting up a fuss."

Josephine went through the motions of dressing, her mind elsewhere. No matter how she tried to blow off Sadie's call, she couldn't deny the fact that TJ hadn't told her about Sadie, which spurred some degree of doubt. Had he hidden their relationship from her for a reason? Her hands began to shake as she applied a little makeup. This is silly. She reassured herself again that TJ would never cheat on her and quickly followed her mother out of the room. Major was waiting.

The FEI Jumping World Cup, held at the Thomas & Mack Center, located on the campus of the University of Nevada in downtown Las Vegas, was just off the famed Strip. After parking and entering one of the long buildings full of temporary stalls, a short walk from the Center, Josephine busied herself with her mount. Having arrived late Monday night, they would just get Major settled in today; a light lunge and a little hand walking around the facility. Little grass was available for hand grazing, but she'd try to find some.

As Josephine stripped Major of his sheet and groomed him while he ate, she reflected on their performance as a team so far. They had done well competing in California. Her favorite moment was making their victory pass following their win at the second show, with a championship sash flapping around Major's neck as she cantered around the stadium. It came in a close second to seeing herself on the silver screen for the first time. She felt confident going into this week's competition. Yet, Josephine was relieved she wouldn't be riding that day. That Sadie call had her feeling off-kilter. But would she feel any better tomorrow? She couldn't allow this nonsense to fester. Confirming her suspicion that Sadie lied out of jealousy, perhaps even as an attempt to break them up, would clear the air so she could focus on Major and nothing but Major that week. She would call TJ as soon as they got back to their room.

While her mother was in the shower, Josephine made her call. Sarah answered the phone.

"Hi, Jo, everything okay?"

"Yes, I just wanted to speak to TJ. Is he there?"

Her heart sank deeper every second Sarah hesitated. "No, Jo. He went out with Talon and some friends last night."

"And, he hasn't come home?" More awkward silence.

"I'm sure he just stayed with Talon overnight. They probably had a lot to get caught up on."

"Sure. Please let him know I called. We're leaving to get lunch, but we should be back to our room by one-thirty." Josephine gave her the phone and room number. "Thanks, Sarah! Say hi to Grandmother and Grandfather for me."

"Will do, good luck this week!"

"Thanks!"

Her mother exited the bathroom and gave her a strange look. "Were you on the phone?"

"Yes, I called TJ."

"That was a record short call for you two."

"He wasn't there. Sarah's going to have him call me later."

"Ready for some lunch?"

"Sure."

Josephine had no appetite, if fact, she felt nauseous. Her suspicions had spiked again. Was it just a coincidence? Had he cheated on her? Or worse yet, had TJ kept their relationship a secret because he still had feelings for her?

When they returned after having lunch at the restaurant downstairs, the phone rang. "Do you mind?" asked Josephine, waiting to pick up the receiver. Her mother smiled and stepped out onto the balcony and slid the glass door shut.

"Hi, TJ."

"Hi, Jo. Sorry I missed your call earlier. What a nice surprise."

"Right." She needed to get to the point of her call and didn't hesitate. "I'm sure you can clear this up. It's about Sadie." She paused a moment, but TJ said nothing. "Guess I should start with the conversation we had in the barn before we left for the West Coast. She told me you two were an item for years, engaged and living together."

TJ froze with the phone to his ear. This news came as a shock. He and Sadie had agreed not to mention their relationship to Katherine or anyone at Two Ponies. At the time, Sadie had her reasons and TJ had his, but that was before he had ended it. He should have known better than to trust Sadie to keep their secret. Stupid!

TJ took a calming breath. "We were only dating, and I did move in with her for a short while, but we were never engaged. I meant to tell you, but everything was going so good, I didn't want to upset you. I never loved her. It didn't mean anything, I swear!"

"It meant something to Sadie. Did you lead her on?"

"Never. I never promised her a thing." Shit this was getting out of hand. Why hadn't he told her? He had nothing to hide.

"I should have heard about Sadie from you, not her!" TJ could hear her anger building.

"What are you so mad about? You're the one that dumped me, remember? What did you expect me to do? Crawl under a rock and die?"

"Can you imagine how I felt being left in the dark? It was embarrassing. It hurt."

This comment touched a nerve. "I think I know exactly how it feels. When were you going to tell me about returning to your acting career in California?"

"What are you talking about?"

"And I should have been the first to learn how successful your last surgery was!"

"I told you it went well. I wanted to surprise you. But wait a minute. We're getting off track. I called you about Sadie. I spoke to her again today."

TJ closed his eyes. In an instant, he knew what was coming next. Sadie had set him up! "What did she tell you?"

"I think you know. She told me you spent the night with her. Did you see her again?"

"I did see her, but it's not what you think."

"Your mom said you didn't come home last night. What am I supposed to think?"

"Sadie called and invited me to join a group at Rudy's. She said Talon was going to be there. I wanted to see him and get caught up. That's the only reason I went. When I got there, there was only Sadie. I drank too much, and she drove me to her place. Nothing happened. I passed out on the couch. I swear it's the truth."

"You expect me to believe that lame story? You never drink that much."

"I was upset after she mentioned you returning to California. She said she even saw it on TV. And she kept bringing up Brad."

"Lies. All lies. I haven't mentioned anything to Mom or Jessie. And there were some reporters in Sacramento, but I never confirmed I was returning to California, or acting for that matter."

"But you're considering it?"

"No! I'm not hiding anything from you, TJ. That's your game. The engagement's off!" And with that, she hung up.

What the hell? Doesn't she know me better than that? TJ had been so emotionally involved in their conversation he didn't realize his mother sat reading in the living room just around the corner during the entire call.

She surprised him as he walked by the living room on his way upstairs. "Who is Sadie?"

TJ sat down with his mother and explained what happened.

"You should have told her."

"I know that now. What should I do?" TJ began pacing the room.

"Go to her, explain in person. It's better that way. She can look into your eyes and know it's the truth. I have some money saved, thanks to all the meat you brought us. Book a flight."

"You need that money to get through the winter."

"We'll be fine. Take it, please."

"I'll pay you back."

"Just go."

"Okay, I'll go."

His mother went to the kitchen and returned with her debit card. "Book the first flight available. I'll drive you to the airport."

"Thanks, Mom." TJ gave her a hug and got on the phone. She was right, he needed to see Josephine face to face.

Katherine could hear Josephine's raised voice but couldn't entirely understand what she was saying. She wasn't deliberately trying to listen in, but she could only go so far out on the balcony. Katherine was quite certain she heard her mention Sadie a few times. She would mind her own business unless Josephine came to her for advice. But, if it involved her employee, she felt justified in asking.

Josephine tapped on the glass, waving her in. "Sorry." She still looked upset, biting her lower lip as her green eyes burned with fury.

"No problem. But I couldn't help overhearing mention of Sadie's name. Is there something I should know?"

Her daughter crossed her arms and began tapping the floor with her foot. "That Sadie. Did you know she and TJ were a couple at one point?"

That took her back a step. "No. I had no idea. When?"

"Apparently, for years until my accident. They were living together even, and Sadie said they were engaged. TJ denies it."

"Well, what's the problem then? You believe TJ, don't you?"

"I did, until I learned he spent the night with her last night. He doesn't deny it, but he says nothing happened, that he got drunk at

Rudy's and she drove him to her place. Why wouldn't she just drive him to his house? TJ never used to drink that much. I've never seen him drunk. But maybe he's not the TJ I used to know. Sarah did say he's changed. His story just doesn't make sense!" Katherine could see Josephine's eyes glistening.

"If that was the case, he must have been pretty upset about something to drink that much."

"Oh, right," she said, sarcastically. "I forgot to mention Sadie told him about the successful results of my last surgery and that you and Jessie said I was returning to California to resume my acting career. Apparently, it was also mentioned on some television show. He got upset that I didn't tell him about the results. You didn't mention anything to Sadie, did you?"

"She overheard us talking about the surgery and Jessie asked me if you would return to acting. I said you hadn't mentioned it."

"Why would he believe her or some show on TV, before me? That says something, doesn't it?"

"Go easy on him, Jo. The wounds from you leaving him the first time may not be entirely healed."

Josephine sighed. "I don't know what to believe." Josephine went on to tell her mother about the exchange she had with Sadie in the barn the morning of her surgery.

"Sounds to me, Sadie is just hurt and lashing out any way she can. If she lied about California, she probably lied about last night too. Why didn't you tell me about all this sooner?"

Josephine explained her reasoning.

"We could have worked it out between Jessie and the other girls," said Katherine.

"I really didn't think much of it until today. I want to believe TJ, but he should have told me about her. The 'why' he didn't tell me is what's so upsetting. I broke off our engagement."

Katherine didn't quantify anything Josephine said as asking for advice, so she didn't give any. "I'm sorry, sweetie. I'm here if you need me."

"Thanks, Mom. I need some fresh air. I'm going to go for a walk."

Katherine hated to see her daughter so upset again. Everything had been going so well for her. "Okay, I'm going to take a nap. I'm still beat from the drive. Wake me up if I sleep past three."

"Okay, I will." Josephine slunk from the room, closing the door behind her.

Katherine wanted to step in, but Josephine and TJ were adults now and they needed to work this out for themselves. That's what Betsy would have said. She just prayed they would, and soon. Her daughter was currently in no condition to give one hundred percent of her focus to her riding, which she'll need to compete at this level. Following the warm-up ride on Wednesday, she must qualify Thursday or Friday to compete in the championship jump-off on Sunday.

Before she laid down for her nap, Katherine searched through the competitors list, running her finger down sheet after sheet until resting on the entry, Kayla Lutz riding Joyous Occasion. Kayla was here! She would locate Erica's stalls when they returned that afternoon. Katherine hoped the girl would be happy to see her considering she never replied to any of her letters. She imagined Karen might have had something to do with that. Would Karen be here too? But first, she needed to get some rest. She had a feeling she was going to need it.

18 – World Cup

Las Vegas, Nevada
Tuesday

When Josephine returned from her walk, Katherine heard her place a call, sigh and return the receiver. She stretched following her nap. "Hi, Jo."

"Sorry to wake you. I tried to call TJ. No answer." Josephine sat on the edge of her bed. "Kind of strange that neither Sarah nor TJ picked up. I know Grandmother and Grandfather are nearly deaf and would have a hard time reaching the phone in time, if they even heard it. I'll try again later. Really need to put this to rest."

"I agree. The sooner the better. Let's go feed Major a little early so we can get back around supper time. We should be able to reach someone then."

On the way over, Katherine noticed Josephine tapping the armrest with her finger.

"What do you think about all this with TJ and Sadie?" inquired Josephine, glancing over to her. "How would you handle it?"

It felt good to have her daughter ask for advice, but now she was levied with the responsibility of offering guidance. "All I can say is, if there is any truth to Sadie's claim about last night, plenty of good people, including TJ, make mistakes. I sure have made my share."

Josephine's mouth formed a painful smile. "You're right. Me too. It's just so hard. I want everything between TJ and I to be perfect like it used to be."

"No such thing as a perfect relationship."

"You and Dad are perfect."

"We're about as close as you can get now, but it hasn't always been that way, believe me. Relationships take a lot of work; patience, compromise, forgiveness."

Josephine nodded. "You and Dad make it look so easy."

"Yeah, now it's easy but we've had our ups and downs."

"I hope TJ and I can work this out. It just all came as such a shock. What are you going to do about Sadie?"

"I'm going to let her go in the morning. I won't tolerate lying. She said things that didn't happen between Jessie and I, deliberately trying to start trouble, and how she treated you at the barn is unacceptable. I called Kaitlin when you were on your walk, I think you've met her. She's going to cover the barn the remainder of the week."

"Yes, Jessie's student that rides Blackjack on Saturdays."

"That's right," said Katherine. "Say, there's something I could use your advice on."

Josephine turned in her seat. "Really, what?"

Katherine explained her history with Karen, starting when she walked out on her trainer and moved to Montana. She gave her a brief rundown of all that happened at the Pan American Games; meeting Kayla, hearing her background, the attacks, learning Karen and her son were behind them, and her decision not to press charges. "Kayla is here."

"Wow, Mom. Do you think Karen is here too?"

"I don't know, but here lies my dilemma. I want to see Kayla, but what if she doesn't want to see me? I have no idea what Karen might have told her. She either never saw my letters or chose not to reply to them. And I'm sure she knows nothing about what happened forty years ago and last summer. If Karen is here, she'll have every reason to keep us apart."

"I see what you mean, but it sounds like you want and need to reach out to Kayla. I hope it works out and I'd like to meet her. She sounds like a wonderful girl."

"She is. And you're right, I do need to try. I wish there was some way for me to help her."

"I think not ratting on her grandmother was a good start."

"I suppose." Katherine pulled into a parking spot. "Can you take care of Major?"

"Sure. Go find Kayla. I'll walk him around the building a bit, feed him his dinner and pick his stall while he's eating."

"Thanks, Jo, I'll try not to be long."

"Good luck!" Josephine hopped from the truck and headed for Major's stall.

Katherine walked directly to the show office to locate Erica's stalls. No wonder they hadn't run into each other. Her stalls were on the opposite end of the show grounds. She was hoping Kayla would be there feeding and tending to the horses, without Karen. Not knowing what her grandmother might have told her, she wanted the opportunity to tell her side of the story.

She looked down their barn aisle and saw no one. Maybe it was a little early. Immediately, she noticed the front of Erica's green and gold stall. Before reaching the tack stall, she recognized the big black stallion that was at the Pan American Games. The name plate on the stall read "Joker's Wild." Katherine stopped to pet the handsome Hanoverian. He snorted and pawed at the door, apparently still waiting on his dinner. Past the tack stall, Joy lashed out at her with her ears laid flat and teeth bared. Catching Katherine off guard, she jumped back. Thankfully, the grated stall front came between her and the mare's teeth. She knew Joy could be difficult, but didn't recall her acting aggressively last summer.

"Be careful, she bites," said a small voice from behind her.

Katherine turned. "Kayla! I was hoping to catch you."

"Kat! I'm so happy to see you. I was hoping to run into you too." Kayla swiveled around checking both ends of the aisle then gave her a hug. "I've missed you."

"I wrote, several times. Didn't you get my letters?"

"No." Kayla frowned. "Grandma. She wouldn't be happy if she knew I was talking to you. She told me things about you I don't believe."

"Is she here?"

Kayla nodded.

"We need to talk."

"Can you wait for me at the tables by the food court?" said Kayla. "I need to feed and pick stalls. We only brought the two horses this time. Shouldn't take me longer than thirty minutes. I'll meet you there." Again, she glanced down the aisleway.

"Sure. See you then."

Just as she was about to exit one end of the barn, she heard voices. Erica and Karen had entered the aisle from the opposite direction. Katherine quickly and calmly walked out of sight. Her curiosity ran wild wondering what Karen told Kayla. Some kind of gratitude, considering she hadn't pressed charges or told her granddaughter what happened in Winnipeg. Yet she could understand Karen wanting to keep it a secret and how complicated it would have been for her if she and Kayla had stayed in touch.

About a half hour later, Kayla approached her table and gave her another hug.

"You hungry? I can order you something."

"No thanks. We're going for dinner soon. I don't have much time." Kayla sat across from her and leaned over the table. "I'm sorry I didn't get your letters."

"No worries. What did your grandmother tell you about me?"

"That she knew you from years ago and that you turned against her and ruined her career. I knew it couldn't be true. You'd never do anything like that, right?"

"It's complicated. I was young, about your age. Remember when I told you about leaving Boston and moving out to Montana?" Kayla nodded. "Your grandmother was my trainer. It hurt her emotionally and financially when I left."

"Oh. But you didn't mean to hurt her."

"No, I was young and too full of my own dreams, I didn't think about the consequences. I feel bad about what happened now. I wish there was some way to make it up to you and your grandmother."

"Maybe I can visit sometime. When I'm on my own. I'm saving money so I can get my own apartment and car."

"I'd like that. Very much." Katherine handed her a business card. "It has my home address and phone number. On the back is our hotel and room number. Let me know when we can meet again, maybe after tomorrow's warm-up course. We're in Stall 202."

"Sure. Are you competing? I couldn't find you listed as a competitor."

"I'm not. My leg got worse after last summer's fall. But my daughter, Josephine, is riding Major."

"I'm so sorry about your leg. But that's great about your daughter and Major."

"I'm glad we're getting to talk. What happened to Joy? She seems very unhappy."

"I'll tell you about it tomorrow. I have to go." Kayla stood up to leave.

Katherine got up and gave her a strong hug. "Good luck this week, Kayla!"

"Thank you, Kat! Good luck to you, Josephine and Major too."

Kayla turned and hurried toward their stall building. It was nice to see her, but Katherine could tell something was off. Kayla wasn't the same cheerful girl she met last year. She seemed sad, depressed even. Especially when she mentioned Joy. Katherine looked forward to seeing her again tomorrow to learn more.

When Katherine returned to their stall, she found Josephine grooming Major with a soft dandy brush. "Did you find her?" she asked.

"Yes."

"How did it go?"

"Good, but we didn't end up with much time to get caught up. I hope to see her again tomorrow."

Josephine exited the stall and latched the door. "Was it what you thought, about her grandmother?"

Katherine filled her in on their conversation. "I'm anxious to hear about Joy tomorrow. But let's get you back to the hotel. You have a call to make and you need a good night's sleep."

As soon as they got to their room to clean up for dinner, Josephine called TJ. Again, there was no answer. Katherine could clearly read the uneasiness returning to her daughter's face.

"That's weird. Not reaching Sarah, at least. I hope nothing happened to Grandmother or Grandfather."

Katherine could understand her concerns, and guessed they probably had little to do with TJ's grandparents. She imagined Josephine had to be thinking along the same lines as she was. That TJ told Sarah what happened, and since Josephine didn't believe him, Sarah might also be upset with Josephine and was not answering her calls. Honor was held in high regard in the Blackfeet community – the one thing no one could take from them. She prayed the couple got the opportunity to work this mess out, and soon!

As Josephine saddled Major for their warm-up course Wednesday, her concentration wavered. Not being able to reach Sarah or TJ weighed heavily on her mind and she knew Major could feel her edginess. She could feel her tension building, threatening her confidence. What if they crashed or fell? Suddenly, she had flashbacks to the dreadful night of her accident. She had managed to keep those fears at bay since she started riding again, until now. She just had to manage her emotions and focus on Major for the next few minutes.

Miraculously, Josephine's course went well considering her mental state and the tight course. Major definitely picked up on her anxiety and wanted to race through the course, but she managed to control him enough to have a clear round, though it wasn't pretty. Thank goodness this was just the warmup and not the final, but now she would have her work cut out for her trying to slow the old racehorse down during the elimination courses Thursday and Friday. Somehow, they must make it through to the final competition Sunday. Josephine didn't want to disappoint her mother after all the time and money she had invested in her riding and competing this year. She needed to either trust or forgive TJ, whatever it took to move on and quiet her mind.

Surprising Katherine, Kayla approached their stall as they untacked Major following the warmup. She and Joy managed a decent course earlier that day as well, going clean.

"Hi, Kayla. I'm so glad you could get away. Great job this morning!"

"Hi, Kat, thanks," she said, turning quickly to Josephine. "Oh, you're even more beautiful in person than you are in the movies."

"Well, thank you," blushed Josephine. "So nice to meet you, Kayla."

"Major looked full of it today," said Kayla. "But he's so talented, it didn't matter."

"That was my fault." Josephine gave her mother an embarrassed glance. "I normally ride him better."

"You did just fine, Jo," said Katherine. "Major is an ex-racehorse remember!" she joked, hoping to lighten her daughter's mood.

Kayla turned to her. "I have only a few minutes."

Josephine must have picked up on the girl's hint and excused herself. "Nice meeting you, Kayla. I'm going to walk Major. Hope to see you again."

"Me too. Nice to meet you," said Kayla as Josephine and Major walked out of the stall and down the aisle.

"Where do you want to talk?"

"How about here in your stall." The girl looked tense.

"Sure." Katherine pulled their two chairs between the six-foot high, solid walls separating the horses, where they wouldn't be seen from either end of the aisleway.

Kayla sat across from her, nervously fiddling with her untucked shirttail in her lap.

"Joy looked happier today."

"A little, but she always tosses her head when jumping. It drives Erica crazy. She's come down hard on Joy lately about her tossing and poor ground manners. It's only made things worse. Erica really wants to sell her. We've had lookers but none of them can get past her disposition."

"But isn't that good news since you're still getting to compete with her?"

"I'd rather see her happy in a new home," said Kayla. "I hope we can do well enough to qualify for Sydney. Maybe then Erica will go easier on her."

"And she'll be committed to keeping her through the summer."

"And that." Kayla smiled. "Enough about me and Joy. Major looks great as always. When did Josephine take over? Where did she qualify?"

"She's been riding Major since the end of January. They qualified in Sacramento. How about you? Where did you qualify?"

"In Wellington."

Even though Kayla wanted to steer their conversation away from herself, Katherine felt concerned about the girl. "How are things going with your grandmother? I saw she's here."

"We all flew in on Monday. The horses were commercially hauled this time. Grandma is helping out. It was nice of Erica to give her another chance."

Katherine tried again. "How are things at home? I worry about where you're living. Sounded pretty rough. Are you safe there?"

"Things are okay." Kayla once again focused on her lap, working the fabric of her shirt through her fingers. When her eyes lifted, the girl looked on the verge of tears. She took a deep breath. "Since we returned from Winnipeg, Grandma has been quiet and to herself a lot. When I ask if she's okay, she says she's just tired or has a headache and she'll feel better soon. But nothing changes. I'm worried about her."

"Do you have any idea what's going on?"

"I think it has to do with my riding and money. It kills her she can't afford to buy Joy for me and that we live where we do… that she can't do better for us. It's gotten worse in the trailer park. There have been a few break-ins and attacks. Even a rape last fall. One of the girls I went to school with. And a man was shot dead over the winter in some drug deal. It's all my fault. If I hadn't gotten sick."

"This isn't your fault, Kayla. It's no one's fault. Her problems might not have anything to do with you."

"Regardless, as soon as Joy sells, or even if she doesn't, I'm going to get a full-time job and get a studio apartment. I need to give up my riding, so I won't be such a burden to her anymore."

"That would be a shame. You're such a talented rider and so good with horses."

"But like you said last summer, I have my whole life ahead of me. Maybe I can return to my riding someday. I should be getting back."

Just as they were pulling the chairs back out into the aisle, Katherine was shocked to see Karen standing out front of their stall. Kayla froze.

"Erica needs you," she said to the girl.

Kayla nodded. "Yes, Grandma." Without another word, Kayla rushed down the aisle.

Karen turned to her. "Please don't take all I have left from me."

"I have no intention of doing anything that would come between you and your granddaughter."

"Well, just leave her alone. Flaunting all you and your daughter have makes it all the more difficult for her."

Katherine couldn't restrain herself. "For her, or for you?"

Karen clenched her jaw. Katherine prepared herself for a verbal lashing, instead she was shocked by her composed response. "I appreciate what you did last summer, or didn't do, but I would also appreciate you leaving my granddaughter alone. I can't compete with you and your movie star daughter. I'm afraid I'm losing her."

"Kayla loves you very much. She feels guilty. Responsible for the hard times you're experiencing. It has nothing to do with me or my daughter. Perhaps if you two sat down and…"

Karen lost her composure. "You have no business giving me advice! You know nothing about hard times. You need to stay out of our personal business!" Katherine could see her eyes welling up. Abruptly she turned away and stormed down the aisle.

Katherine hoped contacting Kayla again hadn't made things worse for the poor girl. She'd never been in Karen's situation and could only imagine how difficult it must be for her, but her old trainer had been wrong. Katherine had seen hard times, financially, and her share of losses. She recalled how Betsy had helped her survive the heartbreaks and how so many friends stepped up to help her and Betsy when they almost lost Two Ponies. Her uncle's book, *The Fellowship*, a story about the strength of community, came to mind. Katherine smiled. She had an idea. She would discuss it with Steven hopefully Saturday, if Josephine makes it to the final.

When Josephine returned with Major, Kayla was gone and her mother was sitting in front of their stall, looking chipper. "Must have gone well."

"No, not really. Karen showed up. She must have guessed Kayla might be with me and looked up our stall."

She didn't expect to hear that news considering her mother's cheerful disposition, piquing her curiosity. "What happened?"

"She doesn't want me to spend any time with her granddaughter. She thinks I'm stealing her away and making her look bad."

"Okay, why aren't you upset?"

"I should be, but I'm not."

"What are you going to do?"

"I'm going to respect her wishes and keep my distance, for now."

"I hear a plan brewing."

"Maybe. But we have enough on our plate at the moment."

Josephine could tell her mother didn't want to discuss it now, so she let it lie and changed the subject."

"Sorry about this morning. I'll do better Thursday, I promise."

"You did fine, really. You were both a little up is all. Are you done? I'm hungry."

"Major is rinsed and scraped," Josephine ran her hand over his soft coat. "But he's not dry."

"Let's get something to eat. By the time we get back, he'll be dry enough to groom and put a sheet on."

They agreed on fish tacos at the food court. When they entered their stall aisle, Josephine could see the back of a young man in a cowboy hat reaching into Major's stall.

"Hey, what are you doing?" she yelled, quickly closing the gap between them.

The young man turned. "Hi, Jo."

Josephine stopped in her tracks. "TJ, what… how?"

He wore a long face. "My Mom flew me out. I needed to see you."

Josephine smiled. Immediately, TJ's eyes smiled back. She rushed into his arms, resting her head on his shoulder. All felt right in the world again. "I'm so happy you came," she whispered in his ear.

TJ held her at arm's length. "I'm sorry, Jo, I should have told you."

"No. I'm sorry. I should have trusted you. I tried to call. I was worried." Again, they embraced. How could she have ever doubted him.

"I love you, Jo."

"I love you too."

"Well, I'm glad you two have that all worked out," said Katherine as she approached the couple.

"Hi, Mrs. Walker.

"Hi, TJ."

"Is the doctor here?"

"Not yet, hopefully this weekend. And you can call me Kat, please."

"Still feels weird."

"I hope you'll soon be calling me Mom," said Katherine with a chuckle. "I'm so glad you came."

TJ nodded with a big grin. Josephine knew her mother had been worrying about her emotional state, not only with her riding, but afraid if anything happened between her and TJ, she might slip back into depression.

"I'll take care of Major. Josephine, why don't you give TJ the tour."

"I'd like that," said TJ. "Sure is a big city. So many people."

Josephine took his hand, smiling, appreciating her mother's subtle way of giving them some alone time.

"How about we meet back here at feed time?" suggested Katherine.

"Sounds good. Thanks, Mom."

As they headed out of the stall building, TJ kept studying her. Unexpectedly, he turned to face her. "Oh, Jo, your face is healing beautifully."

"I was going to surprise you."

TJ guided her to a corner, out of the way of foot traffic and kissed her. "We mustn't ever distrust each other again."

"Deal."

Josephine showed him around the entire complex, ending up in the stadium seating watching a tractor drag the footing in the coliseum.

"How long can you stay?"

"As long as you're competing."

"That's awesome. We hope until Sunday, if I get that far. I'll take you down the Strip tomorrow afternoon. I ride my first elimination round in the morning. My ride didn't go that great today. I'm a littlw nervous about tomorrow, riding against the best in the world. The crowd will be huge."

"Really? I didn't think a crowd would make you nervous after being an actress."

"It's different. You're not acting in front of thousands of people."

"Eventually you do, millions even."

Josephine chuckled. "I never thought of it that way."

TJ's expression turned serious. "Jo, I want you to know. If you ever want to return to acting, I'll support you all the way."

Josephine was shocked. "Really?"

"So long as I'm by your side. I just want you to be happy."

"That's so sweet, TJ. But really, I'm not planning to. I'm happy right here with you."

TJ gave her a gentle kiss. "Let's both look only to the future, our future together."

Josephine flashed a playful smile. "Yes. Let's start with tonight!"

"I don't even know where I'm sleeping."

"Well, I do. With me."

"Aren't you sharing a room with your mom?"

"Yes, but my mom can check into the adjoining room she has reserved for her and dad."

"What would your parents say?"

"We're adults, TJ. Besides, they're tickled pink we're back together."

"Really?"

"Yeah, really. You make me happy and they're happy when I'm happy."

"I'm not sure how I feel about this, but if you say so."

Josephine nodded with a raise of an eyebrow and a seductive smile.

TJ grinned and gave her a hand up onto her feet. "Well then, we better head back. I can't wait to eat and retire for the night."

Saturday

Katherine sat in the stands watching Josephine lightly exercise Major on their off day in preparation for the final competition tomorrow. She couldn't be more pleased with Josephine's rides Thursday and Friday, placing second and third and qualifying her and Major for Sunday's Championship.

She felt equally pleased with Josephine's joyous and positive attitude since TJ. He stood at the north gate, admiring his fiancé. Katherine's heart skipped a beat every time she spotted them holding hands or gazing into each other's eyes. Perhaps her baby stood a chance at achieving the kind of love that lasts a lifetime after all, something so few couples find and even fewer succeed at keeping.

Not one day passed that she didn't thank God to have found Steven. Not once, but twice, they found each other and somehow survived the many tests of their relationship over the years as their love continued to grow. These thoughts naturally led Katherine to anxiously awaiting her husband's arrival that afternoon. She had kept in touch with Steven daily throughout their three weeks of travel, but missed his touch and warmth each night. It seemed with every passing year they became closer, making any separation difficult, let alone for nearly a month.

Steven had offered to meet them in Sacramento, but Katherine felt Josephine was still building her confidence and having her father there might have put too much pressure on her. But now Josephine had several successful courses under her belt and didn't hide her excitement about having both her father and TJ there to cheer her and Major on at the final.

She had told Steven over the phone about Josephine and TJ sharing a room and surprisingly, he hadn't fussed the slightest. After all, they were formally engaged. Yet, when she asked Josephine about a wedding date, she got the same response; undecided. TJ wanted to wait until after he graduated, and Josephine didn't want to wait, wanting a summer wedding at Two Ponies.

Katherine got up and met TJ at the gate just as Josephine and Major exited the north entrance of the schooling ring. At that moment, Katherine noticed Kayla enter the ring from the opposite end, flanked by Erica and followed by her other student riding the black. A moment later, Karen took a seat in the stands near the south gate. "Let's watch them a bit," said Katherine to Josephine and TJ, nodding in the direction of Kayla.

"Sure," said Josephine. "They've been looking good." She parked Major just inside the north gate out of the way.

Kayla had placed fifth and sixth that week, barely making the cut for the final. Katherine had kept her distance from the girl, honoring Karen's wishes, but she didn't have a say about watching her ride. As Joy trotted by, Kayla smiled and hid a wave to her. Katherine returned her smile and nodded her approval.

Next came Joker floating around the ring. Josephine turned and took special notice as the big black passed by. "I love watching that guy go," she said. "He's stunning and he loves to jump! And it's so cute how he whips his tail as he goes around the ring like a wind-up toy, and that high tail swish over each jump just cracks me up! Do you know his breeding?" she asked, unable to pull her eyes away from the stunning animal.

"That's Joker's Wild, Erica's pride and joy. He's a seven-year-old Hanoverian stallion."

"Wow, I didn't realize he was a stallion, he's so well mannered."

"They just need an everyday job and lots of handling. And I'll bet he hasn't done any breeding yet. That has a tendency to wake them up, if you know what I mean."

Josephine snickered, pulling her focus from the black to Major who stood tossing his head. "Someone's not so impressed."

Josephine laughed while patting him on the neck. "Don't worry boy, you're just as gorgeous!"

They watched Joy and Joker work at a canter for a lap, then they headed for their stall. Major hadn't even gotten hot, just stretched out, so he didn't need to be walked or bathed. While Josephine picked his feet and lightly sponged his saddle and bridle marks, TJ put some muscle behind a good grooming, polishing Major's brilliant red coat like an apple.

Katherine checked the time. "We better get going. Dad should be arriving soon."

The kids, if she can still call them that, quickly threw a light sheet over Major and tossed him a little hay to hold him until supper.

"I can't wait to see Dad. I'm so happy he's going to get to see me ride tomorrow."

"He's looking forward to it," said Katherine.

"Aren't we all!" added TJ.

Sunday Morning

Josephine arrived at the Center early to walk the course again. She had paced it with her mother earlier. Now she just wanted to etch the sequence of jumps in her mind one more time.

The course was the toughest she'd seen so far, understandably so. This was the World Cup with the best horses and riders from around the world. Sometimes she felt inferior, like she didn't belong among them, yet here she was, and once she was on board her Pegasus, she felt confident taking on the world. Josephine glanced over at TJ standing at the rail. His smile warmed her like a beam of sunshine. For an instant, she reflected on where she was and what she was doing a year ago. It felt a lifetime ago. Almost like she was looking back on a stranger's past. Yet there were reminders everywhere, like the reporters lined up to take her picture. The photos would show up in some celebrity rag or perhaps on an entertainment television show or a segment of the news. She imagined the novelty of a famous actress surviving a devastating accident to make an unusual comeback on the international show jumping stage would capture readers and viewers but, she looked forward to the day their interest died out and she could live a normal, private life again.

She met TJ at the gate, and they walked hand in hand to meet her parents for an early light lunch at a sushi restaurant just a few blocks from the Center. The heat off the concrete mixed with the smell of two million residents and hundreds of thousands of visitors, confronted her senses. She wrinkled her nose and glanced over at TJ. His expression read the same. TJ had drawn attention among the show jumping crowd at the Center, appearing as though he'd just walked off a Western movie set, but out on the street, he blended in with the diverse throngs of visitors from every corner of the globe. Reporters and paparazzi had confronted them as a couple, inquiring about TJ and their relationship. Josephine proudly introduced him as her fiancé, pleasing TJ and sending the journalists off to make headlines. No longer did she feel ashamed, but proud of her man. Women stared at the rugged American Indian; some with disdain, but more often approvingly, flashing seductive smiles as they ogled his masculine form from head to toe. A few even turned to admire his well-formed buttocks as they passed by.

Just as TJ opened the door to the restaurant, a couple was exiting.

"Well, what a surprise!"

Josephine spun around immediately recognizing the voice. Brad held the door for a blonde model type she thought she recognized.

"Hi, Josie," he said. "You remember Brandy?"

"Sure, hi, Brandy." It took Josephine a moment to recall she had a minor role in *Secrets*.

"And who is this, Josie?" said Brandy, running her eyes up and down TJ.

Brad quickly interrupted. "What are you doing here, Jo?" She felt certain Brad knew the answer, never missing any celebrity news.

"Riding in the World Cup," she said, pointing down the block. "And you?"

"I'm working on a film; *Go*. You might have heard of it."

"No, I'm not really following Hollywood news anymore." Josephine caught Brandy studying her face, which drew Brad's attention.

"You healed well," he said. "*Secrets* is doing great at the box office. Are you going to return to acting?"

"No. I'm writing a screenplay."

"Really? Well, keep me in mind should anything come of it," he said, sarcastically.

"Me too," said Brandy, still drinking in TJ.

"We have to run. My parents are waiting inside."

"Good luck," said Brad.

Josephine nodded. "Thanks."

The couple headed down the Strip, laughing under their breathe.

TJ hadn't said a word, but he didn't need to. He looked as though he might take a swing at Brad any second. And Josephine almost wished he had. But having him out of her life would have to be good enough.

Sunday afternoon, Katherine left Josephine to warm up in the adjoining warm-up ring, while she followed Erica leading Joy and Kayla to the gate of the coliseum. She would be jumping in the final round soon ahead of Josephine. The girl looked tense on Joy as Erica jerked the mare by the reins, attempting to stop her from tossing her head. Katherine noticed Joy now wore a more severe bit than during her last course. She was shocked. Erica should know better than to make last-minute changes, especially with the bit before a competition. Katherine could not hear what Erica was saying, but it wasn't pleasant. Joy began backing into another horse and rider waiting their turn. Suddenly, Joy kicked out, just missing the face of the horse behind them. Erica circled the mare and popped her again in the mouth. Joy stood this time, eyes rimmed in white, nostrils flaring. Katherine had a sinking feeling, fearing for Kayla's safety entering the ring following this display. This wasn't going to end well.

When the gate opened and the previous team exited, Joy planted her front feet, refusing to enter the stadium. Out of frustration, Erica smacked Joy's rear with a crop, sending her rear hoofs flying once again, just missing the trainer. Joy lunged forward and into the stadium nearly leaving the poor girl behind. Kayla gathered her reins and cantered center to salute. Joy would not stand quietly, and Kayla had to salute on the move. Katherine prayed once the pair got on course, they would settle in and focus on the task before them. Reminiscent of their stadium course at the Pan American Games, Joy tossed her head even worse throughout this course, no doubt objecting to the new bit. She could see that Kayla tried not to put too much pressure on the horse's mouth which minimized her control. The pair raced through the course, knocking several poles to the ground. They would certainly be out of the running for a team or individual jumping spot.

Karen stormed by her toward Erica at the gate, her face full of rage. When the gate opened, Erica grabbed Joy by the bridle and led Kayla down the tunnel at a brisk pace in silence, with Karen in fast pursuit. As Erica and Karen blindly passed her, Katherine followed. Erica came to an abrupt halt before exiting the building and Katherine could see harsh words leaving her lips. She moved closer.

"You did this on purpose, didn't you, so I can't sell her?" said Erica in a sharp whisper. "You better enjoy your ride back to the barn, because it'll be your last on any horse of mine!"

This kind of behavior by such a successful trainer shocked Katherine. Erica turned Joy loose and Kayla trotted away in tears. The trainer started for the warm-up ring where her other student and Joker were preparing for their course. Karen seized Erica by the arm, spinning her around. Katherine rushed after Kayla, but not before hearing a few choice words leave Karen's mouth.

Katherine did not find Kayla at her stall. There weren't too many places to go within the fenced off exhibitor area and she found the girl on the outskirt of the parking lot. She had dismounted and stood with her arms around Joy's neck, sobbing.

"Oh, Kayla. I'm so sorry. She had no right saying those things to you."

Kayla turned her tear-streaked face toward her. "I really disappointed her, but she's never spoken to me like that before, no matter how bad I messed up." Again, Kayla wrapped her arms around Joy, who stood heaving and sweating.

"You need to cool her out, and I need to go watch Jo. Walk her to Major's stall. We'll meet you there after Jo's ride. Erica will be busy with Joker for a while. He goes toward the end of the program."

Kayla wiped her face. "Okay, thank you, Kat."

"We'll talk then. You did the best you could under the circumstances. This isn't your fault, sweetie." Katherine gave her a hug and jogged back into the coliseum.

Josephine was searching for her in the tunnel. "What happened?"

"It was terrible. Kayla had a bad ride and Erica accused her of purposely making Joy look bad so she couldn't sell her."

"That's awful. Poor Kayla."

"I told her to take Joy to Major's stall and wait for us there. But for now, you need to focus on your ride. You ready?"

"As ready as we'll ever be," said Josephine. "I just wish there was something we could do for Kayla."

"Me too. I have an idea I need to run by your father." The gate opened. "Just have fun and the let the big guy do his thing."

Josephine reached out and squeezed her mother's hand. "Thank you, Mom, for everything."

She turned and entered the stadium to the roar of twenty

thousand spectators. She knew her course and knew it was a tough one. The confines of the indoor coliseum made for a tight course with sharp turns and short distances between jumps. Tonight's course was designed to find the cream of the crop. Her last thought as she saluted the judge's stand, was to do exactly as her mother had said. She had to ride smart but try to relax and enjoy the flight. Major felt strong under her, but she had settled the rushing issue Friday, trotting some gymnastics. Major might have tested her to the jump in the past, but today she felt they were clicking, one an extension of the other. They were a team!

As she collected the big bay at a canter and circled, for a brief instant, she glanced into the stands. Easily finding TJ and her father standing in the front row, she smiled, then put her game face on and focused on the task at hand. Just one obstacle at a time, she told herself.

"We've got this," she said to Major and herself. "Here we go!" Josephine's heart raced in anticipation, keeping pace with the beat of the Thoroughbred's hooves as they approached the starting line. The crowd silenced and the anticipation in the building was palpable.

She could tell Major felt it too, pricking his ears forward as they approached the first jump. Balanced, she held him just long enough to get their spot, then released the Pegasus, taking a forward position, allowing Major to fully use himself without any interference. She could feel the big Thoroughbred round over the tall obstacle, his hind end lifting and folding under him, landing balanced, front to back, then collecting and preparing for the next jump.

It was an exhausting course mentally and physically with only two big oxer jumps left to clear for a perfect round. They came out of the first one a bit too fast, taking them off her planned track to the last jump. Josephine panicked and turned her head sharply to the right to compensate for her blind spot. And just as her mother had warned, Major turned sharply as well following the shift in her weight, causing him to lose his footing and break stride. Josephine tried to adjust his striding, but the jump was upon them and they ended up too close, feeling like they were jumping from under it. His front end cleared both rails, but she heard a rear hoof hit the second pole. This time just as they landed, so did the rail, making a thumping sound as it hit the ground. Four faults.

She knew that would most likely be enough to put them out of contention for the Games, but still in the money. It had been a gallant effort on Major's part, and she was so proud of him and her mother for all the years of work that led them to that moment. She felt a little disappointed, but she had to remind herself she just completed a sound round at the FEI World Cup ahead of many riders with no impairment. The moment they crossed the finish line, Josephine wrapped her arms around Major's neck. As they trotted toward the gate, she gave him a few pats of thanks.

"Good boy!" she praised. It was a bittersweet moment, though, knowing this would be Major's final Grand Prix course.

She could see her mother smiling at the gate as she approached. "Congratulations, Jo. I'm so proud of you."

"Thanks, Mom. Sorry about that last turn." She shook her head. "It was my fault."

"Don't. That could have happened to anyone."

"Are we out?"

"Yes. There's more to go, but a few have gone clean already. You and Major were awesome. You should be proud."

"I am." Josephine reached down and squeezed her mother's hand. "Thanks, Mom." Then she recalled the incident earlier. "But I feel so bad for Kayla."

"Me too. Take care of Major. Let Joy have his stall for now. I'll be back soon. I need to talk with your father."

Josephine saw that look of determination return to her mother's face. Whatever she was up to this time, she hoped it worked out for Kayla. "Okay. Good luck!"

Katherine wished she could watch Joker and the remaining horses jump their courses, but she didn't have time. She met up with the men outside the Center at their designated spot. "TJ, please help Jo with Major. Kayla will be there with Joy. We'll meet you at the stall." TJ nodded and left to catch up with Josephine.

"Honey, we need to talk."

Steven gave her that "now what crazy scheme have you conjured up" look. "Okay, where?"

"On the way to buy horses."

Steven's brows shot up, his jaw dropping. "What horses?"

"Expensive ones." Katherine started for the other stall building.

Steven shook his head as he kept pace.

"Kayla is in a tough spot."

"Yeah. What happened down there?"

"I'll explain more later. No time." Katherine's words spilled from her mouth as fast as they were covering ground. "She loves that horse and the trainer, Erica, needs to sell her. I want to talk to Karen. Offer to buy Joy and have Kayla move to Two Ponies. She's living in a trailer park with murderers, rapists and drug dealers!"

"Slow down. I know you feel you owe Karen somehow, and Kayla, but what makes you think Karen's going to go for it? Do you really expect Kayla to make the move without her grandmother's approval?"

"I know Karen won't agree at first. But if I can convince her to consider only Kayla's welfare, I think she might give her consent. I have to try. I think we can get the mare cheap."

"You said horses? Expensive ones."

"I want to make an offer on the black stallion, Joker, for Jo as well. Major needs to be retired from jumping at this level and I'd love for Jo to continue competing. I think we can get a good price for them both as a package deal."

"How much are we looking at?"

"I asked around yesterday. She's asking a quarter mil for Joker."

"Whoa! That's a lot."

"We have the balance of Josephine's college fund she never used. That will cover half of it. Can we afford the balance?"

"I suppose. But I'll need to work a couple more years to replace our retirement savings. You've been wanting me to retire."

"Oh, you were never going to fully retire anyway."

"You're probably right." Steven took a deep breath and shook his head again. "I think you just got used to having Jo back home and don't want an empty nest again when she gets married."

"That didn't enter my mind, but good point. I really just want to give Kayla a chance."

"You're a good woman, Kat. Now go, before Karen has the police looking for you and the girl."

Katherine hugged and kissed him. "Thank you."

Sure enough, she found Karen out front of Erica's tack stall talking with a security guard.

Karen's eyes darted toward her. "Where's Kayla? You have her, don't you?"

"Yes, I know where she is. Please Karen, we need to talk."

Karen studied her with contempt. "I don't think there's anything we need to discuss. Where's my granddaughter?"

The security guard placed his hands on his hips. "Is there a problem or not?"

"Not now," said Karen. "Thank you."

"Okay. Good." He turned and started down the aisle.

Katherine stepped closer to Karen. "Where can we talk?"

She turned and entered their tack stall with her arms crossed.

"This isn't about us, it's about Kayla. From what I heard and saw, Kayla's riding days with Erica are over. Am I wrong?"

"No. She's sending Joy to an auction as soon as we return. All her horses and the farm are for sale."

"Please know I'm not judging you. I just want to help. We need to put our past behind us and consider only what's best for Kayla. From what she's told me, you're struggling financially and forced to live in perhaps not the safest neighborhood for a young woman."

Katherine paused for a reaction, but Karen just stood there, straight-faced.

"I want to purchase Joy and perhaps Joker."

"What does that have to do with us?"

"We both know how much Joy means to Kayla. I'm offering to take Kayla on as a working student at our facility in Montana, board and meals included. She could continue to ride and show the mare and it would give you the opportunity to pay off her medical bills, save some money and perhaps move to a better community."

Karen drew in a deep breath and released it. Her jaw clenched and Katherine could see she was struggling with the decision. "How long?"

"She's welcome to stay as long as she wants. Kayla's a grown woman and I could have taken this offer straight to her, but I respect all you've done and sacrificed for her. Besides, I don't think Kayla would accept without your blessing."

Katherine could see Karen's eyes begin to moisten."This is asking a lot. Kayla is all I have left. All I have to live for." Karen paused a moment, taking another deep breath. "It's a generous offer and of course I want the best for my granddaughter." She shook her head, focusing on her feet. When she raised her focus to meet Katherine's, she could see her bottom lip trembling. "Okay," she said, immediately closing her eyes in anguish. "I've failed her."

"No. She appreciates all you've done."

Karen wiped a tear from her check. "I'll miss her."

"You can visit whenever you want. We have a cabin on the property where you can stay."

"Why are you doing this… after what I did?"

"I owe you," said Katherine.

"I believed that for years. I used you as an excuse for all my failures. I don't blame you anymore. You don't need to feel you owe me or Kayla anything."

"I want to do this for Kayla, for you both. Thank you for letting her go."

Katherine shook her hand. Karen offered only a meager smile, but it was a start. The healing between them had begun. "I'm going to wait for Erica to return. Hopefully, I can work out a package deal on both horses. My daughter has fallen in love with Joker."

"Erica needs to sell. She has Alzheimer's."

"I'm so sorry to hear that. No wonder the erratic behavior. Kayla needs to know. She's taking Erica's actions personally."

"I will tell her now. Erica was keeping it under wraps, but under the circumstances, it's time."

Katherine's offer didn't stand long. Erica jumped at the opportunity to move both horses. Joker hadn't qualified either, so she reduced his price by fifty grand and nearly gave her Joy. Since Katherine only had a two-horse trailer, Joker would be commercially hauled to Montana.

When she entered their building, she could see Joy in their stall and Major eating hay in the aisleway between both girls sitting in the chairs and chatting like they'd been life-long friends. She would love to know what they'd been discussing. Horses most likely, and she imagined Kayla would be curious about Josephine's acting career. TJ sat on a hay bale while Steven stood across from him, deep in their own conversation. When Steven noticed her approaching, he met her halfway.

"How did it go? Do we have two more horses and another daughter?"

Katherine smiled. "Yes." She was relieved when he smiled back. "Karen struggled with the decision to send Kayla away, but she finally caved. I felt sorry for her and invited her to visit Two Ponies a couple times a year."

Steven looked surprised. "Wow, didn't see that coming."

"Erica jumped at the offer and we got both horses for the price of one."

"Let me guess which one," he said, sarcastically.

By that time, they were getting curious glances from the kids. Katherine quickly finished at a whisper. "We need to meet up with Erica before dinner to finalize the deal, but first, we need to run this by Kayla, just in case."

"Well, let's get to it."

All eyes were on them as they approached Kayla. Katherine guessed she must have been wearing a silly grin, judging by their expressions.

"Kayla, we have a proposition for you." The girl's face became one big question mark as she scooted to the edge of her seat in anticipation. "I'd like to bring you on as a working student at Two Ponies in Montana, living expenses included." Kayla's eyes widened and before she could ask, Katherine continued. "I spoke to your grandmother and she agreed it would be a great opportunity for you."

"Oh, Kat, it's a dream come true." The girl sprang from her seat and into Katherine's arms. When she broke away, she glanced at Joy then back to her, her smile wilting. Katherine could see the sorrow building in her eyes. "Who would I school on?"

Katherine looked to Steven who was failing miserably at containing the surprise. "Joy, of course!"

The girl stood frozen in shock for a moment. "What? How?" she finally blurted out.

"I'm purchasing her."

It took Kayla a moment to find her voice as happy tears streaked her flushed cheeks. "Thank you! Thank you so much! She really is a good horse. You'll see."

"I know she is, Kayla. She just needs a calm and consistent environment."

"I can't believe Grandma approved."

"I invited her to visit at Two Ponies a couple times a year, whenever she wants, really."

Kayla slipped in the stall and hugged Joy. "We're going to Montana, girl!"

Josephine approached Katherine and whispered, "That was really sweet, Mom."

"It feels good. I had to do something."

Kayla joined them. "Guess I better take Joy back to her stall. Is Erica still mad at me?"

"No. She's not well. Your grandmother will explain. Please don't take what she said to heart. But before you go, there's one more surprise."

The two young women glanced at each other. This caught TJ's attention too. He stood up and joined them. Steven stood beside her, once again unable to keep a poker face.

Katherine stepped away so she could see all their reactions. "I bought another horse!"

"What! Where?" said Josephine.

"It's stalled near Joy." She could read the surprise on her daughter's face, considering her mother could no longer jump safely and the caliber of horses available at the World Cup.

"Is it a dressage horse?" asked Josephine.

"No. He's a jumper."

Josephine looked even more confused. "Oh, so it's a gelding." She glanced at her father wearing a big grin. "Looks like Dad approves."

"Let's follow Kayla over and I can show him to you."

As they approached Joy's stall, no one was around.

While Kayla tended to Joy, Josephine naturally gravitated to Joker's stall, petting his nose through the bars of the door. "Well, which one is it, Mom?" she asked glancing over her shoulder and up and down the aisle. "You can't keep us in suspense forever."

"You're touching him!"

Josephine turned and shrieked, "Oh my God! You're kidding me!"

Kayla joined her. "This is so perfect, Jo. We can school together!"

Josephine turned to her still in shock. "I can't believe it!"

"Major needs to be retired from competitive jumping. I can still show him dressage, but that left you without a mount. I see how much you've come to love show jumping, and you made no secret of how much you fell in love with Joker. You'll make a great team. And who knows, there may still be a gold medal in our future."

19 – Indian Races

June

Josephine studied her face in the mirror. A month had passed since her last surgery. The swelling and bruising had disappeared, leaving near perfect results. Still her face was not as symmetrical as it once was and she still needed to pencil in her one eyebrow, but besides that, she resembled her old self. You almost had to know where to look to see the faint scars. She looked forward to showing TJ when he returned home that week for summer break. It had been a long two months since Josephine last saw him in Las Vegas.

During that time, Josephine and Kayla had become very close, sharing the upstairs of the lodge and schooling their mounts nearly every day together. Kayla picked grandpa's old room at the end of the hall and plastered the walls with photos of Joy. The mare had settled in nicely and was working better than ever in her new home. Joy and Major had become quite the couple, inseparable out in pasture.

Her mother continued to work Major, setting a new goal of competing in musical freestyle classes. As for Joker, Josephine couldn't be more pleased. He was nothing short of a dream to ride and jump. Since their facility wasn't equipped to house a stallion, her father cut an exterior door in Stormy's old corner stall and erected a five-foot-high paddock adjacent to it. Joker seemed as happy with his new digs as she was with her new mount.

That evening after dinner, her mother called her to the phone in the kitchen. It was Roy. He had been checking in on her periodically.

"How did your last surgery go?" he asked.

"Great! My doctors did a fantastic job. I'm my old self again, well almost."

"That's wonderful, Jo. How is your eye?"

"The sensitivity has improved, but I think Mom told you, I'll never regain sight in it."

"Just curious. Is it cloudy, can anyone tell?"

"No, it looks normal. I don't have to wear a patch or anything."

"I'm glad to hear that, Jo." Roy hesitated and she couldn't help but wonder where this line of questioning was leading. "I'm starting a new project this fall in Texas," he added. "It has a great leading lady script."

She should have seen this coming. "Are you offering me the part?"

"You guessed it."

"I'm not interested, Roy."

"You'd be perfect for the role."

"Sorry. TJ will be home from school soon. Everything is going really well. I'm happy right where I am. But there is something I was hoping you might do for me."

"What, Jo Jo?"

"I'm writing a screenplay."

"Really! That's great. Something you might star in?"

"Give it up, Roy. But I'd love for you to read what I have completed."

"I'll tell you what. I have a proposition for you. I'll read your screenplay if you'll read my script. You might change your mind. I'll overnight it to you."

Josephine hesitated. "Okay, it's a deal."

Sadie anxiously waited on her front porch for Matt to return from work. He had recently started a new job at a convenience store and tire shop between Browning and Elkhead where he secretly made long-distance calls. Today he planned to call TJ at school to set a time this weekend to meet with the guys to discuss their practice and race schedule for the summer. Matt wanted to make sure he could get the time off work. Sadie hoped to learn if TJ mentioned anything about a marriage date. Perhaps there was a reason a date hadn't been set yet. She refused to give up on her and TJ so long as he wasn't married. Matt remained crazy about her and even took her home over the holidays to meet his family. She didn't love him, but he paid the rent and he had become her lifeline to TJ now that she no longer worked for Katherine.

When Matt arrived, he looked tired and agitated, slamming the door of his truck.

"Hi, baby, rough day?"

"Yeah, the owner is a real prick. He caught me on the phone today. Almost fired me." Matt passed her by, entering the house. He plopped down on the couch, kicked off his boots and rested his feet on the coffee table.

Sadie brought him a beer. "You spoke to TJ, then?"

"Yeah, he's returning tomorrow." Matt took a swig. "We're meeting on Sunday at noon at the stone house. Noot and Talon already said the time worked for them."

"Great. Can I come?"

Matt flipped on the TV. "No. I don't think that's a good idea."

Sadie returned to the kitchen area and stirred her venison stew. "I'm damn near a member of the team, filling in for TJ while he was gone and keeping the horses in shape through the winter," she said loudly over the television.

"I know, babe. But we'll just be figuring out our schedule."

"Okay." Sadie slipped in beside him on the couch and draped her arm around his shoulders. "Dinner will be ready soon. Say, did TJ mention anything about a wedding date yet?"

"No. Maybe he's finally wised up and is reconsidering. Why are you so curious, anyway? They sure as hell won't be inviting you after what you pulled."

Sadie freaked. "What did TJ tell you?" He surely wouldn't have told him about the night she brought him home.

"That you tried to come between him and Jo with that returning to acting story. I know you hate her for getting you fired and all and I don't blame you for wanting to get even. I don't approve of her either, but she's TJ's problem, not ours."

Relieved, Sadie sprang from the couch. "Dinner's ready."

TJ drove straight to Two Ponies from Fort Collins. Katherine answered the side door. "Hi, TJ. You're early." She gave him a hug.

"Hi, Kat." It still felt strange calling her by her nickname, but now that she brought attention to it, it would be weird calling her Mrs. Walker. "I left early and made good time. Where's Jo?"

"She's upstairs." Katherine walked to the entryway of the great room and called out. "Jo! TJ's here!"

TJ pulled his boots off and lunged up the stairs. He found her bedroom empty but heard giggling coming from within the bathroom. TJ tapped on the door. "Jo? What's going on in there?"

The door cracked open and Kayla slipped out. "Hi, TJ."

"Hi, Kayla. Jo in there?"

Kayla held her index finger up to him. TJ couldn't imagine what was going on. Two knocks from inside the room signaled Kayla to open the door. She waved him in. TJ entered a dark room. "Jo?"

Suddenly, the lights came on. Josephine stood within inches of his face. "Surprise!" she said, framing her face with her hands.

TJ studied her as he traced the right side of her face with his thumb. "Jo, I can hardly find the scars."

"Can you believe it? And I don't even have any makeup on!"

TJ playfully pulled her out of the bathroom, passing Kayla, and into her room by the window to take a better look. He pulled her hair back and kissed her beautiful face. Kayla, who he had momentarily forgotten was standing at the door, raised her eyebrows and closed the door.

"Thanks, Kayla!" called Josephine through the door.

"I'll be out at the barn," she called back.

TJ pulled her onto the bed and kissed her again. "Let's celebrate."

"Not now, TJ. Not here."

"I missed you."

"Me too." Josephine flashed a mischievous smile. "We could ride out to the cabin after dinner."

"It's a date!" TJ sat up, noticing a thick stack of sheets on her nightstand shelf. "How's the screenplay coming?"

Josephine leaned between him and the nightstand. "Great. I'm about half done."

TJ stretched around her to reach for the stack.

Josephine cut him off. "No!"

"What's the matter? Why can't I read it? Just a few pages?"

"Not yet. I want you to read it when it's finished." Josephine took his hand and pulled him off the bed. "Let's join Kayla. I don't want to be rude."

"Okay." TJ glanced at her alarm clock. It read five. "When's dinner?"

"When Dad gets home at six-thirty. You hungry? I can fix you something."

"What I'm hungry for isn't in the kitchen."

Josephine smacked his arm and dragged him out of the room.

After dinner, they pulled an unhappy Bonanza and Dandy from their stalls before they were finished with their hay.

"The temperature is starting to drop," said Josephine. "I forgot to grab a jacket. Can you run up to the lodge while I saddle the horses? A light one. Ask Mom, she'll know."

TJ jogged to the lodge and found Katherine and Kayla finishing the dishes in the kitchen. "Jo wants her light jacket."

Katherine dried her hands and checked the coat closet by the side door. "I don't see it here. Check her closet upstairs. It's navy blue."

Finding the blue windbreaker, TJ was about to leave her room when he remembered the screenplay. He was dying to read a few pages. He picked up the top couple sheets and glanced out the window to see if Josephine was on the drive waiting. When he began reading the first page, he was shocked. This wasn't even close to the storyline she had shared with everyone. Then he noticed at the top of the page below the title read, "By Carly Sanderson." This wasn't her screenplay; it was a script! TJ searched the shelf and hidden under the stack he found a note.

Hope you like it, Jo Jo. It's perfect for you. Let me know ASAP.
Thanks! Roy

Only then did he notice a large envelope addressed to Roy sitting on her desk beside her computer and printer. The envelope was sealed. TJ returned the note and script, picked up the jacket and hurried to the barn. The fact Josephine was hiding the script from him hurt, but he had been snooping around. TJ decided not to confront her about it and give her the opportunity to mention it to him herself.

Following a fun ride and great sex on the old goose down bed in the cabin, TJ became impatient and asked Josephine about her screenplay again. He rested on his side, cradling his head in his hand, admiring her beautiful naked form lying beside him. Enthusiastically, she sprang to a sitting position and shared more about the characters and plot in great detail.

TJ enjoyed seeing her so excited and motivated. He wanted to put his suspicions to rest about the script, but after she hid it from him still, he couldn't help wondering if she was considering the role now that her injuries were no longer an issue. "You think Roy might be interested in your screenplay?"

"I hope so. I'm sending him what I have completed."

TJ recalled the envelope on her desk. "That's great, Jo." TJ couldn't resist. "Would you consider the lead if he likes it?"

Josephine hesitated. "I suppose I've pictured myself in that role as I'm writing it. It helps bring the scenes to life in my mind."

"But would you take the part?" Silence. "Like I said in Vegas, I'd be supportive if you chose to return to acting, in this roll or any other project of Roy's." He was fishing, but he felt justified in doing so.

"I remember and it was a very sweet thing to say, but I don't think you've really thought it through. It would be a terrible strain on our relationship, logistically and emotionally. Any role would require several months, if not years, on location and would most likely involve love scenes."

"Sounds like you've thought it through."

"Yes, I have. And I'm happy right here, with you."

She had a point. He would definitely not be okay with her kissing some pretty boy like Brad, let alone a sex scene. But knowing she had given it that much consideration, frightened him. Perhaps he should give in and agree to getting married this summer before she reconsidered. "Still want to get married this summer?"

Josephine looked surprised. "Well, I've been giving it more thought and think you were right. We should wait."

A day ago, he would have been happy to hear she'd changed her mind, but now it only raised more questions. Was she agreeing for the reasons he'd given her or for her own new reasons? "Are you sure?"

"Yes, it's for the best. Like you said."

TJ couldn't really argue since he'd been trying to convince her to wait ever since he proposed. And it was for the best. He wanted to be able to take care of his wife and currently, he couldn't. She had offered to pay for his tuition and for an apartment in Fort Collins next year, but his pride wouldn't allow it. Now more than ever, he needed to win the Championship this fall so he could afford his final year at CSU and support them as a family.

"I'm meeting the guys Sunday to discuss our race schedule for this summer."

"Do you know your first race date yet?"

"That's the only date I know. June twenty-sixth. Crow Native

Days at Crow Agency in southern Montana."

"That's only a couple of weeks away. Will the horses be in good enough condition by then?"

"The guys have been working them some and Sadie has been helping out."

Josephine's joyful expression turned sour. "Sadie?"

"I told you her and Matt are living together now."

"Does that mean she's going to be there Sunday?"

"No. It'll be just us guys."

"Good. She's nothing but trouble."

"I agree." Mentioning Sadie reminded him he needed to trust Josephine. She's probably just reading the script as a favor to Roy for some feedback. He needed to focus on the two weeks they had together before Josephine, Kayla and Katherine left for shows on the West Coast. "When are you girls leaving?"

Josephine smiled and slid next to him, brushing a few wild strands of hair from his face, her jade eyes sparkling. "I have more good news."

TJ propped himself up on the bed. "What?"

"We're not going to show this summer. We're going to wait and hit the fall circuit."

"That's awesome. What changed?"

"I think we all needed a break, the horses too. But mostly, it was me. I didn't want to leave you. Just think, TJ, we'll have the whole summer together again, like 1995!" Josephine flashed her bedroom eyes, arousing him once again.

TJ glanced out the window. "It's dusk. Maybe we should head back. The horses are probably pawing a hole to China."

Josephine smiled seductively while mischievously peeking under the comforter.

TJ playfully attacked her tummy with a flurry of kisses. "But they can wait!"

June twenty-sixth crept up on TJ and team Piegan Pride quickly. Noot started working at the same store as Matt, Talon worked cattle at a ranch near Great Falls and TJ returned to working at the feed store. Between all four work schedules, they only managed to meet for four practices.

TJ was glad Josephine and the guys' women and their families didn't make the long drive. Crow Native Days turned out to be a disaster. They had trouble loading Sky and arrived late at Crow Agency with little time to warm up. Tomahawk ran out of steam down the homestretch and Sky, in another contrary mood, wouldn't hold still for TJ to mount him. By the time TJ slid onto Moon Cloud's back for the last leg, it didn't matter how well he ran, they were too far behind and finished fifth. The next opportunity for them to race in Montana wasn't until North American Indian Days back at All Chief Park in Browning the middle of July. If they didn't qualify for the Championship there, they had two more opportunities in the state at Phillips County Fair in Dodson the first week of August and back at Crow Agency for Crow Days two weeks later.

He sat with Josephine on the corner glider on her front porch after they returned that night, explaining their race.

"I'm sorry about how things went today," said Josephine. "Sounds like bad luck all around."

"We're going to need to get more practices in to have any chance of winning a race. From what I saw and heard today the competition has gotten stiffer since last year. I'm afraid our string of horses might not cut it this year."

"From what you said, it sounds like they just need to be in better condition, especially Tomahawk. And Sky needs a better work ethic. Horses thrive on a good, steady work routine. What if Jessie, Kayla and I worked them in between your practices?"

TJ turned to her. "That would be great!"

"I'm sure Kayla would be thrilled, but I'll have to check with

Jessie and Dad to see if she can take the time off from the clinic. If not, maybe Mom. We'll figure it out."

"We're going to try to practice every Sunday and Wednesday. If you could work them Tuesdays and Fridays, that would be perfect. But you'd need to go easy Tuesdays, though, so they'll be fresh for us on Wednesdays. All you need to do is breeze them in the pasture. Can you all meet us tomorrow so we can introduce you to the horses?"

"I think so. Let's go ask Kayla and I need to call Jessie before it gets too late. What fun!"

TJ enjoyed having Josephine, Kayla and Katherine watch them practice on Sunday. Jessie was already scheduled to work at the clinic and couldn't get anyone to cover for her. They all met at the pasture where the horses were boarded. After the guys ran a practice relay and a number of transfer sequences, Katherine mounted Noot's reliable Appy, Tomahawk, with a saddle. Kayla was up for the challenge of riding Talon's moody chestnut, Sky, bareback. And Matt put Josephine on his gray speedster, Moon Cloud, also bareback. The women hand galloped the geldings once around the pasture to get a feel for them. They were set to begin breezing the horses lightly Tuesday on their own.

A month later, the horses were working great, turning in their best times ever at the practice track. TJ felt confident they stood a good chance of a win in Browning that day. Everyone was there, Josephine and the Walkers, Kayla and Jessie, even his mom turned out. The guys' girls, Sadie and Cindy were seated with their Blackfeet friends and family. Noot wasn't dating anyone steady, but TJ noticed him checking Kayla out the day they met and the couple times the girls had joined them for their practices. He found it fascinating, Noot interested in a white girl, considering all the grief he and the guys had given him about Josephine over the years. Although, they seemed to have put their indifference aside once the women started helping with the horses.

The Browning race started well with a perfect ride on Tomahawk, putting them in great position on the rail behind the lead horse setting the pace. But the field was tight coming into the transfer area. TJ had a smooth mount onto Sky considering the traffic, but they reached the rail in the middle of the pack. When he tried to slide through an opening on the backstretch, the horse and rider on the outside made a move too, clipping Sky's heels. The crowd gasped as the horse's legs knocked! TJ cringed, feeling Sky stumble, break stride and come up lame on his right rear. Thankfully, the rest of the field avoided running into them as he immediately pulled Sky up and dismounted. The chestnut had no surface injury and TJ was relieved to see he could put weight on the leg, most likely eliminating a break. But any soft tissue injury would probably take Sky out of competition for the remainder of the season.

Within seconds, a veterinarian drove up and parked just outside the track exhibitor entrance as TJ slowly led Sky in that direction. A robust, elderly white man with silver hair and a gimp approached him. "Hi, I'm Dr. Cal Lowry. Do you want me to take a look at him?"

"Sure, but my veterinarian will be here any minute. I'm a vet student myself. I haven't gotten to fully examine him yet, but it looks and acts like a suspensory."

TJ continued to walk Sky toward their trailer where he was certain Dr. Walker would be meeting them. The Walkers had followed them in and parked beside their rig. The doctor examined Sky's leg while they waited.

"Good evaluation, son. I think you're right," said the doctor. "Too bad, though, you were looking good out there. Where are you attending?"

"CSU. I hope to graduate next year."

"Great school. That's where I got my degree." He shook his head in disbelief. "You'll be the first Indian vet I know of. Good to see.

Who's your doc?"

"Dr. Steven Walker."

"Of course, I knew his father well." The doctor patted Sky. "He'll be in good hands."

TJ noticed Matt, Noot and Talon walking briskly toward them leading Tomahawk and Moon Cloud.

"Good luck, kid," said the doctor as he started back toward the track. "Say hi to Steve for me."

"Thanks, will do."

The guys and horses trotted to catch up. "How bad is it?" asked Noot, studying his horse's rear leg.

"I don't think it's serious. He'll recover with rest, but he's out for the season."

"Shit!" said Matt. "Now what?"

"I don't know," said TJ.

Dr. Walker met them at the trailer out of breath. "I'm so sorry, TJ. I came as quick as I could."

Steven had TJ lead Sky so he could study the horse traveling from behind and from the side. Then Steven thoroughly examined the leg. The doctor and student agreed it was a torn suspensory ligament.

Steven turned to Noot. "He'll need stall rest. You're welcome to bring him to Two Ponies."

"Thanks, Doc," said Noot. "I really appreciate it. How much will the board cost?"

"Don't worry about it. But I have a few projects around Two Ponies I could use some help with if you have time."

"No problem. Just let me know."

The rest of their cheering section arrived. Steven filled them in while the horses were tended to and loaded. Matt and the guys followed the Walkers' vehicle to Two Ponies. After running cold water over Sky's leg and wrapping it, they settled him in for the night. Everyone congregated in front of the injured horse's stall.

"Well, it was fun while it lasted," said Talon, shaking his head.

Noot leaned against the front of the stall watching his horse, looking glum.

"We can't just give up. We need to find another horse," said TJ. He couldn't believe this was happening. Too much was at stake.

Matt approached TJ. "What about one of your horses?"

"Red is too old and Cisco isn't in shape."

"I'd offer Dandy, but he is getting up there too, and isn't in any better condition," said Steven.

Josephine stepped up. "What about Bonanza? He's fast and in pretty good shape. We could have him ready in a couple weeks."

"He's a Quarter Horse," said TJ. "Built for short distance speed, not a mile."

Noot turned to join the conversation. "Maybe we can pick up an off-the-track Thoroughbred cheap at the auction next weekend if we all pitch in?"

"That's not a bad idea," said TJ. "We could get lucky."

Rumbling and pawing emanating from their trailer caught everyone's attention. "We better get them back," said Matt. "Let's still meet tomorrow to practice and see how much money we can come up with."

Noot thanked Steven again. "I'll come by tomorrow afternoon to check in on Sky if there's something I can help you with."

"So long as I don't have an emergency, I should be here. We'll start with some fence repair."

"Sounds good, see you then." Noot glanced from Steven to Kayla with a smile.

As soon as the guys left, Steven stepped up. "Don't worry, TJ, if you can't find another horse, and even if you do but come up short for your classes, we'll cover the balance."

TJ shook his head and before he had the opportunity to decline, Katherine, who had quietly stood outside the discussion, approached TJ. "Take Major."

He must have heard wrong. "What did you say?"

"Race Major, he's in great shape and we know he can run. He wasn't retired from the track until he was six for nothing. He has to be fast."

"What about his dressage training?"

"He can use a break. I'm not planning to show him for a while anyway. I can resume his dressage training this winter after the girls and I return."

Still, TJ stood in shock. He'd never ridden a horse like Major, although the thought of racing him was exhilarating. But this was Katherine's baby. She wouldn't even let Sadie ride him. "I don't know, Kat."

"Take him. I trust you with him and Jo can help. She knows him inside and out."

"It'll be fun, TJ. He'll love it," said Josephine.

TJ couldn't help considering it. Major might even be faster than Moon Cloud. Then he considered the logistics. "How tall is Major?"

Josephine looked to Katherine. "He's about sixteen-three."

"Dang, that's three inches taller than Moon Cloud. I don't know if I'll be able to mount him from the ground."

"One way to find out," said Josephine.

"I suppose so. But even if I could, would he stand for me to mount him on the run?"

"I think with practice," said Katherine.

TJ worked his chin between his fingers. "We could run him first so there wouldn't be a transfer."

"Is that a yes?" Josephine was gleaming.

"We'll give it a try," he said to Josephine, then turned to Katherine. "Thank you so much."

"Let's introduce you," said Katherine.

Josephine sprang into motion, taking Major's halter from his stall. "I'll get him." Kayla followed.

Katherine slipped into the tack room and office, returning with his snaffle schooling bridle and a few horse cookies she gave to TJ.

"This will make for a smooth introduction." TJ slipped the treats into his pocket. "He's been ridden bareback by me and Jo so that won't be an issue. But I'd like you to lead him out to the arena and get on him with the mounting block to start."

"Sure. We have to start somewhere," said TJ. Of all the green colts and rank problem horses he'd ridden that were in training with his dad, he'd never been this nervous to ride a horse. When Josephine led Major into the barn beside him, he looked at him in a whole new light. TJ took the lead rope from her. The big bay studied him and took in his scent. TJ blew lightly back into his nostrils. Major snorted, raised his head, then nudged his shoulder. "He's a bright one, isn't he?"

"He sure is," said Katherine.

"Sometimes he knows what I want before I even ask for it," said Josephine.

TJ stroked his silky coat starting at his neck, down his shoulder, across his back and around his rump. Major stood perfectly still, almost too still. Ears flicking back and forth, following his every move. Katherine handed him the bridle. Major let him slip the headstall over his ears with no trouble.

"Okay, we're good," said TJ. "Let's go." He led the way with Major in hand out to the mounting block in the indoor arena. Katherine held him by the bridle while TJ slid onto his bare back. Major flinched a bit and took a couple steps until TJ took up the reins. "I've got him."

He took it slow walking a lap around the ring, then eased him into a trot. It didn't take long before TJ had him going at a good pace. "Holy shit," said TJ. "His trot is huge!" He'd never ridden a horse with such powerful gaits. When he tried to slow it down, Major responded then began trotting in place. "What's he doing?"

"He thinks you cued him for a piaffe. We've been working on that movement lately," said Katherine.

TJ started laughing. He'd felt horses nervously trot in place, but this was so controlled and in rhythm. "He's dancing!"

"Give him a little more rein and cluck," said Katherine. He did, and Major moved out. "Now a little outside leg," she added. Just a touch and Major struck off into a collected canter. "I feel like I'm riding a rocking chair," he called out from the far side of the arena. When he circled back around, he asked for a little more and Major obliged with a bigger collected canter. TJ brought him down to a walk and approached his audience. "I've seen him hand gallop, but when was the last time he ran full out?"

Katherine's face turned white. "It's been a while."

TJ didn't need to ask further. He guessed it had to be when she chased down his father's murderer five years earlier.

"Believe me he'll move out when asked," she added.

TJ nodded. "Okay, I guess I need to find out if I can mount him from the ground before we go any further."

Katherine took hold of his bridle. "I'll hold him the first time. It might spook him." Sure enough, Major scooted away from him his first try. Katherine calmed him with slow strokes of her hand down his neck. "Easy, boy."

The next few approaches, TJ didn't even try to mount Major. He just jumped beside him while grabbing mane and putting pressure on his back. After a few minutes of that, the big bay stood perfectly still.

"Time to try again," he said. TJ stepped a few feet away, took two big strides and vaulted. He didn't get high enough and just slid down the gelding's barrel, but Major tolerated it. More tries, and finally he landed on his belly across Major's back and swung his leg over. Major danced in surprise, but he was on! TJ gathered the reins and asked Katherine to let him go. He walked the Thoroughbred around the ring a lap and mounted him again, repeating this process a few more times.

"Okay, if you don't have second thoughts," said TJ. "I think this might work."

"We'll haul him to your practice tomorrow and see how it goes there," said Katherine.

"Sounds good." The whole idea still seemed surreal to TJ. Racing Major! Wow!

"I'm coming," said Josephine. "I wouldn't miss this for the world."

Kayla joined in, "Me too!"

"Wait until the guys find out," said TJ. "They'll go nuts!"

When TJ arrived Sunday at the training track, the guys were still talking about the longshot of purchasing a replacement at the auction the following weekend. They had pulled together two hundred and fifty dollars and asked TJ what he could contribute.

"Keep your money. I have the solution."

Matt laughed. "What? You going to pull a racehorse out of your butt?"

"Not exactly." The timing played out perfectly as the Walkers' rig pulled up. None of the guys had seen the big Thoroughbred before. TJ wished he had a camera as Major stepped off the trailer, snorting and nearly breathing fire as he took in the new horses and the wide-open field and track. Somehow, TJ felt certain the big boy knew what he'd come there to do. And TJ was not disappointed. It took a couple attempts to mount him with Katherine's help, but once he was onboard, they glided around the track like an eagle.

Katherine watched approvingly from the trailer. "You're doing great with him, TJ," she said when he completed a lap. "And he's loving it."

"He's not the only one," said TJ. "But now we need to try a start." This concerned him since he hadn't tried to mount Major by himself yet. Matt held Moon Cloud and Noot held Tomahawk lined up on either side of him and Major. Talon blew a whistle. As they maneuvered to mount their horses, Major kept scooting away and he found he couldn't hold the reins short enough to keep Major in place, and at the same time, have enough room to get the momentum needed to mount the tall Thoroughbred. "This isn't going to work. Major's going to have to go second or third so he can be held."

"I think we should still finish with Moon Cloud," said Matt. "But how's Major going to do with all the traffic during a switch?"

"We won't know for sure until we're in a race. But we can practice with one other horse. Noot, hold Major. I'll ride in on Moon Cloud alongside of Talon on Tomahawk. Jo, catch Moon Cloud."

Once they were set up for the simulated transfer, TJ yelled "go" and he and Talon raced toward Major. The big bay wiggled a little, but TJ got on. "Okay, we'll run him second."

"Let's run a full relay against the clock with Tomahawk, Major and Moon Cloud, in that order," said TJ. The transfers went well enough and TJ could feel Major's speed under him, his long legs covering ground at an amazing pace. He felt certain Major ran faster than Sky. TJ immediately turned back after the finish to check the time. "That felt fast. How did we do?"

"Record time by three seconds and the transfers weren't even that great," said Talon. "Bet we can shave off another couple seconds with practice."

"That's awesome!" said Matt.

TJ approached Katherine. "Thank you. But I have one more favor to ask. Please let his mane grow in, at least at the withers so I have more to grab onto. It'll help."

Katherine laughed. "Sure, I hadn't thought of that."

Noot shouted, "Championship, here we come!"

Josephine continued to haul Major to the Reservation for Wednesday and Sunday practices while breezing him at home. And the girls maintained their biweekly conditioning of Tomahawk and Moon Cloud. By the first week of August, TJ felt they were ready to win a race.

Since Phillips County Fair in Dodson was less than a two-hour drive east of Browning, team Piegan Pride once again attracted a big cheering section. The Walkers hauled Major over in their trailer and for the first time, TJ felt nervous before a race. So much was on the line; his education, their marriage, Major's safety.

TJ broke away perfectly on Tomahawk, sliding into third place behind two lead horses running side by side ahead of him. On the backstretch, they spread out and he passed one of the lead horses. Racing into the first transfer, TJ could see Major fussing as horses and riders ran up on him. Noot could barely hold on to the strong Thoroughbred. TJ leapt off Tomahawk and it took two tries to vault onto Major. He ended up in sixth place on the rail, at least ten strides behind the lead horse of a stretched-out field. Major passed two horses on the backstretch and another just beyond the far turn. As they raced toward Noot to make the final transfer, the first and second-place riders were already charging for the rail ahead of them. Major tossed his head, grabbed the bit and refused to stop. The old racehorse wanted to chase down the lead horses to the finish. TJ pulled one rein, circling Major until he regained control and returned for the transfer. He reached the rail on Moon Cloud a quarter of a mile behind the field and they finished last. Immediately, TJ knew what they needed to do – finish with Major!

Two weeks later, TJ and the team arrived Friday afternoon at Crow Agency for Crow Days in style. Since Katherine insisted on an overnight stall for Major, considering the four-hour haul south, the guys came up with the cash to stall their horses as well. Matt and Talon brought Sadie and Cindy and got their own hotel rooms, while TJ and Noot shared a room. Katherine and Steven had the room next to them with Josephine and Kayla sharing the next room down. Friday night, they all had dinner together downstairs at the hotel restaurant.

TJ didn't think it possible, but he felt even more nervous the morning of this race than he had at the last race. This was their final chance to qualify in Montana. He would hate for Katherine to need to haul Major out of state. She had done plenty for them already. And the guys couldn't continue to afford hotel rooms and stalls. Hopefully, they would be celebrating their victory that evening.

The race started with the worst possible scenario, Tomahawk getting jammed between two horses as he tried to mount. As soon as he had room, he mounted and raced to the rail. He could see five of the eight-horse field ahead of him on the first turn. The leopard Appaloosa felt strong and gained ground on the backstretch, passing two horses. Thankfully, the transfer to Moon Cloud went smoothly, but so had the switch for the other teams. He parked the gray behind the fifth-place horse through the first turn and passed one horse on the backstretch. The rest of the field was a tight-knit group. He'd be happy to remain in this position following his transfer to Major.

The big bay stood quietly for once, anticipating the switch. He did learn fast. In one fluid motion, TJ slipped off Moon Cloud, ran a few strides, grabbed mane and sprang onto Major's back like a gymnast. Off they flew into a tight pack. TJ found himself once again boxed in going into the first turn. No way would he risk squeezing through an opening and taking the chance of getting tangled again, like what happened with Sky, or worse! Instead, he trusted in the gelding's speed, heart and desire to win and pulled up slightly, just enough to pull out of the pack. But they were already nearing the far turn. If he made his move on the corner, it would be twice as difficult for Major to pass them. But if he waited until the homestretch, would they have enough time to find the lead by the finish line? He waited. Just as the track straightened, he pulled Major open and let the reins slide through his fingers. The old racehorse responded, giving his all. His long strides quickly gained ground on the other horses. His competitors whipped their horses pointlessly as Major easily overtook them one by one down the homestretch. They won by two lengths to the cheers of the crowd, qualifying for the Championship!

20 – The Search

Sadie paced the floor of their hotel room the night of the race. Something must be done! She had watched TJ and the guys win the Crow Days race earlier that afternoon, qualifying for the Championship Race. If they won the Championship of Champions again this year, TJ could afford his last year of vet school. He'd graduate next year and would no doubt intern at Dr. Walker's clinic, where he'd become a partner and one of the most successful Blackfeet of their nation. Next summer, TJ and Josephine would marry, move onto his ranch, start a family and live happily ever after. That was supposed to be her life! Maybe it still could be…

Down the grapevine, TJ to Talon, Talon to Matt, and Matt to her, he learned TJ had found a script Josephine was hiding from him. He had expressed his concern over her possibly returning to her acting career. Music to Sadie's ears. If her career broke them up once, it could come between them again. Too bad she couldn't have hooked up with Talon, TJ's best friend, instead of Matt. Then she'd be getting firsthand information. But Matt would have to do. Besides, Matt had the truck and trailer, which might come in handy.

When Sky came up lame and the guys had no chance of winning the Championship, she thought things were finally going her way. But those damn Walkers stepped in with Major, ruining everything. Now she had to come up with another way of postponing TJ's graduation and their wedding, giving Josephine more time to consider returning to California. If she did, it would never work, and Sadie would be ready to swoop in and mend TJ's broken heart again. But how? What started as a random thought began to take shape in her twisted mind as she paced the room. Without Major, the team would have no chance of winning the Championship. Without the winning purse, TJ would have to work another year, not graduating until the following year. This might be her last chance at obtaining her dream.

Everyone was celebrating their win over dinner downstairs at the bar and grill. No way was she about to sit at a table with Josephine and TJ as they rejoiced and planned their bright future together. She ducked out, claiming she had a headache. Matt would stay late at the bar and drink too much with the guys and come back to the room drunk. Then she would put her scheme into motion.

Around one in the morning, Matt staggered into the room, collapsed on the bed and passed out. Sadie slipped his keys out of his jacket pocket and quietly snuck out of the room. She climbed in the driver's seat of Matt's Dodge and turned the ignition key. The old truck rattled and choked out a backfire of exhaust. Thankfully with the trailer, Matt had to park out back of the hotel, a good distance from their rooms. She sped to the show grounds and parked behind the barn that stalled their horses. Sadie had noticed the night before, there was little security. She quickly opened the back of the trailer and approached Major's stall. Having been familiar with her, the big bay willingly let her halter and load him into Matt's stock trailer. Off into the night she drove toward the nearby Pryor Mountains.

Katherine woke up early Sunday morning feeling uneasy. She shook Steven awake. "Let's wake up Josephine and Kayla. I want to hit the road."

After packing a meal to go from the hotel's continental breakfast, they pulled up to their barn with their trailer. Katherine didn't see any of the guy's vehicles parked at the fairgrounds yet. "Kayla, if you can open the trailer and put a couple sections of hay in a hay bag, I will feed Major his grain while Jo packs up."

Katherine was the first one in the barn. When she reached Major's stall, she found it empty with the door wide open. Terror gripped her chest. Perhaps someone had moved him for some reason. She ran up and down the barn aisle checking all the stalls. "Jo!" she screamed as her daughter entered the barn. "Major's gone!"

"What do you mean, gone?"

"He's not in his stall or any stall in the barn!"

"Oh my God!" Josephine ran to where her father was reading a

USA Today he'd picked up in the hotel lobby.

An older Indian wearing a hat entered the barn from the opposite end and Katherine ran to him. "Have you seen a big bay Thoroughbred gelding?"

"Sure, there's plenty of them here," he said.

"Running loose? Someone leading one this morning?"

"No. I just got here." He continued walking to an open bale in front of a stall and began throwing hay to the neighboring horses.

Steven tossed the newspaper aside and rushed to her, followed by Josephine and Kayla. "Don't worry, honey, we'll find him. I'll call the police."

"Let security know, if there is any," said Katherine, in a panic. "Kayla, stay here in case someone shows up knowing something. Ask the guys if they know anything when they get here. Jo, let's search the rest of the facility, every stall and trailer."

Many of the stalls were already empty and few trailers remained, so they performed a thorough search of the show grounds in about thirty minutes. When they returned they found Steven, a security guard and two county police officers standing in front of Major's stall, which had already been taped off.

Katherine approached them, now in tears. "Find or hear anything?"

Steven wrapped his arm around her. "Not yet. They have a couple vehicles that are searching the grounds and asking questions."

"We already checked every stall and trailer. He's not here. Oh, Steven. Poor Major!" The thought of him being stolen and sold to who knows who took her breath away. "My God, Steven, he could be on his way to an auction or slaughterhouse!" That did it and she began sobbing on his shoulder.

Matt pulled up outside their barn with his rig. Talon, Cindy and Sadie poured from the truck behind Matt, looking concerned with the police car and officers on the scene. TJ and Noot pulled in right behind them. She could hear Josephine explaining the situation to everyone.

TJ approached her and Steven. "Don't worry, Kat, we'll find him."

Josephine, looking as devastated as she felt, gave her a lingering hug. "I'm so sorry, Mom. None of us will rest until we find Major."

Matt stepped up with the guys behind him. "That's right, Mrs. Walker, we'll all help find him."

"Whoever took him is long gone," said TJ. "No sense in searching the grounds again." He turned to Matt. "Let's get the horses home and start our search. Major's going to stick out anywhere in the state. Someone will know something."

"I'll get the word out to all the vets in the state and Mike will notify every law enforcement avenue," said Steven.

Katherine wiped her face and pulled herself together. "Thank you all. As soon as we get home, I'll make up some flyers with a photo and description of Major along with our contact information."

"We'll post them everywhere," said Josephine.

One of the officers approached their group. "We've swept the place. No one saw anything, but most of them didn't get here until after daylight. I would suspect the theft took place in the early morning hours." He gave Steven a card. "Please send us pictures of the horse so we can post them."

"Will do," said Steven. He turned to the group. "Let's get moving. Time is of the essence."

Within minutes, the guys had the horses loaded. TJ rode with the Walkers. Steven drove straight home and called Mike and Chief. The moment they pulled into Two Ponies, Katherine raced into the lodge to pick out a couple photos of Major, a full body shot and a close-up of his head. The gelding had no white markings, but she included his Jockey Club registry number, which is tattooed under his top lip. She included his height, age, sex and a three-thousand-dollar reward. Chief said there was no need setting the reward any higher, so long as it was well above what Major would bring at an auction for meat.

Josephine ran into town to the print shop and had five hundred color flyers printed and purchased several staplers. By the time she returned, Matt and Noot pulled up in their truck and Talon in his, ready to help. Not long after, Mike, Chief, Jessie and Dane drove up. The Two Ponies parking area looked like a used car lot. Everyone circled around the picnic table on the porch to organize. They divvied up the flyers and assigned towns and cities across the state, focusing on feed and tack stores. Mike, Dane and Chief offered to hand deliver flyers to the State Patrol and fax them to all the Montana and surrounding state police departments.

Steven, needing to remain available for any emergency calls, agreed to stay home to man the phone and Kayla offered to care for the horses while Katherine, Josephine and TJ traveled to all the horse auction barns in Montana and a few in bordering states, which would take days. They planned to post flyers and speak to regulars, many of which were kill buyers, who purchased horses to sell for meat.

Each day that passed with no results, Katherine became more depressed. She could see the strain on her daughter as well. Major had become a part of their family, especially for Katherine after all they had been through together. After visiting an auction house in Billings on Monday, they attended one in Bozeman on Tuesday, which was packed with over one hundred horses of every breed imaginable. They split up and searched the pens and trailers, meeting back at the main entrance. She was shocked by how many beautiful off-the-track Thoroughbreds ended up with numbers on their rumps heading to who knows where, possibly slaughterhouses. Becoming more desperate by the minute, they started posting flyers around the property and handing them out to attendees. When they took a break at a food vendor truck parked out front, an elderly man approached TJ.

"Hi, son, I thought that was you," said the robust man with silver hair and a white beard to match. He could pass for a really good Santa with a few more pounds.

TJ turned. "Hi, Dr…"

"Lowry, Cal Lowry."

"Right. Phillips County Fair." TJ turned to her. "This is Katherine Walker, Dr. Walker's wife and their daughter, Josephine."

Dr. Lowry's gaze stuck on Josephine. "I'm sure you've heard this before, but you're a dead ringer for that actress Josie Walker. My goodness, same last name too."

Josephine blushed and smiled.

"Wait a minute, I'd know that smile anywhere. It is you, isn't it?"

"Yes, but…" Josephine placed her finger over her lips.

"I knew it! Nice to meet you," he whispered. Cal tipped his oversized Stetson. "I love Westerns. My wife says I was born a century too late. I've seen all your movies, even the bit parts in your early films. You're even prettier in person." Suddenly, his fuzzy eyebrows resembled two white caterpillars meeting at the middle as he studied her face. "I heard you had a bad accident. I'm so happy to see you're fully recovered."

"Thank you," said Josephine, handing him a flyer. "Say, have you seen this horse around? He was stolen at Crow Days."

Cal studied the image. "Well hell, I was there and saw him run. Beautiful animal. I'm so sorry. I'll keep my eyes and ears open. I get around. I attend auctions primarily to study the behavior of the kill buyer, whose main client is a slaughterhouse, and to provide more transparency to this terrible aspect of the horse industry, which I fervently oppose. Occasionally, I buy a horse."

Katherine had to ask. "What are the chances my horse would end up at an auction, or, heaven forbid, a slaughterhouse?"

"Pretty favorable, I'm afraid. Whoever took him will want to dump him for whatever he can get as soon as possible and isn't looking to sell him where he's going to turn up later. While there is currently no horse slaughter in the United States, auctions like this exist all over North America. From there, they go into Canada, Mexico and even overseas. They are part of the clearinghouse for animals that eventually wind up on dinner tables around the world. But, as I have come to learn, not just any horse will do for slaughter. Kill buyers prefer healthy horses. Consequently, kill buyers often end up bidding against those looking for a horse for their daughter or their farm, which is a damn shame, many of them registered horses including Thoroughbreds. What becomes clear at these auctions is that kill buyers pay a premium for healthy-looking horses. The point is that kill buyers are not simply buying up horses that have no other demand. They are bidding on healthy horses, paying more for those horses as they outbid private buyers and other dealers. A healthy horse bound for slaughter will provide better-quality meat, and more of it, for the meatpacking company."

Katherine regretted asking, her stomach churning. She tossed the last of her hotdog. "Thank you for offering to keep a look out. I must ask, though, as I'm married to a veterinarian, how do you find the time to visit all the auctions?"

"Oh, I'm pretty much retired now. I just volunteer at the Indian races and I'm also a wild horse and mustang advocate. I study the herds, take pictures and keep track of the populations and condition of the horses for the State. Mostly at the Pryor Mountains Wild Horse Range, south of here. I'm heading there now."

"That sounds like wonderful work," said Josephine.

"Thanks." Cal removed his straw hat and scratched his scalp. "Sorry, I shouldn't be taking up so much of your valuable time. I hope you find your beautiful horse."

"Thank you," said Katherine, considering the Santa social butterfly could be helpful, she handed him a stack of flyers. "If you don't mind, here's a few more flyers. Sounds like you get around."

"I sure do, and I'd be happy to do whatever I can to help out. Good luck!"

Cal disappeared into the crowd. "Let's get going. Maybe we can make Missoula by nightfall."

A few days later, the weary and disheartened search team returned to Two Ponies. After a hot shower, Katherine joined her husband and the kids for a home-cooked meal Kayla had prepared for them. No one talked much as she picked at her food. There wasn't much to say. Following a week-long effort by everyone, not one clue had turned up where her lovely boy might be. When the phone rang, Kayla offered to answer it on their portable kitchen phone.

"It's a Dr. Lowry for you, Kat," she said, handing the receiver to her. She couldn't believe her ears. "He saw a horse resembling Major running with a band of mustangs this morning," she shared with the group. She put the phone on speaker. "Where? Can you tell us how to find them?"

"These bands keep on the move, but I'd be happy to draw you a map of where I saw them last."

Steven reached for the phone. "Hi, Cal, this is Steve. Thanks for reaching out. Can we meet you down there?"

"Yes, I have pictures so you can confirm it's him. The horse I saw sure as hell isn't a mustang. I'm at the Yellowstone River Inn south of Billings, just off Interstate 90 on Highway 212. You're going to need horses and the more the better. You might have to separate him from the heard to catch him."

"Cal, this is Katherine again. We can be there tonight, but it'll be late. Do you know where we can keep four horses overnight?"

"No problem. There's a livery stable down the road that takes tourists out to see the mustangs. They should have an open pen you can use. I'll line it up. I'll be here in Room 116."

"Great! Thank you so much, Cal," said Katherine.

"Thanks, Cal!" said Steven. "See you soon!"

Katherine handed the phone back to Kayla. "Can you believe it?" Katherine felt giddy. "How in the hell did he end up running with mustangs?" Then she noticed TJ looking less than happy. "What?"

"I think someone wanted to eliminate the competition. Someone fond of horses just wanting him out of the way. Anyone else would have sold him. I'm so sorry. This is our fault."

"No, TJ. Don't even think that. Please," said Katherine. "We all went into this together. But you're probably right about the 'why,'.

"I have an idea," said Josephine. "I'm going to call Roy. He was at the ranch when we spoke last. If he's still there, I'm sure he'll help us find Major with his chopper."

"That's a great idea," said TJ. "But we still have to ride in to get him once we find him. Who's all going?"

Katherine glanced to Kayla. "Will you be okay here on your own? You can always call Jessie if you need help."

"Sure," said Kayla.

"That leaves four of us. We'll need to take two rigs, one for the search horses and one to bring Major home." said Steven.

"Wish my Mom hadn't sold our trailer," said TJ. "I'll go pick up Matt's stock trailer and load up Cisco. I can be back here in a little over an hour if I hustle."

"Perfect, we'll have Bonanza, Dandy and Blackjack ready to go," said Katherine.

"I'll pack up what you'll need for the horses," said Kayla.

Josephine sprang up from her seat. "I'll be out to help as soon as I pack and call Roy."

TJ was out the door before Katherine stood to clear the table. Roy was at the ranch and gave Josephine the location of an airstrip near the motel where they could meet in the morning. Katherine secured two rooms at the Yellowstone River Inn, packed some sandwiches and drinks in a cooler, repacked her bag with a few changes of clothes and grabbed her riding boots. Steven called Mike and Dane with the latest developments and quickly packed. It was dark by the time their caravan pulled out, heading south.

Arriving at the motel around midnight, they met Cal at his room. Katherine couldn't wait to see the photos. It only took one picture for Katherine to identify her horse.

"That's Major! That's my horse!"

"Wonderful," said Cal.

They followed Cal to the stable where he secured a holding pen for their horses. From there, they moved to a bar and grill next door to the inn. He had a detailed map drawn with a few landmarks easily visible by air. But he warned them, once they got out on the range on horseback, much of the landscape looked very similar and it was easy to get lost and insisted they take his fancy compass. Cal had gotten approval for their search, explaining the situation to his friends with the National Park Service management. When Cal learned the famous Western actor and director Roy Higgins was meeting them in the morning, he got as excited as a kid on the night before Christmas. He insisted on staying until Major was found.

At daybreak, they met Roy at the small airstrip down the highway. After Cal got Roy's autograph and a handshake, TJ and Josephine stayed behind with him while Katherine and Steven rode with Roy in his helicopter. The topography of the Pryor Mountain Wild Horse Range didn't appear to be able to sustain one horse, let alone nearly two hundred. Yet, Cal had assured her Major would do just fine with the diverse shrub-grass vegetation available. He went on to list nearly a dozen varieties that grew amongst the Douglas fir, lodgepole pine, subalpine fir, limber pine, and juniper the horses used for shelter. He really knew his stuff. The man was like a walking encyclopedia.

The view was beautiful from the chopper, miles of blue sagebrush running up to dark green alpine forests with hidden leas. They were heading for one of those meadows now, where the band was last spotted. She tried to imagine her big, spoiled boy out there amongst the coyote, bears and mountain lions scavenging for food. She hoped he hadn't lost too much weight but imagined he would be keeping fit running the open range. Following Cal's directions and landmarks, they flew over the spot he had spotted Major yesterday morning, but no mustangs were in sight. Roy began gradually opening their search. With no sign of the herd by noon, they had to return to refuel.

Cal and the kids were waiting for word at the airstrip and were disappointed to hear they had no luck. The old vet suggested a few other favorite spots for this particular band, run by an old but strong roan stallion he called Bandit. His harem included about twelve mares, their foals and a few young stallions he allowed to tag along until they became a threat to him. She wasn't sure how Major fit in, but he certainly didn't pose a threat to the stallion as a gelding.

Over lunch, Cal entertained their group with the rich history surrounding the Pryor Mountain Wild Horse Range. He explained there are only two areas reserved by the Federal government for wild horses in the United States, one on the Nellis Air Force Base in Nevada and here in the mountains of south-central Montana and northern Wyoming named after Sergeant Nathaniel Pryor. The herd consists of approximately one hundred and eighty genetically unique horses of Colonial Spanish-American heritage, originating in Portugal and Spain, that have roamed freely throughout the Pryor Mountains since at least the time of the Expedition.

He went on to explain the Pryor Mountain Wild Horse Range was created by order of the Secretary of the Interior, Stewart L. Udall on September 9th, 1968. At the time, the Pryor Mountain Wild Horse Range encompassed 33,600 acres of Bureau of Land Management and National Park Service-managed lands in Montana. In the years since, additional land was added. Today, the Pryor

Mountain Wild Horse Range is comprised of more than 38,000 acres.

Josephine and TJ quietly listened as he shared the wild horses' story, brought to the Americas by Spanish explorers, who landed at Vera Cruz in 1519, but it was nearly two hundred years thereafter that the Shoshone Indians became the first Plains tribes to acquire them in 1690, then the Nez Perce in about 1710. Slowly but steadily, the other great tribes began developing their own herds; the Crows in about 1730, the Blackfeet and the Mandans at midcentury, followed by the Sioux and the Plains Cree in 1770. He explained that over the years, the horses crossed with several different breeds, but remain hearty horses still carrying many of the characteristics of the Spanish horses; small ears, wide-set eyes and full manes and tails.

That afternoon, Katherine was thrilled to see the first band of mustangs. When they saw the helicopter, the herd fled at a gallop. Her anxiety was lifted for at least the moment as the beautiful scene played out below them. Mustangs in a wide variety of colors including bay, black, dun, grulla, roan, buckskin and palomino traveled in harmony over the rugged terrain. Katherine leaned, nose against the glass window, searching the heard for a tall lanky bay amongst the short and stocky mustangs.

"There!" she pointed. "There he is to the right, at the back!"

"Yes, I see him," said Steven. "Now to find him again tomorrow morning on horseback. It'll be too late to start out today by the time we get back."

Roy turned the chopper around and headed for the airstrip.

The alarm woke Katherine up to a still dark room. She had a hard time falling asleep and it felt as if she had just closed her eyes. She shook Steven awake. "Let's get going."

She was surprised to hear the kids already moving about in the room next door. Katherine knocked on the adjacent door. Josephine cracked the door open. "We're up."

"Let's meet downstairs. Their breakfast starts in about fifteen minutes."

Josephine gave her a thumbs up and promptly closed the door.

Making quick work of saddling the horses, the expedition departed just after daybreak. The early morning light gave a warm glow to the barren landscape where they entered the range. They would have a long ride up to the meadows where they found Major and Bandit's band of mustangs the day before. Katherine prayed they hadn't wondered too far from their last location.

The mid-day sun beat down on the high desert as they aimed for the middle of two identifiable landmarks, a bald peak neighbored by a pointed pine peak. Having not been used in years, her Western saddle creaked and squeaked to Blackjack's strides. Katherine wiped sweat from her brow, wishing she had worn shorts under her chaps and a cooler top. Her dark riding helmet gave her little relief from the sun. Steven, riding by her side, looked just as uncomfortable, even though he wore a straw cowboy hat shading his face. Katherine glanced back at the kids behind them. TJ rode bareback on Cisco with a browband tied around his head, damp with perspiration. Josephine rode slumped in her saddle, melting beneath her helmet as well. They had ridden for six hours and were just reaching the foothills. Thank goodness they prepared to spend the night.

When they reached their destination, the valley where the horses were spotted the day before, TJ slipped off his Paint and studied the ground. "They were here this morning, but something had them running." TJ walked a distance, stopped and pointed. "Here! Here's Major's shoe track. They were heading south." TJ jumped back on Cisco, now leading the way.

About a half hour later, TJ dismounted again. "Look there," he pointed. "Vehicle tracks. Not a truck, a four-wheeler I think."

Soon they crossed a service road running east and west. TJ glanced down the ribbon of packed soil each way and continued. Not far from the road, TJ stopped. "The herd is walking and grazing again. Hopefully, we can catch up with them before dark."

As they entered a box canyon with a small stream running jagged through its rocky bottom, all the horses hesitated, heads raised and ears forward.

"They're just ahead," whispered TJ. "We found them." He motioned for them to remain silent.

Katherine wanted to trot ahead to find her boy, but she knew they needed to approach the band quietly, as not to alarm them. If they took off at a run, Major would follow.

A short way further, TJ dismounted by a clump of brush near the stream and tied Cisco. "Katherine, come with me."

She followed TJ's lead, slipping off Blackjack and securing him to a willow branch along the creek. She gathered Major's halter and lead and followed TJ. He pointed to a ridge to the left. Quietly, they climbed the stair-stepped rocks to a table rock overlooking the basin.

Katherine searched the band, recognizing the stallion, Bandit, but Major was not among them! She turned to TJ. "I don't see him."

"I don't either. Perhaps the stallion cut him from the herd. Or maybe they crossed paths with another band and Major chose to join them."

Katherine panicked. "Or he's out there by himself making easy prey!"

"Let's cut back while we still have daylight. I might have missed something."

When they returned to Steven and Josephine, TJ explained the situation. Katherine was too upset to say a word, for fear she'd break down in tears again.

Leaning over, TJ carefully studied the perimeter of the herd's tracks from one side while Steven tracked the opposite side looking for Major's shod hoof prints or the prints of another band crossing or breaking off from the main herd. When they came to the road, TJ threw his leg over Cisco's withers and jumped to the hard-packed dirt. He studied the road, then walked a ways in both directions.

"Nothing here to see. Let's find those tire tracks again."

When they reached the four-wheeler tracks, TJ once again dismounted and followed them a good distance before stopping and waving them over. "Someone has Major. Here," he pointed.

Katherine gasped when she saw Major's shod prints following the tire tracks. "Oh, no!"

"The good news is, they're not far ahead of us," said TJ. "They're heading west toward the highway."

"Maybe we can catch up with them before dark if we hurry," said

Katherine.

Steven patted his shotgun. "Sure didn't think I'd need this for anything besides wildlife, but I'm glad I brought it now. Let me go first. These tracks won't be hard to follow."

"I'll be right behind you," said TJ to Steven, patting the knife sheath on his pant leg.

Leading their search party, Steven cued Dandy into a lope across the open range toward the setting sun ablaze on the horizon. The four-wheeler and Major's tracks continued into the dark.

Steven brought Dandy to a halt beside a stream. "I think we should camp here."

TJ followed. "I agree, the horses are tired."

Katherine rode up beside them, giving Blackjack a free rein to reach the water. Josephine dismounted and led Bonanza to the creek for a drink as well. Katherine guessed it was probably an extension of the same creek they had found earlier. As she listened to the horses syphon water from the small tributary, her mind raced with questions. Who took Major? Why? What were their intentions? How far ahead of them were they?

As their posse began to settle in for the night, Katherine felt uneasy. "I don't know if I can sleep thinking someone might be loading Major onto a trailer ahead of us. I could lose him forever."

"I'm going to ride up onto that rise up ahead and see what I can see," said TJ, trotting off as they grazed the remaining horses.

Katherine looked up to the starry sky and prayed they'd find Major in time. A slice of moon provided enough light to see Cisco's silhouette against the night sky. Abruptly, the shape spun around, and she could hear the Paint's hooves clamoring down the slope, capturing everyone's attention.

Before he reached them, he called out. "I see a campfire, about a mile ahead!"

Steven turned to her. "Let TJ and I go. You and Jo wait here."

Katherine didn't have to think about it. "No, I can't."

"Then stay back for now," said Steven. "We don't know what to expect."

Everyone packed back up, and quickly saddled their horses. The men turned and galloped off as the women cantered after them. Within minutes, she could see the campfire and slowed to a walk. As they drew near, a horse trailer could be seen hitched to a pickup truck with a four-wheeler in the bed. From that angle, she could not make out the shape of a horse tied to the trailer. Steven and TJ dismounted ahead of them. The campfire was along the same stream beside some willows. As they neared, Katherine could make out a small tent and an empty chair in front of the fire. Steven waved them closer. The men handed them their mounts and quietly approached the tent, TJ from behind, knife in hand, and Steven from the front, shotgun raised and aimed at the open front of the tent.

Katherine couldn't wait, she handed Josephine the horses' reins and crept around the truck to see if Major could be seen. She heard a horse's shallow snort. It was Major! Shocking her, Major nickered to her. Suddenly, a man exited the tent, a pistol pointed at Steven.

"Stop right there," yelled Steven. "Put down the gun!"

"Why would I do that?" said the man, in a standoff with Steven.

TJ appeared from behind the man, knife cocked and aimed at him. "Because of me."

The man's pistol pivoted between Steven and TJ. "What do you want?"

"He has Major!" yelled Katherine.

The man swung around, trying to find where her voice was coming from.

"We only want the horse. He belongs to my wife. Put the gun down!" ordered Steven, again.

"Why didn't you say that?" The man slowly set the pistol down on the ground in front of him. "I knew he didn't belong out here. My name is Henry Jones. I'm a park service employee. I help manage the mustang herd."

"Then you must know the name of the veterinarian that oversees the herd," tested Steven.

"Sure, old Cal. Dr. Lowry."

Steven lowered his gun while TJ returned his knife to its sheath. "Sorry about that. We had no way of knowing your intentions. Cal is the one who told us our horse was running with the mustangs."

"No worries. You never know these days."

Katherine ran to Major, stroking his neck. Major nudged her. "I sure am happy to see you, boy," she cooed, looking him over from nose to tail. Josephine and all the men joined her beside Major.

"How did he get away from you?" asked Henry.

Katherine stepped up. "He didn't. He was stolen in Crow Agency and somehow ended up out here."

"Really! What the heck?"

"Yeah, it's a mystery," said Steven.

"Look, it's late. There's some hay in the trailer. Feed your horses then I'll run you to your trailer."

"It's parked at the Yellowstone River Inn," said Steven. "Cal is waiting to hear from us there."

"Great, I haven't seen the old coot in months. I sure am glad you found your horse. He is a beaut. I was going to contact State Patrol. I knew someone would have reported him missing."

"Thank you for catching him," said Katherine.

"No problem. He came right to me. He knew he didn't belong out here."

"And for your work with the mustangs," she added.

TJ and Josephine had the horses tied to the trailer eating hay.

"That Medicine Hat Paint sure is a beauty too," said Henry. "Is he a mustang?"

"Yes. My father got him in California from a Nevada herd."

"Yeah, I wish we had some color in this herd, mostly browns, blacks and roans."

TJ glanced at the bed of his truck. "Don't you own a horse?"

"Sure. A mustang, of course. But she's in foal, due any day now. So, I've been using the four-wheeler. Let's unhook my trailer and I'll take you to yours."

Steven and Josephine stayed behind with the horses while Katherine and TJ rode with Henry and drove their rigs back. They were exhausted, but eager to get the horses home and sleep in their own beds that night.

21 – Championship

Two Ponies

TJ accepted the Walkers' invitation to spend the night at Two Ponies when they rolled in after midnight. At breakfast, everyone celebrated Major's return, but eluded any conversation about what would come next. Considering what happened at Crow Days, TJ wouldn't blame Katherine for pulling Major from the Championship Race next month. But if it were a go, it would be helpful to know as soon as possible so he and the rest of the guys could clear their schedules. TJ took out another school loan so he could return to his classes that fall, hoping to pay it off with a win in Washington, but he would need to take nearly a week off school to attend the race. TJ waited patiently through the meal hoping Katherine would bring up the topic herself.

Just as the girls got up to collect their plates, Katherine cleared her throat, getting everyone's attention. She turned and focused on TJ. "I've given it a lot of thought, and I want you to race Major in Washington."

TJ was thrilled, but surprised. "Are you sure?"

"Yes," she said, glancing to Steven who sat beside her, nodding. She must have run her decision by him earlier.

"Thank you! I'll camp outside his stall day and night," said TJ. "No one's getting close to him."

Katherine smiled. "We'll all take every precaution after what happened."

"Awesome!" said Josephine, high-fiving TJ as she passed by to collect more dishes.

They had almost a month to get the horses in peak condition. TJ knew the competition between the only remaining warriors of the plains would be fierce, racing at speeds topping forty miles an hour as they jockeyed for position and fought to cross the finish line first.

Walla Walla, Washington

TJ was entertained by Josephine and Kayla spending all morning grooming the horses the day of the big race. Josephine even French braided Major's mane, all but a chunk for him to grab onto. The tall, large-boned Thoroughbred stood out like a rose in a bouquet of daisies amongst the other horses present that day. Other teams rode Thoroughbreds too, but none of them compared to Major.

Several team members stopped to gawk at the big bay in his stall, as well as all the whites associated with their team. They walked away whispering between themselves. Even though TJ had not grown up on a Reservation, unlike most of the competing and attending tribespeople who had, he was aware of the division between the races. But it was good to see Matt, Noot and Talon making friends with the Walkers and becoming more tolerant of whites in general. The girls volunteering to train the horses and Katherine offering her expensive show horse for them to race had shifted their views. Coincidently, neither TJ nor Talon had to spring Matt or Noot from jail all summer long. And Noot's attraction to Kayla seemed to suddenly render him colorblind. It was all good. TJ hoped as more American Indians got the opportunity to know nice, caring people outside the Reservation and more whites ventured outside their comfort zones, more change would come. But for now, he would settle for the barriers he witnessed crumbling around him every day.

The Walkers and Kayla left for their seats as TJ and his team prepared for the event, including their routine offering of burning sage. TJ lifted the smoke over his head, praying to his father for his blessing and to the spirits to bring them victory.

In addition to the Walker group, Talon's girlfriend, Cindy, and members of the team's family were present. His mother wanted to attend, but she couldn't leave his grandparents for that long.

Strangely, Sadie entered his mind. He glanced at Matt wiping down Moon Cloud's protective splint boots. He had simply mentioned she wouldn't be joining them this trip. TJ got the feeling something was amiss between the couple. He was glad Sadie wouldn't be there. He didn't want anything to tarnish Josephine's experience. His wish from this time last year had come true with Josephine in the stands. She had offered to stay with him all day at the barn until race time, but he wanted her to experience the event as a spectator.

The guys passed the time by playing cards out front of their stalls, keeping a constant eye on Major. During the entertainment and earlier race heats, they took turns walking the horses. They would start to warm them up when the field of horses entered the track for the last heat before the Championship Race.

Katherine sat with her family in the bleachers as the announcer greeted the crowd of spectators.

"Welcome to the Championship of Champions Indian Relay Races presented by the Horse Nations Indian Relay Council and the Confederated Tribes of the Colville Reservation."

Members of the various Nations in full traditional dress, carried US, Canadian and Armed Forces flags as they paraded by the grandstand on horseback. The announcer explained they honor the military since American Indians have the highest percentage per capita of any ethnic group serving in the military today.

Next came the kid pony relay races, which were comical with ponies getting loose and running into each other, yet you could see how serious the young riders took the competition. Many would race as adults and surely dreamed of competing in the Championship Race someday. Several heats led up to the main attraction, like on Derby Day, with a fair amount of betting going on as well in the stands between tribes and team families. Between the heats, tribes took turns displaying their traditional clothing while dancing and chanting to the rhythm of percussion instruments. Katherine noticed a few rows of vendors outside the track selling traditional Indian meals and handmade crafts which she wanted to visit during the lunch break. A variety of enticing aromas drifted through the stands, making her mouth water.

During the lunch break, Josephine and Kayla picked up a hot lunch for the guys and joined them at the barn. Kayla and Noot had become an item over the summer, making a cute yet unlikely couple. Seeing the normally rough and tough Blackfeet young man so gentle and sweet with Kayla surprised everyone. Young love. Katherine recalled Josephine and TJ when they first became a couple, and much further back to the first time she kissed Steven. She had been sure to sit down with the naïve girl when the couple first started dating. Kayla hadn't mentioned their relationship to her grandmother yet, and Katherine had no way of knowing whether Karen had ever had "the talk" with her granddaughter. It was grand to see Kayla so happy; riding Joy, befriending Josephine and experiencing a relationship with a boy for the first time. After she suggested to Kayla she needed to tell her grandmother about Noot, the girl agreed she would soon.

After lunch and a little shopping, Katherine returned to her seat with a lovely turquoise neckless and a pair of moccasins resembling Betsy's old pair. The next heat was about to start and according to the program, the Championship Race would take place next. Katherine felt TJ and his team stood a good chance of winning it all again this year.

Following the last heat, the crowd rose to their feet and cheered as the track entrance gates opened for the parade of champion teams. Piegan Pride, decked out in their red and black colors, entered the track first as last year's champions while the announcer introduced their horses and team members. The other seven teams followed, also introduced to the spectators to the beat of a drum, heightening the anticipation. Katherine smiled with pride as TJ and Major led the procession. Major's finely shaped ears worked back and forth as he took in the spectacle of the event; tribes dressed in bright colors beating drums and shouting for their represented teams. Major pranced sideways beside TJ, ready to race. His brilliant scarlet coat glistened in the sun, showing he had gained back the weight he'd lost out on the range. She nudged Josephine and clasped her hand. Smiling, she gave her hand a good luck squeeze.

The riders attempted to form a straight line with their lead horses dancing in hand, anticipating the start of the race. The remainder of the teams were organized in their designated transfer areas. The horn sounded!

TJ grabbed mane and hopped onto Tomahawk smoothly. The Appaloosa lunged into a good steady pace on the rail in the middle of the pack, keeping pace with the lead horses. He held that position until the backstretch, when the horses ahead of him began breaking away. TJ urged the Appy into another gear to keep up. If he could maintain their place and not lose any ground in the transfer, he'd be happy. Talon, held Moon Cloud steady as he approached.

He couldn't help noticing Noot holding Major behind Talon and Moon Cloud, ready for the final lap. The big bay looked jumpy. He prayed Noot could hold him still long enough for him to make a smooth mount. But first, he needed a good lap out of Moon Cloud.

TJ leaped from Tomahawk only strides away from the gray, effortlessly vaulting onto his back. Out of the corner of his eye, he caught a glimpse of a loose horse. When he reached the rail, he found himself a horse-length ahead. The loose horse must have been from one of the leading teams. Moon Cloud felt strong, his muscles stretching and recoiling beneath him as they quickly covered ground around the first turn. On the backstretch, he placed the gray on the outside of the fourth-place horse, not wanting to get boxed in again. If anyone came up on him from behind, he'd have room to make a move himself. The rider beside him glanced over and asked more of his mount, but the chestnut didn't have it, not at the fast pace they were traveling. It was time for TJ to gain on the leaders.

Going into the far turn, he was on the third-place horse's heels. Out of the turn, he pulled Moon Cloud open and raced toward Major. He dismounted about the same time as the others leaders, all scrambling to remount. As Matt grabbed Moon Cloud, Major's eyes were edged in white, his head held high, but Noot had a good hold on him, his body pressed against the horse's chest. Just as TJ grabbed Major's mane, another horse plowed into them from behind. Major spun around, taking Noot with him. TJ chased them as they circled. Finally, he got a good handful of mane. Pressing into Major's right shoulder, Noot managed to hold him still long enough for TJ to do his two stride and jump maneuver onto the tall Thoroughbred's back. Off they charged!

Another loose horse joined the field without its rider ahead of him. That meant of the eight-horse field, only six remained. As they flew around the near turn in fifth place, TJ could see two horses running neck and neck in the lead at least ten lengths ahead of him. The final lap horses were all fast Thoroughbreds, but Major's huge strides caught and passed the fourth and third-place horses on the backstretch.

Again, TJ had to decide whether to make his move on the corner or wait until the homestretch. He had only seconds to weigh his options. Knowing the caliber of horses, he considered not waiting. But then, Major felt good, testing his rein, waiting for TJ to give him his head to chase down the leaders. Unexpectedly, he heard hoofbeats gaining on him from behind and the decision was made for him. TJ pulled Major open. He would have to pass three-wide on the corner while the two front runners fought head to head for the lead. He let just a little rein slip through his fingers and Major responded, lengthening his stride. Suddenly, one of the lead horses, a liver chestnut, broke away from the mahogany bay. Quickly, TJ closed the gap and passed the second-place horse on the outside, but within the few seconds it took him to take the bay, the chestnut had pulled away by three strides and wasn't slowing down.

He could still hear a horse shadowing him as well. As they broke out of the turn, he gave Major his head, pumping him every stride with his body and arms. Slowly, they gained on the chestnut until they were racing stride for stride toward the finish. He couldn't hear the crowd, only Major's breathing and the sound of hoofbeats. Inch by inch, they gained on the chestnut, passing him. But they hadn't lost their shadow. TJ turned to see a big black horse gaining on them only a few lengths from the finish.

"Go, Major, go!" yelled TJ. Major's big heart answered with a burst of speed, racing across the finish line first by only a neck!

Suddenly, the crowd penetrated his ears like someone had just turned on a blasting radio. TJ let go of the reins and reached for the sky in victory then reached down and stroked Major's neck. "You did good, boy. Real good."

People were rushing onto the track as he slowly cantered then trotted Major to gently cool him down. He could see Talon, Matt and Noot jumping up and down in celebration. As he walked Major toward his team, Katherine, Josephine, Steven and Kayla jogged onto the track to join them.

"What a great race, TJ," said Katherine, patting Major for his part. "He really gave you his all."

"We did it, all of us!" said TJ. "I didn't think we stood a chance after Major got rammed." TJ leaned down and gave Josephine a kiss.

"You rode him perfectly," said Josephine. "I'm so proud of you!"

A few gifts and a check were presented to the team while pictures were taken, then the joyous group headed for the barn to celebrate. Katherine surprised everyone when she pulled two bottles of champagne from a cooler in the truck. Toasts were made as they sang Queen's *"We Are the Champions."* It was a day TJ would cherish forever. If only his father could have been there to see him ride to victory… but perhaps he was.

22 – Wedding

Two Ponies

Josephine gazed at the tree branches swaying above, her head nestled in TJ's lap, as golden aspen leaves showered down around them. Winter would be upon them soon. She didn't feel a chill from the cool breeze off the lake blowing across her naked body. The heat of their lovemaking still lingered. TJ looked down on her with a content smile as he brushed her face free of wild strands of damp hair.

It had been a perfect day, riding together, skinny dipping in the freezing cold lake out front of the cabin and warming each other up while making sweet love rolled in the old quilt on a knoll overlooking the lake. TJ would be leaving to return to his classes in two days. She had missed him terribly the past couple weeks after having spent every day together over the summer. As things stood, she wouldn't see him again until Thanksgiving. Waking up without him was like awakening without air to breathe.

"TJ?"

"What, angel?"

"Let's get married tomorrow."

TJ nearly flung her from his lap getting up so fast. "Tomorrow? I thought you wanted to wait."

"Only because you wanted to."

"I thought you were considering taking a role."

"What? No way. I told you I didn't plan to. If I was going to, I would have accepted a part Roy offered months ago. I read the script as a favor, but I told him no right from the start."

TJ cupped her face in his strong hands and kissed her. "I love you!"

"Then you'll marry me tomorrow?"

"Yes! This is crazy. Where?"

"At Two Ponies, of course. Almost everyone we want to attend is here. Roy and Sandy are still at their ranch. He doesn't leave for production until next weekend. Lisa and Daniel should be able to catch a redeye."

"But then what? I'm leaving in two days."

"I'll return to Fort Collins with you. We can find a small apartment. I'll get a job!"

By this time, they were both on their feet, dancing. Josephine suddenly froze. "But, who can we find to perform the ceremony on such short notice?"

"I have an idea. Would you be opposed to a Blackfeet?"

"Of course not. So long as we're married, it could be Bugs Bunny!"

The couple got dressed, locked up the cabin and hopped on their horses. They galloped toward the lodge, Josephine leading the way, TJ on her tail.

Abruptly, Josephine reined Bonanza to a sliding halt, causing Cisco to run into them. "On horseback!" squealed Josephine. "We'll get married on horseback. It'll be perfect!"

"You don't know how perfect! I used to dream about us getting married on our horses when I was a kid."

"See, perfect! Mom and Dad are going to freak." Again, Josephine took off down the trail with TJ on her heels.

When they broke the news, her parents were speechless.

"Of course, we need your permission to hold it here at Two Ponies," said TJ.

"We just couldn't stand being away from each other for two months," said Josephine. "Or we could just elope if it's too much trouble on such short notice."

"No, no, no, don't do that." Her mother looked to her father.

Steven shook his head, smiling. "Sure, why not. We have twenty-four hours, right?"

"Mom? I need to text Lisa as soon as possible."

"Sure… why not?"

Josephine hugged her mother. "Great, let's plan it for early evening." She glanced at TJ. "When do the guys get off work?"

"Matt and Noot normally work the day shift until three. I think Talon has the day off tomorrow."

"Okay. We'll have the wedding ceremony at five?"

Everyone nodded and got to work. TJ called Sarah to give her the news then left for the stone house to tell the guys. Immediately, Josephine contacted Lisa. While they were texting on the phone, Daniel booked their flight to arrive in the morning. Next, she called Roy. He was thrilled and they would arrive early afternoon.

After Josephine filled her parents in on some of their ideas, the first thing Katherine did was check the weather. Relieved, it looked sunny and clear, perfect for an outdoor wedding. Steven sat at his desk making a list of what needed to be done. He figured the two long tables and benches they once used for the summer camp would work, set up in the front yard. Together with the seating on the front porch, they would be able to accommodate the estimated twenty-five guests. Katherine called a local barbeque restaurant to have the event catered. Everything was set in motion.

Tomorrow, Josephine would marry her best friend!

TJ made record time driving home before heading to the Reservation. His mother gave him a hug, already teary-eyed. "I'm so happy for you, TJ, for you both. You two belong together."

"I can't tell you much more right now besides the wedding will be at five. I need to find the guys and someone to perform the ceremony. I'll be in touch when I know more."

It was a relief pulling up to the stone house and finding Talon's truck parked out front. His best friend was happy for him and agreed to be his best man. Next, he drove to the store where the Standing Bear brothers worked. Noot was fixing a tire and seemed more excited about the possibility of seeing Kayla in a dress than he was about their marriage. As soon as Matt finished checking a woman out at the counter, TJ pulled him aside and whispered a question in his ear, then added, "It's going to be a surprise."

Matt smiled and gave him the information he needed. TJ left for the Blackfeet Council. It all still seemed like a dream. Hell, it was a dream come true. Within twenty-four hours, Josephine would be his wife!

When Matt stepped in the door after work, Sadie was fixing dinner and didn't even stop chopping the vegetables for a salad to greet him. She had been in a foul mood ever since they won the Championship, which for the life of him, he couldn't understand why when he now had the money to pay their rent until spring. He guessed she wouldn't be too pleased to hear about the wedding, but he might as well get the news out of the way, so she'll have time to calm down before bedtime. Sadie had been as cold as an iceberg in bed since they returned from Washington.

Matt approached her from behind in the kitchen, pulled her hair aside and kissed her on the nape of her neck. "Hi, babe."

She swished him away like a fly. "I'm cooking."

"Just saw TJ. I have some news." He knew that would get her attention.

Sadie spun around, always eager to hear any news about TJ or the Walkers. She did hate them all so, which had become an issue between her and Matt over the summer. The Walkers turned out to be good people. Sadie was a spitfire, which he liked, but she could get a bit over-dramatic at times. Like now.

"Don't just stand there. What did he say?"

"TJ and Jo are getting married tomorrow. Can you believe it, with only one day's notice?"

Sadie's eyes opened wide as if she'd seen the devil himself. Her face contorted in ways he'd never seen before. When she finally spoke, she sounded possessed. "To hell with both of them!"

Matt left for the couch to give her some time to cool off. Pans clanged and the floor shook as she stormed around the kitchen, cussing a blue streak, most of which he couldn't understand except the occasional "bitch." Suddenly, a plate crashed against the wall, falling to the floor in pieces, then another. Matt jumped to his feet. "What the hell are you doing?"

She began picking up the shards of glass as if he wasn't even there, her eyes glazed over in anger. "I should have known I could never compete with that rich bitch!"

Matt couldn't believe his eyes as her hand began to bleed and she didn't seem to notice. "I hate her. I hate them both!" she screamed.

It took Matt a moment for the words to sink in. "TJ? You're still in love with TJ. I thought you were over him. You said you loved me!"

"Leave! Get your shit and leave!" she shrieked.

"Oh, now I see. You don't need me anymore, is that it? You've just been using me all along – paying the bills while I act like a spy for you."

Finally, she grabbed a towel and wrapped her hand. "Go!"

Matt felt like a fool, then he began putting two and two together. He had noticed gas missing from his truck at Crow Agency, but just figured someone ran out and syphoned some from his truck. Then there was her reaction to Major missing and finding him that seemed way off base.

Matt stepped up to her. "I should have figured this out sooner. It was you, wasn't it? You stole Major! Was it to get even with Mrs. Walker and Jo, or was it all about TJ?"

Sadie thrust her chin and glared at him with a sinister smile. "Both!"

Matt raised his hand to strike her. "Why you…" but he restrained himself. "You're not even worth the effort." He collected his belongings in a trash bag and slammed the door behind him.

After he got to work the next morning, he took a chance and snuck a couple calls. When he couldn't reach TJ at his place, he tried the Walkers. Katherine answered and called TJ to the phone. Matt felt he should warn him.

"When I told Sadie about the wedding, she wigged out on me," said Matt. "She's still in love with you, dude. Why didn't you tell me she was psycho?"

"What are you talking about? We split on good terms, I thought."

"She started screaming and cussing, throwing shit. She said she could never compete with Jo and hated you both. Then she told me to leave. I moved back to the stone house. Thought you should know in case she shows up at your wedding all crazy. I wouldn't put it past her."

"Thanks," said TJ, sounding confused.

Matt decided not to mention Major. He didn't want to upset the Walkers or TJ on his wedding day. Maybe later, or maybe never.

"I'm sorry, man," said TJ. "You okay?"

"I guess. Sure sucks. I feel like such a sucker. She really had me fooled."

"You deserve better."

"One more thing. Her sister, Sally, just stopped to get gas and told me Sadie is moving to Wyoming to live with some distant relative."

"Perhaps that's for the best."

"I suppose." Matt eagerly changed subjects. "I'll see you later. Wow, you're getting married today!"

"I know. It's crazy. Don't be late!"

As soon as TJ hung up, he felt consumed with guilt. Hearing how upset Sadie got and that she still loved him, he realized how selfish he had been. He had treated her poorly. Sadie must have been holding out, hoping she still had a chance with him. He was no better, using her to pacify his aching heart over Josephine, just as she had with Matt. He had felt the same pain and now understood why she told those lies to Josephine. He needed to see her.

While the women were busy in the kitchen and Steven was raking the front yard, TJ offered to run out to get ice and any other last-minute items. Katherine sent him out the door with a list. Taking the chance Sadie would still be at the rental, he left for the Reservation. Thankfully, her car remained parked out front, heaped full of bags and boxes. The front door stood wide open.

Just as he stepped onto the porch, Sadie filled the doorway, her arms full. "What do you want?"

"Matt told me you're moving."

"There's nothing left of yours here."

"I came to say I'm sorry."

"Sorry! For ruining my life? How do you apologize for that?"

"I never promised you anything, but I'm sorry if you felt I led you on."

"You used me and tossed me aside!" Sadie pushed past him. TJ followed as she tossed a box in the back seat. She turned and stood in his face. Her voice escalating. "I loved you." Then the tears came.

"I don't know what else to say, Sadie. I'm sorry. I wanted you to know I understand why you did what you did." TJ turned to leave, but Sadie followed him, lunging in front of him before he could reach his truck.

"What did Matt tell you?"

"Everything."

"Well, I'm glad I did it! They both deserved it, thinking they're above it all." Sadie started back toward the house.

They both? TJ caught her at the door. "You mean Kat and Jo?"

Sadie's eyes were glossed over, seeming to focus through him. "They needed to feel some pain, some loss. Too bad you had to find him."

"What are you talking about? Him, who?"

Instantly, Sadie's expression flipped from one of anger to one of fear. Suddenly her meaning became crystal clear. TJ could hardly believe she was capable of doing anything so sinister as putting Major at risk, or any horse for that matter. "You stole Major!"

"Oh, TJ. I'm sorry. Really. I was hurting and angry. I wasn't thinking clearly. You aren't going to tell them, are you? Please, TJ!"

Was this somehow his fault? Had he driven her to lose her mind and all sense of right and wrong? "I should. You deserve to pay for what you did. No way can you justify your actions."

Sadie began sobbing and collapsed to the ground at his feet.

Even though anger raced through his veins considering all the pain and trouble Sadie had put them all through with her jealous, revengeful acts, he somehow felt sorry for her. He couldn't see her going to jail, that's if the Walkers would even file charges. He was done here.

"I'm glad you're leaving, Sadie." She raised her head, her face pleading. "Go far away and don't ever come back. I'm not going to tell them. Bye, Sadie."

TJ turned and walked away.

Once again, Josephine stood in Betsy's old room looking in the mirror, nearly a year after her first wedding day. This time she wore her mother's wedding dress, resembling an old Western style design that could have adorned a character from one of her great uncle's books. She lifted the gown and admired her fancy cowboy boots like she had always imagined wearing on her wedding day. Her mother sewed her old veil onto a white, broad-brimmed straw hat trimmed with sprigs of baby's breath.

Kayla ran into the room. "They're ready!" Josephine exited the side door to find Bonanza saddled and waiting for her beside a mounting block on the drive. Jessie and Kayla had him groomed to perfection. Carefully, she mounted him, letting her ankle-length, full dress drape over his rump. Kayla handed her a bouquet of sage, golden aspen and baby's breath, then sped off to take her place among the wedding party, alongside Lisa, her matron of honor, and Jessie. Her father smiled up at her and began to lead her toward the front lawn.

The moment she turned the corner of the lodge, Mukki and Tahki struck up the wedding march, played on a guitar to the beat of a drum. Everyone she held dear stood forming two groups with a wide passageway through the center. The wedding party was already assembled at the front. Daniel led the procession leading Lizzy on Snickers as she sprinkled dried flowers and sage from a basket, followed by Cole carrying a small pooper scooper and long-handled, levered dustpan, just in case. Next, her father led her and Bonanza down the aisle, followed by Lady as ring bearer, with a pillow carrying the rings attached to his harness. Smiling faces, many with tears, looked upon her with love and joy. Josephine felt overwhelmed but she had promised herself she wouldn't cry. The crowd clapped and laughed as the procession made its way to where TJ sat proudly on his his magical Medicine Hat Paint. He wore a Blackfeet headdress and a traditional deerskin outfit, complete with moccasins, he borrowed from one of the performers at the Blackfeet Council Museum. He welcomed her with a broad, gorgeous smile, flanked by Talon, his best man, Noot and Matt, opposite the women. She had managed to control her emotions until she saw her mother smiling through happy tears, looking more beautiful than ever.

When they reached TJ and the wedding party, the music stopped. On cue, Bonanza and Cisco greeted each other with a nicker to everyone's delight, as she took her place beside TJ. Everything was perfect except she didn't see who would be performing the ceremony. TJ had kept it a secret. Josephine searched TJ's face, but he didn't look worried, wearing a joyous grin. Again, a drum began to beat and from behind the crowd emerged a small, old Blackfeet man also dressed in traditional Blackfeet attire. He began dancing and chanting down the aisle in Algonquian.

Since everyone would be on their feet, they had planned a short ceremony. This she did not expect. When the old man stopped, he set the drum down and picked up a pole about the length of his arm and stood holding the staff out in front of him.

"I am Walking Man. Keeper of sacred pipe and teacher of Blackfeet customs and ceremonies. Today we marry TJ Black Feather and…" he pointed to her.

"Josephine Walker," she finished for him, earning a few chuckles from the crowd.

"Pole connect the sky and the earth," he said, raising the rod then returning it to rest on the ground. Then he gazed up to the clear blue sky above. "Now we thank the Creator." Some of their guests looked up, some bowed their heads in prayer. Josephine closed her eyes and said a prayer of thanks.

"What gift do you have for father?" Walking Man asked TJ.

Matt handed TJ a bag. Her groom pulled out a beautiful bridle with pieces of turquoise set in the brow band and handed it down to her father. Steven nodded, let go of Bonanza and joined her mother. Then, Walking Man held up his hands. "Sacred gifts," he said. Noot handed TJ an ear of corn and a stone. Lisa gave her two feathers. "Corn, fertility," he said, signaling TJ to give the corn to his bride. "Feathers, loyalty," he said, motioning for her to give the feathers to TJ. "Stone, strength." TJ handed her a perfectly round stone.

"Say words now," he said, pointing to her and TJ.

Josephine glanced at her parents, holding hands as they smiled up at her. Her mother wore a lovely floral tea length dress, something you might see Audrey Hepburn wear in one of her films. Her father wore khakis, a jean shirt with a navy tie and a navy hunting jacket. They made such a handsome couple, but it was the obvious love they shared that was truly beautiful. She took a moment to take in all the smiling faces one last time: Sarah and Grandmother, who stood proud with her cane, Grandfather in his wheelchair, Jessie, Roy, Mike, and their families, along with Betsy's brothers and their sons. She was told Kimi and Nuna were down with the flu but sent their best wishes.

It was time. She turned her focus to her handsome warrior.

Talon stepped forward and handed TJ the ring. Josephine chose to wear only one ring, so his grandmother's wedding band served as both her engagement ring and wedding band. TJ took her hand in his. "I, Theodore James Black Feather, take Josephine Mary Walker as my wife to love, cherish and honor til death do us part." As TJ slipped the ring onto her finger, he added his own vow. "Jo, you were my dream, my fleeting star that I will now and forever hold in my heart." Josephine couldn't stop the single tear that escaped and marked a trail down her flushed cheek.

She looked into TJ's eyes as she held his hand. Talon handed her

Billy's wedding band that Sarah had given him. "I, Josephine Mary Walker, take Theodore James Black Feather as my husband to love, cherish and honor til death do us part." She slipped the ring on his finger. "TJ, you were the hunter of my heart, my best friend and now you have captured my heart forever."

Walking Man touched each of them and said, "Husband, wife."

TJ pulled her veil aside and kissed her tenderly. Hoots and cheers rang out across Two Ponies and Pine Island Lake! Walking Man began beating his drum while motioning for everyone to follow him. Laughing, family and friends began marching in a circle around them, clapping. Bonanza and Cisco calmly took in the scene. TJ clasped her hand and gave it a gentle squeeze and mouthed, "I love you."

This was how she had always envisioned her wedding day, a joyous and happy occasion. Josephine turned to her husband and gave him the signal. As planned, the couple literally galloped off into the sunset to spend their honeymoon at the cabin.

When TJ carried her over the threshold, they were amazed by what they found. A fire was already burning, and their bed was turned down with fresh new sheets. In the kitchen, champagne was chilling, and a four-course meal awaited them, still steaming. A note on the counter was signed, *Love, Kimi and Nuna.*

Epilogue

Three Years Later
Two Ponies
August 2003

Josephine sat on her gorgeous black stallion in the center of the arena following an early morning schooling session with her mother and Kayla. She still had a hard time believing this beautiful boy was really all hers. Her mother had gifted her Joker on her birthday last year for all the work she had invested in the stallion. About the same time, Katherine signed Joy's papers over to Kayla in restitution for her years of helping out at Two Ponies and on the road as the three of them competed nationally. Her only concession; when both Hanoverians were retired and bred, she got the first foal.

They would leave for the FEI World Cup in Las Vegas next week, where she would compete for a spot on the US Jumping Team for the 2004 Summer Olympics to be held in Athens, Greece. Her mother hoped to qualify in dressage and Kayla in eventing. Kayla halted and dismounted Joy, waving to signal she was done for the morning before heading to the barn. Josephine and Kayla were now best friends, much like her mother and Jessie, she imagined. They shared their love of horses and apparently an attraction to handsome Blackfeet young men. She and Noot were engaged to be married next year. A date hadn't been set yet, all depending on how far she and Joy went in competition. Her grandmother, Karen, visited often.

Joker vibrated beneath her as he whinnied for Joy in her absence. The big black stallion continued to mature and show more interest in mares each year, requiring a vigorous schooling program to keep his mind on his work. Josephine enjoyed the challenge and felt proud of what they had accomplished as a jumping team over the past three years. But Joker had good reason to act studly, with so many mares coming and going. Her mother had begun bringing home off-the-track Thoroughbreds from auctions ever since she saw how many ex-racehorses were run through the auction barns and ended up in trucks headed for slaughterhouses. Next year, she planned to retire Major from competition and focus entirely on training and finding suitable homes for as many of the misplaced animals as possible. She, Jessie and Kayla helped with the training. Two Ponies Equestrian Camp had become Two Ponies Thoroughbred Rescue.

Happy with their workout, their last before heading to Las Vegas, Josephine waved to her mother performing a half-pass across the ring on Major. The big bay seemed to be enjoying the challenge of more difficult dressage movements, as well as her mother, but now and then she still caught them popping over a jump or two out in the back field. It was a beautiful day and she reined Joker outdoors to walk him.

Josephine breathed deep, the familiar scent of horse and pine washing over her as the sun warmed her face. She smiled. She was happy. Looking back, she hated to think what might have happened or where she'd be today, if her sister and mother hadn't encouraged her to reconnect with horses and, hence, herself. She patted her boy's slick shoulder. These magnificent creatures had pulled her from the darkness following her accident. First Bonanza, then Major and now Joker, bestowing upon her the precious gifts of their trust, heart and spirit, allowing her to believe in and love herself again. Funny how it all turned out, she reflected. Perhaps things do happen for a reason. All she felt she had lost following her accident… meant nothing to her now.

As she passed by the lodge, TJ approached her from the front lawn carrying little William on his shoulders.

"Hi, Mister! Look at you," she called to her son. "You're bigger than Daddy."

Will laughed and patted TJ on the head. It made Josephine's heart pitter-patter every time she saw them together. She could hardly believe their miracle baby was already two years old. Named after Billy, everyone said Will took after his namesake; independent, mischievous and already a flirt with the women, flashing the same gorgeous smile.

"You almost done?" asked TJ.

Josephine reached down to feel Joker's chest. He still felt a little hot. "Almost."

"There's an emergency call. I told Dad I'd take it. I'll leave Will with Lisa until you or Mom are free."

"Thanks!" Josephine was so proud of her husband. Following graduation, TJ interned with her father and recently became a partner. Like Mom always said, her father would never retire, but he was allowing TJ to take over more of his clients, especially on the Reservation.

William reached out wanting to pet Joker, so TJ stepped closer so he could reach the stallion's shiny ebony neck. Will was already crazy about horses, but how could he not be, the son of two horse lovers, not to mention his grandparents. It was in his blood. As TJ headed for the lodge, Will turned and waved his pudgy little hand. It made her nervous when TJ carried him so high, but the little daredevil loved it.

As Josephine turned onto the lake trail to walk Joker in the shade of the aspen trees, she recalled her mother's words that no relationship is perfect. But what she and TJ had, felt perfect. Sure, they had had their trials and tribulations as her parents had, but they also had found what her mother and father had found – unconditional, everlasting love.

TJ was a wonderful father as well as the perfect husband. He never complained about caring for William while they were on the road competing or all the hours she spent alone writing at her desk. Roy would start production on her second screenplay that fall, and she was working on her third; another story about a girl and her horse, of course.

Along with the help of family and friends, TJ built a separate house for Sarah on the Black Feather ranch, which Josephine now called home. Sadly, but coincidently, Grandmother and Grandfather passed away within one day of each other a month after they got to meet little William. She loved their home and enjoyed adding her personal touches, but Josephine looked forward to staying over at Two Ponies whenever they got the chance. Like tonight following Mom's birthday party, which was expected to run late.

Her father had decided to hold a big party for her this year, like the ones Betsy used to organize, with all their family and friends in attendance, including a few new faces. In addition to Kayla, Karen, Matt, Noot and Talon, Cal and Henry were driving up that afternoon for the night. TJ had kept in touch with the two men following the stolen Major adventure, volunteering at the Pryor Mountain Wild Horse Preserve and at the mustang and wild horse adoption facility across the border in Wyoming. She looked forward to seeing those two characters again. They always had great stories to tell, but they soon learned, so did she and her family.

The party was a total success, bringing together all those who held a special place in Katherine's heart. The event ran well into the early morning hours with plenty of good food, drinks, music, dancing, laughter and storytelling around the bonfire. Many of their guests spent the night in an upstairs room in the lodge, on couches and a few sprawled out on the front yard under the stars. Traveling guests left Sunday morning for their respective lives except Karen who was spending the day with Kayla and Noot at the cabin, leaving only her immediate family to visit for the day.

Katherine dove into the cold mountain lake, awakening every pore of her being. Even at the end of summer, Pine Island Lake never topped seventy-five degrees, except in the shallow water by the shore where the kids were frolicking. Huge boulders had been removed and sand brought in to form a beach out front of the lodge. She often wondered why they hadn't added the beach sooner. Katherine stood on her tip toes in the neck-deep water, watching Lizzy and Will splash each other, giggling themselves silly. Lisa and Daniel sat in lawn chairs watching the kids. She was so proud of Lisa taking on the project of writing and publishing a children's book with all of Betsy's old Blackfeet stories, illustrated by Sarah. Betsy would be so pleased. TJ and Josephine shared a beach blanket not far from the others, deep in conversation and still so obviously in love. And Laddy lay between the couples, gallantly watching over her as always.

Flipping onto her back, Katherine floated effortlessly as small cumulus clouds slowly passed overhead. In the distance, she could hear the call of an eagle. Using her hands in a figure-eight motion, she turned away from shore to search for the large bird. A bald eagle soared high in the big Montana sky, circling closer and closer to her. Ever since she found the eagle feather on the stump in the tack room years ago, Katherine thought of Billy whenever she saw one of the majestic birds. He would be so proud of his son, married with a family, practicing as a veterinarian and volunteering his time to help the mustangs and wild horses. He often brought one or two home with him to start under saddle and rehome as his father had. Sometimes she would see TJ down by the beaver dam mounting a youngster for the first time in the water, conjuring up the memory of the first day she met Billy Black sliding effortlessly from the gray to the back of the black colt. That is how she always chose to remember him; young, beautiful and astride a horse.

Her teeth began to chatter, signaling it was time to lay in the sun to warm up. But rather than lay on the beach, she swam to the dock. Lying on her back, she recalled the first day she met Steven, laying head to head, studying the clouds as teenagers. That was the day Steven first called her "Kat," a nickname that stuck the rest of her life. What a miraculous journey they have shared together over the years with many highs and lows — now grandparents and still deeply in love. The dock also brought back the dark memory of the night she almost took her life in that exact spot nearly forty years ago. She smiled, though, recalling she felt certain her father had brought her back from the edge with the stroke of his heavenly hand.

Warmed, she sat up and scooted to the end of the dock on her seat. Katherine dangled her legs over the edge and swished her feet through the cool water. Images of Betsy sitting beside her sharing her Blackfeet stories of wisdom swept through her like a warm breeze. She celebrated sixty-three years of life yesterday with everyone she loved and cherished. She had led a full life and any additional years would be a blessing she would not take for granted. But when her time came, she would rejoice in seeing her lost loved ones again.

Katherine stood up, dove back into the lake and swam to the beach where Steven had joined the others. He stood in the water giving turns to the kids, swinging them by their arms in circles through the water. Their angelic laughter echoed off the ancient rock formation standing tall like a guardian over Two Ponies and all who called her home.

The End

Character cannot be developed in ease and quiet.
Only through experience of trial and suffering
can the soul be strengthened, ambition inspired,
and success achieved.
~ Hellen Keller

Strength does not come from physical capacity.
It comes from an indomitable will.
~ Mahatma Gandhi

Sometimes you don't realize your own strength
until you come face to face with your greatest weakness.
~ Susan Gale

This is the final book of the

Two Ponies Trilogy

If you enjoyed this story, a review on Amazon would be greatly appreciated. It's the best way to support any author you enjoy.

Follow the author's progress on her next project on Facebook and on her website at www.susanabel.com.

Made in the USA
Columbia, SC
10 March 2023

13546783R00259